To Jim Lehrer,
Thanks for sharing a Bus of My Own and for your fun [illegible] One Eyed Mack novels. I hope you enjoy your travels through the Algoran Federation even if there isn't a bus in sight.
DonnaLee Wheeler

The Chimes of Resdorn

by
DonnaLee Wheeler

PublishAmerica
Baltimore

First printing

ISBN: 1-4241-3089-1
PUBLISHED BY PUBLISHAMERICA, LLLP
www.publishamerica.com
Baltimore

Printed in the United States of America

Dedicated to Comma Man. Without his help, encouragement and pushing I never would have made it over the mountain.

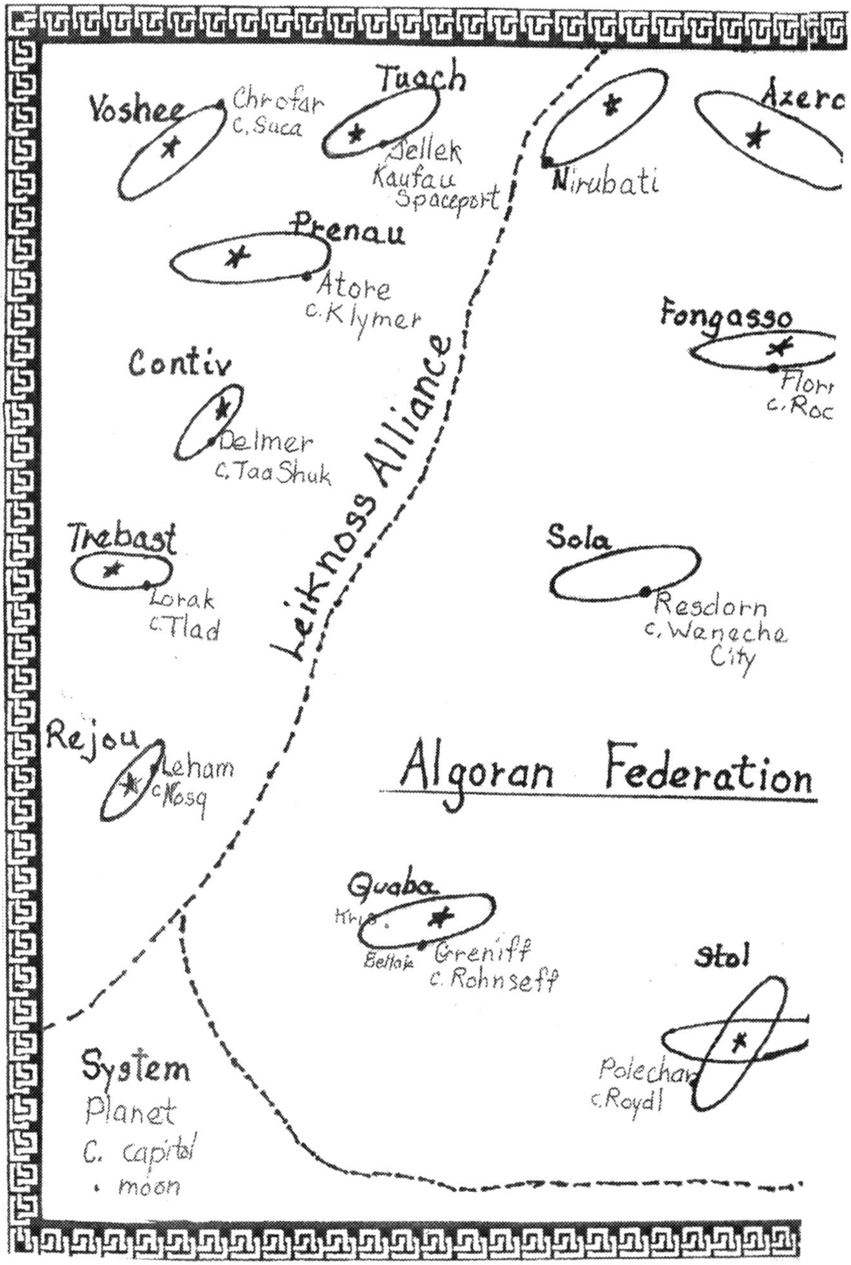

Voshee
Chrofar
C. Suca
Tuach
Jellek
Kaufau
Spaceport
Nirubati
Azerc
Prenau
Atore
c. Klymer
Fongasso
Contiv
Delmer
c. Taa Shuk
Leitkross Alliance
Trebast
Lorak
c. Tlad
Sola
Resdorn
c. Weneche
City
Rejou
Leham
c Nosq
Algoran Federation
Quaba
Greniff
c. Rohnseff
Stol
Polechar
c. Roydl
System
Planet
C. capital
• moon

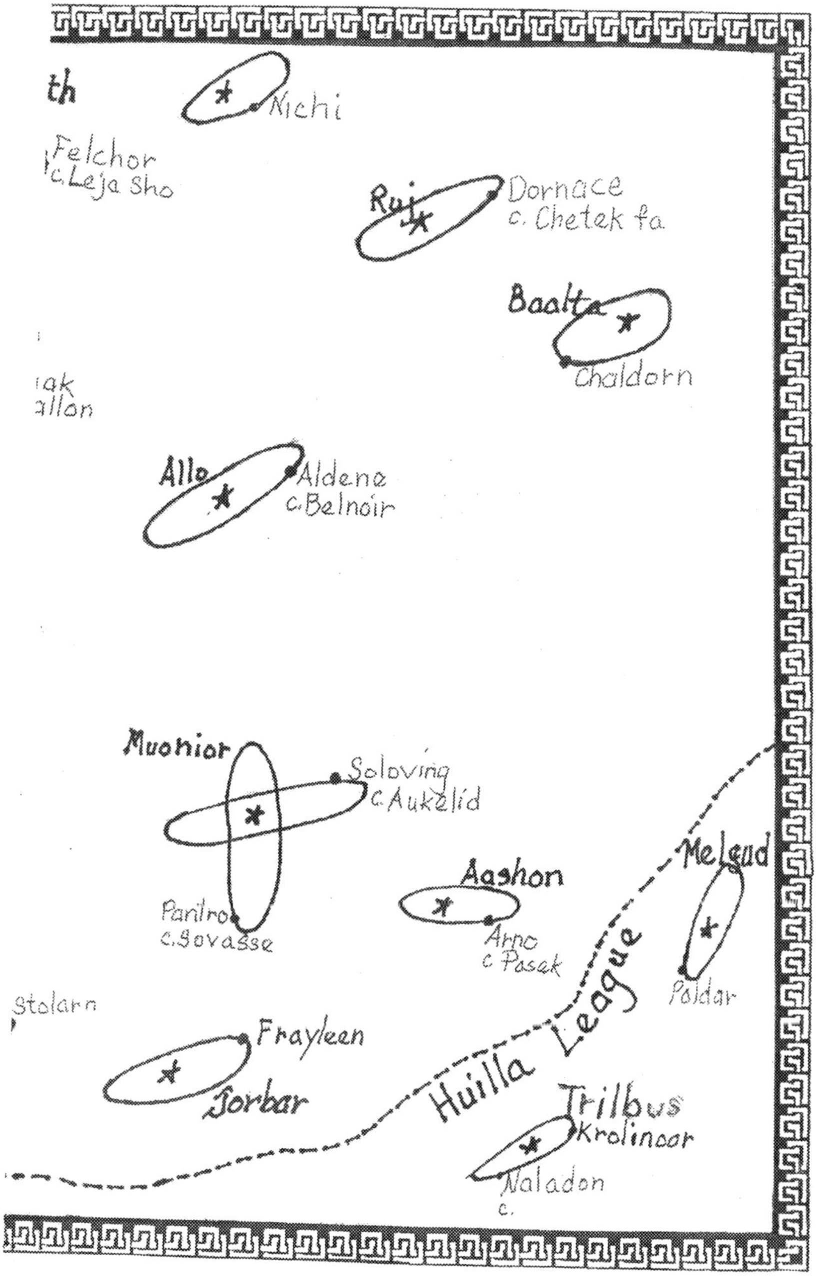
th
Nichi
Felchor
c.Leja Sho
Ruj
Dornace
c. Chetek fa
Baalta
Chaldorn
iak
allon
Allo
Aldene
c.Belnoir
Muonior
Soloving
c.Aukelid
Meleud
Aashon
Panlro
c.Govasse
Arno
c Pasek
Huilla League
Poldar
Stolarn
Frayleen
Jorbar
Trilbus
Krolincor
Naladon
c.

Book One

The Brenev Conspiracy

- 1 -
Best Laid Plans

Coming in too fast! She fought to keep the nose of the flyer up. A clearing. A small clearing just ahead. She headed for it. Up. Up. Keep the nose up. There was a jarring ka-thump as she hit the ground and slid through brush and over rocky ridges with a screeching, ripping sound. The flyer slewed around, skidded into some rocks, slammed into a clump of trees and stopped.

Dulsena sat frozen, her hands clenched on the controls as all around her things popped, snapped and sizzled. Slowly she shifted position and suddenly the whole craft lurched sideways to settle with a bump. Things got quiet and all she could hear was her own ragged breathing. Slowly she raised her arm and tried the door opener to her right. It didn't work. She tried again, this time pushing harder. It still wouldn't budge. She forced herself to turn her head to the left where the body of the pilot lay slumped against the far side. Very carefully, trying not to touch him, she swiveled sideways and started to crawl into the back. The flyer gave another shudder, slid sideways and stopped with a jolt. She looked towards the pilot. The body had slid down leaving a bloody streak on the side window. She closed her eyes and tried to get her stomach under control.

Focusing on the cargo area she saw crates had burst their restraints and were tumbled everywhere. She pushed and tugged them aside trying to get to the side door. It stuck too. Frantically, she tugged and yanked until, suddenly, it jerked open. The body which had been leaning against it slowly tilted backward and fell to the ground.

She closed her eyes and took a deep breath. "Out," she said, her voice loud in the silence. "I've got to get out of here."

A shipping crate still blocked her path and impatiently she pushed it to the ground and started to climb out. She stopped, reached back to retrieve her satchel from the seat she had just vacated, then jumped to the ground. Crack! Something gave way. The flyer shuddered and then slowly, with a grating, metal on metal noise, dropped into a new position. Dulsena staggered forward a few steps then slumped back onto the crate she'd dislodged. She couldn't seem to stop shaking. Her nerves were twanging, her mind racing.

"What a mess," she groaned. "I've shot two men! I'm out here, wherever here is, in the middle of nowhere, and it's getting dark. I'm a lot worse off than I was six hours ago. At least then I knew where I was."

She focused her eyes on the ground at her feet, trying to calm down, but her thoughts careened around, out of control, bouncing from one horrible vision to another. The more she tried not to think of those two men the more she thought of them. Her hand moved convulsively over the satchel lying in her lap and her finger caught in the hole burned into the fabric. She remembered the feel of the small laser that had been thrust into her hand as a stunner. "Stunner," she thought. "How ironic. I'm the one who's stunned. They're dead." She felt the panic welling up again and forced her thoughts away from the still figures; forced herself to take a deep breath, to think.

Things had gone really well until that last transfer. What went wrong then? Apparently that man, the pilot, had been paid by Nayland Brenev to bring her back. Yes, it was Nayland Brenev all right. She was sure of it. He's the one who made everything go wrong. The force of her thoughts propelled her to her feet.

"Well," she muttered, "I'd better see what kind of a mess I've got here." She got up and walked around the flyer hoping against all logic that it wasn't in as bad shape as she thought. It was soon apparent that was a futile hope. It was shadowed on the far side, but she could see that the whole front was stove in where the nose of the ship had plowed into a rock outcroping. All the undercarriage was gone the wheels somewhere back there in the dark.

"Afraid I won't be flying this out of here," she muttered.

She retraced her steps back around the flyer. That side didn't look any better the second time.

"Well points to you Nayland Brenev. You've really messed things up for me this time." She shook her head. Ever since that man had come back to Greniff things had gone wrong. "So Nayland," she muttered,"thanks to you I'm killing people, crashing flyers onto mountain tops in the wilderness and, Great Narm, talking to myself." She started to giggle then checked the rising hysteria. All right, calm down, calm down, she thought. Right now I'm not functioning so well, but I can cope with this. My world has gone crazy, completely crazy, unreal. One thing for sure, the feel of that laser in her hand had been real enough. The dead bodies in that flyer were real.

Suddenly, she was desperately tired. She slumped onto the crate she had shoved out and, taking a deep, ragged breath, tried very hard to think rationally. No question about it, she had been stupid. Stupid and careless and had dropped her guard. But things had gone so well and she was actually at the Rhonseff Port heading for a family friend who would help her. The worst was over, or so she'd thought. "Hah!" The exclamation was out before she caught herself. No, she thought. No more talking to herself. She shrugged her shoulders and settled more comfortably on the crate. So she'd been tired. That was no excuse for sitting there reading cracker boxes while she was being kidnapped. Holy Narm, she groaned, what will Lef Kolek say when he hears about this. After all his training in self-defense how could she have been so careless?

She struggled to her feet and stared at the crashed flyer with its grisly occupants. No. There was no way she could ever explain it to Lef, or to her family and she didn't even want to think about trying to explain at the Fountain of Purity.

"Stupid, stupid, stupid," she muttered. Whap! She kicked at the crate that had fallen out. That didn't make her feel any better, but it did dislodge the top from the base.

She read the lettering on the side of the crate. PITAN. Crackers. Well, they might come in handy since she was stuck out here, Narm knows where. She reached in, pulled aside a layer of padding and pulled out not PITAN, but a small laser, not unlike the one Gutorm had given her. She shifted around trying to get a better look at it in the fading light. Lasers, not crackers. A whole crate full of lasers. Wha…

The sound of a patrol flyer cut through the jumble of her thoughts. She looked up, searching the dark sky. What to do? She had to think of something fast, real fast, immediately. Think.

Stay and try to explain all this to the authorities? No. She had just learned the hard way how far Nayland's tentacles reached. Have to assume he's bought off the police, too. No matter. Once they found those bodies they'd soon be after her. There was enough physical evidence to confirm she had been on the ship. Very soon every law officer on Greniff would be after her and it was very doubtful they would believe she had acted in self-defense. The sound of the flyer grew louder.

Well if there was one thing her mother had drummed into her it was, "When in doubt, don't." She grabbed half a dozen of the lasers, jammed them into her satchel, tied her cloak tightly around her waist and ran. She needed to be as far down the mountain as possible before that patrol landed.

- 2 -
Sweet Memories

Both of the twin Grenavian moons were up, but neither was full, and their meager light did little to penetrate the dark forest. Scrambling and sliding, she went down the slope as fast as she could. It was inky black under the trees and with each leap and slide she was sure she was going to break a leg or worse. "I am not going to end my days under some Sneltzen tree on a planet like Greniff," she vowed. "Keep going, keep going." She repeated the litany over and over.

Scramble, slide, plunge, down she slid through the blackness. The patrol craft landed. Voices were calling. Three more craft landed and soon there were bright beams of light sweeping across the mountain.

Out of time. Have to hole up. They'll be setting up scanners. She looked around. There was an especially dark spot under one of the larger trees. It would have to do. She raced over to it, then stopped and peered into the darkness. What if there was already something under there. She couldn't see a thing. No time to be timid, she though. Besides, I'm probably bigger than anything else that might be in there.

Dropping down, she flung her satchel in, and when nothing objected, wriggled after it as far as she could go. She lay huddled in the dark, her heart pounding, her thoughts racing.

I can't believe I did that, she thought Racketing down that hill like some crazy person. Through a forest full of wild animals. Well maybe not full, but there must be some.

She peered into the darkness around her. Wild animals out there and Narm knows what disgusting, crawly things in here. That thought was not comforting. Fearfully, she reached out her hand and felt around in the blackness. To her relief, nothing moved, furry or otherwise. She did find, however, that the tree branches grew too close to the ground for her to sit up. The best she could do was push some twigs and piles of dried needles around so she could stretch out a bit.

Huddled there in the dark, black thoughts crashed in on her. The two men in the flyer. The laser flashing. The blood. Over and over, in her mind, she replayed that terrible scene in the flyer. Was there something else, anything at all I could have done? She began to feel sick. Putting her head down on her arms she took deep breaths trying to override the nausea. After a few minutes, her head cleared. She swallowed hard and thought about her question. No. There wasn't another way. It was either that or go back to being a prisoner at the Brenev compound and that wasn't to be considered.

She took a very deep breath and let it out slowly. She tried to forget everything else and focus, listen, tried to imagine what they were doing up there. She was worried that even in the dark, they would be able to pick up the trail her wild blunderings must have left. She strained to hear, expecting footsteps, fearing any moment to find hands reaching into her little shelter. Nothing happened.

Occasionally the sound of a voice drifted down and once there was the sound of metal scraping. Time passed. She finally gave up trying to figure out what was going on. She was too tired, too emotionally devastated by everything that had happened. Even though she knew she should stay more alert, the long day, the events of the last few hours, and the mad scramble down the hill were taking their toll. Exhausted, she found solace in memories of home.

Home. Home was clean and ordered and beautiful. Home was where people loved and respected one another. No dirty, hidey-hole under a Sneltzen tree there.

Life had been so different then. She would waken in her beautiful room and see the sheer, rose colored draperies blowing in the breeze, gently touching the prayer crystals. Outside the bright, yellow leaves of the Volnar trees, sparkled in the sun making dancing blue and yellow shadows on the terrace. Down beyond the terrace, a broad sweep of blue-green chlordanzo grass swept outward to the dark green trees on the far hillside.

At the first rays of sunlight, the bell flowers would have opened to welcome the day. From then until nightfall, they made a blaze of color along the patterned pathway leading to the azuroid and copper fountain. Once more, in her mind, she watched as the sprays of water rose and fell, repeating the cadence of the morning prayer.

Then, dressed in pale pink, mauve or cerulean morning clothes, and with her hair twisted in a high, golden chignon, she would join the family for breakfast on the terrace.

She could see her mother, Palomith, looking cool and beautiful in her white robe with the rose patterned borders and her father, in his cream-colored business robe with the dark blue bands. He would be scanning the NewsVu, reading out things that might interest her mother. Scortzi, her brother, in his robe with the pale blue lapel that made his eyes seem even bluer, would perhaps be laughing at some quip of mother's. At her entrance, they would turn and smile.

Smiles, she thought bitterly as she shoved some twigs out of the way. It has been a long time since someone I loved smiled at me. Her heart ached with loneliness. "No," she whispered sharply. "No time for that."

She reached out, parted the heavy branches and peered into the darkness. There were still lights at the top of the hill. Voices called out, and then one craft left, followed shortly by another. Two gone. Still two there. She'd have to stay where she was for a while longer. She retreated back into the darkness. Back into her memories.

Her father was a Merchant who used his occupation like a title. He said it was a very old word full of honor. His Fourth Great Grandfather had been a brilliant student who, after leaving University on Selini, had taken his inheritance and come to Weneche City on Resdorn. Weneche had been a trading center since ancient times and, after studying the trade routes he was sure that, with the increase in interstellar travel, it would become the trade center for that sector. Having decided on his course he wasted no time. Within two years he had set up his business and married the daughter of the leading merchant in the town.

He had been right about the strategic location of Weneche and now, seven generations later she and Scortzi were assuming their responsibilities as the next Kalleni Merchants. Under her mother's tutelage she was learning about the trade in fine art objects, jewels and, of course, the famous Resdorn crystals that were found in the homes and offices of devout Pharosians everywhere. Scortzi had taken his place in the firm under his father, Rimini Kalleni, and the two of them supervised the management of all the other divisions of House of Kalleni.

She preferred the work in fine arts and crystals, not only because of the beauty of the things they bought and sold, but because, with the exception of a few buying trips and conventions, she could stay on Resdorn and let the field buyers do all the traveling. Scortzi, on the other hand, loved to travel, and thoroughly enjoyed it when business took him far along the trade routes. Rimini still accompanied him, of course, however, more and more often he talked of how pleased he would be when he could hand over that part of the business to Scortzi so he could stay home with his beautiful Palomith.

She thought of how her father's eyes sparkled when he looked at her mother. How he used to reach out and gently brush back the heavy, dark brown hair that curled over her forehead. Not long ago Loran had smiled at her and touched her that same way. That thought hurt and she shrugged the cape closer around her. Such a short time ago, when she and Loran had joined in ringing the Chimes of Bonding, life had seemed so perfect.

Irritably she pushed more needles and twigs around trying to get rid of things that were poking her. She remembered the first time she met Loran. It was at Kalleni Gallery where they were showing some of their newest acquisitions. He had introduced himself and before he left they had made arrangements to meet the next day.

A hundred times she had asked herself why she had agreed. She'd never done that before. She had this perfectly good, perfectly logical rule never to mix business and her personal life. She'd never broken that rule until Loran came along, but with him it seemed different. Why?

He was handsome with his dark, thick hair and soft, even features. And those eyes. They were that deep violet color one often saw on people from his home planet, Greniff. He could also be so warm, so charming, so strangely protective. When she was with him she felt like the most important person in the world. From that first day on, they had been together constantly. Those times made sweet memories. She remembered how she had felt, standing with her family and friends, swearing the Vow of Bonding with Loran's violet eyes smiling across the crystals.

Well, they surely hadn't smiled for long. She tried to shift to a more comfortable position and decided she wouldn't think about Loren anymore. She'd wasted too many tears on that man.

What were they doing up at the crash site? Why don't they leave? She strained to stay awake and listen, but finally dozed off. In her dreams the pain of Loran's betrayal crept back in making her feel even colder and more alone.

- 3 -
Good Greniff Wife

Dulsena awoke. One second she was asleep and the next she was awake. It was quiet, but, in her head, she could hear the sound of a patrol craft. She remembered that earlier she had awakened to hear the third flyer leave. So that should account for all four of them.

She was very, very tired. It would be so easy to just close her eyes and drift back...back to sleep. She shook herself and forced her eyes open. No, can't sleep. Dangerous to stay here any longer.

She started to move and found she had curled up into a ball, trying to stay warm. Slowly she unwound and stretched as much as the cramped confines under the tree allowed. The pale blue, first light of morning filtered through the heavy branches and for the first time she could see her little hideaway. She parted the wet branches and looked outside. Everything was misty and foggy with droplets of dew clinging to the tree branches and grasses. The air was damp and heavy. She listened, but couldn't hear any sounds from up the hill. The birds were chirping, and across the small clearing some little, furry animals scuttled about on a downed tree trunk. Everything seemed serene.

Slowly she crawled out from under the branches into the long, wet grass. The little animals scattered out of sight. She stood and stretched, trying to work out some of the cramps and soreness. Her legs and arms were badly scratched and scraped from the precipitous scramble down the hillside, but other than that, there didn't seem to be any serious damage. Her clothes were a mess, of course.

Stooping, she reached back under the tree, pulled out her satchel and brushed it off. Fortunately, the inside was dry and the lunch Leraph had packed, although a little squashed, was still edible. Now, water was the next priority as she was very thirsty. She hoped there would be a stream or spring somewhere near the bottom of the canyon. After that, all she had to do was figure out how to get back to Rohnseff. That's all. No problem.

She started off downhill, her thoughts running faster than she was able to do. First thing, she thought, I must talk to that old friend of father's. He'll help me. If I hadn't gotten into that flyer…If I'd followed my instincts…, If I hadn't let my guard down. If, if, if. Well no point in shuffling the "if" deck. This was a new day. No sense wasting energy wishing she had done something differently.

Slipping and sliding, she made her way down the steep incline. Wet ferns slapped at her legs as she clambered over fallen, moss covered tree trunks. Cone shaped, water filled leaves drenched her whenever she grabbed them for support. They did, however, solve the problem of drinking water as each one yielded a swallow or two. Finally, the ground leveled onto a narrow brush and fern filled valley. As she stopped to catch her breath, she looked back up the hill that rose so steeply and then disappeared in the swirling mist. It seemed miraculous that she had made it down such a slope in the dark without breaking her neck.

But, she thought cheerfully, I did it so I can surely make it the rest of the way. This bit of bravada vanished when she heard a rustle in the bushes to her left. Heart thumping, she ducked down and waited. Hearing nothing more, she inched her way along to where a stream opened into a small pond. The rustling she had heard must have been some animal startled by her approach, for the pond now was deserted. There were what looked like fresh animal tracks around the edge.

She laughed. Come on, Dulsena, what do you know about animal tracks? So all right, she answered herself, maybe I'm not a great hunter, but there aren't any leaves or anything in them, so they look fresh to me. Anyway, whatever made them has left and I'm very dirty so it's my turn. She stripped off her wet clothes, hung them on some bushes to dry and waded into the cool water. It felt good to wash off the soil accumulated in her downhill scramble.

Using one of the cone shaped leaves, she caught some water flowing from a small spring at the edge of the pond. A smooth rock in a patch of sunlight provided a perfect spot to sit while she ate the lunch Leraph had packed the day before. Even squished it tasted good.

After the hectic night, the calm morning was a relief. Although there were no spraying fountains and chimes to greet the dawn, some sort of bird started to sing and the air hummed with insects. She sang quietly, "All god's creatures greet the dawn, With songs of praise da da de da." The words of the old children's song wouldn't come. She tried several variations and finally gave up. She did remember it ended with something about "in their own way, they say their morning prayers." Oh, well. Just another part of her childhood gone.

For now she was warm, and fed and felt a lot better. She rose, shook and brushed her clothes the best she could, then dressed and gathered up her satchel. She looked around the pool and thought I'm ready to go, but where? I don't even know where I am. So what DO I know? For one, the pilot said he was taking me back to the Brenev Compound, so we must have been headed inland to the north. Two, we hadn't traveled far before I saw we were heading away from the port, but, there was the time spent trying to convince him to turn around, and then there was the fight, and after that the crash. Even with all that she didn't think they had traveled for very long. On the other hand, the flyer appeared to be new and fast. How fast? Not knowing their speed she had no way of knowing how far they had come or how close she now was to Brenev lands.

The only thing she did know was that Rohnseff was on the shores of a large ocean. Therefore, it must be downstream. Easy. "Unless you're on the far side of the mountains," a little voice from the other side of her mind put in. She quickly dismissed that thought. "I can't cope with that idea," she muttered, "so for now, downstream it is." I guess I'll soon find out if I'm right or wrong.

The decision made, she settled her satchel over one shoulder and started walking. With each determined step her thoughts kept pace.

When Loran found out she wasn't one of the bodies on the mountain, he'd keep looking. Oh yes. He'd keep looking. She was sure of that. After all, she was a great blot on his reputation. A disobedient wife. She had "shamed him before his family and friends". He'll keep looking until he finds me. "And then he will kill me," she added under her breath. She examined that idea from all sides and knew it was the truth. Yes, as terrible as it seemed she did believe he would kill her. "Shame" had wiped out any love he might have had for her.

Love. Shame. How could those words mean one thing to her and something quite different to Loran? What a fool I've been. Fool, fool, fool. The word echoed in her head with each step. She stomped along the edge of the creek, reliving the highlights of her "education". That's what Loran had called it, her "education". "You must learn how to be a good Greniff wife," he'd said.

It was after the death of Loran's brother, Albar, that her life had started to fall apart. Friends and extended family members had barely left for their homes after the days of parties and receptions honoring Loran and his new bride, when suddenly Albar had died in his sleep. Everyone had come back, this time to mourn. Loran had seemed especially grieved by the death of his brother and retreated from everyone, rejecting even her attempts to comfort him.

Loran's father had been ill for several years and had made the elder brother, Nayland, head of Brenev Industries. Under him, Albar had been in charge of the agricultural holdings on Greniff, and two other planets that she knew of. Loran was head of marketing. That's why he was based in Weneche City on Resdorn. Father Albeg and Mother Farnia had retreated to Circauss, a small island in the tropical region of Greniff. They returned to the home compound infrequently and the festivities surrounding Loran's visit to Greniff on their honeymoon trip was the first time in many cycles that they had been back.

Yes, she decided, it was after Albar's death that her world started to change. First, there was the incident of the new clothes. She had been shocked when Loran had brought in those heavy, ugly clothes to replace her beautiful trousseau. She had complained, of course, but Loran, in a firm voice, had told her that, "Greniff wives do not wear transparent robes and bright colors".

Later that same morning, Loran, acting very strangely, walked her around the family complex to show her "the boundaries of her apartment".

"It is the custom," he had told her solemnly, "for Greniff wives, to keep occupied within the confines of their own apartments until the evening meal with the whole family. The one exception is when there are guests, and then you will wait with the other women in an adjoining room until the guests leave. After their departure the women of the household come in and enjoy their meal."

"The leftovers, you mean," Dulsena had said disgustedly.

Loran had given her an irritatingly patient look before adding, "Greniff wives never eat at the same table or at the same time as their husband's guests."

He had continued on and on telling her what Greniff wives were allowed to do. She was to go out of the family complex only occasionally and then never alone. An older wife must accompany a younger one and both were to be accompanied by a male member of the household. She had stared at him in amazement. She'd been an independent girl all her life, going on buying trips, meeting the public, learning to run a business and now he was telling her she couldn't leave her apartment without a chaperon? Incredible.

A parade of cousins had been introduced to her at the time of their arrival on Greniff. They all seemed to have positions in the family business and they, with their wives and families, lived in the family compound. These women, he added, would show her what was allowed and what was not, and she was to follow their examples.

As he had droned on and on, she had become more and more shocked and outraged. It was appalling. She couldn't believe he was serious. However, one look at the cold expression on his face convinced her he wasn't playing some elaborate joke on her.

He'd left and she had tried to take consolation in the thought that, as galling as these ridiculous restrictions on her freedom were, they were only temporary. They would soon be returning to Resdorn and then her life would return to normal.

"Normal, Hah," she muttered as she splashed along.

The stream had gotten wider and the trees and bushes grew right down to the water's edge. She found she had to wade in the shallow water at the edge. Splashing along, she remembered how excited she had been at the thought of going home to Resdorn.

As the scheduled day for departure approached, she had asked her maid, Naba, to see that her own clothes were returned so she could start to pack. Naba had hurried off, but, soon returned empty handed. In her head she replayed the whole scene.

"Naba, where are the clothes I sent you for?"

"I'm sorry, My Lady, but your clothes cannot be found," she had whispered, all the while wringing her hands and staring at the floor. "What do you mean they cannot be found? Someone must surely know where they have been put." Naba, a quiet little thing, had refused to even look at her when she was first brought to Dulsena. It had taken quite a long time to gain her confidence enough so she would talk at all. Seeing how upset she was, Dulsena had known it would be useless to press her further.

"All right, Naba, I know you tried. Now I want you to go and find my husband. Tell him that I need to see him right away." Naba had hurried away, but it was a long while before Loran appeared.

She remembered how happily she had raced to him and, in a rush, laughingly told him about the impossible maid who could not find her clothes and "would he please, please, please talk to somebody and locate them so she could start packing." He'd made no response, just walked over to a lounge and sat down.

"Loran," she had added, "I need to start packing if we are to be ready. You know how much we carried with us before, and now with the wedding gifts and the souvenirs I have purchased, it will be a task to pack them all. Please, Dear, arrange to have my clothes sent here as soon as possible so I can get started."

Smoothing the fringe on his robe, and without looking up, he had said, in a cold voice, "There's no hurry. We won't be returning to Resdorn for some time."

"Not returning?" she had cried. "Why that's impossible! You know

I have responsibilities there. It was not convenient for me to be gone this long. I must return as planned."

"You don't understand. Albar is dead. Nayland says that I must take over Albar's responsibilities on Greniff. He says that Harallun will go to Resdorn. We will remain here on Greniff."

"Nayland says, Nayland says. What about our plans? Why should Nayland control our lives?" she had shouted at him.

"Dulsena, Nayland is the head of the family, the head of Brenev Industries. I must do what he says."

"Well I don't," she had snapped back. "I'm not married to Nayland. He isn't going to decide what I can and cannot do. And I can't believe you could seriously expect me to. You know what my life was like before I came here. How could you think I would accept such a situation? I can't, all of a sudden, give up my work and interests to live on Greniff. How could you have even thought of agreeing to such a thing without consulting me?"

"Dulsena, Dulsena," he had said in a disgustingly patronizing tone of voice, "you know I love you and want only what's best for you. You are my wife. So," he shrugged, "why should I have to consult you. You will naturally do what I decide is best."

"What you decide is best? What about what I want?" she had shouted indignantly. "How can you stand there and say you love me if you want me to change into someone else? You married me, Dulsena, daughter of Rimini Kalleni. My whole life has been spent training to take over my responsibilities as co-owner of the House of Kalleni. You can't really expect me to stay here on Greniff and forget that." All she had gotten in response was another patronizing look.

"Your father's company is a large one. There are others who can be trained to do what you did. As my wife you now must learn different customs. You must be willing to change. After all, I changed for you when I was on Resdorn."

"You "changed" for me? What do you mean? You "changed" for me? You said you loved me. You stood at my side and took the Vow of Bonding before the Chimes. Doesn't that mean anything to you?"

"Of course it meant something when I was on Resdorn, but, now we are back on Greniff and there are different vows. Surely you can understand that."

Splashing angrily through the stream, Dulsena remembered those words. She hadn't understood Loran then and she still did not understand how he could think that way. A vow was a vow, no matter what planet you were on, and love should be love wherever you were.

She relived that moment again, remembering how she had fought to be calm. Finally, she had managed to say, "I will need to call my mother and make arrangements." Knowing full well that once through to Palomith she would plead with her to somehow get her out of there.

This plan was dashed when Loran said, "That will not be necessary. I have already sent a message saying you will not be returning."

"How dare you. I will talk to my mother myself."

"No, Dulsena, you will not. Not until you have learned your place here. I have given orders that you are not allowed to place any calls off world." Having said this he stalked from the room, leaving her feeling a fury she had never known she was capable of feeling. From then on each day was a battle. Her only hope had been that her father would be able to talk some sense into Loran. He had told her he would stop at Greniff after a business trip to the Allong system. She clung to the thought of seeing him again.

Day after day the fights went on. Filled with anger and frustration she kept to her apartment and Loran kept to his. At meals, in the family dining room, they walked round each other, speaking only when necessary. The rest of the family obviously blamed her for this estrangement and their displeasure showed in every comment and gesture. Mealtimes became very tense and unpleasant. The next time there were guests, her firm and very loud refusal to suffer the humiliation of waiting in the next room with the other "good wives" resulted in her taking all her meals in her own apartment. The only people she saw were her maid Naba and the gardener Bibdag. Other than those two, she was alone, a prisoner.

- 4 -
Nayland's Return

This unhappy state of affairs went on until one evening Loran appeared in Dulsena's apartment. "Good evening, Dulsena," he said, as if he had only been away a few hours instead of many days.

"Good evening, Loran," she had responded formally. "You finally remembered I am still here, waiting to hear when I can leave for Resdorn."

"Dulsena, please don't bring that up again. Look, I've brought you a new robe." He laid the robe on the lounge and smiled at her.

"That's certainly what I need, Loran," she said sarcastically, "Another heavy, ugly robe. I suppose you think I should thank you?"

"Now, Dulsena. It's a very nice robe and I want you to wear it to a special dinner with the family this evening. Nayland has returned and the whole family is gathering to greet him."

He walked over, took her hand and very sweetly said, "Please, Dulsena. This is important. Will you please?" She had looked into his beautiful violet eyes, and, for just a moment, all the old feelings came surging back. Her resolve weakened. Besides, she was tired of being alone. She was used to being with people and had found the isolation frustrating and tedious. Then, remembering the reason for that isolation, she jerked her hand away and said, "I see no reason to honor the man who has made me a prisoner and keeps me from my family!"

Loran, in an irritatingly patient voice, said, "We have not made you a prisoner. You have done that to yourself. If you would only make an effort to learn to get along you would be as free as any of us."

"Free! You're not free. Nayland rules all of you. This older brother that everyone thinks is so wonderful, who couldn't even bother to come home for your wedding reception." She walked to the far side of the room and stood with her arms folded across her chest.

"Dulsena, you just don't understand. But, I promise you, if you go with me to the dinner tonight and try to be pleasant, I will do everything I can to arrange for your father to come and visit."

She watched him closely as he spoke. He seemed sincere, but she still had reservations. He was holding something back. Nevertheless, what were her options? She couldn't do anything the way things were. She had nothing to lose by trying to get some sort of an agreement. At least she would be doing something.

"All right, Loran, I'll go to this dinner with you if you promise to let me talk to my father."

"Of course I will. I said I would, didn't I? Now you hurry and join us as soon as you can."

He walked over and wrapped his arms around her. She stiffened, but offered no resistance. It was the first time in many cycles he had shown her anything but contempt. Stepping back, he gave her a fleeting smile and left with a jaunty step.

She stood there thinking about what had just happened. Something is wrong, she thought. The body language. Something does not jibe. He's sending a lot of mixed signals.

Even with those reservations, she wondered, for the thousandth time, if there was any chance for them to get back together. If they could get away from Greniff, away from this brother who dominated everyone, it might be possible to work things out. After all, at one time they had shared so much love.

If only her father would come. He would help them get away from Nayland. She stopped, motionless, as another thought came to her. Nayland. Maybe I can talk him into letting us go back to Resdorn. This tiny little glow of guarded optimism stayed with her as she bathed and dressed. Fortunately, she had kept her jewelry case with her so it hadn't "gotten lost" and she chose quite a few of her finest, most impressive pieces to wear, both to liven up the drab dress and to irritate the judgemental females who had looked askance at her Resdorn fashions. Finally, satisfied that she looked the best she could in such an ugly gown, she left for this "important dinner".

Their apartments were on the westward side of the main building which was in an irregular star shape with one point missing. The main corridors led like spokes to the central reception areas facing the truncated side and as she got closer to the reception area she could hear the buzz of conversations and an orchestra playing.

The main hall was festive with huge bouquets of flowers and lighted by thousands of glow lights. Apparently all the extended family had come to celebrate the return of the eldest brother, the head of the family. To one side tables were laden with rich delicacies. Some were foods she hadn't seen since her own welcoming dinner and some she had never seen before.

The women of the family, who for the last few cycles had been so contemptuous and disapproving of her, now approached her smiling and seemingly eager to speak to her.

"Dulsena, how nice you could join us. And how are you? You are looking very beautiful tonight. And your health is good, I hope?" All the comments were in this vein and seemed to reflect an inordinate interest in her health. She found this puzzling. The men, as usual, acknowledged her existence with nods, but didn't approach. Finally, after about the twentieth repetition of, "Yes, I'm fine. Thank you for asking."

Loran and his father came in, accompanied by another taller, leaner version of Loran. All three were dressed in tunics of very fine fabric stiffened by elaborate embroidery and gold braid set with jewels of all sorts. She had noticed before that the men did not have the same dress restrictions as the women. They could be dressed as extravagantly as they liked. They, and most of the other men in the room, made quite a sight as the multitude of lights flashed and glittered off their well-tailored tunics.

Nayland's hair was darker than Loran's, his features thinner and sharper. As he came closer she could see even his eyes were sharp looking. He smiled as he greeted the older members of the family in order of precedence, but she had the strong impression that the relaxed affable exterior was only skin deep; a covering for a contained, tightly strung interior.

As they came towards her she could see that Loran was nervous while Nayland seemed very cool. Holding out his hand to touch finger tips with her in the family greeting, he murmured the correct formal phrases and she responded the same way. Just as she opened her mouth to ask for a private interview, the musicians started to play, the crowd surged, and she found herself being led, along with Loran, towards their places at the long table. The moment was lost.

The meal was fantastic. Every type of delicacy that could be had from planets all along the trade routes. Some she knew the value of from having heard her father and Scortzi discussing them. One thing was clear, considering the variety and amounts this meal must have cost a fortune. Nayland, however, seemed unimpressed with this ostentatious display of affection on his behalf. He picked at his food and exchanged languid comments with those around the table. Whenever his eyes met Dulsena's he seemed amused by something. Perhaps he had heard of the problems between Loran and his troublesome wife. Maybe he found it amusing that his brother couldn't "educate" his wife.

Dulsena was uncomfortably aware that Loran added little to the conversation. Only occasionally did he glance at her and then with a worried expression on his face. He also drank more than she had ever seen him drink. She had been warned about the Greniff intoxicants, especially the green, foaming drink they called Smarteg which translates to Scorpion's Tail. Now, Loran filled his glass again and again with it, leaving his food untouched.

Glancing around the room, it was obvious that Loran's actions had not gone unnoticed. The buzz of conversation never lessened, but that was on one level. On another level, looks were being exchanged. Some people seemed amused, others concerned. Dulsena had the uncomfortable feeling she was the subject of this subcurrent of speculation. Eyes meeting her's, too quickly glanced off, and the comments directed to her, while appearing on the surface to be commonplace, seemed somehow veiled and full of double meaning.

By the end of the dinner, tension had built to the point that when Loran's father signaled the meal was over, everyone rose too quickly, talked and laughed too loudly, and practically rushed into the grande salon. All except Loran. He seemed sunk in stupor.

"Loran, we need to go into the salon," Dulsena said. He didn't seem to hear her. He simply sat, staring into his glass.

"Loran," she said a little louder, "we need to go in with the rest of the family."

Only then did he rouse himself enough to look around and see they were alone with only the servants waiting at one side. He rose and with leaden steps walked with her to join the others.

Conversations had resumed and, for once, Dulsena was pleased that they were used to talking around her. She needed to observe and think about what she was seeing. Why had Loran's joy at the return of his brother taken such a turn? What was going on?

After what seemed like an interminable length of time, Dulsena told Loran she would like to retire. He nodded, and bowing to his father and his brother, they left for her apartment. Once there, Dulsena assumed he would leave her alone, but he sank onto a couch and started talking. What he said ended any thoughts of reconciliation and any hopes she still had for her marriage.

Never would she forget his voice saying, "Dulsena, you are now a Greniff wife. Your life here must be in accord with all our laws and customs. Have you learned that?"

"I am Dulsena Ariadne Kalleni of Resdorn, daughter of Rimini Kalleni, Merchant. I am being held here on Greniff, against my will. Granted, I am your wife, however, I shall always be who I am, and no amount of coercion will ever make me forget it."

Loran's face flushed red and he yelled, "Will you get it through your head that your life on Resdorn is over. We now live on Greniff, and as my wife you must keep the customs of my people. There can never be any question about that. My position here depends on you doing your part, and not disgracing me in the eyes of my family and friends. Surely you can see that!"

"I can see that your customs mean a great deal to you, but you must understand that there are basic rights and freedoms and your customs must not deny me those rights."

Flinging himself off the couch he rushed at her, grabbing her arms so hard they hurt and putting his face right up to her's, spat out, "You have no rights, no freedoms except those that I choose to grant you. I'm tired of your talk about rights and freedoms. You will do what I say from now on. There will be no more discussion about it!"

His eyes weren't violet then, they were a deep purple, and his face was twisted with anger. The barely contained violence forced her back in terror. That was when she realized that this man, this man she thought she knew, this man who had vowed his love for her, would kill her to get his way.

Releasing his hold, he'd flung her into a chair and said, "Listen very carefully, Dulsena, to what I have to say. You must be prepared. You have been here on Greniff long enough to understand that the continuation of the family is everything. The death of Albar left just Nayland and me. Now, through your obstinate attitude and the coldness you have forced upon us, six cycles have passed, and you have not been quickened. My brother is now home and he will correct that situation."

"What do you mean? How can he correct the situation? What makes you think he will be able to talk me into accepting this demeaning lifestyle any more than you have?"

Loran looked at her and suddenly, frighteningly, he started to laugh. Straightening up, he stepped away a few paces, still laughing. Then he turned abruptly, and with his hands on his hips, looked at her and said, "Talk you into it? There won't be any talking about it, you fool. He will simply make sure you are quickened. As the elder brother that is his right after six cycles."

The shock on her face made him laugh even harder. "You can't be serious," she whispered.

"Oh, I'm quite serious. Nayland will see that you become a good little Greniff wife and mother, for sure," he gloated.

"Loran," she gasped, "I'm your wife. How can you think to just hand me over to your brother?"

"It is the way," he said. "If I had five brothers they each would have a turn until you were quickened. So you should feel lucky there is just Nayland. It will be easier for you to adjust."

"Easier! Easier!" she shouted as she jumped from her chair. "You are out of your mind if you think I would go along with such an idea!"

"Oh you will 'go along'. One way or another you will 'go along'. You have no choice. Now prepare yourself. It may be tonight or some other time, but Nayland will be calling on you and you will do what is expected of you. You are not a stupid girl, and you know there are methods, not very pleasant methods, of getting people to do what is necessary. Your father and brother do not trade in those things, but many others do. So, the choice is yours. You can decide to do what is expected, or you can suffer greatly and then still have to do what is needed."

His words hung loud and hard in the air between them. Then, after a few moments, in what he must have thought was a conciliatory voice, he said, "I still care for you, Dulsena, and sincerely hope you will make the proper and right decision. We can make a good life here on Greniff, if you will just learn to cooperate and be a good wife, a good Greniff wife. Now you think about it. In any case, be ready for Nayland when he comes." With that, he turned to leave the room. Dulsena leaped to her feet and shouuted,"You are completely mad if you think I will ever submit to such treatment!" Suddenly she found herself stumbling backwards, trying to keep on her feet. Her head was ringing with the force of his blow, an open handed slap of such force that she couldn't focus her eyes. He had struck her! Propelled against the wall she slumped down, and stared at him. scarcely believing what had just happened. He came closer and his face loomed over her and he smiled! He smiled at her and said,"Oh yes, Dulcena, you will learn to obey." He turned and quickly and left the room.

Dulsena stared at the closed door. She felt dazed and numb even though her face was on fire. It was all too much. It couldn't be real.

She seemed frozen, incapable of movement. The door faded as her sight blurred and the only sound was the blood pounding in her head. Then, as things cleared, she found herself shaking with such fury.

"How dare you?" she shouted at the closed door. "I, Dulsena Ariadne Kalleni will not be treated like some brood mare!"

"Wait here for Nayland," she mimicked Loran's tone. "Like Narm I will." Her anger propelled her into action. She had to get away! Her mind was racing. If only she could get to Rohnseff spaceport she could seek asylum with some of her father's trading associates until he arrived and could take her home. But how? How could she do this? When they had come to the Brenev Compound from Rohnseff, they had flown in Loran's personal LRF (long range flyer), and she had been so excited she hadn't noticed distances or direction. On brief sightseeing trips she had seen a range of low mountains and a long winding river. Other than that, she had to admit she knew very little of the surrounding area.

"Well," she muttered, "this is no time to stand around thinking about all the things I don't know. The one thing I do know for sure is I have to get away. Now!"

- 5 -
Flight from Fear

She changed her evening shoes for the sturdiest shoes she owned. Then, looking around she found a soft sketching satchel she had brought from Resdorn. She emptied it and threw in a change of clothes, some personal items and all the currency she had. The only thing available in the way of food was a dish of sweets and the bowl of fruit the maid always kept filled. She tipped these into the satchel. Grabbing the heaviest cloak she owned, she took one last look around, turned off the lights, and stepped out onto the terrace.

The terrace was only dimly lit and she stood for a few moments waiting for her eyes to adjust. The family compound was guarded, and she had often suspected that she, especially, was being watched. She never had seen anyone for sure, but sometimes she'd felt she was being observed. On this festive occasion she hoped that if there were guards, they were off celebrating with everyone else. However, just in case, she held the satchel to her chest and wrapped the cloak around it.

Wandering around the terrace she finally reached her destination, a bench that backed onto a rather large group of bushes that was at the edge of the terrace lights. She sat down with her head bowed in what she hoped would appear to be a sorrowful manner. At the same time she tried to look back over her shoulder to see how dark it was behind her. The shadow from the bushes seemed to stretch quite a ways. She looked the other way and could see nothing that offered any better alternative. Having made her decision, she rose quickly and made her way around the bushes into the shadows. She followed the shadow as far as she could and then hurried across the lawn towards the paved path that she knew surrounded the perimeter of her allotted area. That path was very familiar as she had paced it often enough during the long cycles of her captivity. Further on, straight down from the terrace, she knew there was another, wider path, that led off into the garden where they grew the flowers for the house.

As she got closer she could see where the paving stones of the path made a darker, curving shadow that was just barely discernible in the weak moonlight. Reaching it, she hurried along, checking the edge from time to time, until she could both feel and see where the path led into the garden. Beyond the flower garden she knew there was a vegetable garden, and beyond that were several rows of fruit trees. Past the orchard she had seen large fields of crops of some kind. She had set as her first destination a road she had seen that ran between the trees and the fields. It was narrow, but well maintained as it was used to get supplies in, and the produce out. That road must lead to some main thoroughfare. On a major road she hoped to find some sort of public transport to take her to Rohnseff.

She hurried along through the night scented sweetness of the flower garden, on past the rows of vegetables until she came to an area where there were some storage sheds with produce containers stacked along the sides.

Security devices, she reminded herself. They probably have set up some sort of devices around this area to protect them from pilferage. With that in mind she tried to stay as far away from the sheds as possible without straying off the path which also might trigger some alarm.

She'd almost made it when, just as she was passing the last small garden shed, a hand suddenly clamped over her mouth and a strong arm wrapped around her waist. She lashed out and a voice whispered, "Shhhh, Madame. It is Bibdag, the gardener and a

friend. I not hurt you. I try help you."

Bibdag. Not a guard. She stopped kicking.

"Now, I loose my hand," Bibdag whispered. "Please, not make

calling." The hand came away from her mouth and the arm loosened. She turned and saw Bibdag, with his finger to his lips, motioning her to come with him.

"Well," she said softly, "I hope you are a friend because I surely could use some help."

Bibdag smiled and his large hand reached out and took the satchel. "Come. Very quiet. Stay close." He turned and she followed. Keeping in the shadows, they moved in between the fruit trees until they came to the road. Instead of going along the road, Bibdag crossed it and led her down into a shoulder-high depression which ran along one side. Crouching down, which wasn't easy for someone as big as Bibdag, they went as quickly as they could in that awkward position. Dulsena kept following him until the depression angled away from the road and veered off between two fields.

"Bibdag," she whispered and pulled on his robe to make him stop. "We're getting away from the road. I want to go to the main road. I have to get to Rohnseff!"

"Shhhhh, shhhhh," he hissed. "No road, no road. Very dangerous. Many guards, many, how you say, devices, alarms along road. Must stay in plants, in…in fields, then in trees. Please, trust Bibdag. I help you get away. But must be very careful. Come, please." He started off again.

What he had said made sense, so she followed after him. The depression became shallower and wider. Bibdag got down on his hands and knees and motioned for her to do the same. They crawled along until her hands and knees felt like they were on fire. Finally, when she thought she could stand it no longer, Bibdag rose to his knees and looked around. Grateful for the pause, Dulsena just lay and rested. On Resdorn participation in sports had been a large part of her life. According to Loran, however, such things were "not suitable for good Greniff wives." Now in the cycles of inactivity since she had come to Greniff she had lost much of the stamina she'd had before. Narm, she thought, I'm puffing like I'd played 12 shens of Latz Ball.

She sat up, and as she rubbed her stinging knees she looked around and saw that the gully they had been following had veered off into the trees. She saw Bibdag listening intently. She heard only the usual night sounds and he, too, apparently decided it was safe. Slowly he rose, stood quietly for a few seconds, then, motioning to Dulsena, whispered, "we walk little more".

Dulsena soon decided Bibdag had a gift for understatement as the "little more" turned out to be "a lot more" and her relief at being able to stand was replaced by the pain of walking over some very rough ground in her thin soled shoes. Only Bibdag's whispered, "Little more, little more," kept her moving. That, and the memory of Loran's angry face, helped her put one foot in front of the other.

Suddenly, Bibdag dropped to the ground, pulling Dulsena down with him. They stayed motionless for several minutes. Then, raising his fingers to his lips, Bibdag gave what she assumed was the call of some bird. Soon a similar call came back. Still they waited. He then gave the same call twice. The answering call was repeated three times. Only then did he rise and help her to her feet. Carefully they made their way toward a dark shadow which soon resolved into a small hut. The softest of sounds and a slight difference in the shadow showed a door opening. They slipped through and the door closed behind them. Only then was a glow light activated.

"Safe now here," Bibdag said. "Sit, rest."

Where "here" was she had no idea, and at the moment didn't care. She just collapsed onto the chair he held for her.

A voice, apparently that of an older woman, said, "Poor thing, she is worn out. Here, my Dear, have a drink of this and then you can lie down."

Dulsena wrapped her fingers around the cup that was put into her hand. It contained a warm, delicious broth and after draining the cup she began to think she might survive after all.

By this time her eyes had become accustomed to the light and she could see there were other people in the room besides Bibdag and the woman. For some reason they all seemed to be looking at her and waiting for something. "Bibdag," she said quietly, "what is going on? Where are we, who are these people and why are you willing to help me? I have been trying and trying to figure that out."

"This is hut of barget catcher," he said. "We come far from Brenev house—still on Brenev land. Why I help you? That long story. I, all peoples you see here this room, not from Greniff. We brought here by trouble, all different troubles and kept here by Brenevs. Your maid, Naba, she is one of us, too. She it was who first told us your troubles. For long time we have try think some way to help you if you need.

"All us know of your father, the Merchant Kalleni. All we hear says he is good man. We think maybe, we help you, he learn about Brenevs, maybe he help us."

Although she didn't understand how the Brenevs could have caused these people such harm, she could sense the tension filling the small room. That, and the earnestness in Bibdag's voice, made her believe she was hearing the truth.

Still holding the cup, she rose to her feet and said, "Bibdag, it is obvious that I very much need your help and I am grateful to you. However, in all fairness to you and your friends, I must say that my father is a merchant and the only way a merchant can do business on dozens of different planets is to remain strictly neutral. He never gets involved in the political situation of any planet. He can't afford to and still stay in business. I really don't see how he will be able to help you."

"All us here know many worlds. We know truth of what you say," answered Bibdag. "In truth, if you say, 'Yes, yes, he will help for sure' we maybe not believe all you say. But you not tire our ears with easy promises. You speak truth to us even if maybe lose help you need." He stood very tall and looking straight at her said, "I think Merchant Kalleni taught daughter well." The others nodded in agreement.

Dulsena's eyes filled with tears at his words. How sweet it was to hear these things, the praise for her father, certainly, but, more important, was the idea that these people respected her for being just herself. It had been such a long time since she had been considered anything but a disgraceful wife in need of "educating".

Blinking back the tears, she said, "I can't tell you how much your words mean to me. I don't know what I can do that would be of any help. However, I will give you my solemn promise that when I see my father again, I will do everything in my power to convince him to help you."

"No more we ask of you," Bibdag responded. "Now go with Leraph.

You sleep. Tomorrow be hard day for you, for all us."

The old woman motioned for Dulsena to follow her through a narrow passage which led to another molded hut. There were some primitive sanitary facilities and an old PCU (personal cleansing unit). She handed her a robe and some soft sandals and said that while Dulsena refreshed herself she would clean her clothes.

Clothes off and hair loosened she stepped into the PCU. What a relief it was to remove the dirt of that gully and feel the release of tension in those stressed muscles. Only the abrasions on her hands and knees and her tired feet were left as reminders of that dreadful trip. In spite of the unit being old and slow, she soon could slip into the clean robe the woman had left for her.

Opening the door, she discovered the woman waiting just outside as a mother waits for a small child. Indeed, at that moment, Dulsena felt like a small child, a very tired and vulnerable child.

The kind stranger smiled and led her back through the tunnel into the main room. Bibdag and the others had left and they were alone. Walking to the back of the hut, the woman opened some shutters and showed her the bed that had been built into the wall.

Dulsena protested, "I don't feel comfortable taking your bed from you. You've already done so much for me."

"About that you don't fret yourself," the woman replied. "These are extra beds especially for guests. My bed is across the room. Our quarters are small, but always there will be room for guests in any lodge of Gutorm Anfinru. Even if the lodge is on a strange world far from our home fires. Now here is some salve for you to rub into your scrapes. Rub it in good and then rest. We will talk more in the morning."

Bidding her good night, Dulsena climbed in, closed the shutters and rubbed the salve on all the sore places. They immediately felt warm and the pain subsided. What a relief! Then, snuggled down under the covers she said loudly enough for the woman to hear, "Oh, what a cozy haven this is."

She relaxed for the first time in many hours. The events of the day roiled and tumbled in her brain until they became a big whirlpool and she slept.

- 6 -
The Barget Hunter

The sound of a chair scraping across the floor brought Dulsena wide awake. Light filtering through the gaps in the shutters threw a pattern of broken stripes on the coverlet, and glinted off little dust motes that hung in the air. She could smell something cooking. It smelled wonderful.

She lay there, eyes wide open, clutching the blanket to her chin trying to remember where she was and how she had gotten there. The memory of yesterday's flight, the banquet, Loran's face as he pushed her and mocked her; it all came flooding back. She felt the abraded places on her hands and knees; reminders of that harrowing trip through the gully. Now, here she was waking up in this odd little cupboard of a bed, in a strange hut in the middle of the forest.

Her beautiful dreams for the future had been shattered. She thought she had made wise decisions. How wrong she had been. Loran had not only fooled her, but all of her family as well. Now she had seen Nayland's real character and it was black and ugly. His revelations of the night before had destroyed any love she had had for him. Worse yet, she felt she had lost something of herself as well; a confidence and belief in her own judgement.

If she could have been so wrong about something she had carefully weighed and considered how could she have confidence in herself in the future? She had believed in their love and what had it gotten her?

She had been held a prisoner and finally was forced to run for her life and seek shelter from strangers.

She rolled over onto her side and, reaching over, carefully opened the shutters a bit more. Over in the cooking center she saw the woman who had been so kind to her the night before. A man dressed in tight fitting hunter's clothes was sitting at the table. He sat slouched down on the back of his spine with his legs spread out in front of him, one crossed over the other. One arm was draped over the back of the chair and the other was resting on the table. He was tall and lean with long, very blond hair and had the weathered look of an outdoorsman. Just then he looked up and saw her. He grinned and flicked one finger from his forehead in a casual salute. The old woman seeing him move, turned and saw her, too.

In the daylight, Dulsena could see that the woman had soft, wavy grey hair that framed a rather long face with prominent cheek bones. At one time she must have been very beautiful. Her voice when she spoke, was well modulated, the voice of a cultured woman. That seemed out of place in these surroundings. "Good morning, good morning," she said smiling. "Did you have a nice rest?"

"Oh, yes," Dulsena replied, opening the shutters a bit more, "very nice, but, I fear I have overslept. It seems late."

"Well, yes, it is a little late," the woman said as she gathered up some things and came over to the bed. "But, considering the day you had yesterday, you are entitled to rest

in a bit. Here is your robe and your other clothes. My cleaning unit is old and balky, but at least they are better than before."

She handed Dulsena the clothes and added, "Your shoes are badly damaged. I think it would be best if you tucked them away and wear these instead. They are much sturdier and will be more comfortable for the kind of walking you must do today."

She handed Dulsena a pair of heavy shoes such as those she had seen the workers wear outdoors. They were dark brown with heavy soles and had a wide band across the instep with a pressure closure. They obviously had been worn as there were deep creases across the toes and the soles were worn down on one side. Dulsena wasn't quick enough at hiding her feelings and the woman saw how shocked she was at the thought of wearing someone else's shoes, especially shoes like this.

"I know they aren't fashionable, my dear, but they really will be better for your trip. I have cleaned them thoroughly."

Fearing she had appeared terribly ungrateful, Dulsena hurriedly said, "No, no they are fine. Really. I appreciate your letting me use them." The woman smiled and walked back towards the food preparation center.

Dulsena, feeling quite flustered and embarrassed, closed the shutters and retreated to the back of the bed, still awkwardly holding the shoes. The woman, Leraph, she remembered that was her name, was right, of course. This was no time to balk at something like wearing someone else's shoes. She needed to be dressed appropriately and her own shoes had certainly proven to be very uncomfortable for walking.

That settled, she took a deep breath and started to dress. Slipping on a robe is so easy when you are standing up. Getting one on in the cramped confines of a built-in bed, however, is not easy. After much bumping and bouncing about, she was finally able to escape the tangled covers and emerge, at least mostly dressed. Once out, she slipped on her "new" shoes and got somewhat more settled.

The woman, smiling at her efforts, said, "My son, Gutorm, has gone out to see if it is safe for you to go outside. Your absence may have been discovered by now, even though Naba was going to try to delay that as much as possible. Just in case, though, we think it best if you stay out of sight until you are ready to leave.

"Even if Gutorm thinks it is safe for you to go out, I want you to wear my shawl and try to walk as I do, so that from a distance you will look like me."

Dulsena assured her she appreciated her concern and would try to do as she directed. She then went off to the annex to freshen up. When she came back she saw that the man, now identified as Gutorm, had come back. He was younger than she had first thought. He looked at her, smiled and said, "I'm Gutorm. Bibdag didn't get around to introducing us last night. Now, I'm going to have to ask a question that

I usually don't ask girls that I've just met. How much do you weigh?" At her startled look he added, "If I seem rude please forgive me, but, I really do need to know."

It seemed a very strange question, but she replied as well as she could. He thanked her and added, "We haven't received any reports of an alarm being raised at the compound, so I believe it is safe for you to go out, if you should want to. Just be sure to do as my mother has instructed." Flashing her another big smile, he added, "Just cover that beautiful hair. For sure, it has been a while since Mother had hair that color."

Leraph laughed and, swatting at him with the cloth she held in her hand, said, "Not that many years, you fresh thing. Now get along and let us be about our business."

Gutorm, affecting a servile tone, bowed and backed away saying, "Oh yes, Madame, yes Madame, right away, Madame." Then, adjusting his cap at a jaunty angle, he flashed them a big smile and left.

Leraph, smiling wistfully, said, "For just that moment he was like the old Gutorm, the way he was before…" Then, as if catching herself, she gave Dulsena a wry look and said, "Life takes some strange twists, sometimes, doesn't it?"

Dulsena wholeheartedly agreed to that. She smiled and said ruefully, "Oh, yes, Madame. Twists that one could never imagine."

There eyes met and, for a moment, each recognized the hurt in the other. Leraph, with a wry look, shrugged, then walked across the room and took a dark shawl from the pegs near the door. The shawl was very light in weight and draped beautifully over Dulsena's hair and shoulders. Leraph stepped back to get a better view and then nodded in approval.

"Much better on you than on me," she said smiling.

Dulsena demurred, but Leraph brushed aside her objections and opening the door, encouraged her to enjoy the morning air.

Dulsena stepped through into a beautiful sunshiny day and began walking slowly around the clearing. The air was fresh and the morning light was pale rose and blue. Neither her robe nor the cloak was the correct color for such a morning and no fountain followed the tempo of the morning prayer. The only morning chimes were those of some songbirds in a tree nearby. Nevertheless, it felt good to be there in the sun-dappled clearing.

After a few moments, Gutorm came out of the hut and walked past her saying softly, "Your food will be ready shortly, Dulsena." He walked on across the clearing and disappeared into the woods.

Remembering the little charade, she walked slowly and reluctantly back into the hut. Once inside, she seated herself on the edge of the bed, removed the shawl and rewound her hair. Tidy once more, with the satchel repacked, she was ready for the breakfast Leraph had prepared.

The table was set with a bright yellow cloth, cheerful blue dishes and a bouquet of wildflowers. Her appetite had returned with her confidence and she ate every morsel of the delicious food. Cleaned up and well fed, she was now anxious to resume her flight to freedom.

Gutorm had told her he was making arrangements and that she would leave when he returned. Now, the waiting seemed endless. She helped her hostess with some little tasks, but mostly she fidgeted and fretted despite Leraph's repeated assurances that the men would work things out for her. She got more and more nervous until the inactivity became almost unbearable and all her doubts came flooding back. Having been betrayed by Loran, she now found herself questioning the motives of everyone. Maybe these new friends weren't friends at all. Maybe they were just making a deal with Loran for her return, buying their way back home, using her as hostage. On and on the doubts and worries roiled and tumbled until her nerves were stretched to the limit. She had even begun to think of leaving and starting out on her own when Gutorm finally returned.

He apparently could sense the change in her attitude for he gave her a sharp look when she rose abruptly and said, "Well, what has been done?"

"Arrangements have been made," he said patiently. "First we will eat a little and then we will walk through the back woods to the shipping rail just outside the Brenev boundaries. There you can get a ride to the outskirts of Rohnseff."

Rohnseff, the spaceport. She felt weak with relief. Maybe it would be all right after all.

Gutorm and Leraph exchange worried looks. Leraph said, "Gutorm, must she go right away today? She is still worn out from yesterday."

"Yes, yes," Dulsena interrupted, "I can't bear to wait any longer. It must be now."

Gutorm agreed, and said all the arrangements had been made for that evening. Leraph shrugged and set about putting food and drinks on the table, at the same time saying, "Well, at least you can start out with a full stomach. I've also packed a lunch for you, Dulsena."

Gutorm thanked her and handed Dulsena an old satchel, saying, "Dulsena, I think it would be a good idea to change your possessions to this other satchel. Yours is so obviously off-world that it will draw attention to you. This one is a little worn, but it is the kind everyone in this area uses. It will not look out of place."

She agreed and quickly transferred her things. By the time she was finished, the food was ready. It was meat stew of some sort and a strange green, flat bread. The taste was different, but not unpleasant. Besides, she really wasn't thinking about the food.

The afternoon shadows were very long across the clearing before Gutorm said it was time to leave. She bade goodby to Leraph, thanked her for being so kind, picked up her "new" satchel and hurried after Gutorm.

They left the clearing and started through the woods in back of the cabin. Climbing steadily, they followed a trail that only Gutorm could see. Night was falling and the first moon was already on the horizon before they stopped just short of the top of the mountain for what Dulsena considered a long overdue rest.

Gutorm grinned as he watched her fling herself to the ground and start taking in great gulps of air.

"Not funny," Dulsena said shortly. "A year ago this would have been nothing. I'm just out of shape from living in that prison down there."

"I know," Gutorm said sympathetically. "It couldn't have been easy for you. Rest a bit and we'll go when you're ready."

A minute later she scrambled to her feet saying, "I'm fine now. Lead on." There were fewer trees at that altitude and less undergrowth which made for easier walking. Staying below the ridge line so they wouldn't be silhouetted against the sky, and keeping to the shadows as much as possible, they made their way down to a small valley. Since they were going downhill, Gutorm set a fast pace and they made good time. The new shoes Leraph had given Dulsena, while ugly, were indeed much more comfortable than the ones she had worn the day before and she was able to keep up.

They climbed up and over several hills until, at last they could look down and see the shiny ribbon of the shipping rail. For quite a while, they stayed in the shadows under the trees, watching and listening. Finally, Gutorm, apparently satisfied that it was safe, nodded, put his hand to his lips and directed her forward. He moved very quietly and she tried hard to do the same. Carefully, they came to where a small group of trees grew to within a step or two of the railway. There, in the dark shadows, they sat and waited and rested.

Gutorm, checking his chronos, said very softly, "It shouldn't be too long before your next guide will be along in his shipping car. He will only be able to stop for a few seconds so you must be ready to get in very quickly. You jump in and I will hand you your satchel. At the same time a carton that will equal your weight plus the weight of the satchel, will be thrown off."

Seeing Dulsena's puzzled expression he explained, "The rates on the shipping rail are set by weight and by the time of day. The owner's car is weighed when they access the rail and again at the egress as well as at various points along the rail. There are different rates for those who stop for markets along the way and for those who ship straight through to the market warehouse area in Rohnseff. Your guide always ships straight through and any deviation from this would be noticed. Also, any deviation in the weight from one checkpoint to the next would be marked.

"Once in Rohnseff, he will stop on the outskirts of the market. You will quickly get out, taking your satchel with you. Another man will be ready to put a carton of similar weight back into the car. The man with the carton will then take you the rest of the way to the space port. Is that all clear to you?"

She repeated the transfer routine to him and told him she thought she could manage that. "However," Dulsena whispered, "it seems to me that the big problem will be the guards at the space port. How can I get past them?"

"The man with the carton is a merchant and he will get you through into the freight area on one of his passes. Once there he will hand you over to another trader who has access to the rest of the port. He will take you to the Port Master. Once you have explained your problem to him, he will surely help, since he and your father are good friends."

Dulsena reviewed what he had said and couldn't see any obvious problems. It did involve several people, but, on the whole, it seemed like it might work. The idea of soon meeting a friend of her father made her all the more anxious to get there. She kept watching where the rail wound out of sight and wished the shipping car would come.

Gutorm leaned back in the grass and smiled. "Don't fret," he whispered. "Soon you will be on your way home. And, if your father is willing to help us, maybe we, all those people you saw last night, will soon be going home too."

"Where is your home, Gutorm?" Dulsena asked.

The smile left his face and he sat quietly for a few moments before answering. "My home is in the mountains. Actually in a valley in the mountains. There are beautiful trees, many lakes and rivers and birds and animals of all kinds. It is on a small planet named Frayleen. That is in the Jorbar system. Frayleen never had a lot of industry. We produce only what we ourselves use. So, after we joined the Federation, it was decided that it would be best for us to develop our tourist accommodations. Many people come, have always come, to Frayleen on holiday. They enjoy the moderate climate and our beautiful mountains and oceans.

"For many generations my family has owned a large area of forest land with many lodges and facilities for tourists. We were prosperous and very happy and content until the arrival of Nayland Brenev." The hatred with which he spoke that name said a lot.

"How could Nayland's arrival have changed things so much?" Dulsena asked.

"Brenev is rich and powerful," he answered. "He is used to getting what he wants. He saw our beautiful area and decided he wanted it. Looking back later, we realized he must have been planning for a long time. We never suspected. Not once. He came many times, but, he never let us see him as anything but the friendly tourist. And why not friends? We are a friendly people. "Nayland Brenev, always so congenial, so charming. An oh so satisfied guest at our resorts. And all the while..."

The telling of this apparently caused him great anguish. He pushed himself to his feet and paced rapidly for several seconds before he could continue. Then, squatting down, he balanced easily with his arms loose on his knees. He nervously pulled at the grass near his feet and looked up and down the valley. Then, clearing his throat, he started to speak again very softly.

"Nayland soon made it clear that he was interested in our Dordi, my sister. Dordi was very...Dordi was very beautiful." Here he stopped again and cleared his throat, before continuing.

"Dordi..., well she thought Brenev was charming. He gave her little gifts, told her she was beautiful and then asked her to marry him. To her, it all seemed so perfect, a fairy tale type of love. But, my mother and I, we began to have a lot of doubts about the whole thing.

"Nayland Brenev, why he was a wealthy man, a sophisticated man and our Dordi she was very young. She'd never even been away from home, except for short periods. Such an uneven match, we thought. It did not seem it could be good, this marriage of two people so different. But, Dordi...Dordi saw only what Nayland wanted her to see, and no matter what we said, she was determined to marry him. She was so sure love would smooth out any differences.

"So, they were married and after the wedding he took her away. A long time it was before we had a message from her and then it was a strange, stilted message. Very formal, full of words and phrases not at all like our Dordi. Other messages came at long intervals and then nothing. We wrote, but all our letters were unanswered. All our attempts to reach Nayland failed. We asked our Consul to intercede, but even he was ignored. Nayland would not respond.

"At last we, my mother and I, we decided we must come to Greniff to find Dordi, find out what has happened to her. When we arrived at Rohnseff, at the spaceport, we were taken to a private reception area. Nayland was seated at a desk working with some records. He didn't even rise as my mother and I came in. He just looked up at us in that rude, insolent way he has and told us, 'it is unfortunate you made such a long trip for nothing as Dordi is too unwell to receive you'.

"Naturally, my mother became terribly upset and she told him in no uncertain words that she wanted to be taken to see Dordi immediately.

"No," he said in a nasty, arrogant tone, "I cannot allow that. The strain would be too much for her, I'm sure."

"Mother was furious. 'How can seeing her mother be bad for her?' she asked him.

He just said something about how 'Dordi has been under a lot of stress. Apparently, she thinks the marriage was a mistake'. He went on to say that, considering her attitude, he would be willing to terminate the marriage contract if certain "arrangements" could be made. Well, of course, we asked him what "arrangements" he was talking about. Turns out, he would have the marriage declared invalid in exchange for our signing over titles to all our lands and resorts on Frayleen."

At Dulsena's horrified expression, Gutorm gave a harsh little laugh and said, "Oh yes, your husband's brother is a fine piece of business, he is. He'll do anything and everything if there is a profit to be made."

He paused and then added, "And you know what is really frightening, sometimes there doesn't seem to be any profit involved. It appears that he sometimes does things like this just out of pure meanness.

"Anyway, after he told us what he wanted, we couldn't believe he was serious. See, we didn't know him so well then. But, he was serious. Oh yes, he was. Well, we told him he was crazy and stormed out. We went to the authorities, but they said they couldn't do anything as it was a civil matter. We then sought legal counsel thinking the judicial system could help us, but Nayland has a lot of influence and the judge refused to believe our allegations, or so he said. All the while, Nayland kept taunting us saying that we had better make up our minds to cooperate or Dordi would not be able to come home with us. It was quite clear what he meant.

"Finally, mother and I decided we had to rescue Dordi first and then worry about the court appeals after that. We demanded that Dordi be brought to us before we would sign anything.

"When they brought her to us we could not believe what we were seeing. It was pathetic." Gutorm's voice broke and he had to stop. He cleared his throat and then in a low voice continued, "She was so weak she could barely stand. All she could do was cry at the sight of us. A once beautiful, happy girl who sang and laughed her way through life had been reduced to this…this shell. For the first time in my life I wanted to kill someone. I leaped at him, but those guards of his beat me off.

"There was nothing else we could do, so my mother and I signed his papers. And do you know, as we were leaving, Nayland laughed, saying he didn't think we had made a good deal as she really wasn't worth it. Can you imagine him saying that?"

Dulsena nodded. She was too shocked to speak.

"We went directly to the spaceport," Gutorm continued, "to go back to Frayleen. We no longer had a home or lands of our own, but, we had friends we could go to. Then, just before we were to board our flight, we were arrested. We found out later that for a long time Nayland had been secretly buying up other lands around ours and now, with the deeds to our lands, he had become a powerful landowner. He then had trumped up charges against us of "attempt to defraud". The charges were ridiculous of course. However, we found that the name of Brenev and the money of Brenev works wonders in the courts. Especially in the courts of Greniff where no one knew us and there was no one to speak for us. We were declared immigrants without funds and Nayland bought our indemnity. He bought us. Yes, he bought us. He gave a great sigh and then continued, "I was given a new occupation, that of barget hunter and we were given that hut to live in. My sister, our Dordi, died one cycle later."

By the end of this horrible recital his face was contorted with anguish and his eyes were dark and wild as he looked at Dulsena and said, "Now can you see why we want to get away from here? Why we need someone on the outside to speak for us? Never will we have justice in the courts here!"

Dulsena was so shocked by his recital that it was difficult for her to form the words she wanted to say. "The others…the people I saw last night in your hut, were they treated the same way?"

"Oh, yes, every one of them. Oh their stories are a little different, but there is one common thread, the never ending greed of Nayland Brenev. That man, oh my, he can think of more ways to cheat and hurt than most people could ever possibly imagine."

Dulsena seldom found herself at a loss for words, but what can one say to such a story? Remembering the smile on Nayland's face at that dinner party she could readily believe what Gutorm had said about him. She shivered to think how close she had come to being another of Nayland's defenseless victims. And Loran, her loving husband Loran, had planned to turn her over to him.

Glancing at Gutorm, she saw him still taut and shaken from his recital. Obviously, behind that smile was a man filled with hatred. She put her hand on his and said, "I think Nayland Brenev made himself a dangerous enemy when he wronged you and your family."

He smiled a crooked little smile and said, "I hope some day he too will know that."

Just then they heard the sound of a shipper car approaching. They stood and Gutorm took her hand and pressed something into it.

"I want you to have this stunner in case something happens and you should have to face Nayland."

Before she could speak he gathered up her satchel, took her arm and led her quickly down to the side of the rail way. The car stopped abruptly and the side door opened.

"Quickly, quickly," said a voice from the dark interior. A quick kiss on the cheek and she was lifted into the car and at the same time a large carton was pushed onto the siding.

"Here is your satchel, Dulsena," whispered Gutorm. "Good Luck". The door closed and they were off, quickly gaining speed.

"A person is lucky to have such a friend as Gutorm," said the voice from the back.

The driver nodded in agreement. Dulsena too agreed and touched the spot where that kiss had rested so lightly.

The night outside the window was just a blur of shadows. The men were quiet and she had time to examine the stunner that she still held in her hand. It was too dark to see it, nor did she want the men to see it, but she could tell by the feel that it wasn't a stunner as Gutorm had said: It was a full-power, multi-range laser weapon. She and her father had used these many times in target shooting. Her mother had been very insistent that if she were going to travel off world to all sorts of societies she must be able to defend herself, if necessary. Slipping the laser into her satchel she felt grateful to Gutorm for parting with such a valuable item. Hopefully, if things continued going so well, she would never have to use it.

Over and over she reviewed the plan as outlined by Gutorm. So many people, such precise timing. So many places for things to go wrong and nothing, really, that she could do. She felt like a parcel that was being handed from one person to another. Finally, watching the blur of shadows outside the window, she dozed off.

She awoke to the touch of the man in the back.

"Get ready, My Lady. Throw off your satchel first, then jump after it. There will be a man there to take you the rest of the way."

The car glided to a stop and the door opened. She did as she had been told. A large crate was thrust into her place, the door closed and the car was off. She was alone in the night with yet another stranger.

This new stranger, it was too dark to see him clearly, picked up her satchel before she could and motioned for her to follow him to a merchandise transport that was parked nearby. They climbed in and started off.

After a few minutes the man looked at her and said, "This must be very frightening for you."

This was so unexpected that she started to laugh. He looked sharply at her and said, "You are not frightened?"

"Oh, yes," she answered. "I'm frightened. I'm so frightened it's like there are two parts to me. One half is so scared I can't move and the other just keeps moving, moving, doing whatever I'm told, doing all these strange things I never dreamed I could do. It's interesting really. I never knew I could be this frightened and still move."

Now it was the man's turn to laugh. He turned to her and said, "That, my dear, is what is known as courage."

She thought for a moment then shook her head ahd said, "No, I don't feel courageous. I feel lots of other things, anger, disappointment, rejection, fear, but I don't feel at all courageous."

"Well," he said, "I think you are being courageous and, if you will just continue being brave for a little longer, we should be able to get you back to your family very soon now."

"Oh, I hope so," she said fervently. "I really do hope so, but, we still have to get into the space port."

"Well, we will soon be stopping at a building up ahead. I have a pass into the freight area of the port and you will go in with me. Once at the freight area I will turn you over to another guide who will take you directly to the Port Master."

And that is what they did. Slick as can be they were waved on through the check point into Rohnseff space port. It worked, she thought. We made it.

At the freight area she was transferred like any other piece of cargo to the next guide, who introduced himself as Grafin. Clutching her satchel she was hustled over to a sleek, fast-looking flyer. She stopped and said, "Wait. We're just going to the port authorities, why do we need a flyer?"

"My dear, this is a very large port," Grafin said in a patronizing tone. "Why, the terminal is over 2 kilometers from this freight area. It will be much faster and easier for you if we fly over. After all, you've had a tiring night."

She still didn't see the reasoning behind this, but he kept urging her on and she found herself being lifted into the back of the flyer. Another man, who had been waiting off to the side, followed her in. They taxied to a pad and took off.

The cabin was so packed with crates that she could barely slide into her seat and then her knees were almost up against a crate. On the side of the crate were the letters P-I-T-A-N. The letters were so large that she could either focus on them or let her eyes go crossed.

"What are peetan?" she asked.

"Peetan," Grafin asked blankly.

"Yes, P-I-T-A-N"

"Oh," he laughed, "you mean pie-tan. They are a bakery product made from a green grain mixed with some other ingredients and rolled out into very thin, little, flat crackers."

"Must be those little green wafers Leraph served with the soup," she said. But why, she mused to herself, would Grafin have his personal flier loaded with boxes of crackers when...She glanced out the window and saw that they were heading away from the port.

"Hey! Stop! You are going away from the port!" she yelled.

She tried to get up but the man had come up behind her and forced her down in the seat.

"Stay where you are or you will get hurt, Lady Loran." Grafin said. "We will soon have you back home where you belong."

Back? Back to Nayland? Back to life as a Greniff wife?

"No!" she yelled. "No, you can't take me back! Take me to Rohnseff so I can go to my father. You know of Rimini Kalleni. He will reward you for helping me."

"No, I can't do that," Grafin said. "Nayland Brenev has ordered that you be returned to the Compound."

Turning to the man behind her she pleaded, "Please, help me. Don't do this. My father will reward you far beyond what Nayland Brenev has promised you."

The man just shook his head and then Grafin said, "Just relax. We will have you back at the compound shortly."

Back. Back to Loran and his broken vows. Back to his brother to be "educated", to be "quickened" and made into a "good Greniff wife".

"Like Narm you will," she shouted. She didn't take time to pull the laser out of the satchel, she just grabbed it and shot straight at his back, right through the satchel. Turning she swept a beam across the man at the side. He fell backwards and then lunged towards her again, trying to grab her arm. The flyer was going down at a steep angle and, as she fought with the man, he lost his footing and she shot him again.

Thrusting the laser back into her satchel, she clambered into the empty front seat and struggled to bring the flyer under control. It was no use. They were too low. The best she could do was bring it in level and pray.

- 7 -
Rohnseff Spaceport

The sleek trading ship slipped into the docking bay and the side door slid open. A handsome, muscular man with curly, dark blonde hair stepped through the doorway and stood waiting impatiently as the walkway was lowered into place. The sun glinted off the sprinkling of silver at each temple hinting at an age that the youthful figure belied. He was dressed Resdornian style in a rich cream colored business robe with broad bands of dark blue denoting his status as a member of the Federation Trade Council. The calf length kaiton fit smoothly over his hips and fell in broad pleats in front and back and, as he moved down the ramp, the movement of these pleats emphasized his impatience.

The pleats of the kaiton were repeated in the shirt front and the neckline of the shirt turned back, on the diagonal, to reveal a dark blue triangle. On this triangle glinted the small silver cornucopia which was the insignia of House of Kalleni. The younger man who followed him down the ramp was dressed similarly, except the bands on the bottom of his kaiton and the shirt lapel were a lighter blue. He too wore the silver cornucopia. The strong physical resemblance made it clear they were father and son or perhaps brothers. Both men were very tall and they moved with long ground-eating strides through the terminal. Other pedestrians moved aside and crowds parted as the two walked briskly, side by side, through corridors and offices leaving doors half open and Space Port Personnel scattered in their wake. The Port

Officer's secretary scarcely had time to announce their names before they burst into Captain Xholan's office.

Their arrival, as swift as it was, was not unexpected. The Port Officer had been alerted as soon as the Kalleni craft had docked. Now he rose and, hand outstretched, went to meet the men. He took the older man's hand in both of his, and pulling him close, said, "Rimini, Rimini Kalleni, how good to see you, old friend, but how terrible that it must be under such circumstances."

"Yes, my dear Xholan, yes," said Rimini. "I am so happy to see you. Good friends draw to good friends in times of trouble. Not hearing from Dulsena has caused us great concern."

"Oh, yes, I quite understand," said Captain Xholan. "But please, Rimini, before we talk more of this concern, let us retire to some place more comfortable where we can take some refreshment."

"Yes, Xholan, you are right, of course. That would be a good idea. As anxious as I am to find Dulsena I must admit it has been a very tiring trip. But first, I must apologize. I have been most rude in not introducing my son. "Scortzi, I would like you to meet Captain Rhys Xholan, an old friend. We first met in Lorbar on Nichi when I was about your age."

"I am indeed honored to meet you, Sir," said Scortzi.

"And I you, young man," answered Captain Xholan. "It feels like time is repeating itself to meet you, for you are so like your father when first we met."

"I consider that a great compliment, Sir. Thank you," Scortzi responded with a smile.

A tall, dark haired man had followed them into the room and was introduced by Captain Xholan as Lieutenant Lanti, his Administrative Assistant and friend.

"Now," said Captain Xholan, "let us find some more comfortable spot to relax where we can have some refreshments and catch up with the years."

Leading the way, Captain Xholan directed them to a liftway and waited as the others entered. The liftway was enclosed in a transparent shaft which gave a marvelous view of the harbour and the docking areas for surface and sub-surface ocean craft, and the entrances to the underwater transport systems. Captain Xholan pointed out that docking facilities for inter-planetary and local air vehicles were on the other side of the building. Stepping out of the liftway they avoided the fast moving pedestrian walk in favor of a long winding path paved with multi-colored stones. On either side of the path were neat bushes with bright scarlet and yellow flowers. They had a rather sharp, pungent scent which was unusual, but not unpleasant.

Scortzi, walking along with Lieutenant Lanti, made polite inquiries about the nature of the flowering bushes and then asked about the harbour facilities. Captain Xholan and Rimini were similarly occupied. To the casual observer it would seem that they were concerned only with enjoying the beauties of the day.

Entering a beautiful garden, the Captain led them through an area where many people were seated at small tables. He smiled and nodded at them at the same time saying, "I think you will like the food and drinks here, Rimini. I remember how you liked to try new delicacies."

"Indeed, Xholan, and a most profitable weakness it has been. I like to think that if I find things enjoyable, that others also will like them. Then I take steps to include them in our inventory."

At the far side of the dining area, the Captain directed them into a small, private dining room. A discreet sign near the door marked it as a confi-unit. Once they were seated a human waiter, not a robo-serv, took their order. As the door whispered shut, and the anti-surveillance screen was activated, Xholan said, "You noticed that, Rimini? That was one of the first things that set me to wondering about things here. Why would a planet as advanced as this still have humans performing such menial tasks. Only now, with what Lanti and I have uncovered and the information we received from you, are we beginning to understand.

"It is not safe to speak of such things in my office for I'm sure there have been surveillance devices installed. We also have reason to believe that the security systems of both our homes have been breached."

"Yes, I surmised that when you told me it was unsafe to speak," replied Rimini.

Seeing Lieutenant Lanti's questioning look, he went on to explain, "We both know the secret language spoken by the traveling priests and merchants of old. It is a sign language based on various finger and hand positions and pressures. Messages can be sent that cannot be detected by outsiders. In ancient days trade agreements were made by both merchants placing their hands in a bag and doing all their negotiating under cover. That way no other traders could see the prices offered or accepted. These same hand signs have been converted to a written language and it was in this way that we communicated first in the message Xholan sent to me, and then again with his handshake.

"I have taught this language to Scortzi, although on most worlds such stealth is no longer needed." Turning to his son he smiled and said, "You see, Scortzi, I told you that such knowledge might come in handy sometime."

"It already has been useful, Father," laughed Scortzi. "Dulsena and I used it many times to confound professors at the University."

The waiter returned as the other men laughed at Scortzi's admission. After serving them their food and drinks the waiter left, sealing the door behind him.

"Now, Xholan," said Rimini, "What have you learned of this matter?"

"Rimini, no one could be more shocked than I have been to learn the extent of Nayland Brenev's activities," responded Captain Xholan. "When I was first transferred to Greniff I heard only of the wonders of this beautiful planet with its abundant natural resources. As I learned more I began to see how the net of Brenev Industries has woven throughout every facet of industry and trade. They control things while at the same time they personally keep far enough in the background so as not to be obviously connected.

"After I picked up this thread of subterfuge, it seemed best for me to pursue it on my own, with only the help of Lieutenant Lanti who has been with me for many years, and whom I trust completely. As for the rest of my staff, it is the same as when my predecessor was here, and I have not been here long enough to know whom I can trust.

"It has been very difficult for us to pursue our search without being detected and yet we felt we had to continue. Much of what we found could not be confirmed. There were just suggestions, innuendos, little pieces of information that in and of themselves did not seem particularly important. It was not until we started putting them together that a pattern began to form."

"We needed proof," Lanti said, "but we were unsure how many records we could access without revealing our searchings."

"Lanti is right," Xholan agreed. "You must understand, Rimini, much of what Lanti and I were going on was suspicion, a gut feeling, if you will. Starting out, we knew something was wrong, but we didn't know what.

"And there were times," he laughed and looked at Lanti who smiled too, "when frankly, we wondered if we were chasing shadows, imagining things. However, your message confirmed our suspicions and we increased our efforts."

"Yes," sighed Rimini, "It took us a long while to believe that Loran Brenev could actually be refusing to let us see Dulsena. We had felt only admiration and affection for him when he was on Resdorn. Never in the slightest action had he shown us this side of his character, this total lack of compassion and, yes, though I'm reluctant to say it, this unbalanced state of mind.

"He had us all fooled. He seemed to sincerely love Dulsena and told us of their plans to return to Weneche. Loran was to continue as Trade Manager for his family's business and Dulsena, as you know, was training to take over the fine arts trade for House of Kalleni. They had everything all planned. It just seems incomprehensible that he could change so drastically in such a short time. It's like he is a different person."

"Well," said Captain Xholan, "You have heard about the death of his older brother, Albar, have you not?"

"Yes we heard about it, but we don't understand why that changed things," Rimini said.

"The first thing to understand is that their business is run by family and there's a lot of family."

Lt. Lanti nodded and said, "When we started listing everyone involved we were shocked. There seems to be no end to the cousins etc. who are involved."

"Li's right," the captain laughed, shaking his head. "You should see that family tree. Anyway, for years Albar managed the agricultural interests for the Brenev's. When he died, unexpectedly, they had to reshuffle assignments. The family decided that Loran would be moved from Resdorn back to Greniff and another cousin was assigned to replace him as Trade Manager on Resdorn. Well, obviously, this meant a big change for Loran. He would no longer be living in the free and easy society of Resdorn. Now that he was 'back in the bosom of his family', so to speak, he and his new bride would be constantly under observation. It was essential they keep all the old laws and customs of Grenechan socity and, most important, their conduct towards his family had to be above reproach. I doubt if it ever occurred to him to question whether his wife would agree with whatever he chose to do. In Grenechan society the idea that a wife would refuse to do what she was told was inconceivable."

"Well," said Scortzi, "anyone knowing Dulsena could have told him there was no chance she would agree to such a thing."

"It seems to me," Lieutenant Lanti put in, "that the older brother, Nayland, has a very powerful hold over his brother. In fact he rules the whole family including his own father. Under his cover as a charming, indulged, rich man's son, he has amassed tremendous power over numerous worlds. It has always been true that there are people of a certain type who flock to men like that. They are willing to do anything he wants in exchange for riches and a little power for themselves. Right and wrong do not enter into their thoughts."

"You are quite right," Rimini said fiercely. "And it is a terrible thing for the whole of society when a man such as that can run rampant, breaking both Federation and planetary laws and subverting the court systems of countless planets as well. He must be stopped and he must be stopped now, before anything worse happens to Dulsena, or anyone else. Now let's put all our facts together and see what sort of a solution we can come up with."

It was late afternoon before they emerged from the confi-unit, shook hands and separated to put their plans into action.

- 8 -
Dulsena

The thick, dark Sneltzens had given way to slender, yellow trunked trees that lined the stream in thick stands. Sometimes the trees followed the banks and other times wandered into the water. Stiff, twiggy, rust colored bushes grew in amongst the trees and made it hard to tell whether they stood on the ground or in the water. After several missteps Dulsena was soaked to the waist and gave up trying to follow the shore. She just waded along in the stream.

She slogged on muttering, "I really hate this. I really, really hate this." Her little litany, while not very original, did keep the adrenalin flowing. It also kept her from hearing what she should have heard before. Voices.

When they did get her attention, she quickly dropped on all fours and frantically worked her way into the bushes, hoping desperately she had not been heard.

The voices of two men came from just up the hill. It sounded like they were moving along parallel with the stream. Could they, she wondered, look down into where she was hiding? She pressed down even further into the muddy ground scarcely daring to breathe.

The men were speaking Greneche. Another voice called out from further up the hill and the men near her answered and then left, leaving her weak with relief. After waiting a bit to get her nerve back, she started to rise.

"No, Dulsena." The sharp stage whisper scared here so that she went right back, flat into the mud.

"Who the Narm are you?" she hissed. Her thoughts were racing, trying to make sense of what had just happened.

"Stay down, Dulsena, they have sensors set up on the ridge and are scanning this area," the voice whispered. "You don't know me, but I am part of the group working under Gutorm. We heard about Grafin's flyer crashing. When there was no report of your having been found at the crash site, we thought you would be trying to make your way on foot and hoped to intercept you before Brenev's men found you. I had just picked up your trail and had almost reached you when those men came over the ridge.

"Now then, here we are and here we will stay for a while. When we do move you must follow my instructions exactly. Understood?"

"Yes, I understand," she whispered back.

She lay listening intently. The men apparently had left. At least she couldn't hear them any longer. The only sounds were the bubbling of the stream over the rocks and the whine of insects. It was warm and she'd had very little sleep last night. Since she couldn't move she figured she might as well rest, if the insects would allow. Easing her arms under her head, she pulled the hood of her cloak over her head, buried her face and dozed. Movement was limited to the occasional flick of a finger to discourage a too adventurous flying or creeping insect. The time seemed to pass very slowly.

The sun was much higher in the sky before she again heard the voice whisper, "Dulsena, Dulsena. Do you hear me?"

"Yes," she whispered back.

"Soon we will move. First, I want you to think of how animals move. We will become two animals who have left the stream and now are moving slowly up the hill. We do not move in a straight line from the stream to the top, we go this way and that, we stop where the cover is heavy as if we are browsing. We will come together, we will separate, drifting slowly to the top. Do you see how this can be done?"

"Understood," she said.

And when he said, "Now, move, slowly, slowly," she moved slowly,

slowly. She sensed that her unseen friend was doing the same.

It seemed a very long time before they topped the hill and started across the fields toward the shelter of a dark stand of Sneltzen trees. What a relief to clamber beneath the dark fringed branches and stretch her complaining muscles. The other “animal” crawled in beside her, and a nice looking animal he was, too. Young, dark curly hair and blue eyes with thick dark lashes and, although he was slender, he had broad shoulders and the look of an athlete.

He rolled onto one side, smiled and said, “So, this is the fair Dulsena. Somehow I hadn’t imagined you with mud all over your face and bugs in your hair.”

At her look of indignation, he rushed to add, “Well don’t fret about it. I also can imagine that once you are cleaned up you might be quite presentable. At any rate I think we did very well, at least we don’t seem to have aroused any suspicions.”

Despite his woodsman’s clothing his speech indicated a well educated man from the Stolarn System. She had met trade representatives from there, in Resdorn at the trade marts.

“What is a nice young man from Stolarn doing under a Sneltzen tree on Greniff?” she asked sweetly.

His eyes widened with surprise and he said, “Ahh, You are a sharp one. Gutorm said he thought you were. Why am I here? Oh that is a long story, too long for here. My name is Derek, by the way, and I’m just one of the many who have had their lives turned inside out by Nayland Brenev. But, I tell you what. Since you are obviously dying to know all about me, when we’re safely away from here we’ll arrange to spend some nice, quiet time together, just the two of us, and I’ll tell you all about my wonderful exploits and deeds of daring-do.”

At her rather inelegant snort of disgust, he blithely said, “No, no, that’s quite all right. It won’t be any bother at all. Now however, as much as I would like to spend more time with you in this cozy bower, we do need to move. We have a way to go yet before we’re in the clear. I know you’re a fragile city girl, so I will try to take it easy. Are you ready?”

She definitely was ready. Fragile city girl. Take it easy, would he, she fumed. All her life she'd managed to keep up with Scortzi and his friends. Some University boy from Stolarn wasn't going to have to "take it easy" for her. Grabbing her satchel, she followed him from their shelter and they started through the woods.

He moved like Gutorm, quietly, with long easy strides that, she was chagrined to find, left her hard put to keep up. Her shoes were soaked and squished and slid as she walked, adding to the problem. From time to time, he would stop in some sheltered area and, leaving her, would go back a different way to check whether they were being followed. She tried to seem indifferent to these rests, but they did give her a chance to catch her breath and try to do something with the increasingly uncomfortable shoes.

When forced to move out of the trees, he kept to shallow areas or followed along the rocky outcroppings. No matter where he went, she was determined to keep up and smiled brightly each time he looked back to check on her.

Late afternoon she lay on another hillside watching yet another hut in the center of a small clearing. Derek was once again checking their back trail. A bush moved and he slid into place beside her. She hadn't even heard him coming.

Stretched out beside her, he dropped his head to his arm to rub away the perspiration from his forehead and eyes, and pulled out his pentrascope. "Anyone gone in or out?" he whispered.

She shook her head and mouthed "no".

He watched a bit longer and then, putting his scope away, motioned for her to follow him. They went to the door of the hut, knocked, and went in. No one was there.

The hut was another of the molded units similar to the one used by Gutorm and Leraph. The furnishings were simple, but in the adjoining room was both a clothes cleansing unit and a PCU. At the moment that was all she cared about.

She closed the door on the world, stripped off her filthy, mud covered clothes and threw them into the cleaner. She stepped into the PCU and luxuriated in the warmth and the welcome relief of being clean. If only, she thought sadly, along with the dirt from that creekbed, I could wash away all the betrayals and the fears. Wash them all away and go home to Resdorn where things were what they seemed.

Suddenly, cutting through all the memories of home, there was the sudden knowledge that there was something she wanted even more than going home, she wanted to make sure that the Brenevs were stopped. Stopped, so they could never hurt her or anyone else again. At that moment she realized she had became one with the exiles, or rather, the other exiles, for she, too, was now an exile. It was a sobering thought. Anger at Loran and the other Brenevs wasn't enough. Anger must be transformed into action.

Standing tall, head high, she slowly and softly said, "I swear, by all I deem Holy, I will do whatever I can to help these people bring Nayland Brenev to justice." She was hit with the thought at how ludicrous she must seem standing stark naked in an old PCU making noble vows. However, her resolve was firm. Their goal had become her goal.

She stepped out of the PCU, changed into her cleaned clothes and retrieved her cosmetic bag from the satchel. She brushed her hair until it shone, added a little color here and there then stepped back from the mirror to check the effect. Much better, she thought. No more smudges and bugs. Maybe now even that smug Derek will consider me "presentable".

She gathered up her things and went out. She was surprised to find a number of people were there sitting around talking. It appeared they were waiting for a meeting to start. As she entered, all eyes turned her way and the talk ceased. So many people had crowded into the small room that it took her a moment to see Gutorm. He was seated at a table, as before, leaning back in his chair just looking at her. Their eyes caught and he gave her a slow smile that made her breath catch.

Uh oh, she thought, I haven't felt like that for a long while. What was even worse, she could of all things, feel herself blushing. Flustered and annoyed with herself, she deliberately turned away and saw Derek who seemed quite pleased with her transformation.

Willing herself to move, she smiled sweetly, and sat down in the chair that Gutorm offered her. Then in a very business like voice said, "We really must stop meeting like this."

After the laughter had died down, Gutorm spoke, “Dulsena, I’m so sorry things did not go right for you. We had no idea Brenev had gotten to Grafin.”

“I’m sure it wasn’t your fault,” she said. “I know you tried.”

“Thank you, Dulsena. Hopefully, next time things will work out better. Now,” he went on, “I was about to bring everyone up to date on the reports we have been receiving. From all over Greniff we are hearing of unusually heavy inter-world traffic. Many of the incoming people have temporary employment permits and are being absorbed into various Brenev Industries offices and their agricultural holdings. Some of these facilities have increased their staffs by four or five times.

“Also, a suspiciously large number of people, claiming to be merchants and traders, suddenly seem to be interested in opening markets on Greniff. In addition to that, the tourist facilities are booked to capacity.

“This influx is world wide and what each report emphasizes is the excellent physical condition of each of these ‘office workers, traders, and tourists’. There are few older females and no children in the groups.”

“That’s probably why they are shipping in lasers,” Dulsena said.

“Lasers? What lasers?” Gutorm asked.

“The ones in the cracker boxes,” she said.

“Crackers,” croaked Derek.

“Well, peetan, or pietan, or whatever you call those green wafer-like things. Anyway, there were several crates marked P-I-T-A-N on Grafin’s flyer. When I opened up one of the crates there were lasers inside. They look to me like a new style, at least I’ve never seen any quite like them.”

She took the lasers from her satchel and handed them to Gutorm who passed them on to the others to examine. This new development caused quite a stir and Gutorm said, “This influx of what I think we can assume are troops, coupled with your information about the lasers, Dulsena, seems to confirm our suspicions that Nayland Brenev is about to implement a coup to take over the government of Greniff.”

“Has Governor Sechem been told of this?” she asked.

“In order to get to the Governor one has to go through so many levels we fear that if one of us tried to see him, we would be discovered before accomplishing anything. And, by trying, there is a strong chance we could jeopardize our whole organization.

"We're almost certain that Nayland Brenev has men working close to Sechem to make sure he doesn't get any information that they don't want him to have.

"So, Dulsena, this is where you come in. When we heard of the crash and the fact you were not found at the crash site, we came up with this plan and…"

"Wait just a minute," Dulsena protested. "How could you know I'd make it back here? I could have been out there wandering around on that mountain, or lying under some bush with a broken leg. Which I Narm well almost did what with racketing down a steep mountain in the dark and then slip sliding the rest of the way down through wet bushes. So, how could you make plans for me?"

"Well, I'll tell you, Dulsena, we just didn't think you were the kind to let little things bother you," Gutorm said calmly. "We figured you could take care of yourself and when Derek found you, and we were sure he would, he would get you back here without any trouble."

She stared at him and then at Derek and then the rest of the people in the room. They seemed to find his comments perfectly reasonable.

"Little things. Right. Like shooting people, crash landing a flyer, being lost in the woods."

"Well, you're here, aren't you? So we were right." He turned back to his notes as she shook her head and gave up trying to argue with him.

"So, as I was saying," Gutorm went on, "If we can arrange for you to meet the Governor, and speak with him personally, perhaps you could apprise him of this danger. As the daughter of Rimini Kalleni you should have a good chance of getting his attention."

"Of course, I'll try," Dulsena said. "I only have to make it back to Rohnseff and then to the Parliament House wh…"

"No," interrupted Gutorm, "To the Governor's Palace. He is hosting a ball inaugurating the opening of the second session of parliament. We think we can slip you in as one of the guests."

"All right," she conceded. "Assuming that this time I get to Rohnseff I could maybe get into the Palace if I had an invitation and if I had the appropriate clothing."

"The invitation won't be a problem. As for clothes, your maid, Naba, retrieved some of the clothes that were taken from you and Bibdag brought them here to Leraph. "Leraph, do you have them with you?"

Dulsena hadn't seen Leraph seated at the rear of the gathering. Now she stood and said she had the package and was sure there were things appropriate for Dulsena to wear to the palace.

"Good," said Gutorm. "We will try to get you as close as possible to the Governor and then, making very sure you are overheard by others, you will demand asylum, thereby obligating him to protect you until the claims are answered. Ask to speak to him in private, in a confi-unit. Once it is secure you will tell him of the reports and our suspicions. Tell him that the people who have been wronged by Nayland Brenev are ready to help him in any way they can to remove this menace to his government. Do you think you can do this, Dulsena?"

"If you can get me in to see him, I will do my best to convince him," she said.

The next few hours were busy, indeed. The people were assigned various responsibilities and, one by one, slipped out of the hut. Gutorm, Derek and a woman named Aasa, briefed Dulsena on what she was to tell the Governor.

She and Leraph looked over the clothes that Bibdag had brought and discovered that Naba had chosen well. Not only were there several gowns, but cloaks as well. They selected an appropriate costume and rolled it very carefully into a small parcel which was then fitted into a lightweight back pack. With this backpack on and a dark hooded robe of Leraph's over the top, it took only a slight stoop and the slow hesitant step she had copied before, to transform Dulsena into an old woman, at least from a distance. Theatrical makeup would have helped with the disguise, but, since they hadn't any they made do with the makeup she had in her satchel and hoped the dusk and coming night would mask the rest.

The trip back to Rohnseff started the same way as the one she had made a few days before. As the shipper raced through the darkness, she hoped this time it would end more successfully. She didn't want to make this a habit. Fortunately, everything did go well. However, instead of going to the spaceport she was taken to a small apartment in one of the worker's quarters located underground near the city center. Someone was on vacation and it was available. The next day she rested and prepared to be the star of the ball.

Traveling in a musician's transport, stuffed in with instrument and music cases was not a stylish way to go to the ball, but it got her in. Backstage at the Governor's Palace, she fussed about carrying music folders, trying to look busy so no one would doubt that she was part of the band.

Finally, all the musicians went into the ballroom leaving her waiting nervously in the suddenly quiet, musky smelling dressing room. Only the thin sounds of music drifting in from the ballroom and an occasional footfall in the corridor broke the silence. The dim glowlights reflected eerily in the double row of dressing table mirrors and glinted off the clasps on the instrument cases piled here and there. She sat in a straight chair whose back was too short to allow her to relax, and each time she moved the light glittered off the silver threads in her robe.

Time dragged and it seemed forever before she heard the music of the Governor's March announcing his arrival. No longer able to sit, she paced back and forth waiting for the musicians to take their first break. Finally, they were there, filling up the small dressing room, assuring her that the Governor had arrived and the hall was full.

The talk went on in a flood with comments about the uncomfortable chairs and the bad acoustics and jokes about something Sully, the Blenitzen Rughe player had done.

Drinks were passed around and everyone seemed to be talking at once. Clasps popped and snapped on the cases as they cleaned or changed their instruments. Then, when the leader called time and they went back in, so did she.

The Governor's table was right up front and, in her presentation robes, no one noticed Dulsena until she was right in front of him. As his guards grabbed for her she shouted, "Please, Your Excellency, I am

Dulsena Ariadne Kalleni, daughter of Rimini Kalleni and I demand asylum."

The room went quiet. The Governor waved off his guards, slowly rose and, in a formal tone, gave the required response,

"Dulsena Ariadne Kalleni, I hear your request and honor it."

"Thank you, Your Excellency. Now, please, I need to speak with you in private."

"NO." His aides pushed forward all of them saying that it was impossible. With another wave and a glare, the Governor silenced them and said, "I see no reason not to grant her request."

Still the aides remonstrated with him.

"Gentlemen, I WILL talk to Dulsena Kalleni. Turning to his still mute guests he said, "Please, everyone, do not let this interrupt your enjoyment of the evening. Musicians, play. Friends, friends, go on, enjoy, enjoy. We will be back shortly, after we have had our little talk.

"Now, Dulsena Kalleni, we will retire to my private apartments where we can talk."

"Do you have a confi-unit there, Your Excellency?" she whispered.

"What you have to say is so important, then? In that case, we had better use the one in my office instead."

In his office, sealed in his confi-unit she gave him the information Gutorm's group had acquired. His patronizing attitude was replaced by a look of deep concern.

"Are you absolutely certain of the validity of this information?" he asked.

"Absolutely, Your Excellency."

"How did you get involved in this, Dulsena? I know you came here just a few cycles ago, as the bride of Loran Brenev. Now, here you are, working with a group of exiles, accusing your husband and his family of treason. There must be more to this."

For the next few minutes she tried to give him some idea of what had happened after the death of Albar, of her "education", and her flight from the compound. It was the recital of her abduction by Grafin, the crash, and her discovery of the weapons that finally convinced him.

"Have you informed your father?" was his next question.

"Loran blocked every attempt I made to get in touch with him. Father told me he was going to visit here on the way home from a trip to Allong System. However, I have heard nothing from him and I suspect the Brenevs have kept any messages from me. But, I just know he would keep trying to see me, Governor, and I'm worried about him. From what I've heard, Nayland Brenev is capable of anything and I fear he may have done something to my father."

"Well," the Governor said, patting her hand, "on that regard at least I can put your mind at rest. Your father is here on Greniff. Your brother, too. A merchant I met with late this afternoon gave me a message from him, and I have an appointment to see them both here privately, after the ball. I do not understand why he didn't contact me directly at my office."

"Your Excellency, we have reason to believe your staff does not pass on every request to you."

"Yes, I was afraid that might have been the reason."

"Please, Sir, do not mention your appointment with my father to any of your aides. Talk to him first and let me talk to him before you make a decision about whom to trust. The lives of many fine people depend on your discretion."

"Dulsena, don't think for a moment I doubt your report," the governor said, "Other things have happened which tend to support the allegations you have made. I will, of course, wait until I talk with your father, and maybe together we can work out a plan which will be mutually beneficial. Now, I must return to my guests and I think, under the circumstances, it would be safest for you to return with me. No one will harm you in such a public gathering. Just stay close to me and my daughter, Raynelle."

Breaking the seal on the confi-unit, they walked back towards the main salon. As they walked, he very quietly said, "I think it would be best if we act as if whatever had been troubling you has now been resolved. Now to all observers we are only concerned with having an enjoyable evening. Do you agree?"

She agreed and with smiles and feigned casualness, they made their way back to his table. The musicians were playing, the guests were dancing and his aides were glowering. The Governor chided them for their long faces and they made a small show of addressing her politely. However, during the rest of the evening they seemed very restless and there was much coming and going and the exchanging of muttered comments in passing. When the Governor wasn't watching they looked like they were eating glass. Governor Sechem, all the while playing the genial host, did not miss these looks and whispered exchanges.

His daughter, Raynelle, was a sociable girl who tried to make Dulsena comfortable, and the evening was such a pleasant change from being held prisoner in her apartment by a horde of glowering Brenev relatives, or scrabbling through the woods that she found herself enjoying it all. A large part of her good humor was the thought that kept running through her head, Father and Scortzi are all right and they're here. They're here on Greniff and I will see them soon.

- 9 -
The Coup Begins

Dulsena wasn't the only one having a good time. The music was good, the drinks were flowing, and the party was in full swing. Some very happy people came crowding back to their places at the next table and in the crush someone bumped into her table tipping her drink over onto her lap. Leaping to her feet, she dabbed at the spreading stain with her napkin.

"Oh, Dulsena, your lovely gown," Raynelle cried. "Hurry, let's go to the lounge where there's a cleaning unit. We'll get it out before it stains.

They threaded through the tables and had just started down the corridor when they heard the musical fanfare for an announcement.

"Oh dear," said Raynelle. "That's the signal for my father's final toast and thank you speech. I must, as his hostess, be there."

"That's all right, Raynelle," Dulsena said, "Please, go ahead, I'll be fine."

Raynelle patted Dulsena's arm, turned and hurried back towards the main salon as the guests responded with applause and laughter to something the governor said. The laughter abruptly changed to screams of horror and shouts of, "He's been shot!"

"The governor's been shot!"

"Grab him! He shot the governor."

Dulsena didn't wait to hear more. She hitched up her gown and ran to the dressing room. Grabbing her satchel and cloak she dashed out the exit nearest to the musician's transport and clambered in. The door had just barely slid into place when people began bursting out of every palace exit. The night was soon filled with shouts and sirens.

"Narm," she muttered. "Narm, Narm, Narm. Doesn't anything ever go right?"

Peering out she could see the Palace Guards trying to form a cordon around the building and get things under control, but guests continued to force their way out. Once out, they scattered everywhere to ground transports and VTF's and took off willy nilly. She saw several near misses. It was chaos.

Dulsena's thoughts were just about as chaotic. What was she going to do now? Was the governor dead or still alive? If seriously wounded he could not meet with her father, and, even if his injuries were minimal, his aides and medical advisors, not to mention the palace guards, would not allow anyone to get near him. He hadn't had a chance to act on the news she had given him so it looked like the exiles were right back where they started.

For what seemed like a terribly long time, she sat huddled in the dark watching the people leave. Official vehicles, their sirens blaring, came and went, media units disgorged dozens of people who milled about attempting to interview the shocked partygoers who were only interested in leaving. Finally, the back door of the transport slid open. Wolking, the leader of the band, climbed in and turned to lift in an instrument case that was being handed to him. He turned to put it in place and saw her. Although obviously startled, he simply put the case in front of her and continued to load the other instruments as they were handed in. The musicians crowded in and took their places.

The door closed and the vehicle started to move.

Wolking, bobbed his head in her direction and the other musicians turned to see her back in the same old spot. The driver, too, had seen that she was back, but his attention was now on getting a place in the long lines attempting to exit the palace grounds. The guards had started checking every vehicle as it exited, but, they gave only a cursory look at the musicians before waving them through.

Wolking, said, "I did not know that we would be honored with your company on the return trip, Dulsena."

"Sorry to be such a bother," she said, "but, after what happened in there, I thought it best to get away before the authorities started interrogating people. Tell me, was the governor killed or wounded?"

"I'm not sure," Wolking said. "The trauma attendants took him out. I saw that his daughter went with him. Do any of the rest know anything?" he asked his men.

None of them had seen or heard anything to indicate the Governor was dead. Most had gotten the impression he had only been wounded, but no one knew anything for sure.

"Can you take me back to where I spent last night?" Dulsena asked. "I need a place to stay until I can contact my father."

After some discussion, much head shaking and repetition of the words "bad snarf", they concluded that perhaps that was not too wise. The best thing they could think of, was for her to go home with Wolking, the band leader. Apparently, from the jokes and laughter, the presence of a female in his quarters would not be considered unusual.

So, rather than ending her evening in a joyous reunion with her father, she would once again spend the night in the sub-level workers quarters, hiding in yet another strange place. Wolking brought her to the door of his quarters, keyed in his identification, opened the door, and then left, saying he would stay with a friend.

Dulsena closed the door after him and looked around. Wolking's room was small and furnished with some rather bizarre items from several planets. Several movi-cons battled for attention against strong, and to her eye, clashing colors. The room seemed to move and shift each time she moved. "Eerie," she whispered.

The bedroom was done the same way. Searching for the PCU she happened onto another very small room. Unlike the others, it was a somber grey. The few pieces of furniture were functional and very austere looking. The walls were lined with hundreds of record spools. Above the spool racks there were Aud-Vues of old musical instruments. One showed an ornately carved stringed instrument. She touched the sound bar at the bottom of the frame and beautiful mellow tones filled the room. Going from one Aud-Vue to another, she heard excerpts and passages of classical music from several systems. Some were old familiar favorites while others she recognized only from her university studies. This was obviously the collection of a serious musician.

Picking up one of the record spools she was surprised to see the label was in Dornatz. Her knowledge of the language was limited to reading order forms, but she picked up several spools and tried to study them out. One said something about "stores", another something about ships or vessels and on yet another was a word whose root seemed to indicate something to do with mines. Only a few were music spools. "Well," she muttered, replacing the spools, "an interesting man, our Mr. Wolking."

She turned on the News-Vu and found that the shooting of the governor was the big news. "There has as yet been no official statement as to the Governor's condition. His daughter, who accompanied him to the hospital, has refused to be interviewed.

"The governor's Chief Executive Assistant will neither confirm nor deny reports that the attacker, who was killed by security officers, was an ex staff member. We here at Rohnseff Report will keep you informed as to any new developments on this tragic event."

She turned up the volume and went to find the PCU and prepare for bed. Some time later, after watching the same scenes over and over, she turned off the News-Vu and slipped into bed. Feeling very depressed, she thought, "If he is dead the exiles are right back where they were before and I've done all this for nothing."

As tired as she was, the thoughts rushed around and around in her head. She thought about the scene at the ball. She thought about Wolking's strange apartment. She thought about Gutorm and how he smiled at her. She thumped the pillows and flopped this way and that. When she finally did sleep she tossed and turned from nightmares, reliving in scrambled form all the horrors of the previous few days.

The next morning, eyes bleary and feeling groggy, she turned on the News-Vu to find the broadcasts still focusing on reports about the governor being shot. The governor was "in serious, but stable condition". The governor's daughter was still refusing to comment and his aides simply mouthed set phrases, saying a lot, but giving no new information. She raided Wolking's meager food center and found some fruit and what looked like energy bars. Munching, she sat and watched the News-Vu and tried to get her thoughts in order.

First, she thought, I need to get to my father. But where is he? I don't know. She munched on one of the bars and thought some more. He might be at a hotel, but I don't know which hotel. Or he might not even be in a hotel. She knew Kalleni maintained apartments on many planets for the use of their representatives, but, she couldn't remember if Greniff was one of them, if indeed she had ever known.

"Why don't I know that?" she said angrily,waving the bar at the NewsVu screen. "I should know that." She slumped back in the chair and wondered why she hadn't taken the time to learn more about Kalleni operations here on Greniff. The obvious answer was she had been thinking only of Loran and her bright, wonderful future. "Hah!" she said, bitterly.

She chewed angrily on the stale bar. Truth was, since she didn't travel very much, there were a lot of things about the company that she didn't know. Well, one thing she did know was that she couldn't just call Kalleni's. Nayland was sure to have all communications to and from the House of Kalleni Office monitored and a call from Wolking's apartment would get him involved. It would also alert those who undoubtedly were watching for her.

"No, I'll have to go there," she told the unresponsive News reader. "I'll go, but not as Dulsena Kalleni Brenev. As Dulsena I'd never make it to the offices. They'd pick me up as soon as I walked in the store, if not before. But, thanks to Leraph, there just might be a way." The NewVu reader didn't seem the least bit interested.

She finished the bar and hurried into the bedroom. She stood in front of the mirror pushing her hair this way and that and then twisted it into a tight knot on top of her head. She dumped out all the cosmetics she had in her satchel and went to work. She darkened her skin and added wrinkle lines around her eyes. Not enough. She added more lines dulled her natural high color. Finally, she stepped back and looked again. "Have to do," she muttered. She rolled the ball gown and put it into the backpack. Then, feeling rather uncomfortable about it, she started rummaging through Wolking's closet. She found a gown, no doubt it had been left there by one of the band leader's lady friends. It was too long, but she managed to bunch it up at the waist so she could walk.

She fastened the backpack in place and then put on the hooded cloak that she had worn on the trip to Rohnseff. The image that looked back from the mirror looked nothing like her.

Not bad, she thought. Good enough to get me past Nayland's spies if I keep in character.

She looked up the local address for House of Kalleni in the communications directory, grabbed her satchel, and left the apartment. Once again she dropped back into the, by now familiar, slow, dignified old lady's walk. No one looked at her twice as she made her way up to the surface and headed over to the nearest Directional. She had never used the public transport on Greniff and hoped she could figure it out. She was relieved to find it was a standard grid selector and, other than the directions and names being in Greneche, it was the same as others she had used.

She knew Greniff was an agricultural planet and that the people had been quite adamant about controlling the population of their cities. Even Rohnseff, the capitol, appeared to have only 20 levels.

She encoded the address of Kalleni Greniff and the grid lit up with an orange line showing the route she was to take. The transport request signal flashed on and off and, after she confirmed her request, there was only a short wait before a small four person unit slid to a stop before her.

Not having a local identification card, she used her Merchants travel card. This was the crucial part. She was afraid that Loran had perhaps withdrawn her clearance from the system, but the card was accepted with the usual "welcome to our planet" speech and an announcement that travel information was available in all standard Federation languages by calling such and such a number. That was a relief. Loran had probably forgotten she even had it. None of the women at the compound had their own cards.

There was one other person in the unit, so she made a great show of climbing in and settling into a seat. A few stops later the other passenger got off and she was able to relax as she rode alone to her exit. Once there, all she had to do was get from the stop into Kalleni Building. Nayland might have men watching for her, but they wouldn't have been told to watch for an old woman.

The unit stopped and the directional flashed the route from the stop to the address she had keyed in; only a few meters down to the next grid and over four entrances.

Once again assuming the slower movements of her new persona, she stepped out and at a dignified pace, made her way there.

Once inside the building she walked slowly over to the public lifts and only at the last minute did she turn aside to the private lift and tap in her code number. The guard reached the door just as it closed. She guessed there would be another at the top of the lift. There was and he got a little aggressive, but did nothing to stop her when she strode past him into the manager's reception area. She walked up to a very surprised receptionist and announced she was Dulsena Kalleni and wanted to see Siburi Myre immediately. When he started to sputter, she leaned very close, looked him straight in the eyes and said, "Immediately."

He blinked, pressed the communicator and spoke briefly. Then, motioning for the guard, who had followed her, they entered Siburi's office.

Siburi Myre was seated behind a pale lavender desk covered with silver bas relief. Rising slowly she looked like a cool lily in her white robes with the lavender bands.

Dulsena was very conscious of the difference as she stood there in her old woman's makeup and bunched up dress. She dropped her dirty beat-up satchel on the pale yellow carpet and said, "I know we have never met, Siburi Myre, but my father has often spoken of you. I am Dulsena Kalleni. Is your receptionist cleared for private communication?"

"Yes," Siburi Myre answered, "he is cleared." She pressed a button under her desk and the verification panel on the desk top lit up. "You may proceed," she said.

Dulsena walked forward, pressed her palms onto the plate and said, “I am Dulsena Ariadne Kalleni,identification Rolandspar 5.”

The light remained constant and a voice said, “Good Morning, Dulsena Ariadne Kalleni. You have been cleared for all levels of communication.”

The light went out. Dulsena looked at Siburi Myre and said, “I need your help.”

- 10 -
House of Kalleni, Rohnseff

"Dulsena, please, relax," Siburi said, smiling. "We know you need our help. We have been trying to find you. The last we heard…"

Just then the door slid open and Scortzi burst into the room and swept her up in a great hug. "Dulcy, Dulcy, am I glad to see you. Great Lomax, Dulcy, what's happened to you?"

Crying and laughing at the same time, she rubbed her fingers across her face and said, "It's makeup, Scortzi, see, just makeup. I'm fine now that you're here. Where's father?"

"He's on his way," Siburi said, touching her small ear receiver. "He just received Anselm's message and said to tell you to stay in one place for a change."

"He needn't worry," said Scortzi. "I'll keep her here." He gave her another hug.

Disengaging herself from Scortzi's bear hug Dulsena said,

"Siburi, you mentioned you were looking for me. How did you know I wasn't still at the Brenev Compound?"

"Oh, we were told about you showing up at the ball," Scortzi interrupted. "When we came here almost a cycle ago and Loran refused to see us, Father sent out inquiries on the network. But, until last night.. Well, that's a long story. I'll wait and let father tell you that part. "From the looks of you, you've had a hard time of it."

"Oh," she laughed, "I look much worse than I am. These clothes may not be attractive, but they, or ones like them, have gotten me into and out of a lot of places I couldn't have gone otherwise."

"Well, you weren't wearing them at the Governor's ball last night," said Scortzi. "We got a report about the beeeauuutiful Dulsena Kalleni making an evvveeer so dramaaaatic claim of asylum and all the excitement it caused." He laughed as she made a face at him and poked him in the chest.

"Anyway," he went on, "we were on our way there to meet the Governor and you when we heard about the shooting. You can imagine our frustration when, by the time we could get into the palace, there wasn't any sign of you."

"I thought it best to get out of there. The Brenevs seem to have influence everywhere, and they may even have the police on their side, too. I didn't want to take the chance. How is Governor Sechem?"

"As far as the public is concerned he is mortally wounded. Actually, he is going to be all right. His daughter, Raynelle, just wants to keep him isolated for now."

"She has called twice this morning," Siburi added. "She has been very concerned about you."

"Where is she?" The sound of Rimini's voice roared through the open door and then Dulsena was enveloped in such an embrace.

"Dulsena, Dulsena, my dear girl. Are you all right?"

Holding her at arm's length he said, "Oh, my child, you look terrible! What's happened to you?"

"It's makeup, father. See it rubs off. I'm fine, really I am. I'm so happy to see you."

"Well we're certainly happy to see you," he said pulling her close for another hug. "They are sending a message to your mother, right now, to give her the good news. We were so worried." This statement produced more hugs, with more laughter and even a few tears.

Wiping his eyes, her father said, "As much as I want to know all about what has happened, there is no sense having you repeat it a dozen times. So, "old woman", why don't you go and get cleaned up and we will have some lunch. By then the others will be here and you can tell all of us what you've been doing and we will do the same."

She was very happy to agree and gladly took the hand Siburi held out to her. "Please, come with me, Dulsena, and we will try to make you comfortable."

Dulsena gathered up her satchel and followed Siburi into a beautiful suite that was all cool yellow and white with lavender accents. Then, after showing her around, Siburi, left her to, as Dulsena put it, repair all the damage.

The PCU in Siburi's private quarters was about as different from Leraph's as one could imagine. She emerged feeling wonderful and found a new robe had been hung in the dressing area for her. It was a beautiful midday robe of pale yellow with a dark yellow pattern woven in. Smooth and soft to the touch, it was everything she had longed for while wearing the clothes that Loran had forced her to wear.

With the proper makeup on and her hair brushed into a thick coil she once more looked like Dulsena Kalleni, of Weneche on Resdorn.

The chimes of midday were ringing as she was welcomed into the manager's private dining room. Rimini and Scortzi were waiting. Rimini rose and said, "Ah, welcome back, daughter. That's more like it. Do you like the robe I selected?"

"It's lovely, Father, thank you."

Her father beamed as he led her to a seat. "Your mother sends her love, too," he said as he kissed the top of her head. "She is anxious for you to be home again. Now, first we eat and then we will compare information and decide what we must do."

Lunch over they moved to a large room where several people were talking. Taking her arm, Rimini said, "Dulsena, I want you to meet Henri Dakkon, Federation Special Services."

Dakkon was a slight, older man, unremarkable in every way except for his eyes which were dark and piercing. Dulsena bowed and moved on to a petite, dark haired lady her father introduced as Lisbet Bornach, Delegate to the Algoran Council. She nodded her head abruptly in response to Dulsena's bow. Then Rimini introduced her to the man she had tried so hard to reach, Captain Rhys Xholan, Rohnseff Port Master. Dulsena had just started to tell him how glad she was to finally meet him when the door opened and another man came rushing in.

"Uncle Luiz," Dulsena said, as he rushed up, gave her a big hug and said, "Dulcy, Dulcy, You've given all of us such a scare."

Luiz Roncallo wasn't really an uncle, but an old friend of the family who had been like a second father to Dulsena. He and Rimini had known each other since school days and Luiz was now Kalleni's Vice President for Personnel Services. For Dulsena, feeling his smooth cheek and smelling the scent of his familiar cologne brought back hundreds of memories of sitting on his lap and being petted and indulged. Luiz Roncallo was a man who made life exciting for everyone around him. That he enjoyed his wealth was obvious from the heavy gold chain on his wrist and the extravagant gold and diamond cornucopia rings he always wore.

Rimini came over, put his arm around Dulsena's waist and, patting Luiz on the shoulder, said, "Isn't it great to have her back, Luiz." They stood grinning idiotically at each other until Rimini remembered his manners and showed all his guests to their places.

They were seated in the inward curves of a large serpentine-edged conference table. To the left of each place was a small information monitor and to the right of that lay a small electronic slate and stylus for taking notes.

Rimini took his place at the head of the table with Henri Dakkon on his right and Lisbet Bornach on his left. Scortzi was at the foot of the table with Dulsena on his right and Luiz to his left. Captain Xholan was between Luiz and Henri Dakkon. To Dulsena's right was an empty chair, but the screen and slate were on and ready for use. Rimini caught her questioning look and said, "Your friend, Raynelle, will join us shortly. Her father has asked her to be his liaison with us. Until his investigation is finished he will trust no one on his staff."

After the preliminary comments usual at the start of any meeting Rimini said, "First, Dulsena, we will tell you what we have discovered and then you will tell us what has happened to you and the Brenevs and about this group of exiles you told Governor Sechem about."

The reports were long and detailed. The gist was that on ten different planets, all major marketing terminals, Nayland Brenev had recruited or imported what appeared to be huge mercenary forces. These mercenaries were working under cover in various positions waiting for the signal from Nayland when, it was believed, they would attempt to take over key Federation positions.

"At first," Lisbet Bornach said, "we couldn't explain the reports we were getting. They didn't make sense. Then Rimini reported that Luiz's assistant had picked up on some really strange personnel shifts on Greniff and Dornace. "It was only after we talked to him that we began to understand."

"You see," said Henri Dakkon, "we had quite by accident discovered information concerning the manufacture of illegal weapons on a small planet beyond our boundaries in the Huilla League. We instituted a surveillance and discovered they had indeed set up factories to make proscribed weapons and these weapons were then being smuggled across the borders into the Algoran Federation."

"That's when I came into the picture," Lisbet Bornach said. "The Federation President asked me to verify this report. We kept running into trails which seemed to link Brenev Industries with the smuggling activities, but neither we nor the Huilla authorities could prove anything."

"Not that the Huillas were trying very hard," Dakkon said wryly.

"Well yes, the Huillas have their own interests," she smiled and went on. "In the meantime, Dulsena, your father and brother had become suspicious of the Brenevs and had instituted their own investigations."

"You know how that works, Dulsena," Rimini put in, "Merchants talk amongst themselves—the same with manufacturers. They know their own territories. We got a little information from this one, and a little from that one, and when we put it together we knew we had to get it to the Federation."

"Thank goodness they did," Lisbet said, "Their information filled in enough of the gaps so that Henri and I could present it formally to the Federation Council.

"The Council agreed with our conclusions and Federation forces are even now being brought to within striking distance of each of the ten planets."

"Now, Dulsena," Henri Dakkon said, "timing is the thing. We don't want to move until Brenev shows his hand and we have some better idea of who is involved. Still, we must be ready to stop them before they can take control. This is where you come in. We need to know what this group of exiles is planning to do so we can coordinate their activities with ours. They must not force us to make a move until we're ready."

Just then Raynelle came in. She bowed to all and then went directly to Dulsena, kissed her on both cheeks and said,"Dulsena, I'm so pleased you are safe. We were concerned about you. My father said to be sure to give you his regards."

"Thank you, Raynelle," Dulsena responded, "I'm glad to see you too and especially to hear that your father is recovering."

"Yes, thank you. He is very lucky."

Rimini introduced Raynelle to each of the others. She acknowledged the responses and said, "I do appreciate your asking me to join you in this meeting. Please excuse me if I seem abrupt, but I can only be away for a short time. I believe I just might have some information that may help.

"First let me explain. My father and I, for various reasons have for some time felt something was very wrong in the governor's office. Matters were not being handled in the usual manner, the proper channels were not being used. Most especially, my father had become more and more dissatisfied with the actions of some of his aides. At first we talked of this, just the two of us. Then one of his aides made a few veiled comments to me, and then to my father, which led us to believe that he too was concerned about something.

"We decided to take a chance and took him into our confidence. He confided there was indeed an elaborate scheme to by-pass my father in certain affairs of the planet and keep him occupied with minor happenings. Audiences were being refused and communications diverted without his knowledge. Reports about immigration, population shifts and shipping records were being altered or filed without his ever seeing them. This confirmed our worst fears. After discussing this, the three of us agreed that we would say nothing to anyone else and continue to gather whatever information we could. Then, on the day of the party, this aide did not report for work. When my father asked about him he was told that he had requested a transfer. My father asked for a confirmation, which he received. However, we didn't believe it. We are afraid that someone found out he was helping us. "Then, at the party, Dulsena, you showed up with your public claim for asylum. I think that was when they decided my father could not be allowed to talk to anyone else and tried to have him killed.

"Fortunately, the attempt failed. Now, under the guise of the grieving daughter, I have contacted family and friends whose loyalty we can count on. They have gathered here and are setting up a network to protect us. Also, some of the older guards, who transferred here with my father, and are fiercely loyal to him are helping to keep him isolated. Also, from them we have learned which officers are not to be trusted.

"In addition to the governor's staff, we also have serious doubts about some of the local law enforcement officers not only here in Rohnseff, but in other cities as well. We believe quite a few of them have gone over to Brenev.

"One other thing that might be important, we have been hearing rumors of a network of exiles who have set up in opposition to the Brenevs. You can imagine how excited my father was when this was confirmed by Dulsena. We hadn't been able to locate their headquarters or learn who is leading them. We are hoping Dulsena can give us that information."

"Maybe I can," Dulsena said. "I have met the leader and know there is quite a group who want to get rid of Nayland Brenev. They have tried to use the legal system, however, they received no help. Although I do not know this personally, I believe things are escalating to the point where they are planning to resort to violence. Actually, what they really want is for the government to help them." This announcement caused quite a stir.

"Perhaps," she went on, "if I recount my experience with the Brenevs and how I met the exiles, it will help put things in perspective." For the next several minutes, Dulsena recounted what had happened to her. Her father and Scortzi listened with growing anger as she recounted how Loran and his family had treated her, but also with obvious admiration for what she had done to escape.

Dulsena's recital also confirmed all their suspicions. Now it was clear how imperative it was that they talk with Gutorm.

"Gutorm," Dulsena said. "I hate to admit it, but I can't tell you exactly where Gutorm is. Although I feel I am intimately acquainted with a stretch of creekbed and some Sneltzen trees, I don't know where that area is in relation to Rohnseff. I can give impressions and clues, but not enough information to pinpoint it exactly.

"The rides on the transport rail," she told them, were in the dark. She had no way to gauge how far they had traveled. Disappointment was reflected in each face around the table.

"Well," Rhys Xholan said, "we know where the compound is and we can approximate distances. But we really do need something more accurate than that. So any suggestions as to how we can get in touch with this Gutorm."

A pall settled over the group which was dispelled when Dulsena blurted out, "Wolking. We can get in touch with him through Wolking. He's the bandleader who took me to the governor's palace. He's part of the network and can probably get a message through."

"How can we talk to this Wolking without putting him in danger?" Rimini asked.

"Hire him," said Scortzi.

"Yes, but that would be too obvious if a Kalleni contacts him," Lisbet said.

Henri Dakkon said, "Lisbet and I aren't even here officially and Raynelle is the worried daughter concerned only about her father. So who then?"

"Glarin Stortz," said Luiz Roncallo. "He is always having parties and he was at the Governor's ball. He could say he heard them there."

"Stortz flew out this morning to Borage," Rhys Xholan said. "I happened to see his clearance, myself. But, there is another, a friend of mine, Merchant Corrinon. You know him, Rimini. He is a good man, very sociable and he entertains a lot."

"Fine, you take care of it, Rhys," Rimini said. "Then shall we all plan to meet back here at say 7:30. Is that all right with you Lisbet and you Henri?"

They agreed, but then Dulsena said, “Father, Wolking won’t tell Luiz or Captain Xholan anything. He doesn’t know them. I need to go. He knows me and will trust me.”

Luiz objected, but Rimini said, “No, Luiz, what she says makes sense. Rhys, you make an appointment with this Wolking to meet at Merchant Corrinon’s home and then you, Luiz and Dulsena will go with him. Luiz, you can take one of the Kalleni flyers. Oh, and take Jonas and Kiku with you.”

Luiz said surely it would not be necessary for the Captain to take time away from his work for such a simple errand nor did they need the guards. “I can watch out for myself and Dulsena,” he declared. Captain Xholan, however, responded that it was no trouble at all for him to go and he would like to do it and he thought the guards were a good idea. Rimini agreed and said, “Fine, that’s it then. We’ll meet back here tonight at 7:30.”

“As for you, Dulsena, Siburi has invited you to stay in her private apartment here at the store for as long as necessary. So Rhys and Luiz will pick you up here.”

He rose and taking Raynelle’s arm, ushered her out saying, “We’d better get that mourning robe you came here to buy, hadn’t we Raynelle. We have to make it look good for those who are following you.”

They left, followed quickly by the others. Scortzi put his arm around Dulsena’s shoulders and walked her to the door of Siburi’s apartment. “Try to get some rest, Dulcy,” he said. “You look worn out.”

She had to admit she was tired and quite satisfied to retreat back to Siburi’s lavish bedroom and sink onto her luxurious M.U.S.E. The warm modulated-ultrasonic-sleep-envelope, that was one of Kalleni’s best sellers, closed gently around her and the world slipped away.

She awoke and for a few moments could not orient herself. She had been waking up in so many strange places lately. Looking towards the chaise, she saw a splash of color and boxes and packages of all sizes.

Releasing the M.U.S.E., she rolled out and walked across the soft yellow carpet to where a selection of robes and cloaks had been laid out. Spread across the satin seat, they made a bright rainbow. A stack of beautifully wrapped lavender and silver boxes held lingerie, hose and sandals. She held one of the robes against her face. So soft. So smooth. To think that at one time she had taken clothes like this for granted.

Just then the door opened quietly and Siburi peeked in.

"Ah, Dulsena, you are awake and have found the things, I see. I thought you would need new clothing so I had some things sent over. Do they suit you?"

"Oh Siburi, they're lovely, thank you so much. I really do appreciate your thoughtfulness. He took away all my clothes, you know."

"Loran did?" Siburi said in a shocked tone. Dulsena nodded.

"You were wearing Resdorn gowns when he met you. He must have liked you in them then. However, I do know many Greneche are still very conservative and want to maintain the old, traditional culture. Thank goodness many of the younger people have more modern ideas. With them, and the off worlders stationed here for their governments or businesses, we have enough customers here at Kalleni to do very well."

"I think it was Loran's brother, Nayland Brenev, who objected and it seems that whatever Nayland says is law. And, of course, the old women of the family followed his lead and were determined to make me conform to their idea of what was proper. So after many cycles of having to wear those ugly old things I am thrilled to be back in beautiful Resdorn style robes. I really do appreciate your taking the time to select these for me. It was very considerate of you."

"You are quite welcome, my dear. I had fun doing it. I love shopping with someone else's money." They both laughed and then Siburi said, "Oh, mustn't forget, I came to tell you that Luiz called. He will be here very shortly. They have arranged to meet the band leader at Corrinon's house."

"Oh good. I'll hurry and be ready, Siburi. Thank you."

Not long after that, Luiz and Captain Xholan arrived, and together with Dulsena they went up to the top level of the city to the private Kalleni flyer pad. Jonas and Kiku were waiting by Luiz's VTF (vertical town flyer) which already had been brought up into position. Jonas smiled a big welcome when he saw Dulsena and Kiku even stopped frowning long enough to say he was happy to see her again. They had known Dulsena since she was a little girl.

They climbed aboard the luxurious craft. Captain Xholan settled into the pilot's seat with Jonas to his right. Luiz and Dulsena sat in the rear seats, Kiku in a small seat near the door. It took only a few minutes to fly across the city to the pad on the roof of Bertrand Corrinon's house. Kiku insisted they stay in the flyer until he had checked the landing pad and the entrance. Only then did he allow them to make their way to the entry. Just inside the entrance was a lift which carried them down to a small, but tastefully decorated reception area where the Merchant Corrinon was waiting to greet them.

"Dulsena Kalleni, I am honored to finally meet you. Welcome to my home. Luiz Roncallo,how nice to see you again. And Rhys, old friend, you know you are always welcome. Come, I've arranged for you to meet Wolking in one of the smaller conference rooms. Here we are."

The door slid open to reveal a very small room furnished only with a table and four chairs. "This entire room is a confi-unit," Master Corrinon said. "I will have Wolking brought here so you can be assured of complete privacy. Perhaps your men would be more comfortable just outside?"

"Yes, Thank you," responded Luiz. "This is perfect. Jonas, Kiku, would you please wait outside and show Wolking in when he comes?"

Kiku ignored this suggestion until he had made a complete circuit of the room with his security scanner. Then, nodding to Jonas, they both left. Luiz shrugged and smiled in apparent amusement at their zealousness. Captain Xholan smiled too, but said, "Well, they are very good at what they do and it is for our benefit."

"Yes," Dulsena said, "I wish they'd been with me the last time I was in a flyer."

Just then the door opened and Jonas introduced Wolking. As soon as the door was back in place the activator started to hum. Wolking looked surprised at that, but even more surprised when he looked beyond Luiz and Captain Xholan and saw Dulsena.

"It's all right, Wolking," she said, "nothing's wrong. This is Luiz

Roncallo, an old friend of our family and Captain Rhys Xholan, Rohnseff Port Officer. We have asked you here because we need your help."

"My help, Dulsena? You need a band?" He asked with a gentle smile.

"No, we don't need a band. We need to talk to Gutorm."

"Who?" said Wolking, looking truly puzzled.

"Wolking, two days ago I was with Gutorm. I was put on a transport rail, transferred to a guide in a ground car and then to one on a public transport who brought me to you. Now I must get back to Gutorm or get a message to him to meet me. I think you know how we can do this. Please, please help us. It is vitally important for us to see him. The safety of the whole exile's network is at risk. In fact, the whole Federation may be in great danger."

Wolking was quiet for several minutes just looking back and forth from Dulsena to Luiz to Xholan. Finally he shook his head and said, "I don't know any Gutorm, Dulsena. I just know my contact, the woman who brought you. All I can suggest is that you give me a message and I will tell her to pass it on to her contact. It may eventually get to this Gutorm person you want, but, of course, I can guarantee nothing."

"All right. We can do that. But, Wolking, please impress on your contact that it is vital that this message gets to him."

"I understand, Dulsena. I will do the best I can."

"That is all we can ask, of course," said Luiz. "Please, if you would kindly wait outside for a few minutes we will prepare the message for you."

The door whispered open and Wolking slipped out. The door closed and Luiz reactivated the unit.

Taking a small pen sized recorder from his pocket Luiz asked, "This Gutorm, he does have a receiver?"

"I don't know for certain, but I should think he would have," she answered.

"We will hope so," Luiz said wryly, as he passed the unit to her. Pressing the panel she said, "Barget hunter, this is the old lady. It is urgent that I speak with you as soon as possible. There is great danger.

Do nothing, NOTHING, to further your plans until we speak. The safety of all depends on this. Follow the known path to family."

She finished and handed the recorder back to Luiz. He removed the tiny spool and sealed it in a carrier.

"Now then," he said, "let's hope that works."

With a nod to her and Captain Xholan, he de-activated the unit and they went out to where Wolking, Jonas and a servant were waiting.

Luiz slipped Wolking the spool and at the same time said,

"We've decided to hire you for our party provided you can clear up those little problems. Of course, we must know right away as there is still much to be done and many people to invite."

"Yes, I understand," said Wolking. "I'll do my best. I hope our playing pleases you. Thank you, Gentlemen." Bowing, he turned and the servant showed him towards the front of the house.

They were heading out of the reception room when on an impulse Dulsena said, "Excuse me just a moment," and ran back to where Wolking was just disappearing through the other doorway.

"Wolking," she called. "A moment please."

He turned and waited as she hurried up to him. Dulsena asked the servant to please continue on down the corridor and then wait there for Master Wolking.

Turning to Wolking she said hurriedly, "In my message I asked Gutorm to come to House of Kalleni to see me. I don't know why, but I've had second thoughts about that. Could you arrange with your contact to have him brought to you?"

He looked at her quizzically and then said, "Certainly, I'll make arrangements."

"Thank you, Wolking. I feel better about that. In the meantime I will try to think of some way we can get him into Kalleni Building without being seen. I'll get back to you. Oh, and thank you again for your help." She hurried back to where the others were waiting in the hallway, smiled and said, "Sorry to keep you waiting, I just wanted to thank him again for being so kind to me. I really was a bother, you know, putting him out of his room and all."

Jonas led the way back to the flyer pad with the Captain. Luiz and

Dulsena followed and Kiku brought up the rear. A few minutes later they were back in the Kalleni Building.

Now came the hard part, the waiting, the questions. Would Wolking get the message to his contact? Would the others act quickly enough so Gutorm would receive it before setting the exile's plans in motion? Had they jeopardized the security of the network by contacting Wolking? If they had, Wolking and his contact could be picked up by Brenev's men.

Henri Dakkon and Lisbet Bornach had gone back to their ship to catch up on the latest reports from Aldene. Captain Xholan had gone back to the Spaceport. Dulsena was in a small data room supervising three SKIPPYS, actually S-C-I-P-U-S, Self Contained Information Processing Units, which were decoding the messages from the merchant's network. Rimini and Scortzi were ostensibly on company business, but were actually evaluating the decoded reports being sent to them. They had pressed Luiz and his assistant into helping them and the four of them had been closeted together all evening. Raynelle, still by-passing her father's aides, continued to access the main government data base and transmit data to Henri Dakkon's assistant.

Everyone was busy. But all the time Dulsena was working, she was worrying about Derek and Leraph and especially Gutorm. She had talked to Siburi and they had worked out a plan to get him into the building, but first he had to get to Rohnseff. The Brenevs would have everyone out looking for her, which would make it much harder for anyone to get around without being observed. Would he make it all right? She found herself repeatedly checking her chronos while the time dragged by.

- 11 -
Gutorm

"Where are they all coming from?" Gutorm muttered to Derek.

"From all over I imagine," Derek said quietly, "and a lot of them are off-worlders".

"Yes," said Gutorm. "That's my impression, too. They must be the ones that Nayland Brenev has brought in."

"That group back in the draw there were sure interested in what we were doing," Derek said, "Good thing we had a good day's catch to show them."

"Right. Well, I think we have just seen proof of that report about the influx of mercenaries. Nayland must be getting ready to make his move real soon."

"That's going to make it a lot more dangerous for us," Derek said. "We don't have that kind of manpower. Maybe we've waited too long."

"Maybe," Gutorm replied, "but then again it might be to our advantage to wait until there is an actual confrontation between Brenev and the Federation. We then could throw our manpower in with the Feds. Maybe that would make them listen to us."

"The men have been on alert for quite a while," Derek reminded him. "All these strangers coming in and nosing around are bound to make them more nervous. I hope they don't precipitate some incident that could..."

Something was wrong! They had just entered the clearing near the hut when Leraph, looking very upset, entered the clearing from the other side and started hurrying towards them as fast as she could. They quickly strode forward to meet her.

"Oh! Thank God you are here," she gasped.

"What's the problem?" Gutorm asked. "Why are you hurrying so? Come in and sit down." He led her into the hut and pulled a chair around for her to sit on. Derek followed, closing the door behind him.

"A message. I have a message for you, Gutorm," she gasped.

"A message? From whom? Cleidah?"

"I don't know. Anthorp met me as he was coming here and gave me a spool case. He said someone on the transport line had given it to him and that it was very important you got it right away. Here, here in the bottom of my basket, under the pulau leaves."

Gutorm found the spool case and crossed the room to an old fashioned sideboard. From a hidden recess at the back, he took a small reader. Slipping the spool from the case, he fitted it into place, at the same time thumbing the volume control to soft.

Dulsena whispered to them from the speaker, and they could sense the urgency in the brief message.

Gutorm rewound the spool and they listened to the message again. In the silence that followed, they sat thinking of all the problems involved in making the trip she had urged him to take.

Leraph looked concerned, "Are you going?"

"Yes."

"Are you sure we can trust this girl?" she asked. "She seemed very nice, but she is married to a Brenev."

"Oh yes, I think we can trust her," Derek put in hurriedly.

"I think so, too," Gutorm added, "and besides, we really have no choice. We must know what is so important that she would take this chance."

They each knew that going meant risking another call to their contact for the transport rail, who would, in turn, have to call his contact, and so on down the line. Each call added to the danger. Also, with so many strangers in the woods the pickup would be difficult.

"Well, nothing for it," Gutorm finally said, as he stowed the reader back in its hiding place. "You will go with me, Derek?"

"Sure," Derek said, and to Leraph added, "Don't worry, Leraph, I'll keep him out of trouble." Leraph just threw up her hands and said, "I've never yet found anyone who could do that." She went off to the food service area to prepare the evening meal while the two men made arrangements. Gutorm got the transmitter from its hiding place in one of the sleeping alcoves and tapped in a number. A voice answered and after Gutorm gave the proper identification he hurriedly explained what he needed and broke the connection as quickly as possible. Turning to Leraph he said, "We will leave as soon as it is dark."

With nightfall, Derek and Gutorm were back in the woods. "I hope they've all gone home for dinner," Derek whispered.

"Not all," Gutorm whispered as he pointed towards a small light on the next ridge. "They don't seem too concerned about being seen." Taking a long circuitous route through the woods, they did come to the rail line and were picked up and rode without incident through the night.

The second transfer also went smoothly. When the third switch in Rohnseff also went smoothly they began to think they might make it.

Their new guide had just led them onto a branch of the public transport beltway when they hit. Three of them. One pushed the guide off, then tackled Derek. Another one slashed at Gutorm with what looked like a Felgan blade. Rolling to one side Gutorm hit him with a shot from the laser Dulsena had given him, and then turned to see the third man coming at him with a Nervcept Wand. The flash of the laser crossed the Nervcept and the explosion threw the attacker backward off the beltway. In the meantime, Derek had flipped the other one sideways onto the line heading the opposite direction.

People were yelling and they could hear the fast bleep, bleep of the security watch coming in fast. Derek tried to calm the bystanders down while Gutorm rolled off the beltway and ran back to where the guide was lying, surrounded by people. Pushing through the crowd he turned the man over and could see he was in a bad way. Gutorm spoke to him and he opened his eyes and tried to say something.

"No Kalleni. No Kalleni." Then he gasped something that sounded like "walking the musician".

"What are you saying? Tell me again."

"Walking the musician. Find h…"

He either fainted or died. Gutorm didn't dare take the time to find out which. The bleep bleep had stopped and he could see uniforms headed his way. He ran, trying to get lost in the crowd. Knowing he absolutely must not get caught, he ran like he never had before. Down the moving walkway, then onto the stationary walkway he raced, threading his way through and around the pedestrians. He could hear shouts and a hand reached out and grabbed his shoulder. He swung around and stopped just short of landing a blow when he realized it was Derek.

Together, they raced down the walkway a bit further, slid in front of a large group of shoppers, then veered off, slowed and half walked, half staggered through the doorway of a men's store. A large fabric display offered a chance to catch their breath.

Derek was grinning and shaking his head. "Welcome to Rohnseff," he whispered, as he fingered some material.

"Yeah," wheezed Gutorm, "I'd have settled for a little more quiet reception." He looked back the way they had come, saw there was still some commotion and said, "Let's get out of view."

They walked towards the back of the store looking here and there at the displays as casual shoppers would. Approaching a clerk, Gutorm, in an outrageously exaggerated upper-class Dornatzian accent, said. "I would like to see something in an Algoran robe, please."

The clerk bustled him into a selection room and Derek, trying to look urbane, trailed along after him. Gutorm was carefully positioned before the tri-view and his image was recorded. The clerk coded in the style numbers, all the while keeping up a running commentary on how nice the new materials were that had just come in, and what the latest colors were, and how decorative the new borders were.

While Gutorm watched, his holograph appeared attired in the new, sample robes. The clerk then asked Derek to step towards the tri-view.

"Oh, no I'm just helping my friend to…" He stopped as Gutorm was gesturing trying to get his attention.

"No, no, no don't back out now," Gutorm said in a joshing tone. "You know we both agreed we needed new clothes. Make new men of us, so to speak," he said jovially. "Go ahead," he said to the clerk, "and get his measurements too. Goodness knows from the looks of him he could use something." He smiled broadly as Derek's black look changed to one of comprehension.

Soon they were both watching intently as their holograms turned and posed. It's doubtful the clerk had ever had such careful shoppers. Between the two of them, they asked every question anyone could ever think of about the fabrics, the textures, the styles, the cut, everything right down to the history of the designs on the bands. They looked at first one and then another. They went back and forth until even the clerk ran out of things to say. Finally, they made their selections. They both hoped enough time had gone by that the patrol was now off looking elsewhere.

While the clerk went off to get the new robes they stripped off their old clothes, rolled them around their lasers and were waiting when the clerk came back with their selections.

With much assistance and many pats and tugs the attentive clerk made sure each was suitably attired in "absolutely the newest color, with the latest bands".

Gutorm finished dressing first. He then released the knot holding his hair and gave it a quick brushing changing his long hunter style hair into an approximation of the new "Lion Mane" style. No doubt about it, he did look different. He just hoped there was enough difference. Derek's hair was much shorter and curlier so he was more limited in what he could do, but by brushing the curls forward over his forehead and sweeping the sides back, he did effect quite a change.

The clerk found it all terribly fascinating and was still patting and adjusting and chirping away as Gutorm gave him enough notes to more than cover the cost of the robes. While the clerk went off for a receipt, they retrieved their lasers, dropped their old things in a refuse chute, and walked out a side door.

There was no sign of any security activity. They caught the beltway and rode in silence for quite some time.

"Breakfast," Derek said succinctly and nodded his head at the sign up ahead. Gutorm saw the self serve and said, "Food and some thinking."

After the server left, Derek said, "All right, Gutorm, did the guide say anything to you, give any hint as to where we were going?"

Gutorm shook his head. "Nothing that made any sense to me. All he said was, "No Kalleni", which could only mean we weren't to go to the House of Kalleni as we had been told to do. Or at least that's what I think that means."

"Yes," Derek agreed. "I think that's probably right. Nothing else at all?"

"Well he then said something about "walking the musician." What could he have meant about walking the musician?"

"A walking musician," Derek suggested, "you know like the ones that play in the town squares or in front of the museums?"

"No, I don't think so. Besides, he hadn't said A walking musician he had said walking THE musician."

They sat and thought and then Derek said, "Perhaps waking the musician? It isn't night time, but don't musicians sleep during the day and work nights? Could it have been 'waking' the musician?"

"I don't know," Gutorm said. "Whatever it was he thought it was important enough to use his last words to tell us.

"Musician. Musician. Where to start?"

Suddenly Gutorm slammed down his cup and said, "Of course!"

"Of course what?" Derek asked.

"A musician makes his living playing for other people and they get those jobs by advertising, or through an agent.

"We talk to an agent and…"

"Right." Gutorm said. "We talk to someone who is in the music business and find out if what the guide said makes any sense."

There was a communication booth in the hallway and Derek scanned the directory, checking for musical agents. Picking one, he gave the number to Gutorm who encoded it. When a man answered he asked, "Does the term 'walking the musician' mean anything to you?"

"Yes, it does," the man answered. "It means money for my

competition, that's what it means."

"Why is that?" Gutorm asked.

"Because if you want to hire Fedor Wolking you need to talk to Hartshes."

"Hartshes?"

"Yes, Hartshes. They're his agency. But you don't need to. I've got a dozen groups better than his at a better price. How about Lorenz Risher and His Algy Swats? They are a great little group or…"

"No, no thank you," Gutorm interrupted. "I want Wolking. Thanks anyway."

Derek was already looking up Hartshes in the listings. He found it and Gutorm quickly coded in the number. It rang four times before someone answered. By that time they both were ready to crawl through the communicator.

"Hartshes Talent"

"Good morning, Do you have a musician named Wolking?"

"Oh yes, indeed we do. Fedor Wolking and his Welcome Melodies. A fine group, too. Do you wish to hire them?"

"Yes I do, but I want to hear them first. Where are they playing?"

"They have an engagement at the… let me see… oh yes this is…no that was yesterday…yes here it is The Pa Ashur Lounge. That is the one on 12-165th, 23rd level, not the one on 14th. That one went out of business last year, you know."

"Yes, of course, the one on 12-165th, 23rd level. I can find it. Thank you."

"Well after you listen to them I'm just sure you will like them, so could I have your name and the dates you have in mind and I will see if they are free and go ahead and draw up the preliminary paperwork and…"

"That's all right. I'll listen to them and get right back to you," he interrupted and broke the connection.

"It's a name, Derek, a name, Fedor Wolking. He and the Welcome Melodies are playing at the Pa Ashur Lounge."

"Great! Where's that?" Derek said as he followed Gutorm who was heading for the door.

"I have no idea, but we can look it up on the grid."

At the nearest grid directory they dialed in the address. The directions appeared and it was only a short while, after confirming the request, until the correct color coded unit slid into place. Gutorm fed in the Identi-card, which the unit accepted without any delay. It wasn't his card. It belonged to a man who was a member of the network. Several of the leaders had copies to use in case of an emergency. The unit was empty and after they started to move they could relax and try to plan their next move. The car came to a stop and the directional read, "12-165th, 23rd level, to the right". They climbed out and went as directed.

The Pa Ashur Lounge was a large eating place with several dining rooms, but they headed towards the main dining room where they could hear an orchestra playing.

The maitre d' swooped towards them, smiling and anxious to seat two gentlemen dressed in the latest fashion.

"Later, thank you," Gutorm said. "Right now we just want to listen to the musicians." They were assured that they could hear the band just fine from their table and be much more comfortable. He seemed quite disappointed when they said they would wait for a few minutes, but finally shrugged and backed off.

"He must have liked our latest patterns, not to mention our fabulous hairstyles," Derek whispered. Striking a nonchalant, but affected pose he added, "Obviously, any eating establishment would be honored to have us in their dining room."

Gutorm gave him a look, shook his head and said, "What is obvious is you've been out in the woods too long. Come on."

They walked over to a small alcove where they could stand and be a little less conspicuous. Soon the musicians finished playing and exited through a door on the far side of the stage.

Derek and Gutorm circled around the edge of the room to that door and went in. They were immediately set upon by a rotund, agitated little man. "Oh no, Sirs. Sorry, Sirs. This is for staff only, staff only." The little man bounced up and down, trying to hustle them back out the door.

"Just a minute, Just a minute," Gutorm said, "I'm supposed to meet

Fedor Wolking here. His agent sent me."

"Oh my. Not at all usual. Not at all usual," the little man exclaimed. Since Derek and Gutorm were still walking forwards the excited man had ended up walking backwards as he protested. Finally he said, "Well, all right. All right, I suppose, I suppose. If you must."

He reluctantly turned and scuttled ahead, leading the way down the hall, all the time rubbing his strange, yellow-orange hair this way and that, until it stood up in little spikes all over his head.

"It's just not usual, you know," he spluttered over his shoulder. "No one is supposed to be in here but staff. Only the staff. Well, and the musicians, you know. I'll probably get in trouble for this, you know."

"No, no surely not," Gutorm responded calmly, "and if you do, this will help won't it?" He slipped him a five drek note and the little man pointed to a door and scuttled off saying "that's all well and fine, but I'll still probably get into trouble, you know, it's just not done, there'll be trouble".

The man and his monologue of woe exited through a door at the end of the corridor and the hall was quiet. Gutorm listened at the door for a moment. Hearing nothing, he nodded to Derek and knocked. At a muffled response, they went in.

"Excuse me," Gutorm said, "We're looking for Fedor Wolking."

"I'm Wolking."

"I'm glad we found you. We're looking for a girl named Dulsena."

The seven of them were fast, real fast. Gutorm and Derek didn't have a chance.

- 12 -
The Gathering Forces

"Dulcy, There's a call for you." Scortzi's voice came over the intercom. "Line 26, no identification."

She picked it up and heard, "Wolking here. About this Gutorm person…"

"Yes, yes," she interrupted. "Have you heard from him?"

"In a manner of speaking. At the moment, Hobard is sitting on him." Hobard was the drummer in Wolking's band and was easily 130 kilos.

"Good Heavens! Is he all right?"

"Oh, I think he probably is. But before we get too concerned about that, can you tell me what this Gutorm looks like?"

She described him the best she could and then heard Wolking say, "Hobard, you can let him up now, that seems to be the right man.

"Do you want to talk to him, Dulsena?"

"Yes, please."

There was quite a wait before she heard a sort of ragged, breathless voice say, "Dulsena, you have good friends. Big, but good. Will you tell them I'm harmless and to please send me to you."

"Yes, Gutorm, I'll do that. I'm glad you got the message and got here so quickly. We're all anxious to see you. Now put Wolking on again and we'll see if we can get you the rest of the way."

"He's the one, Wolking. Will you please see that he gets to the Schertzer warehouse, 12th—23rd, sub level 2. Talk to a man named

Largan. He will bring him to House of Kalleni with his regular delivery. Someone will be there to meet him."

"Sure thing, Dulsena. But there are two of them."

"Two of them? What do you mean?" Dulsena asked.

"There's another guy with this Gutorm. Not so tall, black curly hair. Pretty city type."

"Who does he say he is?" Dulsena asked.

"Derek. He says his name is Derek. Know him, Dulsena?" Wolking asked.

"Oh yes, I know him," Dulsena replied. "Stolarn accent, right?"

"That's the one," Wolking answered.

"He's ok, Wolking. Send him along with Gutorm."

"Will do. I'll have Hobard bring them to you."

The thought that Gutorm was on his way was a happy one, and she would even be happy to see Derek again. She smiled to herself. The idea of these very self-sufficient woodsmen being sort of hand delivered by Hobard was very amusing. There was one thing, however, that she found puzzling. What could Wolking have meant by Pretty City type? She certainly would never have thought of describing either Gutorm or Derek with those words. Strange.

Leaving the Skippys to their work, she went to Rimini's office and told him and Scortzi the good news. A call was made to each of the others, and it was agreed they would meet in Siburi's conference room.

Scortzi went down to arrange with security for Gutorm and Derek's arrival, and Dulsena went to Siburi's apartment for a quick fresh-up. She was thinking that Gutorm had never seen her in her own clothing, only the things Loran had allowed her to wear. Now she found she was very nervous at the prospect of this meeting.

She was still trying first one robe and then another when the intercom announced their arrival. Quickly she settled on the patterned yellow robe her father had selected for her, gave her hair a fast brush and hurried out. Coming down the corridor she could hear Gutorm's voice and was surprised to find herself rushing because she was so anxious to see him. "This is ridiculous," she said out loud, and forced herself to stop and wait until she had regained her composure.

"I can't imagine what is keeping her," she heard her father say. "She has been so anxious for you to get here. "Ah, there you are, Dulsena. We were wondering about you."

"I'm sorry if I kept you waiting," Dulsena said, trying her best to look like Siburi. "Hello, Gutorm."

Gutorm's face was a sight to cherish. A guarded expression changed to surprise and then to clear admiration and pleasure. She was so glad she had taken time to change clothes.

"Dulsena, how nice to see you again. You look marvelous."

She could see Scortzi and her father exchange glances as she took Gutorm's hand and smiled. "You do too. My, that's quite a change from your hunter's clothes."

He laughed and said, "Protective coloration for the city." Turning towards Derek he said, "Derek here had a hard time deciding what to wear. He looked so good in all of them."

Dulsena laughed and said, "I'm sure he did. Well it suits both of you. Even people who know you well would have a hard time recognizing you in your city finery."

"We were sort of hoping that would be the case." Gutorm said wryly.

"Well I'll find out more about that later," Dulsena said, "right now I'm just glad to see you survived your encounter with Hobard."

"Oh, don't remind me," Gutorm laughed, rubbing his ribs. "I wasn't sure I would ever be able to breathe again. "He turned to Rimini and said, "Your daughter has some big, powerful friends."

The intercom purred and they were told that Henri Dakkon and Lisbet Bornach had arrived. Walking into the large conference room they found two others waiting with them, Commanders Rich Balnger and Dwina Pirtle, both of the Algaron Fleet.

The meeting was a revelation for Gutorm and Derek. To find that others, besides their group of exiles, were trying to stop the Brenevs was a wonderful surprise. Just after they started, Raynelle came in and it was her report that excited Gutorm the most. Governor Sechem was not only not in the conspiracy with the Brenevs, he was trying to sort out who was, and who had remained loyal to Greniff and the Federation. Her remarks also supported their belief that the governor's staff, or most of it, was working for Brenev.

Gutorm spoke out, "Finding out that the Governor is with us and that the Federation has been investigating Brenev's activities on ten different planets, all of a sudden makes our mission seem much more feasible. We have been feeling very alone in this struggle, thinking no one in the government cared what was happening to the people. To suddenly find we have this support is…is…overwhelming." His voice broke and it was clear the tension this man had been under.

Derek took over saying, "Gutorm speaks for both of us. We want you to know that we, and a lot of others who have been victims of Nayland Brenev, are determined to do everything we can to stop him. You just tell us what you want us to do."

"Well believe me," Henri Dakkon said, "we're just as glad to find you and your group here. Your expertise about the local situation will make things much easier for us."

"Please, Gutorm Anfinru," Lisbet said, "will you tell us about what happened to your family and give us some background on the others in your group. We need to know which worlds in the Federation are the most involved."

Gutorm's recital of what he knew about Nayland Brenev's activities was a sobering one. Clearly, Nayland's tentacles had spread through far more of the Federation than the leaders had thought.

"Raynelle," Lisbet Bornach asked, "can you help us find out which of the local forces may be trusted?"

"I'm sure my father and the few old friends on his staff who are loyal will have some ideas about that." Turning to Rhys Xholan she asked, "Could we work together on this? I'm sure as Port Master you have your sources and, as an outsider, you may be more objective."

"My assistant and I have indeed gathered some information and formed some opinions. We will be happy to share what data we have been able to find. Working together we should be able to get a pretty good idea which way the locals will go in any confrontation."

While it was decided what each group would do, Henri Dakkon excused himself to call Federation Headquarters. When he returned he said, "I think you will all be pleased to hear The President has ordered a full scale Federation-wide alert as of now." He smiled as Derek slapped Gutorm on the back and shouted, "At last!" The others smiled their approval.

Dakkon went on, "Admiral Toomey has been placed in charge. Commanders, his orders to you are to assist in coordinating the efforts of your forces with those of the exiles and any loyal, local forces. Operations will commence with an attack on the Brenev Compound in 24 hours. Meanwhile, there is much to be done."

Having had their duties and responsibilities delegated, they dispersed to put the plans into action. As Gutorm was leaving, he and Dulsena touched fingertips in the formal Greniff manner but then, turning his hand, he caught hers and kissed her palm. His other arm slipped around her waist and he pulled her close. Kissing her forehead, he whispered, "Dulsena, sweet Dulsena, you did it. You came through for us." Abruptly he released her, turned and strode from the room, leaving her weak kneed and trembling.

Rimini's voice boomed out, "Come on, Dulsena, there's work to be done if we're going to get those polchars." That brought her from her reverie and after that there was no time for such romantic thoughts.

- 13 -
The Brenev Compound

Twenty four hours later Dulsena was back in the same ravine that Bibdag and she had traveled in her flight from the compound. This time, under cover of darkness, combined Federation and exile troops had made their way across Brenev lands to just outside the compound and taken up positions around the perimeter.

"I never dreamt I'd be back here and certainly not like this," Dulsena whispered to Derek. It was too dark to see any of the small group she was with. She knew they were there, dispersed behind a large farm building waiting for the signal to advance.

Like everyone else in Derek's group, Dulsena, was dressed in a Federation support uniform. Each one was wearing PGU's (personal gravitation units) and heavily armed, thanks to the supplies the Colonel had arranged to be brought in.

A few of Colonel Czerny's men, with heavier weapons, were interspersed immediately behind them. They would be supported by an airborne group which would be dropped at the time of the attack. Altogether, it wasn't a large group, but should be more than enough. Dulsena had told them there were approximately 125 family members and about 175 others including security people, servants and the ground staff. Once again, in her mind, she went over the names, checked her tally and hoped she had guessed right.

The troops waited quietly. She laid her head on her arm and tried to relax. Just two hours earlier, she and the Federation troops under the command of Major Jhurgy had been flown over the valley just beyond Leraph's hut. The flyers had come in low to drop them and they had used PGU's, to come in the rest of the way. It had been a very fast transfer and, everyone hoped, one that had gone undetected. Shields had been put in place before they had moved into the gully to prevent detection by the security system at the compound.

Now they were in place, ready and just waiting for the signal. Czerny's plan was to have troops all over Greniff move at the same time. He had emphasized he wanted that advantage of surprise. There must have been a delay somewhere.

Derek had been there when she landed and seemed pleased to see her, but, except for a smile now and then, they hadn't had time for any personal conversation. He'd been far too busy distributing arms to the exiles.

In the planning sessions, Dulsena had already given the Fed Officers all the information she could about the layout of the compound. Given it with the understanding she would come with them. There had been protests, especially from Rimini and Scortzi, however, Dulsena had insisted that her knowledge of the compound would be helpful. Now, however, as she lay there in the dark, she found she was having very mixed emotions about it all. She could remember how she had felt coming to this compound for the first time, so in love and wanting to make a good impression on Loran's family.

She wondered again, for the thousandth time, how things could have gone so wrong in such a short time. Love changed to distaste and then to contempt. Loran and his family turning mean and hateful, leaving her no choice but to flee for refuge. Her only thought then had been to get away and never have to see them again. Now, here she was, coming not alone but with armed soldiers, waiting to invade that same compound, waiting to arrest her husband and his traitorous brother.

The evidence was undeniable against Nayland and, remembering his cold mocking eyes, she did not doubt it. As for Loran, she still wasn't sure he was in on his brother's schemes. If he knew, and disapproved, he certainly had done nothing to stop him.

Her thoughts tumbled about. How sad that this beautiful compound, and all its luxuries she had so admired, had been obtained through extortion, greed and at the expense of other people's lives. She remembered Gutorm recounting Nayland's treatment of his sister. A beautiful, loving, trusting girl destroyed because of his greed. And there was Gutorm's mother, torn from her home and comfortable position into a life of drudgery and deprivation. She wondered about the women in Nayland's family; Did they know what was going on? Knew what Nayland had been doing? Knew how he had treated these innocent people.

And the children. What about them? The apartments were full of children. Could they be kept from harm? Was she, their cousin, if only by marriage, going to put them in danger. These and other questions hammered about in her head, even as her body lay immobile in that dark, quiet night.

Her laser was digging into her ribs and she couldn't find any position that was comfortable. Trying to ignore that, she focussed on Derek. Derek, as Gutorm's second in command, was leading the exiles in this area while Gutorm was with Commander Balnger coordinating the activities of the exiles assigned to other Federation troops. Gutorm and Derek. Derek and Gutorm. That too was a muddle. Oh, it was all too much to think about.

After twenty four hours filled with hectic activity it was hard to just lie still and wait. However, several times Colonel Czerny had impressed upon them how essential it was that everyone hold their positions until ordered to move.

So, Dulsena thought. We wait. The night air was scented with the pungent aroma of clay and the musky smell of ripening grains and garden vegetables. They had been in position long enough for the normal night sounds to resume, and she heard only those, plus an occasional muffled sound as someone shifted position.

She hoped that Bibdag, Naba, and the other servants had done their jobs. Bibdag, the gardener, was to have seen that the fruits for the evening meal had been soaked in a strong sedative, which should have put everyone to sleep by now. A helper in the main kitchen was to have dosed the evening drink with the same sedative. When most were asleep,

Naba was to open the terrace doors of all the apartments on the back side of the compound. Another man, having worked his way into a position of trust, had access to the security system and was to have turned it off as soon as the guards fell asleep. If things went as planned, there shouldn't be a problem and no one would be hurt.

To her left, Derek shifted position and put his mouth close to her ear. "You can still go back, Dulsena." She shook her head and he said, "All right, then, are you ready?" She nodded. Just then the Major's voice came through the headpiece, sending them surging forward.

The compound was dark and quiet. There wasn't a sound other than light rustlings as their PGU's skimmed them across the fields. No alarm was raised. Apparently their plan for de-activating the security system had worked. Looking up, Dulsena could see troop carriers starting their approach in order to drop men with PGUs directly onto the flat rooftop. They reached her old terrace garden and tried the door. It was open and she slipped through into her old apartment. An arm suddenly circled her throat in a choke hold. Desperately, she grabbed the arm, dropped to her right knee and threw the attacker over her shoulder. He slid into a piece of furniture with a crash. Shu-luke was not necessary as he had apparently been stunned in the fall.

"I think," whispered Derek, "that the plan called for us to be very quiet."

"Thanks a lot," she whispered back. "Give me some light I want to see who this… Oh no! It's Loran!"

"Put restraints on this man and take him back to field headquarters," Derek whispered to a pair of soldiers who had come in. Then he and Dulsena crossed the room and slipped out into the hallway with the soldiers following closely. So far, other than the attack by Loran, they hadn't seen anyone.

As they reached the end of the corridor, they saw the body of a woman lying on the floor. Hurrying to it, Dulsena turned it over and was shocked to see that it was Naba and she was dead. Just then the lights came on, and Nayland's guards hit them. Hard. The night was filled with the cries of wounded men, the splintering, crashing sounds of walls being breached. Powerful explosions shook the whole building.

It was obvious that the sedative ploy had not worked. Not only were they not asleep, they were expecting them! They'd been warned! Someone had betrayed them. The Federation troops pressed forward, but Brenev's troops had the advantage of being on home ground. The battle was fierce. Dulsena had gone into this with the idea of being a guide in an easy takeover and now here she was fighting for her life. Many times in the next few minutes she was thankful for the hours she had spent learning how to shoot. At one point she found herself thinking, "I must remember to tell Mother she had been right about learning to defend myself."

They fought hard for each corridor, trying to work their way to the main salon. But they just didn't have the needed manpower. The backup support from the airborne troops wasn't there. Later they found out that Nayland's troops had been concealed on the roof tops, under shields to foil the sensors, and had decimated them as they landed. It was a disaster.

It wasn't long before the code for retreat came over the headsets and they fought their way outside, gathering up their wounded as best they could. With grav-units on full power they retreated to an area about two kilometers from the grounds. There the Robo-MedTecs had set up a medical station and were treating the wounded and arranging for their transfer back to Rohnseff.

They had barely brought in all the stragglers when a warning signal sounded and a voice came over the set telling them to take cover. Within seconds, the sky was lit up with brilliant flashes. A trooper told Dulsena they were LSL's, Large Scale Lasers. Their incredibly powerful beams swept the compound destroying everything in their path.

"Old Pirtle's brought the Fed ships in," one trooper yelled.

"What about the women and children in the compound?" Dulsena cried out.

"None there," someone answered.

"Narm! They was gone 'fore we even got here," someone else hollered.

"Someone tipped 'em off, that's for sure."

"Yabbut who and how?" That was the question that haunted all their thoughts.

- 14 -
Exile and Compensation

"Dulsena Kalleni, report to Commander Pirtle immediately," the order rang over Dulsena's headset. Wearily she got to her feet and with the PGU on full power made her way to Gutorm's hut which was serving as a temporary field headquarters. There she was told to take a shuttle to the command ship.

Once there, the shuttle bay doors slid open and she was surprised to find Hobard waiting for her. "Hobard," she said. "What are you doing here?"

"Wolking sent me. I'm sort of a liaison officer between him and Commander Pirtle."

"Wolking?" Dulsena said. "Hobard, I'm very confused. What has Wolking to do with all this?"

"Ah, Dulsena, he fooled even you, didn't he. Wolking is the leader of the exiles on Rohnseff. He and Gutorm have been working together for years."

"But Wolking didn't even know Gutorm when he came to the lounge and asked for me," she said.

"That's true. You see they had never met in person," Hobart answered. "They had only communicated using their code names, Barget Hunter and Cleidah."

"Well," Dulsena said, "in one way it is a surprise to find out about Wolking, but it also explains all those record spools about ships and mines. Please, give him my regards, Hobard, and thank him again for helping me. Now, excuse me, but I must report to Commander Pirtle."

"Yes," said Hobard, "I'll go with you, as I too have been summoned."

On the bridge, Commander Pirtle came right to the point. "Your husband has been captured and we are trying to get him to cooperate. So far he will not answer any questions. We had hoped you could talk to him. We must know where Nayland Brenev has gone and what his plans are. See what you can find out. Also, see if you can find out how they knew we were coming."

"I've wondered about that," Dulsena said. "Didn't the scanners show they were there?"

"They used thermal blockers," Commander Pirtle snapped. Seeing Dulsena's questioning look she added, "It's a new technology. Something that they shouldn't have even known about. It's still restricted information."

"But, how…?"

"That's what we have to find out, Dulsena. Hobard, stay with her. I think that man can be dangerous."

"Talk to Loran?" Dulsena muttered to Hobart. "I don't want to talk to Loran. I don't even want to see him again."

"I understand, Dulsena," Hobart said. "I know it may be painful. Yet, Commander Pirtle was right, we have to find Nayland, and Loran is sure to know where he is."

They were joined by two guards and escorted to a small room in the security section. Loran was brought in. He took one look at Dulsena and then deliberately looked away. He walked over to a chair on the far side of the small room, seated himself and with a look of total disdain, refused to acknowledge her existence.

She walked over to him and said, "Loran. Loran, look at me."

Turning away from her, he smoothed his cuff and ignored her.

"Loran!"

He turned suddenly and glared at her. "I wish I'd never looked at you," he hissed. "Look what you've done to me, to my family."

"What I have done?" she said in amazement. "I haven't done this to your family. Your brother is the one who did this, not me."

"Oh no, You are a wicked, wicked woman. You've betrayed me and my family. I should have killed you before you had a chance to disgrace me. That is why I stayed behind, to correct that mistake."

The venom of his remarks was incredible. She was so shocked that for a few seconds she couldn't even move. Then the anger came. "Disgraced you! Disgraced you! Why you poor, pathetic, miserable excuse of…Let me down! Put me down! The gall of that…put me down!" she screamed. Hobard had picked her up by the waist and lifted her into a corner where he set her on her feet.

Very calmly he said, "We can't have you injuring Federation prisoners, now can we Dulsena."

"Did you hear that man?" she yelled. "I disgraced him! Of all the nerve!" She was yelling and crying at the same time.

"Dulsena," Hobard said quietly, "Think. Is he worth getting upset about?"

She stood there with Hobard holding both of her arms. Slowly the anger drained away because she knew he was right. Feeling her resistance gone, Hobard let her loose.

"There now, center down, Dulcy. You know you are not to blame for this. Loran is the one who made wrong choices. You acted in good faith; he did not. Hold your position and be strong in yourself."

"Yes. Strong in myself," she thought. She knew she was not, nor could she ever be, the type of woman Loran had tried to force her to be.

"Now," said Hobard, "you go and talk to him and try to find out what we need to know."

Taking a deep breath, she walked back to Loran, sat down, and looked at him. As calmly as she could, she said, "You know this is all futile, Loran. The Federation Forces will never let Nayland get away with this. If you help us now it will save a lot of bloodshed on both sides."

Loran just sneered and said, "Nayland is stronger than you know. He will succeed. He has the men and the arms. The Federation won't always win. They think they have all the power, but the people want to control their own planets."

"And you think that Nayland, if he wins, will let the people on each planet rule themselves? Surely you're not stupid enough to believe that. Especially knowing Nayland as you do. He will become a dictator, a tyrant controlling a lot of little tyrants and the people will be much worse off. Only Nayland would benefit. Even now all of your family have been torn from their homes and taken off somewhere."

"That is only temporary," Loran said disdainfully. "When he is victorious they will return."

"You're fooling yourself, Loran. He won't win. We can't let him win. Now, tell me where he is."

"I told Nayland you would be more trouble than you'd be worth. He wouldn't listen to me. He thought only of the hold he would have on the great Rimini Kalleni to have his daughter with us when we made our move."

A cold shaft of fear swept through Dulsena. "What do you mean?" she whispered. "Is that why you changed towards me and tried to make me over into a compliant, obedient wife? You thought I would get my father to go along with you in this crazy scheme?"

Loran just looked at her and then laughed. "You still don't see, do you? You are such a pampered little fool. That is why Nayland had me marry you in the first place."

She drew in breath as if she had been hit very hard in the stomach. "No, Loran, tell me you don't mean that. Please, Loran. You could not mean that."

His eyes were dark purple and the mocking expression on his face was like the one she had seen on Nayland's face.

"All the time you were making love to me it was on Nayland's orders?" she whispered.

"Oh, there were some benefits to the whole charade," he laughed.

She felt sick. She looked at him. Saw his mocking smile and wondered how she could have been so stupid, so naive. This man had lied to her, deceived her, reached down inside her and mocked her most sacred innermost feelings. All because his brother had told him to. He was a weak nothing of a man and she felt such loathing for him. Slowly she rose to her feet, brushed past Hobard and went back to the bridge.

Commander Pirtle seeing her come in asked, "Did you get anything for us?"

"No, no I didn't and I'm sure I won't. He won't go against his brother. You will have to use the interrogation room."

Commander Pirtle looked sharply at her and said, "Are you sure, Dulsena?"

"Yes, You won't get anything from him any other way."

They both knew what the interrogation room did to people, but just then Dulsena wanted Loran to hurt as much as he had hurt her.

Commander Pirtle nodded to one of her men and they went to get Loran. Dulsena followed them back to the security area and waited. When they came out to go to the flyer, Loran was in a full length restraint.

"I hope they get their information, no matter what they have to do to you," she said softly. Her fury steeled her resolve as she watched the flyer take off. She turned on her heel and reported for re-assignment. She was determined to do whatever they asked of her, whatever was needed. They could not let Nayland Brenev win.

- 15 -
A Traitor in Our Midst

"They knew!" Lisbet Bornach slammed down the report, "In spite of all our efforts to make it a coordinated surprise attack, they knew ahead of time! How? Where was the breach of security?"

"We're trying to find that out," Commander Pirtle responded.

Lisbet Bornach stabbed at the report with her index finger, and said, "We had better find out. They knew enough ahead of time to not only warn Brenev here on Greniff, but all the other wolds too. That was a lot of lead time for him which means thatwhoever it was who warned him was in on things right from the first."

"Well, with so many worlds involved and so many messages being sent there is always the possibility that security could be breached somewhere along the line," Pirtle responded.

"That's true," Henri Dakkon said, "but I think what Lisbet is saying has merit. I think the leakage was very early on and to begin with there just weren't that many of us who had that knowledge."

Pirtle said, "You mean at the first meeting with Dulsena and that group?"

"I think," Dakkon replied, "that we should seriously consider that possibility.

"We'll get security to start focusing on that premise, but surely you don't think it was Dulsena or her family, do you?" Pirtle asked.

"No, no," Lisbet answered, "not at all, but there were others there.

As for Dulsena, she has been invaluable to us. It was thanks to her information that we were able to take over the Brenev enclave on Circauss. It will be a tremendous help to us if she can find out from those people where Nayland Brenev has gotten to."

"What about her husband, Loran, did they get anything from him about his brother?" Pirtle asked.

"We've no report yet," Dakkon answered, "I imagine that…"

The door opening interrupted his comment. Lisbet's secretary announced that Dulsena Kalleni had arrived.

"Good. Please show her in."

"Dulsena, thank you for coming," Lisbet said, motioning her to a seat. Dakkon and Pirtle nodded to her.

"Well, Dulsena, they found a good many of the Brenev family on Circauss Island where you told us they might be. Nayland wasn't there, nor any of his men, but the parents, most of the women and children, and a few men were. They are being very obstructive and we want you to go and talk to them. We need to find out where Nayland Brenev has gone."

"Oh, Counselor, I really don't think that would work," Dulsena answered. "They won't tell me anything. You can very well imagine how they feel about me. And, really, as for me I don't want to see any of them ever again."

"I'm quite aware of all that, Dulsena, but you know more about them than anyone else we have. You know who would be most likely to know something, who to concentrate on. We really think you are the best hope right now and we would appreciate very much if you would try. Use their anger towards you. Maybe their anger will make them careless."

Dulsena sighed and looked very skeptical. She shook her head and said, "All right, Counselor. If that is what you want. I'm not optimistic, but, I will try."

"Good," Lisbet said. "Commander Pirtle has arranged for Derek Donovan to go with you. You two seem to work well together, and, of course, some Judicial Clerks. An armed escort will be assigned to you when you arrive." She stood in dismissal and said, "Thank you, Dulsena, good luck and do take care. That animosity you spoke of might trigger something besides words."

Commander Pirtle smiled and said, "I'm sure you will do well getting those people to talk, Dulsena. Now Corporal Ektin is waiting outside and he will escort you to the compound. He's a good man and you can trust him. Good Luck."

Dulsena wished she had some of their confidence in her ability. Reluctantly, she was escorted to the shuttle bay where she found Derek and four Judicial Clerks were waiting.

Judicial Clerks were noted for their amazing memories and astute perceptions. They were the heart of the Federation judicial system and testimony given before them was used by Judges to help determine guilt or innocence. Intelligent, impartial, inscrutable and totally incorruptible they insured fair and swift justice for every citizen of the Federation. The incredibly difficult training in mnemonics, psychiatry and behavioral science combined with the stringent lifestyle insured that only the most qualified and dedicated candidates survived to wear the long, hooded, grey cloaks of a Judicial Clerk. Their mere presence was intimidating to those being questioned.

It wasn't long before they landed at the Brenev compound on the small island of Circauss. Stepping from the transport they could see the situation there was very chaotic. Part of the main building had burned to the ground and what remained was badly damaged, as were all the other outlying buildings. Long sections of the compound's wall were down and much of the forested surrounding area was still burning fiercely. In addition to the fire control units, Fed mop up units were busy searching the ruins for hold-outs, while Robo-MedTecs were treating and removing the injured.

Four soldiers had been assigned to take them to where the interrogations were to be held. Led by Corporal Ektin, they went into the one wing of the house that seemed the least damaged, but they still had to thread their way along corridors filled with rubble.

"They fought hard," Corporal Ektin said. "There were a lot of casualties on both sides. Fortunately, we had a larger force."

"You know," Derek said, "looking at all this it's obvious there's no way our exiles group could have beaten Brenev without the Federation Forces help. We knew Nayland had brought in a lot of troops but we had no idea just how many. And the weapons he had! He must have been building up his arsenal for years. Where did he get them all? Great Lomax, I hate to think what would have happened to us if we had tried this operation on our own. If you hadn't gotten to us, Dulcy, I don't know…"He gave her shoulder a squeeze and managed a rather wan smile.

The soldiers led them to a doorway and the Corporal spoke to the Judicial Clerks, "If it is agreeable to you, Sirs, we planned to form two groups; two Clerks with Lady Brenev and two with Derek Donovan. There will also be two soldiers with each team. Is this all right?"

"Quite satisfactory," one of the Clerks said and the others nodded.

"All right with you folks?" Corporal Ektin asked Dulsena and Derek. They each nodded and a soldier opened the door. A wave of noise broke over them. The room was full of restless people milling about yelling at each other or the guards. Children were crying and demanding attention. The commotion was deafening. Someone noticed Dulsena, her name flashed around and then the whole room exploded. The women rushed at her, calling her names—traitor, witch, and much worse. The soldiers stepped forward, weapons at the ready, and stood between Dulsena and Derek and the mob of angry women.

"That's enough! Shut up, all of you or we'll put you in restraints in isolation." Slowly they subsided into a sullen silence. As bad as Loran's looks had been, their glares were worse. They formed into a ragged line, arms folded across their chests, defiant, daring them to use force.

"We won't get anything from them if they are kept together," Dulsena whispered to Derek.

"Right," he agreed. "We'll have to talk to them one at a time."

"Corporal," he asked, "do you think your men could find us a couple of rooms, each with a table and some chairs, where we can talk to these people in a little more orderly manner?"

"No problem," the Corporal said, and motioned for two of the soldiers to go and take care of it. The group remaining now stood frozen in a silent tableau. Two armed men, two civilians and four Judicial

Judges in a silent face-off with the angry women and a few half grown boys. A large group of children stood sullenly behind the women.

One of the soldiers came back and said, "There are two rooms down this corridor that will do, Corporal." The two teams followed the soldiers down the corridor. The rooms they had found were small and in a shambles, but each had a table that could be used as a desk and some chairs that were still usable.

"Derek," Dulsena said, "why don't you start with the boys and the older women and I'll take the younger women. Then we can trade off."

"Sounds like a place to start. Is that agreeable with you?" he asked the Judges.

With no objections raised the soldiers went off to bring the people in one by one. Dulsena had already told Derek, in private, that she was sure that most of the older women were quite aware of all that was going on. She wasn't as sure of some of the younger ones. She thought perhaps they saw what Nayland wanted them to see and thought what he wanted them to think.

Once each person was seated, Dulsena followed the proper legal procedure introducing herself, the two Judicial Clerks, and the occasion for the interrogation. This was properly confirmed by the Judicial Clerks. Their long, dark grey, hooded uniforms and expressionless faces had such an intimidating effect that even the most obstreperous of the women answered her questions albeit grudgingly.

However, despite the presence of the Judicial Clerks, not one of them would give a straight answer. Everyone of them blamed Dulsena and/or the Federation. "All this terrible destruction is your fault," was the litany repeated over and over. Dulsena tried very hard to be patient because she understood how afraid they were for their husbands and sons. She knew this fear increased their hatred for her.

One by one the women were led in by the soldiers to sit before her and the judges. Sullen and uncooperative, they declared over and over that "we are only wives and, therefore, knew nothing of the men's business".

After three hours of hearing the same story, Dulsena was very glad when Derek stuck his head in the door and called, "Time for a break."

Even the Judicial Clerks seemed glad to stop for a while.

Corporal Ektin had found a slightly larger room where they could eat the lunch Commander Pirtle had sent down for them. The judges were not allowed to comment on the proceedings, however Derek speaking quietly, said to Dulsena, "I don't know what you're getting, but all I'm hearing from the women is 'we're just wives and know nothing of the men's business. All this trouble was caused by that woman Loran brought home. Our family has done nothing wrong'. On and on and on."

Dulsena laughed and said, "My goodness, what a surprise. I wonder where I've heard that one."

"Meaning you've been getting the same thing," Derek chuckled.

Dulsena nodded. "What about the boys? Were they any more forthcoming?"

"No, just variations on the same theme. 'We are not old enough to know Nayland's business activities. All these charges against him have been trumped up by 'that Kalleni woman' and 'we' were only trying to defend ourselves and our families against Federation aggression'."

"I'm beginning to think this is all a waste of time," Dulsena said. "They won't tell us anything."

"Well," said Derek finishing his lunch, "we can't give up yet. They must be getting as tired of us as we are of them. Let's go through it all again. They may tell us something yet."

Back once more in their rooms, they talked to each of the children over the age of twelve and then started all over again with the women and the boys. Through all the denials and declarations of ignorance, a thread slowly began to show. It became clear that they did know about Nayland's plans. Some knew more than others, but they all knew the general idea.

After another break Derek said, "All right, enough of this. Now we get tough."

"Threaten them with the interrogation booth?" Dulsena asked.

"Right."

Finally, the hard approach began to pay off. The threat to take them all back to the dreaded interrogation booths in Rohnseff, resulted in a few answers. Even more importantly, they started to get names of others who had known Nayland. One of those names Dulsena got from several sources and it came as such a shock that she could scarcely credit what she was hearing. No wonder they knew we were coming, and when. It explained everything.

Finally, the last woman was taken back to the main salon. From there all the witnesses would be taken to detention areas to await the results of their trials. All of their testimonies, given before the four Judicial Clerks and properly recorded, were binding on them in the courts where Federation Judges would hear their cases and determine sentencing.

"It will not go well for them," Derek said as they were walking back to the shuttle. "The charge of treason against the Federation is considered the most serious of crimes."

The seats on the shuttle were soft and comfortable and Dulsena was so bone-deep weary that she leaned back and closed her eyes, thinking to sleep until they landed. However, as soon as her eyes closed, words, scenes, phrases ran through her mind; all the things she had seen and heard began turning over and over in her mind in one giant maelstrom. Love, betrayal, duty, deceit, friendship, betrayal; around and around in her head. Lost in the bitterness of her thoughts she was startled when she realized the Clerks were preparing for landing.

She forced herself to move, to try to overcome the heaviness of the news she was carrying. "I have to give shape to this terrible fact," she thought. "Reduce it to words in a report. Words naming a traitor."

"I'm glad that's over," Derek muttered as they made their way to the Records Section. "We'll transfer this information, make a copy for the Commander and then get some sleep".

"I hope so," Dulsena agreed, "I need some."

Unfortunately, a message had been left for them that they were to report to Commander Pirtle as soon as they arrived.

"Oh no," Derek groaned. "Not another assignment. I'm so tired my brain has turned off."

They were told Commander Pirtle was on the bridge so after taking formal leave of the Clerks, they went directly there.

The tension was evident as they walked in. Derek saw a lieutenant he knew and asked what was the latest news.

"We're getting reports from all over, some good, some not so good. Third Air Division around Dornace met fierce opposition and one of the largest Federation ships was lost. Fighting was very heavy on Chaldorn, but ground troops have moved in and are making headway. Nirubati and Flornak still have pockets of resistance. Felchor and Nichi are secure as are Polchar, Frayleen and your home planet, Stolarn. Brenev never had too many supporters there at any time."

"What about Resdorn?" Dulsena asked.

"Secure there, too and…" He was distracted by something on the large communication screens which were running statistical data and upgrading reports. "Excuse me. Have to get back." He hurried to where another officer was holding out a report.

Derek and Dulsena stood to one side waiting. Their minds were reeling with all the unanswered questions that hung so heavily in the air: Where was Nayland Brenev? Had he been captured? How had things gone in the other battles? How about the other worlds the lieutenant hadn't mentioned. Would this all soon be over and done, or were they in for a long siege?

"Dulsena, Derek," Commander Pirtle acknowledged their presence. They hurried forward and handed her the copies they had made of the interview reports. She read the brief summaries at the top, stood quite still then, looking piercingly at Dulsena, asked, "Dulsena, you are quite sure of this?"

"Yes, It was confirmed by more than one," Dulsena said sadly.

Commander Pirtle said, "I know how hurtful this must be for you, Dulsena, but it does support some other information we have received. Turning to her Security Officer she said, "Pick up Luiz Roncallo".

"Commander," her second called and she gave nods of dismissal to Dulsena and Derek who immediately made their way off to the side.

Dulsena was feeling completely drained and sick.

Derek leaned over and whispered, "I was given that same name. Who is this Roncallo fellow?"

"My father's best friend and business associate," Dulsena answered.

"A man I called "Uncle Luiz". A man I thought of as a second father. A man I now find out I did not know at all. Oh, Derek, I don't know how I can tell my father. This news will just devastate him."

She leaned against the bulkhead, her eyes stinging. "What a rough thing to find out," Derek said. He put his arms around her and pulled her close. Enfolded there she welcomed his strength and support.

Suddenly there was a stir on the bridge. A Captain appeared on screen and said, "Attention. Admiral Toomey will speak to us."

All eyes were riveted as Admiral Toomey's face appeared on the screen. There was silence for a moment and then, in his deep, gravelly voice, he announced, "Combined Federation and local units have prevailed in most of the initial engagements to quell this rebellion. As you know, we had hoped for an element of surprise, however, this was denied us due to a breach of security. Even without this advantage, our troops have managed to neutralize large numbers of the opposition and gain significant, strategic sites. A great number of Brenev's forces have surrendered and masses of contraband war materiel have been recovered.

"As in any large-scale military effort," he went on, "there have been casualties on both sides. We are, however, pleased to announce that among Federation forces those losses, while grievous, have been relatively few."

Dulsena's thoughts went to Naba and Bibdag and all those killed at the compound. "Relatively few" they might have been, but still so important as individuals.

Toomey went on to say that, "obviously there is still much to be done, but I have no doubt that the Federation forces along with the invaluable support of not only local government forces, but that of various irregular units will soon rout this traitorous band of rebels."

Dulsena assumed the reference to irregular support units included all the fighters from Gutorm's exile's group.

As she looked around she saw Admiral Toomey's good news reflected in the faces and attitudes of those present. The taut desperation she previously had sensed, had been replaced with, if not exactly an air of jubilation, at least a strong sense that the balance had swung against the rebels. Now it was just a matter of time.

"I believe he is right," Derek said as he turned and firmly led Dulsena off the bridge. "We've made a good start and, eventually, right will prevail. As for us, we have done all we can for the moment and we're heading back to your family."

- 16 -
Lost Friend

"I don't care what they say, I just don't believe it!" Rimini's voice boomed out. "I will not believe that Luiz Roncallo would do something like that. Why we've been friends and business associates since before you two were born. How can you think something like that of him?"

Dulsena looked helplessly at Scortzi. They were in Rimini's room at the inn where they were staying until it was safe to return to Resdorn. Scortzi, who was leaning against a column with his arms across his chest, sighed and said, "I understand how you feel, Father, I felt the same way when I was told. It does seem incomprehensible, especially knowing how he seemed to feel about Dulsena. But, if you will look back at the events you can see that they support the allegations."

"What support?" Rimini countered, "I see no support."

"Remember when we were trying to contact Gutorm?" Dulsena asked. "Who was it that first suggested someone hire Wolking?"

"Rhys," Rimini said, "he knew that man, what was his name…Corrinon, Bertrand Corrinon, who had been to the Governor's ball."

"No," Dulsena said, "first Luiz recommended Glarin Stortz. Then Rhys told us that Stortz had left from Rohnseff just that morning. Remember he said he'd seen his flight papers? That is when Rhys suggested Corrinon."

"Oh, yes," Rimini said, as he stopped pacing and listened intently.

"Well," Dulsena said, "Glarin Stortz has been implicated in the rebellion."

"And obviously Luiz knew that," Scortzi put in. "That's why he was trying to get you to go to him."

"Right," Dulsena said, "And when that failed and the decision was made to go to Rhys' friend, Corrinon, Luiz did his best to arrange for him and me to go alone. Remember how he tried to convince you that it wasn't necessary for Rhys to take time off from work to go with us? But Rhys said it was no problem and he wanted to go.

"So next Luiz tried to convince you that it wasn't necessary for us to take Jonas and Kiku," Dulsena added.

"Oh no," Rimini said as he sank into a chair and stared at her, "You are actually suggesting that if only you and Luiz had gone that maybe you would not have made it to Corrinon's house?"

"I'm afraid so, yes," Dulsena answered.

"Oh, Dulsena," Rimini moaned, shaking his head. "I just can't believe that Luiz would have hurt you. Why Luiz…Luiz has been like a member of our own family. He…Oh I can't bear to think of it." He sank into a chair, his head in his hands.

"I know, Father," Scortzi said, "but the facts seem to indicate that he has been working for the Brenevs for quite a while. His trip here, for instance, at just the right time was too much of a coincidence. Even more damning is the fact that he wasn't the one who turned up the information on the population shifts. His assistant did."

"There was one other thing," Dulsena interjected, "From what Loran said I believe that my meeting with him was arranged." At their surprised looks she added, "Remember, Loran said it was all Nayland's idea for him to marry me. He and Luiz could have arranged for us to meet at the gallery. Luiz knew my schedule."

"As to why Luiz would do such things," Scortzi said, "it's hard to tell. Maybe Nayland Brenev had some information that Luiz didn't want made public and was using it to blackmail him. Or maybe Nayland made him an offer he didn't think he could refuse. We all know what expensive tastes Luiz has."

Rimini started to object again and Scortzi said, "Now be honest,

Father. You and Luiz are old friends, but you have led quite different, separate lives. You, we, don't know everything he does."

Rimini sighed, and said, "Yes, you're right. And that other thing you said about Luiz is true, too. He was there, wasn't he? Each time." He sighed and said, " All right, I guess I have to believe it. But, it's hard, so hard. All these years I thought he was my friend."

He sat slumped, dejected, then rose abruptly, went over to the window and stared out into the night. "I don't think we ever will understand unless he chooses to tell us himself."

"No we won't. And, personally, I don't think we'll ever know," Scortzi said softly.

Rimini sighed and said, "No, nor will I ever understand."

There was a long pause then Rimini squared his shoulders and in a brisk voice asked, "This Stortz that Luiz wanted you to see, you say he has been implicated. Is he in custody and if so can he tell us anything?"

"He probably could, but he isn't in custody. He has disappeared, too. No one has seen him since he left Rohnseff Spaceport."

- 17 -
Fears and Joys

Three cycles of hard fighting had proven the Admiral was right, the nightmare wasn't over quickly. Nayland's forces had proven surprisingly strong. Federation forces had quickly regained control of Rohnseff City, the port facilities and all of the Harsham Continent. They were still getting reports of fierce fighting in other areas of Greniff. Being Nayland's home planet, he had had years to build up support for his ill conceived venture.

Rimini and Scortzi, given the opportunity to get back to Resdorn on a Federation transport, had left. They had urged Dulsena to come with them. However, in spite of their arguments, she had chosen to stay on Greniff. The war had receded and the city of Rohnseff was fast recovering from the damage that had been inflicted. Dulsena was comfortably ensconsed in the executive suite at House of Kalleni.

On a beautiful warm morning, she was sitting on the balcony having breakfast and watching the NewsVu when a call came from security.

"A person to see you, Lady Loran. A Derek Donovan."

"Send him up please," Dulsena responded, as she thought to herself, "Derek here. That's unexpected."

She walked to the door, opened it and watched as Derek came into sight in the clear view lift. "Derek, what a nice surprise," she said happily, giving him a big hug. "It has been far too long. Come in, come in and let me get you something. Have you had breakfast?"

"Yes I have, Dulsena, thank you," he said as he kissed her briefly on the cheek. "But I will have something to drink, if it isn't any trouble."

"No, no trouble. I just made a new pot of tea." She watched as Derek slumped onto the nearest chair. He was thinner, his clothes were rumpled and there were lines around his eyes that hadn't been there before. "There you are," she said, trying to sound cheerful. "Now what brings you over here so early in the morning?"

Derek took several swallows of tea, then asked quietly, "Did you hear about the skirmish over near Maashout?"

"Yes the story was on the NewsVu just a few minutes ago. What about it?"

"Gutorm was there. He was hurt."

The color drained from Dulsena's face and she could barely ask, "How badly?"

"It's pretty bad, but they think they have him stabilized now. They're bringing him into Rohnseff. In fact," he said, looking at his chronos, "they are probably here by now. I came to tell you as soon as I could."

"Leraph? Have you told her?" Dulsena asked. Before the attack on the compound, Leraph had been taken aboard one of the Fed ships. After Rohnseff had been secured from Brenev's forces Raynelle had arranged for her to stay in a small suite at the governor's palace.

"I didn't, but one of the other members of the unit did."

"Good. Derek, I'd like to go to the hospital."

"Yes, I thought you might. But, Dulsena, you understand he is pretty badly hurt. You might not be able to see him."

"I know, but I want to be there if only to be with Leraph."

* * *

Dulsena jerked awake. She had dozed off again. In the shadowed waiting room she couldn't tell if Leraph, who was curled up on a lounge near her, was awake or not. She got up, stretched and walked over to the windows. It was still black outside with the city lights sparkling far below. There was a bright glow on the horizon showing the unceasing activity at the spaceport. Yawning, she checked her chronos and was surprised so little time had passed. The two of them had been there all the day before watching as the medical staff and Med-Tecs had worked with Gutorm.

She turned and walked across the waiting room towards Gutorm's room. This area was constructed in concentric circles with the nurse's station in the center, the patient's rooms in the middle and the waiting rooms on the outside perimeter. The walls were glassed so it was possible to see all the way through from the waiting area to the center section. She could see Gutorm, lying quietly, surrounded by the monitoring equipment with its pulsing lights and dimly glowing graphs. Yesterday's bustle of activity had finally ceased and the pain and trauma replaced, hopefully, by the recuperative power of sleep.

As night had fallen, the lights had been dimmed and still they waited, she and Leraph. Watched and waited, feeling helpless isolated beyond the glass wall. Others checked and monitored and comforted while they could do nothing to help him. Through the hours they had talked of all that had happened, the battles, the victories, the defeats and what it all meant. Talked out, they had sat, each wrapped in her own thoughts, fighting back her own fears.

She was turning away when suddenly lights came on in Gutorm's room and nurses hurried in to adjust the machines and confer with bent heads and soft voices. Leraph, roused by the lights, was suddenly standing beside her. "What's going on?" she asked in worried tones.

"No idea. Whatever it was they apparently have it under control," she added as the lights once again were dimmed. A Nurse seeing them there came over and spoke to them through the intercom. "He's all right. Just a problem with one of the monitors. Been taken care of now." He turned and strode away. The nurses were all men, for on Greniff it would have been unthinkable for women to be caring for strange men. They were assisted by Robo-MedTecs.

Leraph still stood watching as a MedTec checked another monitor and turned to leave. "They don't tell you much, do they?" she said to Dulsena.

"No. He does seem to be resting and that is the best thing for him right now." There was a pause and she added, "The Federation Medical officer I spoke with yesterday will be in tomorrow and maybe he will explain more. For now, you must try to get some rest. You can't help Gutorm by getting all worn out." She led Leraph back to the lounge and took a seat near her.

There was no sound for several minutes and then Leraph spoke, "The last time Gutorm was back in Rohnseff, you and he spent a lot of time together."

"Well, not a lot. He only had twenty four hours," Dulsena replied.

"And the time before that?"

"A few hours. What are you getting at, Leraph."

"I guess I just wanted to know if you two are serious about each other," Leraph laughed, softly. "Don't be angry with me, Dulsena. I'm just acting like a mother."

"I'm not angry. It's just that we don't know yet how we feel. Besides, I am still married and there's a lot of sorting out to do before we can even think about getting serious."

Still married, still married. The words kept going around and around in Dulsena's head. After all that had happened, after what Loren had said about the marriage having been a sham, just another plot of Nayland's it was hard to believe, to feel she had really been married. Legally it would be quickly dissolved. That wouldn't be a problem, but the emotional hurt would take a while. She had always been so sure of herself and her feelings so it was hard to accept the fact that she had been so fooled—a naïve little fool, Loren had called her. I guess I was, she thought. She stood looking out at the lights below, seeing all the activity at the port. Since it was Nayland's home planet there was a very large power base of his supporters. She'd been told that apparently many of his troops having been forced from areas retaken by Federation forces had fled back there. Still loyal to Brenev they were making a fierce stand. She could only stand and watch while counting hours in the unnatural hush of the hospital night. Suddenly she didn't want to be quiet. She wanted to yell and rant at the stupidity and idiocy of men like Nayland Brenev. Movement caught her eye and she turned and watched as nurses responded to someone else in need of care. Gurtorm lay quietly. That was good. She watched his still figure fighting its own battle to win. Ignoring the activity outside the window she curled up on the lounge opposite Leraph, muttered yet another heart felt prayer and let herself slip into a much needed sleep.

Several days later Derek and Dulsena were once again seated on her balcony. "So he's ready for visitors," Derek said.

"Yes, and if we don't get going he'll think we have forgotten him. Finish your drink and let's go."

A little later Dulsena stood at the bedside of a very wan looking Gutorm. "You really are going to be all right?" she asked again.

"Yes, really," Gutorm said softly, smiling at her. "Now stop looking so worried and tell me what you have been up to."

She gave him a brief review of her activities and then it was obvious that she needed to leave.

Derek was waiting outside the doorway. He waved goodbye to Gutorm and he and Dulsena left. Derek was gratified to feel Dulsena's hand reaching for his. They walked, hands clasped and shoulders touching. "He looks so pale," Dulsena said somberly.

"Yes, but he looks a lot better than he did." They walked on without speaking, each caught in their own sadness: Her in her worries about Gutorm, him in his fear that her concern for Gutorm might end forever any chance that she would someday turn only to him. Certainly, Gutorm was his friend and yes he was concerned for him. However, he loved Dulsena more and more each day and there was nothing he could do about it, but be there for her. As long as Gutorm was lying there in the hospital he couldn't very well press his suit with her. That wasn't fair. He couldn't do it. He would have to wait.

- 18 -
Impasse

Cycle after cycle passed and the battles raged on. On many worlds of the Federation there were still pockets of resistance, but the Federation forces were gradually getting the upper hand. Each day the news was a little more encouraging and after each newscast Gutorm fretted and grumbled at his slow recovery. He wanted to be back with his troops.

Derek checked in with him whenever he was back in Rohnseff, coming sometimes with Dulsena, sometimes alone. Now Gutorm was working out in the physical therapy room as he did every morning. The Robo-MedTec stopped one exercise machine and indicated Gutorm should move to another one. Silently he positioned him and said, "Please, you will now walk for twenty minutes, then we will be finished for this morning."

"As if I didn't know that," fumed Gutorm. "As if I haven't heard that same thing twice a day for two cycles." RoboMedTecs were very efficient, but not much for conversation. They had been programmed for little socialization and didn't even talk about the weather. Derek walked in just then and Gutorm looked up scowling and asked, "Do you think robots worry about the weather?"

"What?" Derek said blankly, stopped in his tracks by this odd question.

"Do robots worry about the weather? Do you think maybe they worry about shorting out in the rain or something?"

"There isn't any weather in the city and I think you've been here too long."

"You're right about that," Gutorm said as he stepped off the walker and toweled off. "So I'm leaving."

"Really? That is good news. When?"

"Now. I was just waiting for you to come."

They headed back towards Gutorm's room and found Dulsena there ahead of them. "Good morning. You're looking good, Gutorm."

"You hear that, Derek?" Gutorm said, elbowing Derek. "I'm 'looking good', while you, on the other hand are still thin and ratty looking." He had never said so, but he too had been concerned about Derek looking so worn out.

"Now that's not what I meant," Dulsena protested. "Derek looks fine although I was going to ask both of you when you were going back to that shop you went to when you came to the city that time. You must admit you could both use a new kaiton. Perhaps you could check on what's the latest in borders and..." She walked around them both, eyes narrowed, lips pursed. "Yes, definitely. A visit to the hairstylist would also be in order."

"Will you just listen to her?" Gutorm said, shaking his head. "It's not enough we should be conquering heroes, we're supposed to be stylish, too. Did you ever?" They both managed to look terribly aggrieved, at the same time trying hard not to laugh.

"All right, you two. Gutorm, your satchel is packed, I see. So, let's get you out of here."

As they reached the door it opened, a nurse came in and said, "Wait. You'll want to see this." She turned on the News[a]Vu. "...Toomey," an officer was announcing as the familiar craggy face appeared. "As you all know, for ten full cycles we have waged a long, hard fight to suppress the Brenev Rebellion. Now I am pleased to announce that as a result of several decisive engagements over the last few days, Federation Forces have overcome the last major strongholds of the rebels and a capitulation agreement has been signed by the rebel leaders.

"Unfortunately, Nayland Brenev is not at this time in custody.

However, a concerted effort is being made to expedite his apprehension and we will let you know as soon as we do so."

Admiral Toomey, looked up and smiled, "I am proud of all our brave forces who have served so well in this enterprise and proud that on this day, that we have looked forward to for so long, I can stand and announce, "We have suppressed this rebellion and peace will soon be restored on our home worlds."

- 19 -
What Goes 'Round

"I heard the decision of the courts." Rimini's voice sounded reedy and thin on the radio call from Resdorn. "The penalties seemed fair enough, but I do hate to think of Nayland Brenev off somewhere alive and free. That's really galling after all the pain and suffering he has caused. We can take some comfort in knowing that someone that evil will get his dues some day. Anyway, that aside, when will you be coming home, Dulcy?"

"I wanted to talk to you about that, Father. I know this won't please you, but I don't plan to be back on Resdorn for some time. Something else happened when I was on Aldene that you should know about. The Federation, I think it really was Lisbet Bornach's idea, has stripped the Brenevs of all their real and personal property and have given me title to everything. I now own Brenev Industries."

"Oh, Dulcy, that is a huge responsibility," Rimini said, in shocked tones. "Are you really sure you want to do that?"

"Father, I've thought of nothing else since they told me. I've looked at it from all sides and one minute it sounds like fun and the next I'm scared to death. One thing I do know, I will need some help. For example, I don't think I can work with a lot of the administrative and technical people who were close to Brenev so I'll need to bring in new people. I was hoping I could pull some from Kalleni, on a temporary basis, of course, to help me during the restructuring. There are some businesses I want to keep and even expand and others I want to drop altogether. At the same time, I would still like to maintain close ties with Kalleni and I wondered if we could work out some arrangement in exchange for technical advice."

"You don't need to worry about paying for technical advice; you know we will help any way we can if you decide on this course."

"I know that, Father, but I want it to be on a business basis. If I'm going to have this responsibility I want to start off right. You can understand that, I'm sure."

"Of course, I can. So, what do you need exactly?"

They talked for a few more minutes and then both decided that it would be better if Rimini came to Greniff and saw the situation firsthand.

That evening Dulsena met Gutorm for dinner. She was full of plans for the future. Gutorm was too, but Dulsena talked faster and now sat, eyes shining waiting to hear his response to all her ideas for Brenev Industries.

"Doesn't that sound like a workable idea, Gutorm? Or at least the start of a plan." She waited while Gutorm finished his drink and set it down, carefully aligning it on the napkin, aligning the napkin with the table edge.

"Gutorm?"

"I'm just a little surprised, Dulcy. I've been visualizing something quite different." He looked up and saw her questioning look. He reached out and took her hand and said, "I was hoping your plans included coming back with me to Frayleen."

"Oh, Gutorm, are you serious," she said. "Are you really asking me to marry you?"

He raised her hand and kissed her wrist at the same time drawing close until their lips were almost touching. "You must know how I feel about you. I think I fell in love with you the first time I saw you peeking out of one of my beds." She giggled and said, "That sounds terrible when you put it that way."

He smiled, reached out a finger and smoothed a curl on her forehead. "Well I did. You weren't quite awake and your hair was loose and tumbling all around like a golden cloud and your eyes were wide and so blue. You looked like an angel. Then later, when I saw how you tamped down your fear and went on to do whatever was necessary, that was when I really began to see beyond the sweet angel to the truly wonderful person you are."

"Oh, Gutorm, how sweet. I didn't fall in love with your hair, even though it's very nice hair." She laughed as he flipped his head and said, "Of course, especially when I comb it in the latest fashion."

"Oh, especially then. But it wasn't just your hair, or the way you walk. Now don't look surprised. You know you have a great walk, especially from the back when you're wearing those leather pants of yours." He threw his head back, laughed and in a strangled voice said, "I've never seen me walk from the back."

"Well you do, but it wasn't just that. It was the great grin. When I was 'peeking out of one of your beds' and you grinned at me I knew right then you were something special. Oh, Gutorm."

The rest of the evening was a blur. They had walked, hands entwined, and talked of hopes and dreams and watched the fountains by the governor's palace reflect in each others eyes. It was only much later, in the dark of the night, that reality intruded. "I don't think there would be any problem having your headquarters for Brenev Industries on Frayleen. Of course, you realize I will be traveling a lot but that…"

"Wait. What do you mean you will be traveling a lot?"

"Dulsena, you don't think the people that Brenev wronged are going to just let him get away with all this? We've gotten together and formed a group we call The Brenev Exile's Network. Each of us has vowed to work as long as it takes to find him and bring him to justice."

"What about your resorts, your lands on Frayleen? Surely you will be taking care of those?"

"Of course, but our first priority will be to find Brenev."

"For revenge," Dulsena said flatly.

"For justice, Dulsena, for justice," Gutorm said firmly.

"Thc Federation will find him."

"Perhaps, but we must do this."

"No, you don't. How do you think you can have a normal, happy life if your first priority is revenge? It can't be done, Gutorm."

"Yes it can."

"You're fooling yourself."

On and on the argument raged until they parted at dawn. The happy, loving mood of the night before dissolved in the bright light of morning.

- 22 -
Changing World

Dulsena walked briskly along the street, hands thrust into the pockets of her robe. She hadn't gotten to bed until first light and then had slept poorly, tossing and turning, going over in her mind all that had happened with Gutorm. Finally, she had given up, dressed and gone to the chapel provided for Kalleni employees. There, walking the path, with the fountain sprays synchronized with the Midday prayers, she had received the guidance she needed.

Afterwards she felt the need to get out, to move, to go for a long walk. Striding along through the crowds, she had reviewed the situation once again, looking at the problems from all angles. She came to the same conclusions. It was going to be hard, but in her heart she knew what she must do. Lost in thought she didn't notice the approving glances of the off-worlders or the disapproving stares of the Greneche. Her gown, very modest by Resdorn standards, was a light yellow with sprays of silver-white flowers. The dark yellow robe complimented the gown and brought out the gold highlights of her free swinging hair. She looked much too bright and frivolous by Grenechan standards.

"Her hair's not even bound," one older, darkly robed Grenechan woman hissed to her companion as Dulsena approached. "These off-worlders have no taste or sense of decency." At that moment three Dornatzian women entered the roadway from the moving beltway. Their bright Federation Blue robes swirled about them as, laughing and joking, they jostled past the somberly clad Greneche. The older woman narrowed her eyes and pursed her lips in distaste. Her companion said, “They look so young and happy. What is wrong with looking pretty?” This comment earned her a sharp glance and the order, “Don’t dawdle. You’ve been out quite long enough.” Never the less they both glanced back at Dulsena as she hurried into House of Kalleni.

Someone else had been watching Dulsena. He had just moved in behind her when she turned, with several others, into the Kalleni Building. He paused a moment, then followed, staying close enough to keep her in sight without appearing obvious. He could be patient.

As Dulsena hurried towards the lifts she bumped into what appeared to be a large purple wall. “Oh, excuse me, I…Hobart?…what a surprise. What are you doing here?”

“Why we’ve come to see you, Dulsena.”

“Hello, Dulsena,” a voice said. She swiveled to see Fedor Wolking standing quietly to one side.

“Oh, this is such a wonderful surprise. Come on up to my apartment where we can talk. Have you had lunch? I haven’t. I’ll have some sent up and we can talk. Oh, this is great.”

“Dulsena, we really would like to, but we are on our way to the spaceport. We just wanted to say goodbye before we left.”

“Are you sure you can’t? I have so many questions. Where are you going?”

“Back to Dornace,” Hobart rumbled. Have to get back to work.”

“And to his family,” Wolking said. “He has three children waiting to see him.”

“And your wife?” Dulsena asked. The smiles disappeared and Hobart said, “No, not my wife. She died shortly after the problems with Brenev. The boys have been with their grandmother.”

Dulsena put her hand on his arm and said, “I’m so sorry Hobart.” Turning she asked, “What about you, Wolking?”

He smiled and said, “No wife, no children, just a job. They’ve offered me my old job back teaching at the University in Chetek City and…maybe I’ll be doing a little conducting.”

“More than a little I hope,” Hobart said. “If I’m lucky I’ll be back playing with the symphony orchestra, I play the Cherimora and…"

"And plays it very well, too," Wolking interrupted.

"Well," Hobart laughed, "I used to. Now…who knows? It's been a long time. Anyway I want to work under Fedor again. He is a fine conductor and a great composer."

"That explains all the spools of classical music in your apartment," Dulsena said.

"Well yes, and my collection of AudVues," he said, smiling. "That's one of the reasons we stopped. I wanted to pick them up before we left."

"Oh, you really want them back?" Dulsena said teasing him. "I've grown so very fond of them I was hoping you might have forgotten all about them."

Hobart threw his head back and laughed a great roaring laugh that caused heads to turn. "Fedor's as likely to leave them behind as I am to take up interpretive dancing. He collects those things everywhere we go and has trundled them all over the Federation."

"Well follow me and I'll gather them up for you," Dulsena said, adding, "I really appreciate your letting me play them while I was storing them for you." She turned towards the lift with the two of them following. Hobart drew close to Wolking and under his breath said, "Check the man in green, right rear." He had no sooner spoken than the man pushed some people aside and pointed a laser at Dulsena. Hobart knocked his arm up, deflecting the strike at the same time Wolking stunned him with a blast from his laser. Some woman screamed and people pushed and shoved trying to get away from the scene, fearing they too might be caught in the violence. From a distance they watched as Hobart bent over and pried the laser from the man's hand and then checked the man's pulse. "He followed her in," he muttered to the security guard who had rushed up and was kneeling beside the downed man.

"Let's get him to the office, away from all these people," the guard said. "We'll want to talk to you two," he added. Walking over to where Dulsena still stood he asked, "Are you all right?" She nodded and he asked, "Do you know him?" They watched as the guard and Hobart half lifted, half dragged the still inert man out of sight.

"No, I don't recall ever seeing him before." Wolking came over to stand beside her and she asked him, "What happened? I was walking away and didn't know anything was wrong until that woman screamed. Where did that man come from?"

"He followed you in." He looked around at all the curious faces and said, "Let's get some place where we can talk and not bother all these people." He smiled at the shocked faces and led her in the same direction the guard and Hobart had gone.

Meanwhile, in the office, the guard checked the setting on the laser Hobart had taken from the man. "It's set on full power." They looked at each other. They knew what that meant. That man had meant to kill Dulsena.

- 21 -
You Can't Please Everyone

Derek, Gutorm, Dulsena and Siburi were in Siburi's office. Derek was fuming. "They warned you this sort of thing could happen," Derek said. "Didn't you take them seriously?"

"The rebellion is over. Nayland Brenev lost. I figured the people had had enough of him and would get on with their lives. Besides, nothing had happened so I just sort of forgot about it."

Derek threw up his hands and said, in an incredulous tone, "She forgot about it."

Gutorm spoke up, "It's my fault. I know what these followers of Brenev are like and what fanatics they are. They hate Dulsena and I should have known they would try to get back at her."

"Gutorm, it's not your fault," Derek protested. "You were off in the hospital most of the time. I should have taken better care of her."

"Hey, wait a minute," Dulsena said, hotly. "Neither you Derek, nor you Gutorm, were responsible for watching out for me. I should have had enough sense to take more precautions. Lef Kolek has pounded security procedures into my head since I was a little girl, so I should have known better. I was the one who got careless and now I'll take care of it. I'm sure Siburi knows some reliable security people I can use."

"Yes, of course," Siburi said, "and I will run some extra inquiries to make sure they were not Brenev supporters. All the security in-house will be increased as well."

"So," Dulsena said to the two scowling men. "Don't worry about it."

Neither Gutorm nor Derek were about to "not worry about it", but they let the subject drop for now. There was an uncomfortable silence and then Siburi asked, "When is your father due in, Dulsena?"

"He said he'd be here within the cycle."

* * *

The time went past very quickly. Dulsena tried to wade through all the information on the Brenev Industries, spending hours reading personnel profiles, damage reports and estimates on repairs for those businesses damaged in the fighting. That was intellectually hard. What was emotionally draining was trying to get Gutorm to understand her decision to not continue their relationship and to stay on Greniff and run Brenev Industries.

Finally, accepting her decision, he left for Frayleen. For Dulsena, knowing it was the right thing to do didn't do much to lessen the feeling of desolation that swept over her as she watched his ship lift off and disappear from view.

She trailed back to her flyer with her new security guard, staying close and watching everyone who got anywhere near her. Gutorm's words were still ringing in the guard's ears, threatening him with awful, dire punishment if anything should happen to his charge.

Late that night she was sitting on the floor surrounded by trays of record spools and mountains of hard copies when the intercom sounded. "Too late to come up, Dulsena?" Derek's voice asked. "I'm downstairs."

"No, Derek, it's not too late. Come on up, but I'm afraid I won't be very good company."

When Derek walked in he stopped short, "Looks like you've been busy. What are you doing?" She explained and told him about her father coming and what she hoped to have done before he got there. "So, maybe I can help," he offered.

"You know about business?"

"A little. I've heard you talk about your ancestor who came to Weneche, well mine came into Soloving. He owned a publishing house and one day had an argument with his paper supplier. Ended up with him buying his own paper processing plant, then his own bindery and then after that it all sort of got out of hand. Each generation added new companies and whoever wanted to was trained to work somewhere. I was trained for the fabric and carpeting mills."

"My, I'm impressed," Dulsena said.

"No," he laughed, "if you want to be impressed you need to meet my sister who is into heavy machinery. Big stuff, mining, terra-forming you know that sort of thing. She loves anything really big."

"Maybe you could introduce her to Hobart," Dulsena laughed.

"That's a good idea, but she doesn't care much for music."

They laughed and then Dulsena said, "So all right. Let's go to work. There are annual reports, financial reports, prospectuses, damage reports, personnel records…" Once Derek had the basic layout of her piles figured, they worked for several hours until Dulsena cried, "Stop! enough. My head is bursting." She flopped onto the lounge. "You get going on this stuff and you sound just like Scortzi," she said, laughing.

"First time in a long time I've had a chance to look at this sort of thing. Guess I sort of missed it. However, you are right. It's definitely time to quit. If you want me to I can come back tomorrow."

She quickly took him up on his offer. After he left and she was in the PCU she thought, "It sure is easier with two people bouncing ideas around and Derek is really good at this stuff. Shame he'll be going back to Soloving."

- 22 -
Shadows

Rimini Kalleni swept into Rohnseff Spaceport in one of the larger Kalleni executive transports. Dulsena, who was there to meet him, was surprised to see him leading a large contingent of people. Rimini introduced them as his Chief Financial Officer with five of his auditors, his Director of Management Information Systems with six data engineers and information analysts and, of course, Lef Kolek. Siburi Myre arranged accommodations near House of Kaleni and the next morning after an orientation breakfast they were hard at work.

When Lef learned of the attack on Dulsena he assigned another agent to Rimini and, with Rimini's encouragement, set about investigating that incident himself. Derek agreed with Lef's plans and told him, "I'm glad you're looking into this because I believe there's more to it than just the act of a single disgruntled rebel." So, while the others worked over their computers and print-outs of spreadsheets and reports, Lef was closeted with the Security Chief for House of Kalleni, Greniff.

The large security observation room seemed small because every inch was filled with surveillance monitors. In a small space at the back, Lef and Porlis, chief of staff security, were running the films showing the front area of the store on the day the attack occurred. Again and again they had watched the arm holding the laser raise, saw Hobart knock it upward and Wolking knock him to the floor. Finally Lef said, "Wait. Stop. Go back a little to before he attacks. You see there? He appears to be looking at someone, don't you think? Get a wider view of that will you, please?" The operator widened the view, pulling back to show more of the crowd. "There he is," Lef said, "and there, I think he is looking there, yes, at that man. They exchanged glances. Move in on that man, can you?" Slowly the shot narrowed as a man glanced towards the attacker and then away. "Can you hold it there and give me an enlargement, please?"

The enlargement showed a man of medium height, medium weight, dark hair, totally unremarkable from hundreds of other Greneche. "Recognize him?" Lef asked softly. Porlis shook his head. "What's that on his tunic pocket?" Lef asked. "I can't make it out." The operator zoomed in on the tunic and a small emblem could be seen. "Mean anything to you?" Lef asked. "Nothing," the other two said.

Lef stood, legs apart, arms across his chest, eyes narrowed, and peered intently at the screen. "Pull back again, please and let me see the shot with both of them."

They all stared at the screen. "I really do get the impression they were looking at each other," Porlis muttered.

"Yes, I think so too. All right then," Lef said, briskly, "let's mark that man and run him through all the other security files and see if we can make a match." The computer whirred and stopped at a scene much like the other, but the attacker was not there, only the unknown man. "Get a tight focus on his tunic," Lef ordered. "Yes there it is. It's the same man. Any others?" The computer whirred, and stopped once again.

"There, right there. Same man," Porlis said. "Again," Lef ordered. Again, and yet again, the same man with the emblem on his tunic appeared looking about the front area.

"He never seems to buy anything," Porlis muttered. "Never is carrying any packages, never talks to the clerks or enters anything into the order unit."

"Comes in, looks around and then walks out again," Lef agreed. "Did either of you notice anything else interesting about those shots?" The others thought a moment and then shook their heads.

"The times," Lef said, "the times were all about the same, just after mid-day."

"Maybe he was on his mid-break."

"Maybe he works near here."

"I don't suppose we can get that likeness run through the police Match'n Search?" Lef asked.

Porlis shook his head. "Not without more reason to connect him to the incident."

"Didn't think so," Lef sighed. "So, if you will, please, make us some hard copies of that guy and let's see if anyone in the area recognizes him."

"You know," Lef mused, "Loran Brenev and his family who helped Nayland in his conspiracy were sentenced to life on Perdita, the prison planet. The women and children underwent reprogramming and have been re-located on separate planets throughout the Algoran Federation. They are out of the way. But we must remember that Nayland Brenev has not been found. The same for Luiz Roncallo. He left Greniff before the authorities could apprehend him." He frowned and added, "I knew Luiz Roncallo for years. I don't think he would ever deliberately set out to hurt Dulsena. But, Nayland Brenev's another matter. He could very well be orchestrating these attacks from wherever he has gone. He's the type who would seek such vengeance."

"Well let's get going," Porlis said, gathering up the pictures, "the sooner we track down this man, the sooner we can find out who is behind all this."

* * *

It was late in the afternoon, and a lot of people had been shown the picture and a lot of questions had been asked before they got a positive response from the owner of a dinette in an office building two blocks down. He took one look at the picture and said, "Sure, he's the Burgho soup with two pietans. Always the same, except on Alaffday when we have Piloosh. He likes our piloosh."

"Do you happen to know his name?" the Chief asked.

His assistant had come up and, while reaching across Lef to get a pad stylus, glanced at the likeness. “Relarde,” she said, smiling and dimpling her dimples at Lef. “His name’s Relarde.”

“Know his second name?” Lef asked, smiling back.

“No. You see he wasn’t my type.” She had accented the word ‘he’ and the implication was clear. “He was friends with Solane and all I ever heard her say was Relarde.”

“Well, that will help us, I’m sure, unnhhh,” he peered at her name tag.

“Lurese. I’m Lurese, and I just love your kaiton,” she added, showing her dimples again.

“Thank you,” Lef said, smiling back. He didn’t have any dimples, but he did the best he could without them.

“I was on Rohnseff once,” she went on, “with a theater group I was touring with and I thought the men were so handsome. I’d like to go back if I ever make enough money”. She turned and gave her boss a hard look before continuing “to get away from here. I’m Dornatzian you see. We know how to have a good time.” This time her smile held infinite possibilities.

“Oh yes, I’ve been on Dornace and I know what you mean, Lurese.” He drug out the syllables of her name. “You say this Relarde wasn’t your type. So what type was he?”

“Oh, he was just weird,” she said waving the stylus. “Some crazy religious fanatic, like a lot of these Greneche. He was always telling her she didn’t dress right and she shouldn’t do this and shouldn’t do that. A real pain.”

Lef smiled sympathetically and said, “Some men just don’t appreciate a good thing when they see it.” The dimples reappeared. Lef smiled and moving even closer asked, “Lurese, do you happen to know where he works?”

“Big complex with the copper tiles. Or anyway I think he does. I saw him going in there one day.”

Porlis’s loud voice broke up the cozy tete a tete when he abruptly thanked the owner for his help and turned to leave. Lef graced Lurese with another slow smile and said they might be back if they had any more questions. Once they were outside, the security chief grinned and gave a snort of amusement which he quickly stifled on seeing Lef's glare.

All along the street, doors were closing and grills were sliding into place. It was the end of the workday. Relarde would have to wait until tomorrow.

- 23 -
Shortcut to Vengeance

"No problem," Rhys Xholan said, when he heard of Lef's search. They were in Rimini's room sharing an after dinner drink. "You give it to me and I'll send it to Governor Sechem. He can run it through the system for you."

Rhys was right—no problem. The next morning Lef stood with a printout of Relarde Olun from the government's viewpoint.

"According to this," he said to the Chief, "this man was a perfect citizen. There's nothing here but info about schools, memberships in professional organizations, etc. There is one separate notation…he was a member of…won't try to pronounce it, but it's apparently some religious organization. Why would they include that?" he muttered.

The Chief, who had been looking over his shoulder said, "Not surprising when you consider the date of entry of that piece of information. That's after the rebellion was quelled and that organization is a very conservative, some might even say radically conservative, group who supported Nayland Brenev."

"Aaahhhhaa," Lef said, and Porlis nodded in agreement. Lef smiled. "Some sort of religious fanatic, our Lurese said. That fits. That fits just fine."

* * *

The man who attacked Dulsena had been completely uncooperative. It was only after the interrogation booth that they learned of the plan. "He doesn't know a lot," the interrogation booth monitor said as he gave Lef a copy of the session. "He was a very minor player and knows only that he was on 'a great mission', to save Greniff from the evil Federation."

"Maybe the other one will give us something to go on," Lef said, hopefully, as he started to leave. "You know how to reach me."

Relarde, the perfect citizen, was scheduled for the booth later that day. He never got there. The mere thought of the booth had apparently been quite enough to start him talking. By the time he finished, the governor, the Federation and all the Greniff Occupation Forces were moving in the biggest operation since the rebellion.

- 24 -
Uncertain Dreams

It was a beautiful night and the view of the city from the restaurant atop House of Kalleni was spectacular. Dulsena listlessly moved her food around the plate, unaware of the view and only half hearing Rimini's comments on some bits of data he had uncovered. "All in all, it's going very well," he said cheerfully, "don't you think so?" There was no response. "Dulcy? Are you in there?" he asked, laughing.

Dulcy looked up and said, "I'm sorry, Father. Yes it does seem to be working out. With your help."

Rimini waved his hand and said, "Well now, you and Derek had a pretty good plan of action before we ever got here. We just helped gather data and put things together." He paused, took a drink and added, "That Derek, he's a very smart business man. Too bad he's leaving." He took another drink, watching Dulsena over the rim of his glass.

"Yes, but he has his own businesses, his own life to get back to," Dulsena said quietly.

Rimini leaned over and took her hand. "Are you sure that's what he wants to do?" She shrugged. "Are you sure that's what you want him to do?"

"Oh, Father, I don't think I know what I want. That's the problem. I thought I wanted Loran and look how wrong I was about him. I thought I wanted Gutorm, but I can see now we really aren't right for each other. Now I think I don't want Derek to leave, but how can I be sure of anything."

"There is one thing I think you can be pretty sure of," Rimini said. "Derek loves you. And I don't think he is anxious to go back to Soloving."

Dulsena looked at her father, her eyes filling with tears. "Oh, Father, do you really think so? I would really like for him to stay here. If we could work together…"

"Well, why not?" Rimini said. "I think it's a good idea. I'm sure we could put together an agreement we could live with. From what he's told me about his businesses, I believe it could be quite profitable to merge our interests. Wouldn't hurt to ask him, would it."

She shook her head. Tears overflowed and rolled down her cheeks. "He might not want to," she whispered.

"Quite right. He might not. But, there's no harm in asking, is there?" He leaned forward, took her hand and in a soft, serious voice said, "Dulcy, for now, keep it on a business level you feel comfortable with. If it develops into something else all well and good. Give yourself time to be sure." There was a long silence, then he gave her hand a sharp tap and said, "Now, let's finish with some of that torte I had the other day. It was delicious."

* * *

The last of Rimini's experts trailed out of Dulsena's office. For over a cycle they had been working very long hours organizing findings, hammering out the wording on a Teaming Agreement and making a good start on a Policy and Procedures Manual. Now, with a groan, Derek stretched out on the lounge while Rimini raided the drink cabinet. Dulsena made some final notes, turned off her station and said, "I hope the people going to Arno and Pantro won't have a problem getting there in time."

"They'll get there," Rimini said as he read the labels on bottle after bottle. "We checked. They'll all be in place and ready to move." Their plan was to have the new managers for each business on site at the same time thereby eliminating any opportunity for accounts to be renamed or postings changed out of line before the new management took over.

"Don't fret, Dulcy, it'll work," Derek said sleepily. "Too bad," he broke off with a big yawn, "too bad about the name change. There was a lot of name recognition with some of those older companies."

"Yes, all negative after Brenev's treasonous activities," Rimini said, as he poured himself a drink. "I think KalVan works fine. Kal indicates the association with House of Kalleni and Van from Donovan for you and your businesses that have been brought in. Sounds good. Catchy. New management, new name, all works out." He plopped into a chair and looked at Dulsena. "All very businesslike."

- 25 -
Deadly Business

KalVan, KalVan the name had been running through Dulsena's head as she worked. She could see the new logo, the new script, the new colors. Already Derek's paper manufacturing and printing plants were turning out supplies showing their new identity. Kalleni's large public relations and advertising departments were preparing the news releases and advertising promotions that would go out as soon as the official announcement was made. All over the Federation people would be made aware that Brenev Industries was no more and KalVan was now there to fill their needs.

* * *

"This is a particularly beautiful one," Reesa's voice broke through her thoughts. She was holding up a well crafted chime cabinet. She and Dulsena had been unpacking a shipment of crystal clusters and cabinets that had just come in from Resdorn. Dulsena had wanted to be there since her mother had personally selected the items that were included. They had just finished hanging all the crystal clusters and adjusting the display lights and had begun to unpack the cabinets for the clusters.

"Oh, it is special, Reesa, and look at this one." She bent over to take another cabinet from its foam cocoon when there was a shrill shrieking sound followed by a ka-whaump and a huge hand flung her to the floor. Shards of crystals flew through the air, Reesa screamed in pain and then was silent.

Slowly Dulsena tried to move. Her neck and back felt as if they were on fire. "Reesa," she whispered and tried to get up. Crystal shards cut into her hands as she braced herself against the foam crate, fought to get her legs under her, struggled to stand. Slowly, she heaved herself to her feet and stood reeling. She couldn't see. Everything was blurry. She raised her hand to rub her eyes. It came away sticky, covered with blood.

Suddenly there were all these people wanting to know if she was all right, telling her not to worry. Again she whispered, "Reesa. See if Reesa is hurt."

Suddenly she felt herself being lifted up, being carried. She could hear crystal crunching underfoot, see the ceiling moving crazily overhead, faces looking at her, voices shouting, sirens and then…nothing.

* * *

Lef Kolek paced back and forth as he had been doing since they brought Dulsena to the hospital. "Sit down, Lef, you're wearing yourself out," Derek said in a tired voice. Lef threw himself into a chair and pounded his fist into his thigh. "We thought we had everything covered," he said, for the twentieth time.

"You did what you could," Derek said, again. "You couldn't have known they would try something like this."

"Relarde had plenty to say, but he didn't say one word about another attack on Dulsena."

"He probably didn't know. When the first attack didn't work someone must have come up with this idea. You…" He broke off as the doctor appeared.

"She will be fine," he said, as he strode toward them smiling. "She sustained a great many cuts from the flying shards, some quite deep, but we were able to close them. She was lucky that she had knelt down to remove something from the crate, and most of the shards went over her head. Unfortunately, the young woman with her was standing very near. We couldn't help her."

As Dulsena slept she couldn't know that all over Greniff, Federation forces, acting on the information given by Relarde, had been waiting for the saboteurs to strike. The only one they missed was the attack on Dulsena. An attack that utilized an ultra high frequency signal to the chip buried in the top of each crystal cluster. A signal so high that it shattered the crystals into sharp, lethal projectiles.

A short time later, Security Chief Porlis ran the security tapes and spotted the man watching the girls as they hung the crystals, saw him leave the area immediately after the explosion. A quick check of personnel records gave them an address so they were able to find him very quickly. He wasn't hard to find. He was sitting in front of the NewsVu, dead by his own hand. A pad and stylus lay nearby with the cryptic note, "I failed. She lives. May Lord Brenev forgive me."

- 26 -
Loving Comfort

First there were the strange sensations, the pain in her back and her head, the disoriented feeling of not being quite there, wherever there was. She opened her eyes. It was dark, but dim light was coming from somewhere overhead. It was all very strange. She tried to move her arms, but felt so weak. Finally, with great concentration, she was able to raise herself up on her elbow. Oh, someone was sitting there. A man. He was so close his head and shoulders rested on the side of the bed. She tried hard to focus her eyes. It was Derek and he was asleep. Why was Derek asleep beside her bed? Why was her back hurting so?

"Concentrate," she told herself, "concentrate". Slowly little flashes of memories started coming back; that horrible noise, being thrown forward, Reesa screaming, people talking to her, sirens and confusion, someone telling her over and over that she would be better soon. It had been early afternoon when she and Reesa were hanging the crystals, now it was nighttime. And, there was Derek, keeping watch over her. She reached out her hand and touched the curls tousled over his forehead. He stirred and looked up. "Dulcy, darling, are you all right?" He clasped her hand and held it tightly.

"Oh, Derek, I'm so happy you're here," she whispered. It seemed completely natural for her arms to slip around his neck and her face to nestle in his shoulder. His arms gathered her in and held her tight. "Ooooh, not my back," she yelped.

"Oh, Honey, I'm so sorry," he said in shocked tones. "Don't be," she laughed, "but for now, just hug something else or kiss me, or something." Derek was glad to oblige. Dulsena finally pushed him back and whispered, "What are you doing here? It must be late."

"You don't think I would be anywhere else do you? I was so worried about you." He smoothed her hair and gently stroked her cheek. "You do love me then," she said, with wonder. "Father said you did."

"Your father is a very smart man," he laughed. "You should always listen to him. Of course I love you. I think I've loved you since the first time I saw you all muddy and frazzled, with bugs in your hair." He smoothed her now shining hair and smiled, "especially when I saw just how presentable you were once you were cleaned up." They both laughed, remembering that meeting in Gutorm's hut.

This tender moment was interrupted by a nurse saying, "Good evening, Miss. The sensors indicated you were awake and experiencing some pain. Let's take care of that and then you need to get some sleep." She looked at Derek and added, "both of you." Derek, taking the hint, rose and said, "I'll see you tomorrow. Sleep well." At the door he turned and said, "Don't worry. Lef's man is just outside."

The nurse gave her something for the pain and she relaxed again. "Lef's man is just outside," she repeated in her mind. She examined that statement carefully and reluctantly came to an unsettling conclusion; whatever had happened, she was irritated with herself for not asking Derek just what had happened, but whatever it was, it was an attack against her. Another one. She had been lucky. Reesa, what about Reesa? She called to the nurse who was just leaving the room. "What about the girl who was with me?"

"I don't know, miss. I wasn't on duty when you were brought in. Now try to sleep."

"Send in the guard please."

"Now, Miss, you really should sleep. You can talk to him tomorrow."

"No, now. I can't sleep until I know." The nurse shrugged and soon Lef's man was asking, "Yes, Miss?"

She asked him about the girl who had been with her in the store. At first he was reluctant to tell her anything, but he soon saw she wouldn't let it go. She had to know. What she learned did not help her sleep.

- 27 -
Uncertain Hope

"Oh, Dulsena, I do hope you don't do that," Raylene leaned forward, the earnestness of her words reflected in her serious expression. "We need you here on Greniff. Tell her Siburi."

Siburi shook her head and looked unhappy. She was after all an employee of Rimini Kallenni and felt she could not very well tell his daughter she should not heed his counsel to move the headquarters of KalVan to Resdorn.

"I'm sorry, Siburi," Raylene said, seeing the troubled expression on Siburi's face. "I'm putting you in a difficult position. It's just that I feel so strongly about this." She had made her position very clear in their talk at luncheon. She and Siburi both felt that with the Federation presence so strong on Greniff, especially in the larger cities, there was finally an opportunity to expose the women of Greniff to new ideas, new products. She felt there was no question that if the women could see Dulsena, a woman, running KalVan it would inspire them to enlarge their dreams, to see their potential. House of Kalleni could also help fill that need by hiring women and giving them responsible positions.

"I've talked to so many women who told me in confidence that they welcome the Federation people being here. They view it as a way to loosen the domination of the men. They desperately want to know what women are like on other worlds, what their lives and options could be if Greniff were more like other parts of the Federation. There is no one in a better position to get those ideas across than you at KalVan and Siburi at House of Kalleni."

"I have received my share of criticism for being in business," Siburi said quietly, "even though I am Aldena working for a Resdornian based company. On the other hand, I have also been, to a certain extent, sheltered by the Kalleni staff and keep a relatively low profile. In all the years I have been on Greniff I have never experienced physical attacks such as those on Dulsena. Unlike us, Rayleen, Dulsena, as the ex-wife of Loran Brenev, is the person many Grenevians think destroyed the Brenev family. She does not have the option of anonymity. Everything she does is noticed and she has become the focus of a lot of hostility. Surely, Raylene, you can understand her father's concern."

"Of course, I can. It's just that I can also see that there is so much good that could be done." She sighed, shook her head and looked at Dulsena. "I'm sorry, Dulsena. I shouldn't be trying to tell you what to do." She rose and gathered her things to leave. "You must make up your own mind."

After the girls had left, Dulsena walked out onto the terrace and looked over the city. "Make up my own mind," she thought. "That sounds so easy."

* * *

Dulsena, under heavy security, and accompanied by a phalanx of clerks and secretaries, arrived at the rather non-descript headquarters of Brenev Industries and was led to the conference room. All the Executive Directors were waiting for her. She stood in the doorway and nodded formally. They rose and bowed.

Stepping firmly, Dulsena made her way to the head of the table at the far end of the room where there were two empty seats. Every eye was focussed on her, assessing her.

"She's so young," some thought.

"She's inexperienced. We can influence her."

"The company can never survive under this, this WOMAN. It will fragment and fall apart." The ones who thought this made their displeasure known by their unfriendly expressions. For a number of them, their main concern was how they could come out of it with their fortunes and careers intact. And yet there were others, who knowing the strengths of House of Kalleni, were quite prepared to believe the stories about the legendary Kalleni Traders who had been tremendously successful for so many generations.

Each one, no matter their opinion of her abilities, was quite aware of the attacks that had been made on her life. At some time, each had wondered how they themselves would have reacted to such threats.

Now Dulsena stood alone at the head of the large conference table and took a moment to survey each face. "Which of these men are my enemies?" she wondered. She had pored over their biographies and work records until she felt she knew far more about them than they knew of her. "Well, we shall see."

She seated herself, the others followed suit. There was a rustle as everyone settled, then silence. Dulsena raised her head, took a deep breath and said, "Brenev Industries is no longer. It is now KalVan and its headquarters will remain here on Greniff." She noted the little signs, the expelled breaths, the glances exchanged as the men received the news.

"This new name," she went on, "reflects the merger of the Kalleni name with Donovan Corporation, a conglomerate of businesses owned by Derek Donovan of Soloving,...my husband."

There was a collective intake of breaths and heads turned to watch as Derek now walked the length of the room and took his seat to the right of Dulsena.

"Gentlemen," Dulsena went on, "the Secretaries are now passing out sealed envelopes. We ask that you each retire to the lounges the clerks indicate and consider the contents. This meeting will reconvene in one hour." She stood. The others rose and began filing out. The expressions on their faces ranged from dazed to outraged. The door slid closed and Dulsena and Derek sat in the quiet.

* * *

One hour later, Dulsena again stood at the head of the long serpentine, conference table. A number of the chairs were now empty. Those who had been seated there had been escorted from the building. Their sealed envelopes had informed them there would be no place for them with KalVan.

Now the monitors lit up at each occupied position and secretaries began placing hardbound copies in front of each man.

"Gentlemen, you will find on your screen and in the hard copies placed before you, the new Policy and Procedures Manual, reports of the Chief Financial Officer and the Director of Management Information Systems, also copies of all other findings and agreements pertinent to this merger. The positions held by previous colleagues will be filled by House of Kalleni consultants until such a time as new Presidents and Directors are installed. As they are already aware of this data, this meeting will serve to bring you up to date. Before we start, however, let me say thank you for accepting our offer and welcome to KalVan.

The next few years were busy ones and many changes were made, all directed from the newly redecorated KalVan headquarters.

Dulsena and Derek also had the old Brenev compound renovated and executives who wished to do so made their homes there. The lovely, quiet countryside made a pleasant change from the city and it was within easy commuting distance by flyer. The compound wasn't as lavishly furnished as before the rebellion, since anything that could be salvaged was sold to reimburse those exiles wronged by Nayland Brenev. It was beautifully furnished, however, and, as Dulsena was fond of saying, "we now live with things legally bought, not stolen."

Although Rimini and Palomith were disappointed Dulsena did not return to Resdorn, they accepted her decision to stay with Derek on Greniff.

As for Dulsena, she was pleasantly surprised to find she thoroughly enjoyed the responsibilities and challenges of running a large business. It would seem she was indeed a "Kalleni Trader." She often laughed and reminded Rimini she certainly should be able to do the job since he and Palomith had trained her well.

Derek had proven himself to be a warm, loving, supportive husband, and, as would be important to any Kalleni, a very smart businessman. The two of them worked well together and took great joy in their two children. They traveled frequently to Resdorn to visit and brought back to Greniff the strong moral teachings embodied in the Chimes. Each day for them ended with the family walking the path in the proper order, as the chimes rang and the azuroid fountain rose and fell following the cadence of the evening prayer. The wounds of the Rebellion were healed and at last there was peace and harmony. They prayed it would prevail.

The End

Book Two

The Crystals

Prologue

The huge Astrodome was filled to overflowing. Over 145,000 people had crowded into the covered amphitheater to hear the President of the Pharosians, the largest religious denomination in the Algoran Federation. Church authorities from dozens of planets were seated on the curved raised platform. A 500 voice choir, in their celestial blue robes, provided the perfect background for the speakers.

It was the close of a very successful series of instructional and inspirational meetings. Feelings and emotions were at a high point as the congregation joined with the choir in singing the beautiful Hymn of the Chimes.

All Glory to Thee
Oh God of All
Thou provides a body
for our seeking spirits
Thou provides worlds for our mortal forms
Thou provides the light of a million suns
and the bounty of untold numbers of planets
to fulfill our earthly needs.
For the Glory of God
For our immortal souls

The fervent tones rang out, clear and true while overhead the huge cluster of exceptionally fine, large crystals rang their interludes. These particular crystals were the most perfect specimens ever found of the famous Resdorn Crystals. They were euhedral quality, hexagonal, bypyramidal crystals of unparalleled clarity that were found only in the mines on Resdorn. Their color and Piezo-electric values stabilized in a curing method developed over the centuries, they symbolized God's gifts to mankind. Hung in every home and public meeting room, they were rung morning, noon and evening to call the faithful to walk the path of harmony and be reminded of God's Hand in all things.

Now in this huge hall, instead of the usual fifteen crystals (the sacred number) there were 15 of each tone. Each of these had been perfectly matched so the tones were true. They hung suspended from thin golden wires and rang and flashed their colors in response to each programmed signal sent to the minute chip embedded in the top of each crystal.

The crystals, even as large as they were, were far too small to be seen by everyone in this great hall. So, as the cluster turned and flashed, a holographic projection, magnified ten times, was projected to 15 places in the amphitheater. It was incredibly beautiful as the crystals turned and their colored lights flashed, illuminating the high vaulted ceiling and the upturned faces of the worshippers.

The hymn ended and the High Priest rose to conduct the final prayer. But before he could begin, screams of horror burst from thousands of throats as great flames leaped across the wall behind the choir and raced around the sides of the amphitheater. The sound system went out leaving the High Priest shouting unheard in the bedlam. The worshipers rose as one and flung themselves toward the exits. Noxious fumes roiled forth filling the hall. People, choking and coughing, crumpled to the floor only to be trodden over by others frantic to reach the exits. Exits that, for some unfathomable reason, held firm against the force of thousands of panic consumed bodies pushing against them. The hastily summoned fire fighters fought in vain against the mountain of flames which lit the night sky.

By morning's light only blackened rubble marked the site. Rain began to fall mingling with the tears on the soot blackened faces of the huddled mourners.

Later, some of the crystals were found buried in the debris. No longer pale, pure colors, when the black soot was rubbed off it was seen that they were now blood red.

Some dissenters, who had long opposed the Pharosians, gathered the crystals and took them to their leader who held them aloft and joyfully shouted, "Thus you see our cause affirmed. Justice is all. Only by complete obedience, only by the sacrifice of blood can we make our worlds Holy Places. God will not be mocked. These crystals the color of blood are our sign. Rally. Rally to our cause."

From that time on the blood red crystals were the sacred symbol of the Black Knights, sworn enemies of the Pharosians.

Or so the ancient legend goes.

- 1 -
Unwelcome Disruption

It lay there stunning them with its appearance. About 20" long and 2" in diameter, light glinted from its faceted sides, changing, wavering, shifting as the viewers themselves trembled. It was something they had thought they would never see. Something they had never wanted to see.

Outlawed for more than 500 years, this objectification of all that was evil lay there on the white viewing pad and seemed to pulse with some hidden power; seemed to gain strength from the very exhalations of the breaths they could no longer hold. Breaths that had caught in their chests as, glistening, it had slid out from its black velvet cover, like some evil mystic thing coming to life. A blood red crystal.

"Is it real?" Palomith's voice cut through the silence. "Is it real?" she asked again, a bit louder. Her hand with the pale lavender nails reached out to take hold of the crystal.

"Mother," Scortzi said sharply. It was the first time anyone had heard him call her that while they were in the office. That he had done so now revealed his discomposure.

Palomith looked at him, eyebrows upraised in surprise, even as she continued the motion of picking up the crystal. "Scortzi, it's only a crystal." She turned towards the window and held the crystal up to the light, turning it this way and that. "The only evil in it," she went on, "is in the minds of those who choose to find it evil, who make it a symbol for all their evil thoughts. To anyone else it is just a crystal. I assume you haven't had time to make any sort of analysis?" Scortzi shook his head. Well that must be done right away. Londine, where is the man who brought this to you?"

Londine, his eyes still focused on the crystal, looked up startled that she was addressing him. He cleared his throat and waving his hand weakly, stammered, "He's a…he's in my office…waiting. I uhm… asked him to wait…in there."

"Alone?" Scortzi's voice brought him sharply to his senses.

"Alone? Oh, no, no. Not alone. Jenkar is with him."

Palomith turned from the window, walked to the table and slid the crystal back into its black wrapper, at the same time saying, "Londine, tell us about this man. What is he like and what did he say when he came to you?"

It was as if the act of putting the crystal away, out of sight, had released all of them from some spell and they started to move and shift. "For goodness sake," Palomith said, "all of you sit down and relax so we can listen to what Londine has to say."

Henri Londine was Vice-President of Acquisitions for all items, other than fine art and comestibles. He supervised the agents who sought out and acquired the products that kept Kalleni customers happy year after year. At Palomith's direction, he had slumped into a chair. Now, he rose slowly and looked at the others seated around the large conference table. He had spent most of his adult life with these people. They were more than business associates, more than friends, more like family.

Across from him Albrech Falen, head of the Division of Testing and Product Assurance, was perched on the edge of his chair looking at him expectantly. Falen, small in stature, ran his laboratory like a benevolent despot. Behind his back, his staff called him "Ferocious Flea". Falen never let on that he knew, but was privately amused. It was his lab that tested all new products for safety and standard requirements and worked with Palomith's staff of appraisers to authenticate fine art. The huge food division had its own testing laboratories located in another part of Weneche City.

To Henri's left, at the end of the table nearest the door, was Lef Kolak, Chief of Security for Kalleni on Resdorn. A big, heavy shouldered man, Lef said little and saw everything. He also supervised security routines for all branches of the House of Kalleni. Now, arms folded across his chest, he swiveled back and forth in short abrupt arcs. His heavy black eyebrows were drawn together in a scowl. Obviously he did not like anything about this black crystal business.

On Henri's right sat the beautiful Palomith, wife of Rimini Kalleni. Palomith was in charge of Fine Arts for Kalleni. Sleek, elegant and graceful she seemed as much a work of art as any of the exotic wares acquired. Her pale cream complexion appeared translucent in its frame of dark chestnut hair that swept back in waves into a large chignon at the nape of her neck.

House of Kalleni, one of the largest merchant houses in the Federation, had been founded eight generations before by Rimini Kalleni's fourth great grandfather. The eighth generation, Scortzi and Dulsena, had been reared in the business and were now preparing to take over whenever Rimini and Palomith decided to retire. Palomith's department included the sale of the famous Resdorn Crystals that were such an integral part of life in almost every corner of the Federation.

Scortzi, to her right, had his mother's temperament and his father's good looks. He was tall, well built, with strong even features topped by a mass of blonde curls styled in the classic Resdorn manner. Easy going and soft spoken, Scortzi was a canny businessman who knew every facet of company operations. He had spent his life training to take his place at Kalleni. Already he had assumed the duties of President and General Manager while his father Rimini Kalleni retained the title of Chief Executive Officer and President of the huge Kalleni Foods Division.

Now, he, Scortzi, was seated at the head of the table as his father and grandfathers had been before him. He looked around the table into the face of each person there. He knew each one was quite aware that the actions of one of their agents had jeopardized all their careers. In fact, it was not exaggerating to say that the very existence of House of Kalleni might be in jeopardy.

Londine cleared his throat and began to speak. "Rolf Blenton is our buyer for the Soloving District. He's well educated, personal, gregarious. In short, everyone likes Rolf. He's been with the company for twelve years and has a fine record. He has a keen eye for unusual things that sell well and he usually negotiates a good price for us."

"Yes," Palomith said, "I remember him now. He's the one that got us the Drellix Mobiles a few years ago."

"Yes, he's the one. When he came here today, not only was I surprised to see him, but I was shocked at his appearance. However, when he showed me what he had brought, I could understand why he looked as he did. As soon as he told me how he came to have the crystal, I rang the conference bell and brought it straight here."

The conference bell he referred to was a signal that rang in each of their offices and was used very rarely to call the top staff together. In the past ten years it had been rung only four times.

"Thank you, Londine," Scortzi said. Turning to Lef he said, "Lef, please ask this man to join us here. Oh, and bring Jenkar with you when you come back." He keyed the door and Lef strode out.

"Well," Palomith said, "I'm anxious to hear what this man has to say." There was a mutter of agreement followed only a few moments later by a discreet tap on the door. Scortzi keyed it open and Lef walked in followed by another man. Jenkar remained just outside the door.

Rolf Blenton's appearance matched Londine's description. About 35, well built with pleasant features, it was easy to imagine that most of the time he would be affable and gregarious. Now, however, there was a nervous tic at the corner of his eye and he moved stiffly. His skin was grey and he seemed to be completely exhausted. Londine cleared his throat again and introduced him to the group.

Scortzi waited while Blenton took the seat Lef indicated and then said, "Rolf Blenton, we want to thank you for taking the initiative in bringing this matter to our attention. Now, would you please tell us how this crystal came to be in your possession."

Blenton took a deep breath and began to tell his story clearly and without any dramatic embellishments. "I attended a dinner party given by an acquaintance and there met a man, named Nevron Coldene. We chatted only briefly so I was surprised when five days later, when I was at work, he came to see me. I was shocked at his appearance. He looked a nervous wreck, fearful, very agitated. He said that his business partner had died and when he was going through his things he had found a crystal hidden in his office safe. A blood red crystal. He said he was stunned, didn't know what to do. He said he was afraid to destroy it. He didn't want to take it to the authorities as then it would be a matter of record and everyone would know his partner had it. He was worried that the resulting scandal would not only ruin his company, but then he too would become suspect. He certainly couldn't take such a thing home not with his family there. He just wanted to get rid of it somehow." Blenton took a deep shaky breath and drank from the glass of water Lef had poured for him. With great care he replaced the glass, folded his hands and continued his story.

"He said he had then remembered meeting me at the dinner party and knew I was a buyer for Kalleni. So, he had brought the crystal to me, hoping I could take it off his hands or at least know how to get it to the authorities without implicating him.

"Well at first I refused to have anything to do with it, but, well you should have seen the man, he was begging and pleading, saying his life would be ruined if I didn't help him out, and on and on. Frankly he was in such a state I was afraid he would fall apart right then and there.

Finally, I agreed to take the crystal and see what I could do with it. He dropped it on my desk and literally ran from the office. Well, he hadn't gotten out the door when I immediately regretted my decision. Especially when it occurred to me that maybe I'd been set-up. That's when I started being as frightened as he had been."

"Surely," Londine asked, "you realized that if you were caught with such a crystal you could be charged with dealing in a proscribed product?"

"You bet," Blenton answered. "I had visions of being brought up on charges and my career, everything I had worked for, going right out the window. That's when I decided I needed to talk to you, Londine, but how? I couldn't talk about such a thing on an open channel and if I'd been set-up by one of the other merchants, an Ocam transmission wouldn't be safe either. It seemed the best way was to bring it to you here on Resdorn."

"You were taking a terrible chance, traveling with such a thing," Lef growled.

"Don't I know?" He stopped and ran his hands through his hair. "You can believe I thought about nothing else for the four days it took to get here. I'd figured out a pretty good way to hide the crystal in my sample case but, still, I kept imagining what would happen if I got caught in the customs check after landing. As it turned out, I got through without any problems and came directly to House of Kalleni."

He now sat, hands clasping and unclasping, waiting for someone to break the silence. The others sat immobile, each one evaluating what he had said. His recitation left a lot of questions unanswered. It also expressed some of their fears. They all were quite aware that just by having this crystal in their possession, not only they, as individuals, but the whole of House of Kalleni could be open to charges. The laws concerning proscribed products were very strictly enforced.

Scortzi cut through their thoughts, saying, "Thank you Blenton, for your report. We appreciate how trying this must have been for you.

"I believe," he continued, "the first thing we need to do is have this crystal analyzed to find out where it came from."

"No. I don't agree," Lef said. "We do need to contact Federation Security immediately and get rid of this thing."

"Lef," Palomith cautioned, "if we go directly to Federation Security we still will be in trouble because one of our agents accepted this crystal. And, once reported, I doubt there would be any way to protect Blenton."

Rolf Blenton's head came up sharply and he stared at Palomith in panic.

"I suppose you're right," Lef said. He thumped his hands flat on the table and said, "There is another question we have to ask. How likely is it that one of the other merchant houses could have contrived all this? Maybe to cause us embarrassment?" Every face reflected what a shocking thought that was.

"I suppose there is that possibility," Scortzi answered, slowly, "but, I would hate to think anyone has done so. Of course, as one of the largest, most prestigious houses in the Federation there will always be some who are jealous of our success. For the most part though, I think we're on excellent terms with the other merchants. Aren't we?" All at the table made comments that affirmed his evaluation and no one knew of any trading house who would do something so devious.

"Yes," Palomith agreed, "I can't think of any merchant who would resort to such a trick." The others nodded in agreement. However, Lef's question hung there in each of their minds. Could someone actually be that jealous of their success? Jealous enough to set them up for official censure and public recrimination? Could they at any moment expect a visit by the Federation Regulation Board?

Scortzi broke the silence saying, "I want to find out which mine this crystal came from and when and where it was cured. Over and beyond our need to know if one of the other merchant houses is behind this, we need to know if security has been breached at one of the mines or curing facilities. If it has, it's unlikely that just one was made. There may very well be others like this."

"Not necessarily," Palomith countered. "It could be so old that it was cured before the proscription."

"Yes, that's a possibility," Londine said hopefully. "Maybe this is a very old one that has just recently surfaced. However, I do agree with Scortzi, we need to know where and when it was cured. If we find that out we will know better how to proceed."

"Yes," Lev said firmly. "We certainly do need to know if there has been a breach of security in the curing process."

"We might very well find it has indeed resurfaced after hundreds of years," Falen said hopefully. "That would determine how we handle the whole matter."

"Yes," Scortzi said, "I agree that knowing when and where is the key. As much as I don't want to think any of our associates are involved, if there is someone out there unscrupulous enough to try such a game we need to know and protect ourselves.

"There is one other consideration," Palomith said quietly. "If security has been breached, our chime crystals are in danger."

Her remark set up a babble of comment. Since chime crystals were the basis for the whole Resdornian economic system, any breach of their monopoly was serious indeed.

"We all agree. We must know more about this crystal," Scortzi said firmly. "Albrech, do we still have that shipment of Ronavian pearls and Krellix shells in the safe?"

At Albrech's nod, he continued, "I realize it is already late in the day, but I don't think we should wait. Put out the word that because of a hurry up order you will be doing quality testing on those tonight. That will give you an excuse to be in the lab after usual hours. Send your regular staff home and you do it yourself." At Albrech's startled look, he added, "I know it has been a long time since you did any of the actual testing, but you know what needs to be done."

Scortzi rose, picked up the wrapped crystal and, walking around the table, handed it to Albrech. "How soon do you think you can have something for us?"

"Shouldn't be long," Albrech answered. "It's pretty straightforward stuff."

"Good. Let us know as soon as you can. Before we do anything else we have to find out how old this crystal is and which mine it came from. Then tomorrow we'll turn it over to the Federation."

Turning to Lef, he said, "Use the excuse of the Ronavian testing to have extra security on duty tonight and keep everyone away from that lab."

Turning to Blenton, Scortzi said, "We will do all we can to protect you, Rolf, and again, thank you for bringing this matter to our attention. We appreciate your efforts. Now consider yourself our guest and try to enjoy the remainder of your stay."

"Londine, will you please see that Blenton is settled into one of our guest apartments." The two men rose, bowed and left the room.

As the door closed, Scortzi turned to Lef and said, "See that Blenton doesn't leave his apartment or make any outside calls. Screen any in-house calls. We still don't know what role he plays in all this. Increase security around the whole building.

"As for the rest of you, all of you, stay close to your own security people and use your apartments here rather than going home tonight.

And, please, keep alert. Right now, we have no idea where the next surprise may come from. Report anything at all that is unusual or out of the ordinary, no matter how insignificant it might seem.

"We'll meet back here as soon as Albrech has something to report. In the meantime, I'm sure you don't need me to tell you that not a word of this goes beyond us here, to anyone. You know what could happen if this isn't handled right. Once we have Albrech's report we can pass it on to the proper authorities and get back to work. Everyone agreed?" At their nods he keyed the door.

They all rose to leave. Lef spoke to Jenkar who then followed Albrech to the lab while Lef went the opposite way towards the security office.

Scortzi and Palomith went into Scortzi's private office where Scortzi flopped onto the lounge. Palomith sank slowly into a conform unit, rubbed her fingertips across her forehead and said, "Well, this has turned out to be a rather interesting day."

Leaning back with his hands locked behind his head, Scortzi looked at her fondly. "Mother, mine," he laughed, "you have a real gift for understatement."

- 2 -
Crystal Unclear

Scortzi sat alone in the stillness of the conference room. It was very late, in fact it was already tomorrow. Apparently the testing had taken Albrech longer than he'd planned. The subdued lights gleamed on the long, grey, serpentine table and reflected off the dark window behind him making the room seem cold. He pressed the button to clear the window and the bright lights of Rohnseff sprang into view. House of Kalleni was on one of the topmost levels of the city so most of the lights were downward. Above the inner city, the dark of night was grayed by the maze of lights and now and then streaks of light cut through marking the flight of ships heading off world. Scortzi pressed a button and the draperies swished closed, shutting out the night.

He turned the lights up to a more cheerful level and began roaming around checking to make sure the monitors were on and the water pitchers were filled. He knew he didn't really need to, the staff would have seen to it, but he was restless, couldn't sit still.

Having confirmed that everything was ready, he once more slumped into his chair. He squeezed his eyes shut and rubbed them. They felt gritty. He and Asa, his personal secretary, had been working steadily trying to get other matters out of the way; getting a running jump on the next day so he would have time to cope with this crystal business.

There couldn't have been a worse time for something like this to happen. The big holiday season was coming up and everyone was already under stress. There just weren't enough 12ths in the day to get everything done.

Now, suddenly there were all these questions about that blasted crystal. All evening he had tried to push them out of his mind, but in the quiet they came flooding back. What had Albrech found? Which mine had been subverted? Would they be able to keep Blenton and House of Kalleni out of trouble over this? How could he somehow distance Kalleni from the whole unpleasant business; He just wanted to turn it over to the authorities and get back to minding the store.

A soft chime sounded and a voice informed him that Albrech was on his way to his office. Slowly the others, responding to Albrech's summons, began to file into the conference room and, in silence, take their seats. Scortzi watched each one carefully without appearing to.

Palomith, looking strained, nodded to Scortzi and took her seat to his right. She folded her hands in front of her and stared straight ahead, looking at nothing. Londine seated himself to Scortzi's left, adjusted his monitor and checked his stylus; going through all the normal motions one does before a meeting. Only the dark circles under his eyes and his hunched, tense shoulders belied the normalcy of this meeting.

Lef Kolak came in with Rolf Blenton. They nodded to the others and took their places while Jenkar waited just outside the door. Lef didn't look any better than Londine and Scortzi guessed he had been up all night keeping an eye on Albrech.

Rolf Blenton, not surprisingly, looked much better. After four days of worrying about getting caught with that crystal, it was easy to understand why he was relieved. He'd been able to do what Scortzi himself wanted to do; turn his problem over to someone else.

Scortzi leaned back in his chair looking relaxed, but he missed none of the nervous movements made by the others. His training in Ocam had made him very sensitive to the body language of people.

Blenton, for instance. While he looked more relaxed, he definitely was not at ease. He smoothed his lapel, moved his stylus, looked here, looked there. "Very nervous," Scortzi thought, "from being in a little over his head or from something else?"

Finally, Albrech came in, shocking them all. Usually neat and very nattily dressed he now was unshaven and his eyes were bloodshot. His hair was more smoothed than combed, as if it had been done on the run, rather than in front of a mirror. His hands shook as he laid down a sheaf of notes and laid the black wrapped crystal on top of them.

Attempting to pour himself a glass of water the pitcher bumped the rim of the glass and water spilled out before he could right it. Hastily he pulled a tissue from his pocket and ineffectively dabbed at the spill.

"Ho, Albro," Lef said, in a strained effort at jocularity. He jumped up and got a towel from the sideboard. "I'll get that." He mopped up the water, dropped the towel in the disposal unit and gave Albrech's shoulder a squeeze as he came back to his seat.

Albrech nodded absently, took a drink, very carefully set the glass back on the table, and then, clasping his hands tightly on top of the black wrapped package, stared straight ahead. All of this had occurred in an unnatural silence. It was almost as if it had been a staged tableau, a mime.

Palomith took a deep breath, breaking the silence and Scortzi looked up as if suddenly brought from a spell. Sitting up, he cleared his throat and said, "I want to thank all of you for being here so promptly in spite of the early hour. But then, I'm sure you're as anxious as I am to get this matter cleared up so let's start right in. Albrech, were you able to complete your tests? Can you tell us how old that crystal is and where it was mined?"

Albrech raised his head and said, "Yes, I finished the tests and I can tell you the crystal was cured only a few years ago. As for where it was mined, that I can't tell you."

"I thought that each crystal was marked somehow to identify the source and curing station," Londine said in surprise.

"That's true," Albrech said, "of our crystals."

"Well," said Londine, impatiently.

"Well," said Albrech, mimicking him "this isn't one of our crystals."

"What do you mean? 'Not one of our crystals'," Scortzi asked.

"This crystal..." he stopped, swallowed and took a deep breath. "This crystal is not from Resdorn."

"Not from Resdorn?"

"That's crazy! Impossible!"

"It has to be from Resdorn!"

"No one has ever found crystals like that anywhere except in the mines of Resdorn!"

"Yes, for thousands and thousands of years, the only place."

"There must be something wrong with your tests."

Everyone was talking at once and didn't stop until Scortzi spoke, "Wait, wait, quiet, please. Let Albrech explain."

In the quiet that followed, Albrech raised his chin and looked defiantly around the table.

"My tests were not defective. This crystal is not from Resdorn. It's very like the crystals from our mines, however, there are differences in both structure and composition. Differences that make it flawed. It would never be considered pure by our standards."

"Is there a chance that it is very old and has been exposed in some way to alter it?" Palomith asked.

"No," he responded, "there are basic differences in composition."

"Well then, where did it come from?" Lef shouted.

There was silence while all eyes focussed on Albrech.

"I don't know where it came from," Albrech said very slowly and quietly. "However, I can tell you this, if someone has found another source for crystals and has set up curing facilities, it would, as you well know, be devastating to the economy of Resdorn. Worse yet, if these mines are being operated by the Black Knights there will be repercussions far greater than the economic ones."

"Oh, no," cried Blenton, putting his head in his hands. "That's what I was afraid of. I kept telling myself that the BKs had been suppressed for hundreds of years. I wanted to believe that crystal was just an old one that had turned up. But, I've had a bad feeling about all of this ever since Coldene dumped it on my desk."

"What do you mean, Blenton?" Londine said sharply. "Do you know something you're not telling us?"

"No," Blenton said. "It's just that when I saw it I realized that lately I've heard more about the BKs than I have in a long time. Nothing you could really quote, just little snippets, comments, you know."

"Scortzi, Palomith," Lef said sternly. "This does it. We have to go to the authorities."

"You're absolutely right, Lef," Scortzi agreed, "but not to the local authorities. Blenton got this crystal on Soloving and brought it to Resdorn. I think we should take this right to the top, straight to the Algoran Council."

"You're right, Scortzi," Palomith agreed. "You worked with Lisbet Bohrnach during the Brenev Rebellion, when she was President of the Algoran Council. She is now a Chancellor. Can you get through to her and ask for an interview?"

"Oh, I'm sure she would agree to see me," Scortzi responded, "but it's such a bad time for me to be gone."

"Don't worry about that," Palomith assured him. "The trip shouldn't take long and Rimini will be home tomorrow or the day after. We can certainly manage things here until you get back. Take Asa with you and go as if it were any other business trip. That way your visit to her would be considered a courtesy call from an old friend."

"You really are the one to go, Scortzi," Lef agreed. "Blenton and I will go with you. You two can tell her what we have learned and then it will be her responsibility to decide what to do. It will then be out of our hands and we can head home.

"In the meantime," Palomith said, "we will keep the crystal in our maxi-security area and try to keep things looking as normal as possible to allay suspicion."

"Alright," Scortzi said impatiently. "Of course you can do without me for a few days. As for the staff…Albrech, no one saw you working on this last night, did they?"

"No, or at least I don't think so. Lef kept a close watch."

"Good," Scortzi said. "It might be a good idea to drop a few remarks about those pearls and new gemstones or something that would warrant the extra security."

"Easy to do, Scortzi, no problem," Lef said, "But about this trip, I don't think Blenton should travel under his own name. Someone may have discovered why he left his office so abruptly."

Scortzi agreed and turning to Blenton said, "Another thing, Blenton. Normally you would check back with your office while you are on a trip to find out how things are going at home, wouldn't you?"

"Yes, of course," Blenton responded.

"Have you done that since you got here?"

"No, I was too upset when I got in yesterday."

"Well, I want you to make that call and give some excuse for not calling in before, maybe something about getting sick on the flight, I'm sure you can think of something. But first you get together with Londine and think of some reason for you to have made such an unexpected trip. Remember, whatever it is, it must sound plausible, so give it some thought. Tell your office they can reach you through Londine. He will be here to field any calls for you and convince them you are here on Resdorn, but just happen to be out of the office.

"Londine," he added, "what about your assistant, Clarendon? Can we let him in on this?"

"Clarendon?" he answered, "well, he knows everything that goes on. But something like this…"

"Well," said Scortzi, "concoct something. Maybe make him think it's necessary to keep Blenton's whereabouts a secret in order to make a really good buy somewhere, or something like that. Right?"

"Right, I'll think of something."

"Lef," Scortzi continued, "Asa will take care of the travel arrangements, but you'll need to do something about other travel papers for Blenton. In the meantime, I'll call Chancellor Bohrnach."

"Scortzi," Palomith said, "Dulsena and Derek need to know what has happened."

Dulsena was Scortzi's sister. She and Derek, her husband, were the co-owners of Kal-Van, a subsidiary of Kalleni with headquarters on Greniff. Dulsena had been granted ownership of the huge Brenev Industries after her husband, Loran Brenev, and his brother, the infamous Nayland Brenev had been convicted of Treason against the Federation. She had chosen to maintain the headquarters of Kal-Van on Greniff rather than return to Resdorn.

"Yes," Scortzi agreed, "they should know, but it would be best not to send any messages, even through the merchants code. It would be safer if we came up with some reason for them to meet us on Aldene. Dulsena became very friendly with Lisbet Bohrnach during the Brenev rebellion and she sees her whenever she goes there. Another visit would not be considered unusual."

"Yes," agreed Palomith, "I'll arrange it through Rimini."

"Now, Blenton," Scortzi continued "are you willing to go with us to tell your story to Chanceller Bohrnach?"

"Certainly," Blenton said, "if you think it will be of any help. But, I'm not sure I like the idea of traveling with false papers. On top of everything else I've done, if I'm caught with those I could really be in trouble."

"I think," Scortzi reassured him, "that Lef can fix up something that will get you through to Aldene without any problems and after that Chancellor Bohrnach will protect you."

"Other than the papers, do you, any of you, have any questions about these arrangements?" Scortzi asked, looking around the table.

There was silence until Albrech raised his head, looked at Scortzi and asked, "Do you want me to go with you?"

"No, my friend," Scortzi answered. "We need you to stay here and run the lab so everything will appear to be normal However, that will start tomorrow. For today, the word will go out that you have some minor ailment that will confine you to your quarters for the rest of the day. You go home and let Leda baby you. You've earned it."

"Hey, no fair," Lef barked. "I was up as long as he was."

"Do you think Leda would baby you too, Lef?" Scortzi said, laughing.

"Well, now that you mention it…" Lef said. Everyone laughed as it was common knowledge that he and his sister Leda did not get along at all.

With that welcome release of tension, they stood and filed out of the room. At least now they knew what the problem was, and they had a plan. No point in mentioning that the plan so far consisted of asking for help.

- 3 -
Pass to Aldene

Scortzi left Asa to gather up all the spools and other records. Out in the corridor he walked along scrunching his shoulders and flexing his back. He was stiff all over and it felt good to be out and moving. For the three days of the flight to Aldene, he and Asa had scarcely been out of his suite.

He headed towards the lounge, but before he got there he met Lef and Blenton coming towards him.

"So, you two moles have finally decided to come out, have you?" Lef asked. "We were beginning to think you had been locked in."

"Well," Scortzi laughed, "I think Asa thought so too. But, there's a lot to be done before the mid-season rush. Where are you two going for the landing, to your staterooms or the lounge?"

"Let's go back to the lounge," said Lef. "The view is better from there. All right with you Rolf?"

Blenton nodded—It was fine with him. The one hour warning bell had rung and people were gathering up their belongings and saying goodbye to shipboard friends. Once the landing bell rang, everyone would have to be in their seats confined within their webbing.

They had just gotten comfortable when the landing signal rang and they hurried to fasten their webs. The re-entry was quick and after only a short while the window covers, that had been lowered for the descent, were raised and they could see the lights of the spaceport growing brighter and brighter until they finally folded around them. They landed and soon were threading their way along the maze of moving walkways.

"You know," Scortzi said, "although I'm used to the bustle of the port on Resdorn, I'm always impressed by the immensity of the facilities on this otherwise very small planet. Just look around. It's only by the application of the latest in personnel and materiels transport that they're able to get all these people from one place to another in a reasonable amount of time."

"Of course," Asa muttered to Rolf, as they were quickly ushered through reception, "being a Kalleni helps speed things up a bit." They exchanged tight smiles.

At the Inn, located on the top level of Belnoir City, Scortzi, Asa and Blenton waited in a small reception area while Lef checked the rooms. Scortzi considered this excessive caution, however, he had agreed to let Lef have his way about security on this trip. Chafing at the delay, at the same time he appreciated Lef's attention to detail and reminded himself it was for his benefit. He slumped further into the chair and tried to relax and watch the NewsVu that Asa had turned on.

Rolf Blenton, meanwhile, was having a great time. Never in his wildest dreams had he ever thought he would be traveling to Aldene with Scortzi Kalleni, the President of the company, to see one of the Chancellors of the Federation.

As the others watched the NewsVu he watched Scortzi. THE Scortzi Kalleni, he thought. The heir to the famous Kalleni Mercantile Empire sat there looking so calm, so in control, so beautifully dressed and perfectly groomed. He saw Scortzi make some casual comment to Asa about the reporter on the NewsVu and they both laughed. Relaxed, casual, he appeared to be totally at ease. And yet, Rolf thought, as friendly and easy going as Scortzi Kalleni was, he somehow never let you forget that he was a Kalleni. He seemed to take all the little perquisites of his position as being quite natural. Rolf wondered if he even noticed half of them; how doors opened and routines were altered to ensure his convenience. He was handsome, rich, young and powerful and had never known any other life.

For the hundredth time Rolf wondered what he was doing with this group. Would this be his big chance to prove himself or would he end up back on Soloving, once again a little frog in a little pond. Well, not too little a frog. Being a Kalleni Representative was a very good job. He'd been perfectly happy until he'd seen things from this level. He shook his head and thought to himself, "don't be stupid. The Feds could still come after me for even accepting that crystal let alone smuggling it all the way to Resdorn. I'll be lucky to see Soloving and my office again."

Lef came back and they followed him to their suite where they found their luggage being put into place.

"Come see this, Rolf," Scortzi said as he led the way out into the garden adjoining the penthouse suite. "As far as you can see there are trees and greenery. Hard to believe we're 20 levels up and what we're seeing are roof top gardens of the surrounding buildings."

A robo-serv brought cool drinks and they sat in the flower scented, cool, blue night enjoying this world of the very, very rich.

"Remember we're relaxed and comfortable on an ordinary trip," Lef reminded them. He was referring to the decision they had made that, just in case they were being watched, they would try to give the impression that this was just another trip regarding trade legislation. Nothing urgent or out of the ordinary. The natural thing, they had decided, would be to dine in the main dining room rather than in their suite.

Reluctantly they left the view from the terrace and went down to the main floor. Scortzi led the way into the large, beautifully decorated dining room which was filled with dignitaries and government officials from all over the system.

"Remember, Gentlemen," Scortzi reminded them again as he opened the large ornate menu, "we are here to enjoy ourselves. The chef is famous and the wine cellar outstanding. Enjoy. Right Lef?" The others laughed and the dinner conversation was relaxed and pleasant. Afterwards, Lef leaned back and said, "Well you were right, Scortzi, the food here is indeed delicious and the service is excellent."

"Glad you enjoyed it," Scortzi said smiling, "and I'm sure that even more than the food you enjoyed watching and listening to those Aalong light harpists."

"Yes, Scortzi," Lef said with a very sincere expression, "thrilling, truly thrilling."

The others burst out laughing and they left the dining room looking decidedly relaxed and comfortable, just as Lef had ordered.

* * *

The next morning, after a quiet breakfast on the terrace, Scortzi, pushed back his chair and said, "Asa, I hate to leave you here to enjoy all this beauty by yourself, but we must be off. Lef, Rolf, five minutes."

"Yes, Asa, try not to be too lonesome for us," Lef joked as he pulled himself away from the table. "I'll just take this last pastry so you won't have to worry about it."

"Nice of you, Lef," Asa said wryly. "I know I'll never have to worry about leftover pastries with you around."

Lef grinned at Rolf and strode off. Soon they were onboard a company shuttle and climbing into the blue gold morning sky heading for the Council Complex.

"Have you been to Aldene before, Rolf," Scortzi asked as they left Belnoir City limits.

"No, no I haven't," Rolf replied. It's beautiful and so green. Somehow I had imagined it would look more urban, all full of government buildings and facilities. But look," he said pointing out the window, "there are vast stretches of forest and park land. I never expected to see that. Only here and there can you see buildings."

"Yes that has always impressed me too," Scortzi said. "We know that all of Aldene is given over to the government of the Algoran Federation. The Presidency, the Choitarem, the Council of Delegates, the Algoran Supreme Court, all the government agencies and information support groups necessary for running the coalition of twelve systems are based here. The only industry is what is necessary to provide for their own use and it is very strictly regulated, so there is none of the pollution that is common on some heavily industrialized planets."

"Of course," Lef put in, "there are those who claim that any planet devoted to politicians, certainly has air pollution." They all laughed, knowing this was usually said without rancor as Algoran Federation was known for having a very progressive and responsive government.

"Most of the buildings are under ground," Scortzi went on, "and, as you've probably noticed, most of them are made of that same sparkling white material you see in those buildings below. See how low they are with rounded edges and how they curve in and around the landscape. As a result they appear to be adornments rather than intrusions on the land."

They passed over clearing after clearing before the flyer descended to a small landing area. They climbed out and started towards the main entrance.

"Watch," Scortzi said. Rolf looked back in time to see their flyer being lowered underground. The surface closed over and the landing pad was once again a terrace. Enjoying Rolf's expression, Scortzi added, "all service areas are also underground so nothing will intrude on the beauty of the surroundings."

Once inside the building they were greeted by an attractive receptionist whose amethyst colored, faceted eyes betrayed the fact that she was not human. These Algoran androids were so advanced that many people seeing them for the first time, found it hard to believe they weren't human. Scortzi, Lef and Blenton each introduced themselves and stated that Chancellor Lisbet Bohrnach was expecting them. They were welcomed and directed to another desk where they could pick up their guide.

As they walked over, Lef said to Rolf, "Security in these buildings is very good. The efficient little android who welcomed us was also checking our retina patterns even as we spoke. If the patterns had not checked with those on file we would have been restrained and removed from the premises with that same quiet efficiency. That's why you could not use your "traveling" name."

He grinned and went to pick up their guide, a short rod that had been programmed for Chancellor Bornach's suite of offices. He held it in front of him and a bright line appeared on the corridor floor which they were to follow.

"If we should deviate from this designated path," he said, "security would be alerted and the corridor closed off around us."

Rolf was very impressed as were all first time visitors to Aldene.

The corridors followed the contours of the building, curving around and opening occasionally into small patio areas with fountains and seats. The Aldonair's love of nature was reflected in the decorating. Sinuous plants, flowers and animal bas reliefs decorated the walls and glowed in the stained glass windows and sky lights. There were live plants and trees everywhere and the effect was so natural that at times it was difficult to tell if one were inside or outside the building.

Entering Chancellor Bohrnach's reception area they found Dulsena and Derek had arrived before them. "Dulcy," Scortzi shouted, as he gave her a big hug, "it's so good to see you! Hey, let me look at you. Well, not too bad for an old married woman. Obviously your hectic life agrees with you."

With his arm still around Dulsena's waist he turned to Derek to clasp his hand, "And how are you, boy? You look great as usual. Not even a speck of grey in those dark, curly locks. Dulcy must be taking good care of you."

It was all Scortzi could do to restrain himself from running his hand through his own hair. He had a quite unfounded concern that his own hair was growing thinner each day.

He introduced Blenton to Dulsena and Derek. Lef had known them for years.

After everyone found seats. Scortzi watched Derek sitting next to Dulsena with one leg crossed towards her and his arm behind her. While Derek was telling all about their children's antics, Scortzi was thinking, "Goodness, Dulcy positively purrs whenever she looks at him. And no wonder. He certainly is a handsome man and he has those incredibly blue eyes. He also has a great personality, is a good talker and very intelligent. No wonder she loves him and no wonder they've made such a success with Kol-Van. People didn't suspect that this casual, relaxed young man could be such a clever business man. At least not until he'd gotten the best of them in some deal. Easy to see, he thought, why Rimini was so pleased with the match Dulcy had made. Good for her. Good for Kalleni. Scortzi had lost track of how many times Rimini had lectured him on the importance of having a wife to back him up in his work. Someone like Palomith, someone like Dulcy. Someone like Celia.

"Celia is a lovely girl," he could hear is mother say.

"Celia is smart and will make a good wife and a good partner."

"Celia is a merchant's daughter. She knows what your life is like," his father would say.

Celia, Celia, Celia. Good old Celia. He'd known Celia forever. He and Celia and Dulcy had been inseparable as children. They'd gone everywhere together. Celia was a great girl, a fun girl, but she just didn't interest him romantically. He knew she loved him. He knew everything about her and how she felt about things. That was the problem; he knew her too well. She was so predictable, so…so boring. Well not boring exactly. More like a sister. He'd never been able to explain that to his family and certainly not to Celia. Not that she'd waited to be told.

Bad train of thought, he said to himself. He was happy to drop it and tune Derek back in as he told about Garrett's and Selene's latest escapade.

Chancellor Bohrnach's receptionist chose that moment to rise from behind her flower shaped desk and announce that the Chancellor would see them now. She led the way into a lovely conference room done in pale yellow and green.

Lisbet Bohrnach, a petite, dark haired, very intense woman, rose to greet them. She was still as pert as ever, but there were streaks of grey in the hair at her temples. After introductions were made and they were seated she turned to Scortzi and asked, "Now what is so important, my friend, that we must have this very secret, very hurried visit?"

"Please, Chancellor," said Scortzi, "I think if we could have your permission to set up a projector, we can show you why we felt the need for a meeting."

"Certainly, certainly," she responded, "anything to make it convenient."

Lef quickly placed a small holographic projector on the desk, activated it and the image of the dark red crystal hung over the table. It turned and twisted showing every facet, glinting blood red in the light as Lef read Albrech's report.

All eyes were on Lisbet when he finished. Scortzi, Rolf and Lef had expected her to react as they had done on seeing the crystal and hearing the report; as shocked as Dulsena and Derek now looked. However, Lisbet remained silent and composed. Her short, delicate fingers moved her slate slightly as if to align it with some pattern only she could see. Finally, clearing her throat, she looked up at them and said, "I can see you are surprised at my reaction to this object. Believe me, the first time I saw a crystal such as this my reaction was very strong indeed. However, this is not the first one that has been brought in. It is the third."

"The third," Scortzi whispered. They looked at each other in amazement.

"One," Lisbet went on, "was picked up in a regular security check at the spaceport on Dornace and the other was brought in by your old friend, Gutorm. A man on Flornak had found it in his daughter's room. Not wishing to get her involved he took it to a friend, that he knew was a member of the B.E.N., the Brenev Exiles Network," She clarified for Blenton. "That man in turn, took it to Gutorm who brought it to the Presidency. That was one and one half cycles ago. Ever since then we have been trying to find out where they came from. So far we have not been successful.

"We had been receiving reports of renewed activity among the Black Knights and these crystals provided the proof of these reports. F.I.S., Federation Investigative Services, has been conducting the search, but, so far, we haven't been able to find the source. This crystal you have is probably from the same place as it's very unlikely that there is more than one additional source."

"Excuse me," Dulcy said, "You say that Gutorm brought one in. Is BEN working with FIS on this?"

"Yes, they are now," Lisbet replied. "They're concentrating their efforts on Dornace and most particularly on Flornak.

"FIS has been checking shipping in and out of those two planets and trying to find some pattern. So far, all they have come up with is a little heavier travel than usual in and out of Felchor, in Azeroth and Chaldorn in Necho. Both are relatively minor planets. A man named Burrus, a merchant, has been named in several reports, however, we can't find any evidence tying him to the crystals. I have a picture of him somewhere. Yes, here it is. It isn't a very good picture. It was taken by a surveillance camera at quite a distance."

She handed the picture to Scortzi who looked at it and handed it on to Lef. Lef looked carefully, shook his head and handed the picture to Rolf. Rolf glanced at it and said, "Burrus?" This is Carradyne. Arnhalt Carradyne. He's Chairman of Faraday on Soloving."

"Are you sure?" Scortzi asked, looking at the picture again.

"Yes, quite sure. I've met him at several trade affairs. As you know, Faraday has more than forty outlets on Soloving alone."

Turning to Lisbet Bohrnack he added, "As you probably know, Faraday sells mostly family fashions and home furnishings and maintenance. They do not have the variety that Kalleni has, but they still command a very large Federation wide market."

Retrieving the picture from Scortzi, he looked at it again, very carefully, "Yes, I'm sure that's Carradyne. No doubt about it."

"Why would he be using the name of Burrus?" Derek mused.

"This "Burrus/Carradyne", where was he when this picture was taken?" Dulsena asked.

"On Flornak," Lisbet answered. "He was photographed coming out of some freight offices that F.I.S. had under surveillance. They checked and found he had been recorded at customs as a merchant from Dornace."

"Dornace, Flornak, and Soloving, three places where crystals have turned up and Burrus/Carradyne is connected with all three. Very interesting, don't you think?" Dulsena asked.

The others agreed.

"Rolf, what do you know about this Carradyne?" Scortzi asked.

"Not a lot. He's very rich, of course, and has a good reputation. I believe he even holds a position as a counselor in the World Trade Commission. Your Head of Sales on Soloving, William Manchester could tell you more about him than I can. I believe they have worked together on various boards."

"It might be a good idea, considering the circumstances, to talk to Father about Manchester before you contact him directly," Dulsena suggested.

"Yes, I agree," Scortzi said, "I have met Manchester, but really know very little about him."

"Let's get back to this heavier than usual travel to Flornak, from where was it? Chaldaron?" Dulsena asked.

"Chaldorn," Lisbet corrected. "A captain by the name of Schwecker has added both Felchor and Soloving to his route. His invoices list only products regularly imported and exported by those worlds."

"Felchor in the Azeroth system, Flornak in Fongasso, Dornace in Onati, Chaldorn in Necho and Soloving in the Muonior system," Derek mused. "A long, rather ambitious, but, not unreasonable circle for a very fast ship. However, I think I would like to see schedule times and shipping weights for this Captain Schwecker."

"Yes," said Lisbet. "The addition of Soloving may just have added the piece we needed to connect this puzzle." She keyed the monitor and requested the analysis they wanted. She was told it would take only a few minutes for the information to be retrieved. Scortzi rose and asked if he could put in a call to his father on Resdorn. Lisbet led him out to her receptionist and instructed her to find an empty office for Scortzi and place any calls he chose to make. She then returned to her office to find the others deep in speculation.

As they talked a discreet bell chimed and the computer asked if she wanted a hard copy of the information now available. This was confirmed and immediately a long sheet of data emerged.

Scortzi returned and reported that his father had given Manchester a vote of confidence, but had reservations about Carradyne.

Lisbet Borhnach raised her eyebrows, but made no comment. She began to scan through the data sheet reading the most pertinent parts.

"Captain Hugo Schwecker born Cassel, Librecht Province, Dornace. Married to Aldrys Vlietan, two children Joran and Sardrys. Educated Librecht Academy; received papers from Dornace Flight School; ship the Ulisse registered Dornace 2109FC. Minor reprimand for delay in docking, otherwise clean record. Then there follows a listing of all trips for the last 24 cycles, including schedules, pay loads and weights. The breakdown in graph form shows that in each case he spends more time on Dornace, which is normal considering that is his residence, and the times spent on Soloving have always been somewhat irregular. The one variation which the computer notes is that starting 11 cycles ago the run between Felchor and Flornak has averaged 1/2 day longer than before. No indication of why."

"You know" said Dulsena, "before this I don't think I've ever heard of a planet named Felchor."

"Not surprising, Dulsena. It is a very small planet in the Azeroth system. Really terrible climate, hot, swampy, very oppressive heavy atmosphere. Poor soil that won't grow much of anything except nago nuts which are its only major export. The population is kept small because of living conditions and the fact that they must import all but the most basic requirements."

"Doesn't sound like any place Kalleni would consider setting up an outlet," laughed Derek.

"That's true," Scortzi agreed. "I imagine Captain Schwecker's visits are the most excitement they have."

"If that's the case why is he spending more time there?" Dulsena asked.

"A romantic dalliance, perhaps?" Lef suggested

"Perhaps, perhaps. Something to check into," Lisbet mused.

They went on discussing the report, focusing finally on the variable schedule on Soloving. On checking the report it was discovered that the Ulisse often carried cargo for Faraday, Inc. After deciding that there certainly could be a tie-in between Captain Schwecker and Carradyne, Scortzi made a proposal. "I could go to Soloving with Rolf and somehow arrange an introduction to Carradyne. I also can tap into the merchant's network and maybe come up with something that the Federation agents haven't noticed."

Lef didn't go along with that at all. In his opinion it was too dangerous. He finally agreed when Lisbet suggested that FIS provide a security backup.

"It will have to be very discreet or it will just place Scortzi in more danger by linking him with the investigation," Derek commented.

"Right," Lef agreed, nodding his head vigorously.

"Scortzi," Dulsena said, "do you really think you could accomplish anything by getting involved like this? You know that Kalleni and Faraday compete in so many areas that relations have always been somewhat strained between us. It's not likely that you could find out anything from Carradyne."

"Well, I don't see how it could hurt to go with Manchester and take a look around and listen to what is going on. There will be other merchants there besides Faraday and who knows what they may have noticed. They certainly wouldn't take suspicions about another merchant to the FIS, but they just might open up to a fellow merchant, especially to a strong "friendly rival" of Faraday's.

"Ordinarily, Scortzi," Lisbet said, "I wouldn't consider having a civilian involved in such an investigation. However, it is the opinion of the Federation Council that the old proscription against the Black Knights is a valid one. They preach sedition and rebellion more than religion and as such, are a menace to society. We feel this latest effort to revive the cult must be stopped before it gains any more momentum.

"If you are willing to go to Soloving and try to get some more information about this possible tie-in of Carradyne to the BKs then we certainly would be grateful. As for your safety, I'll arrange for FIS to provide as much protection as they can without jeopardizing your position. Besides, you will have Lef with you. She smiled at Lef and said, "would you feel comfortable with those arrangements?"

"Comfortable? No, but I will go along with them."

Lisbet smiled at him. "Good. Now, Dulsena, Derek, I could see that you hadn't heard anything about these crystals. But what about the Black Knights? Have you heard anything about them becoming active again on Greniff?"

Both Dulsena and Derek shook their heads and said they'd no idea that people were trying to revive the cult. "But then," Derek added, "we stick pretty much to business and our home. We aren't involved with the sort of people who would be interested in such a revival."

"There were plenty of people who were willing to follow Nayland Brenev," said Dulsena. "And, there are bound to be some who were sympathetic to his attempt, who were never caught. They might be the type who could be recruited by the BKs. and, in turn, recruit or convert others. I think it might be a good idea if we, now that we are aware of the problem, see what we can find out about such activities on Greniff," she added. "What do you think, Derek?"

"That was my thought, too, Dulcy. Scortzi is right in that often we can pick up on things much faster than the officials can. It has occurred to me that if there is such a revival of interest in the BKs it will reflect itself in other ways, too. We need to think about this a bit more and see what other signs or trends might be significant."

"Excellent," Lisbet said. "This little visit may prove to be very productive. Now let's get together with the head of the investigation and see how we can work together on this."

The next three days were busy ones and by the time they parted at Aldene Spaceport they had their strategy planned.

- 4 -
Impatience Dampened

The wind whipped and roared around the building matching Nayland Brenev's mood as he stood staring out the rain streaked window. Lightening streaked through the sky flashing great jagged blue-white light on the violently lashing trees. In the blackness after the flash he re-focused his eyes on his own image reflected in the dark glass. He saw a long face with a high ridged slender nose. Long ridges running from the high cheek bones to the sides of his thin mouth made him look even leaner. His dark hair was pulled over his left ear and then wound into the tight top knot typical of the P'Toran. As he turned his head, the gold ring in his right ear flashed in the light from the small glow bulb on his desk. A sudden band of light flashed onto the window as the door to the corridor was opened.

"Nayland?" Georgg stood in the open doorway peering into the gloom.

"Yes, I'm here. What is it?" Nayland growled.

"What are you doing in here in the dark?" Georgg asked, at the same time pressing the light plate. He walked over to Nayland's desk and laid down the pile of records he had carried in, then walked over to the windows and pressed the panel to close the draperies.

"Don't tell me you are in one of your moods again," he said.

Nayland snorted and slumped into the chair behind the large black desk. "Living in this miserable place is enough to put anyone in a 'mood'," Nayland snapped. "I don't see how any atmosphere can hold this much rain. Rain, rain, rain, day after day, after day. Why did we ever come here? Surely there were other places we could have gone." He slumped even further, put his cheek on his fist and glared at nothing in particular.

Georgg sighed, walked behind Nayland's chair and started to massage his shoulders. "Nayo," he said softly, "you know perfectly well why we came here. Nirubati is small, obscure and of no interest to the Federation. Its officials don't like it here anymore than you do. They only come here if they're low man on the lists or are assigned here as punishment for messing up somewhere else. That is definitely an advantage. Also it has a small population, most of whom, unbeknownst to those same disinterested Federation officials, are faithful followers of our "great and good friend" the Black Knight who also graces the planet with his presence. All in all that makes it a perfect place for us. Maybe it isn't much like Greniff, but, as long as we work quietly, nobody bothers us. "Besides, it won't be much longer. The way things are going we soon will be able to go wherever we want." He gave Nayland a final pat and added, "So, cheer up and look at these latest figures on the crystal transports."

"All right, all right, I know," Nayland grumped. "Let's see what you have that is so exciting."

"Well," Georgg said, laying out the records. "You can see that our shipments have increased. Both curing facilities are working around the clock and the matured crystals are being sent out as soon as we have transport. That is actually the hold-up now, transport. Captain Schwecker is giving us problems."

"Problems?" Nayland asked. "What kind of problems?"

"He says this trip will be his last one for us."

"The last one? But he agreed. Does he want more money? Is that it?"

"No, we offered him more money, but he wouldn't take it. It would appear that his conscience is bothering him."

"His conscience? His conscience? Oh deliver me from men and their consciences." He abruptly reached across his desk for a small silver-chased jar and took out a few nago nuts, the main crop of Nirubati. Popping one into his mouth he crunched it and added, "Well, we shall have to find something to override Captain Schwecker's prickly conscience, won't we. He has a wife and several children, I believe. Where are they?"

Georgg looked at Nayland, smiled and said, "I thought you might ask that. I therefore took the time to look up their address. They live in a small town near the spaceport on Dornace."

"Who do we have on Dornace that is reliable?" Nayland asked.

"Narig Velson, is there. I checked and he isn't on assignment just now. I think he might do what is needed," Georgg replied.

"Velson, yes," Nayland agreed. "Velson will do quite well. You will see to it?"

"Right away."

"Well," continued Naylan, munching another nut, "assuming the Captain's conscience is put to rest, we should have regular shipments going out from now on. There's no problem with the other Captain, Captain Brillig, is there."

"None at all. He is a very devout Black Knight and is sure he is involved in a holy work."

"How nice for the good Captain," laughed Nayland. "He can make very good money and feel righteous at the same time. An enviable position, for sure."

"Well," agreed Georgg, smugly, "we do try to make people happy."

They both laughed. Nayland went over to a panel and pressed the center of a gilded flower. The panel slid back revealing an assortment of bottles. He poured a green, foaming liquid into two glasses and handed one to Georgg.

Georgg grimaced and said, "I'm going to stop doing nice things for you if all you give me is smartegg."

"No, Georgg, you won't stop." They exchanged fond smiles. Nayland resumed his seat, leaned back and said, "As for making all those people happy, I'm not so sure that old Marridon is still happy."

"Oh, really? What makes you say that?", Georgg asked.

"Nothing in particular, just his attitude. I get the impression that he doubts that my conversion to the true faith is as sincere as it might be."

"Well," said Georgg. "He may doubt, but he won't act on those doubts as long as we control the crystal production. He needs those crystals for this holy war of his and he needs us to get them for him. Until then I think he will be able to set his doubts aside."

"Yes," Nayland agreed. "Just as long as he needs us and not one second longer. In the meantime, we must make sure he can't do without us. At least, not until we can do without him."

- 5 -
Requisite Godliness

The Council of True Disciples filed out leaving Marridon, the current Black Knight and Derrachem, his High Councilor, alone in the high vaulted chamber room.

Marridon was a tall, aesthetic looking man. He wore his long grey hair pulled back into a braid and then tightly wound over the crown of his head, emphasizing the gauntness of his face. It was not an attractive hairstyle for him considering his overly large ears, however, if someone had suggested this he would have scoffed at the idea that anyone could be concerned with such matters. Vanity, he would have been quick to point out, was not one of his sins.

Still seated in a stiffly upholstered, high-back chair, he raised his long legs and stretched them out in front of him. At the same time, with his hands together, he stretched his arms out as far as he could to ease his cramped muscles. He relaxed, lowered his legs, and placing his hands together fingertip to fingertip, made a tent of them. He bent his head down and his index fingers just fit into the hollow below his rather full lower lip. Watching, one couldn't help but wonder if the hollow had always been that pronounced or if years of conforming to those fingers had increased its depth.

Derrachem, a big man gone to flab, had hooked a chair around and now sat completely relaxed with his feet up on the facing chair.

"Nayland Brenev," Marridon snorted suddenly, raising his head and glaring at Derrachem. "Is he really stupid enough to think we would believe his protestation of faith in our cause?"

"No," said Derrachem, yawning. "Ruthless, callous, conniving, devious, yes. Stupid, no. He knows full well we will suspect him. He's merely using us for his own ends."

"Just as we are using him," Marridon said sharply. "Well, I would treat with Narm himself in order to get those crystals. We need them as a rallying point for the new converts. Most people aren't swayed by doctrinal niceties; they need signs and symbols to focus on, something to appeal to their emotions. Understanding doctrine is not high on their requirements in a religion.

"They are perfectly happy having someone else do their thinking for them. Someone to make the rules and tell them what they must do. And rightly so. Far too many souls are lost when you have anyone and everyone deciding for themselves what they want to believe.

"You and I saw that when we were young men in training, as you well remember. Yes, laxness, that's at the root of it all. Laxness and free-thinking everywhere. Laws not kept, prayers and ordinances a matter of form only. No control at all. Disgraceful."

"I suppose so," Derrachem said, "At least now it looks like people are beginning to question what's been happening under the Pharosians with their ideas of "free choice".

"Free choice," Marridon hissed. "A license for heresy, I say. But, I think you are right. People are beginning to see the need for conformity, for vigilance. Yes, he mused, maybe having free reign for so many hundreds of years will ultimately be those false priests' downfall. The people can see where their laxness has led them."

"Once it is pointed out to them," countered Derrachem. "That, of course, is where we come in. We just have to get a lot more people out there exposing these fallacies. And you're right, we need those crystals to show them the way."

Marridon nodded in agreement. He sat up suddenly and fumbled through the record spools lying on the table. "Where are the production records for the last cycle? Are you certain the curing facilities are working at absolute maximum?"

"They are working around the clock. It isn't something that can be hurried, you know. It takes time to get the crystals from the mines on Felchor. Their transport in the raw state is a tricky thing, and loss through breakage is high even with the most careful wrapping and packing. Then, after they do get here the curing process has multiple steps, each one finely timed. We've shortened each procedure as much as we dare and still maintain the standards. We just have to remember that everyone is trying, Marridon."

"Yes, yes, Derrachem," Marridon said, pushing the spools aside. "How about our little project on Resdorn? is there any way we can get more of those crystals out? We need those true ones for the shrines."

"No way. It's slow I know. They can only take out a few at a time because the security on Resdorn's very good. We'll have to share them out."

"I just get so impatient," Marridon sighed. Then, seeing Derrachem about to speak, said, "I know, I know, we are limited by having only three ships available for export. Captains Schwecker and Brillig can only transport a certain number of crystals and still maintain their regular shipping schedule and Enferdeem Swadi has his problems. I realize that. If only the spaceports weren't so well regulated."

"Yes, how many times have we said that?" laughed Derrachem.

"Well, God is just," Marridon said piously, "He will provide, if we have faith in our labours."

"Well, let's hope our captains continue to labor and prove their faithfulness. I suppose we should be thankful for their devotion so far."

"Yes, thanks be for that." Marridon muttered, "Still, I would feel better if we had another transport. If one of them were to get caught smuggling crystals we never could keep up with our orders. We really do need another ship.

"We've tried," Derrachem said.

"Then we must make this need a matter for our prayers." Marridon said firmly. "A solution must be found."

Rising abruptly Marridon moved swiftly around the table and headed towards the door. Derrachem sighed, got slowly to his feet and followed him as he left the chamber and strode down the dimly lit corridor. As Marridon opened the door to the garden, the wind and rain lashed their faces and their long black cloaks billowed about them. Pausing to adjust his hood, Marridon stepped out into the rain and hurried across the terrace towards the chapel, leaving Derrachem fighting against the wind to close the door. Splashing through the puddles they both were soaked by the time they reached the arcade at the rear of the chapel.

"Rain, rain, rain," muttered Marridon, shaking the rain from his hood. "How can the heavens hold this much rain?"

"Be grateful for the rain," Derrachem said, "remember that without the rain on Felchor we wouldn't have our crystals."

"Well, let it rain on Felchor, not here on Nirubati," Marridon snapped.

"Perhaps we should add that to our prayer list," jibed Derrachem. He began to chant in an exaggerated, theatrical voice, "Please, God, for the comfort of our dear leader, Marridon, not to mention the relief of his loyal councilor, Derrachem, please temper the rain and thereby his displeasure. Amen, Amen, Amen."

"Levity, Derrachem, will be your downfall," Marridon said testily. He shook his cloak vigorously and swept into the chapel leaving Derrachem with a wry smile on his rain streaked face.

- 6 -
Never Rains but Pours

"Pilferage! Pilferage!" the deep bass voice boomed out. "Nonsense! We can't be having pilferage! The checks built into the system have worked perfectly for hundreds of years. What are you basing such a wild statement on?"

Rudolf Porter, Managing Director of Windswept Mine, all two and one half meters of him, quivered in fury at the suggestion that his mine was being run incompetently.

"The records for the last cycle show that production is 10% under the estimated figures," Bertram Williard, the Production Manager, repeated patiently.

"Estimated, estimated!" Porter scoffed, "there's your problem. This is a new shaft. We have no precedents on which to assume average production. We have only your "estimates". Rather than assume pilferage, why not assume that your pre-production "estimates" were incorrect?" Porter threw himself back into his desk chair and glared at the man who had dared malign his operation.

Williard ignored the yelling and the glare. He was used to the Director and his legendary displays of temper. Once he had come to understand that the Director felt very proprietary about HIS mines they no longer bothered him.

"As you well know, Porter, the techniques for determining crystal deposits are very advanced. With the newest sonograpic and spectral analysis procedures we are able to pinpoint deposits with great accuracy. The evidence leads us to conclude that not all the crystals taken from the shaft are making it to the curing rooms."

"And does your so-called evidence show how the security checks are being deceived?" Porter growled.

"We have some theories about it, yes."

"Theories!" The director threw his stylus onto the tablet, lurched to his feet and strode over to the window. For several seconds he stared out, seeing nothing but rain falling into the courtyard below. Finally, he turned, looked hard at Williard, and in a low, hard voice, said, "You're really serious about this aren't you? You really think that we could have such a problem?"

"Yes. I checked it out very carefully before I mentioned it to you."

The Director turned back to the window. He brushed his hand across his forehead and over his hair. "Why now?" he said tiredly. "Why the Narm now? I'm due to retire in 18 cycles. Eighteen Narm begone cycles. Now this."

There was silence as he watched the rain splashing against the window. "I suppose The Brethren know of this?"

"I haven't said anything to them," Williard said softly. "However, they do have their own records as you know."

"Yes, I know, I know. How much time do we have?"

"That's hard to say. It would look better if we had some sort of investigation initiated before they hit on it."

"I suppose you have some ideas on that, too," Porter said angrily as he resumed his seat.

"Why, no, I haven't," Williard answered mildly. That is your department, Director."

"Hah. All right let's see what Briggs says about this." He angrily punched in a code on the intercom and looked up. "Sit down and stop hovering like some Snarvian Wraith." He turned back and spoke quickly to Security Chief Briggs, briefly reciting Williard's theories and warning him to prepare for a review, probably with the Brethren.

Williard sat quietly and watched as Porter talked to Briggs. Snarvian

Wraith? he mused to himself. That's a new one. He's never called me that before. The wry smile that was beginning to form was wiped out at the sound of the receptionist's voice softly announcing the arrival of Brothers Eindal and Harrik to see the Director.

Williard flashed a glance at the Director who simply shrugged and said softly to the Security Chief, "Briggs, it seems that review is now." Giving the last word two full syllables and much import. "Eindal and Harrik are already here." The word 'Here' also rated two full syllables.

Turning to Williard he said, "Briggs is on his way. I assume you are prepared to share your views on how we can handle this problem." He didn't wait for an answer but turned back to the intercom and said heartily, "Of course, Zela, show the Brethren in."

Brother Eindal, a short round man, swept into the room, his smooth round face full of bonhomie and kindness. Brother Harrik followed, carefully closing the door behind him. He stood smiling quietly as Brother Eindal shook hands with the two men and then sank with a sigh of pleasure into the proffered easy chair.

"Harrik, Harrik," Eindal said, looking behind him, "where are you? Come in, come in. You should know the Director and Manager well by now."

"Yes, of course, it is very pleasant to see you again," Harrik said softly as he extended his hand diffidently to each. Some might assume that Brother Harrik was shy. He was not. He just preferred to observe rather than participate in most events. He found he learned a great deal more that way. He had, from time to time, remarked to his good friend, Needham, that "so many subtleties are lost when one scuttles around being terribly involved with things". Needham was a Judicial Clerk and understood perfectly. In fact he had considered it a great loss when Harrik had chosen Ecclesiastical Administration rather than Judicial Clerking as a career.

Now Harrik took a seat to one side and sat smiling benignly as Brother Eindal clapped both hands on his knees and said, "Now, what is all this about production being 10% less than anticipated?"

"Ah, yes, Brother Eindal," Porter said, "Williard and I were just discussing that. Of course, as you realize, that percentage was based on pre-production estimates and doesn't represent any real loss since we have no actual production figures with which to compare. However, we always want to be on the safe side and you'll be happy to know we have already instituted an investigation into the matter. Not that we expect to find any irregularities, you understand, just as a formality."

"Good, good. Glad to hear it," Brother Eindal responded heartily. He leaned back in his chair with his hands clasped over his ample middle. His right hand moved up to his face and the fingers rubbed up and down as if feeling for stubble. Then they moved down to the back of his neck, massaging, massaging. Porter and Williard leaned forward expectantly. Harrick smiled benignly. The silence grew heavy.

"It's just that, ah…I must admit, that we, that is Harrik and I…were a little troubled by this…this…ah…discrepancy. And, of course, I'm sure you can understand our concern. It's the timing, you see. The timing."

At their puzzled expressions he continued. "Yes, the timing. In light of this other matter that has recently been brought to our attention, you see."

He looked at Williard and then at Porter. "Of course, this is just between us," he said lowering his voice to a conspiratorial rumble, "but we have been told of rumors—-rumors of a resurgence of interest in the Black Knights."

Seeing the shock on their faces, he shook his head and continued, "Yes, I know it seems incredible, but we have been hearing more and more about some groups being formed and meeting in secret."

He shifted position, leaned forward, hands clasped on his knees and added, "Unfortunately, that's not all." He paused, watching as they now hung on each word. "That's not the half of it. We have heard," he paused to look at each one, "we have heard, that the Narmists are also active again."

Having delivered this bombshell, he sat back and watched as Porter and Williard gaped at him in shock.

"Noooo," Porter said shaking his head. "Not after all these years, surely not."

"Unfortunately, I'm afraid it is so," Eindal sighed. "At first, we hoped the reports had been exaggerated, but subsequent investigations have since confirmed them."

Silence filled the room as rumor transformed into reality in their minds. The silence was broken when Williard cleared his throat and said, "Assuming these reports are true, then are we to understand that you suspect these production figures indicate that either the B.K.s or Narmists are pilfering crystals from our mine?"

At the word "pilfering" Porter glared at Williard, while Eindal nodded his head slowly, in agreement.

"I say they MAY indicate that. At the moment that premise has not been proven. However..." The word hung there. "They would want them, you know," he added softly.

A discreet buzz broke the silence that followed this comment, and the receptionist announced the arrival of Security Chief Briggs to see the Director. Briggs was shown in and, after the usual greetings was given a brief review of the Brethren's concerns. He then asked if he could set up a display of the new shaft and excavation areas. With their permission he set up his equipment and soon, over the director's desk, a three dimensional view of the new shaft appeared. Briggs then proceeded to point out, step by step, all the security procedures from the excavation area to the curing rooms.

"Chief," said Porter, "we know all this. We've grown up knowing about the crystals. Those of us here are completely familiar with each step of the mining and curing. Why are you telling us all of this?"

"I thought," Briggs said defensively, "that going through this review was a simple way to refresh our memories and help us review how the safeguards operated."

"A commendable idea," Brother Eindal offered, "A little review of procedure might be just what we need. Let's do it again."

Briggs, mollified by this support, ran the program again. Twice, three times they went through the drill. Studying, considering, asking where was it? Where could a breach be made? At the end of that time, when the viewer was turned off, they found they did have a few questions, but mostly they were baffled. The safeguards certainly seemed adequate and had worked well for hundreds of years. What was different now? Even the ebullient Brother Eindal was somber as they parted, still puzzling over what they had seen.

Porter sat alone in his office, the rain beating at his windows. "No easy drift into retirement for you, boy," he said to the empty room.

The midday chimes began to ring as he keyed the intercom and said, "Bring me the cutaways for all of Windswept—oh, and all the topographical surface maps too." He was about to key out when he paused, and added, "and have some lunch sent in. I won't be going out this afternoon after all."

- 7 -
In a Darker Vein

It was dark as the PersVan drove up to the guard shack at the entrance to the new Windswept mine. The guard switched on the floodlights revealing two men in the cab. Grumbling, he put on his rain cloak and helmet, and walked out into the rain. Approaching the vehicle, he thrust the identification reader through the window that had opened at his approach.

Porter pressed his fingertips on the plate and gave his name. He then handed it to Williard who did the same. The guard nodded as clearance came through his head phone. "Sorry, Sir, I didn't recognize you in the dark."

"Of course not, Feldi, no problem. There will be another PersVan along shortly with Brothers Eindal and Harrik. Send them on through, all right?"

"Yes, Sir, I'll be watching for them."

The guard stood looking after them as the PersVan moved off into the dark. It was a cold, rainy, renewal evening and other than the few perimeter guards huddled in their little cubicles monitoring the screens, the area was completely deserted.

"Strange," he thought, "now why would they be havin' a meetin' with the Brethren here, at the mine? And on a Sabbath night?" Well, not his job to think about such things. He remembered Briggs giving the whole staff a tongue lashing about 'maintaining security' and then, in private, reaming Evans and him out good for talking about work over a few drinks at "Purkeys". He slammed the door on the guardroom and shook off his wet cape.

"What they doin' out here on a night like this?" Evans asked.

"Beats me, but I'm not goin' to waste time worryin' about it. For all I care, the Directors and the good Brethren can go dance a tardanta on the loading dock—stark naked—in the pourin' rain and I'll not say one Narm Begone word about it. Me, I'm stayin' right here and mindin' my own job."

"Just like old "Cat's Eye" told us to do," added Evans.

"So right. I like this cushy job and if it means keepin' my ideas and my…what was it, my spec-u-la-tions, to quote ol' Briggsy, to myself then that's what I'll Narm well do, all right. So, let the old scoofs do whatever they want. Me—I'm goin' to watch the rest of the Latz Ball Finals."

Meanwhile, on the other side of the dark yard, Porter drove the PersVan as close to the shaft house as he could, swung the vehicle around, and backed in towards the entrance. He and Williard climbed out and opened the rear doors. They off-loaded several crates and stepped back as Briggs jumped out. The three men carried the crates inside and were just loading two of them onto a lift when Eindal and Harrik arrived.

After short, muffled greetings, Eindal asked Briggs, "Are you sure the guards will keep their own counsel?"

"Yes," Briggs answered "I assigned those two specifically. No problem."

They stepped into a dressing area, slipped off their business suits and put on regulation one piece thermal suits and the LAGS, Light Amplification Glasses, they had brought with them. They then stepped into the elevator and, from niches in the walls, pulled out drop down seats. At the controls, Briggs dialed in the number of the first level. That was the larger of the two crosscuts and the first to be extracted. The area that was being cleared was about two thirds of the way along the cut. Further along, at the end of the cut, was a chute for waste material which was lifted to the surface to be used later to fill in depleted cuts.

In spite of being closest to the surface the crosscut was over 500 meters below ground and this elevator moved very slowly since it was used to transport crystals as well as men.

No lights were allowed in the unexcavated areas, of course, and the only illumination was from the small safeglow lights lining the elevator shaft. Their faces were dark blurs under their helmets while the small red lights coming and going made grotesque patterns on their bodies.

They rode in silence. Each person in the elevator had grown up knowing the story of the crystals. Now, this ride down into the dark mine, and their reason for taking it, brought all the old stories to mind. The discovery of the crystals had been lost in the mists of pre-history. Brief historical references in ancient epigraphy told of the mining of the crystals. In early times, many crystals were lost because the people hadn't known how to handle them. That's why the priests became so important. They were the ones who developed the technology needed to mine and mature them with a reasonable margin of safety.

These marvelous crystals with the rare properties that made them suitable for chimes were found only on Resdorn and their production was carefully monitored to control the market.

An incredible type of apatite, the crystals were found in clusters and only at great depths. Extremely fragile in their natural state, they were removed with utmost care, by hand. No robotecs would ever work the crystal mines as positions were hereditary and jealously guarded. Some families had worked the crystals for over five hundred years.

Removing the crystals was a tedious process. They shattered easily so had to be removed while still embedded in some of the surrounding material. The pads, as they were called, were carefully cut away from the background material and gently placed in a light proof bag. Each bag was loaded onto an air pallet and taken to a central collection area. At the collection area, the bags were placed in thermal containers that maintained the same temperature as that of their parent site while being lifted to the surface and transported to the curing facility.

Once the clusters were sealed in the controlled and lightproof environment of the maturing facility, the outer thermal bag was removed and the crystals left for one cycle to mature in the 16 C. air. There was a second cycle at 26 C. then held at 38 C. for yet another cycle. During that period the bonding between the crystals and the surrounding material becomes weakened and the crystals can be separated. Since this separation is done in a darkened room all personnel used LAGs. Occasionally crystals are left for another half cycle.

After the last maturing, while still in a darkened room, the crystals are mounted in a circle on an exposure frame. The mature hexagonal bi-pyramidal crystals vary in length, but all have exceptionally long oscillatory faces, some as long as 3 meters. The diameters vary, depending on the over all length.

The exposure frames are segmented on the top so the top flap can be lifted. The crystals are set in with the bottom point in a 0.2 centimeter dimple in the bottom. The top flap is then lowered, catching the top point in a similar dimple in it. Thus each crystal is held by a minimum support, allowing maximum exposure to the light. The top and bottom units revolve slowly so all sides of the crystal are exposed evenly. Once the crystals are in place the lights are turned on and the crystals start revolving.

In ancient times the crystals were hung outdoors, but this made crystals that were not pure in color due to weather changes and differences in the quality of the light. Now the curing was carefully controlled, using light in the segment of the spectrum desired for the finished crystal. For example morning crystals are exposed to the lights of the rose, pale blue, lavender, and pale yellow spectrums. Evening lights were exposed to those in the darker oranges, blues, purples, etc. Needless to say, no red crystals were ever made.

Before the Days of Enlightenment, some crystals were exposed to the light of the full moon on a summer night. These crystals were a dark grey with mottled white. These were used in ceremonies by the Narmists, a small, secret cult left over from the time of the old religions. As with the red crystals, these gray clouded crystals were outlawed and never made. There were rumors that a few still survived as oddities. They would have to be of great age as they had been made in the dark days before technology, when superstition and nature worship was popular. Few people gave credence to the rumors that there were still Narmists around to use them. It seemed so highly unlikely.

In homes and places of worship crystals were hung according to the time of day. In the old days, when the crystals were rung by hand, they were hung, when not in use, in a special cabinet. Removing and replacing them was done with appropriate reverence and ceremony. Now, with automated electronic controls for the chimes, a full color spectrum was hung with only the appropriate ones activated at the proper times.

One of the things which makes the crystals of Resdorn so valuable is their incredible piezoelectric qualities. The tonal value of each chime is stabilized during the curing process by varying the pressure in the curing room. Generally the tones of each type are quite distinct, morning crystals having a light clear sound, while evening crystals ring with a throatier, fuller tone.

The "crystal families" zealously guard knowledge of the mining and curing processes and only a select few know all of the procedures. Positions within the families are guarded and only rarely are new acolytes admitted to their closed communities, and then only after careful screening and training. And, as in olden times, all crystal production is supervised by the priesthood.

It had been over 500 years since the last revival of the Narmists. The Pharosian doctrine was dominant and, being unchallenged, the religious aspect of the crystal culture had somewhat faded and been replaced by something closer to a cultural habit. Now, at least on Resdorn, the crystals were commercial commodities, the planet's economic structure, in large part, being based on the sale of the rare and beautiful Resdorn Crystals.

The lives of all of the men riding down into the dark mine were centered around the production of crystals. Porter and Williard, born into "Crystal" families, had always known they would work in the mines. The priesthood representatives had been selected for their positions because of their administrative abilities. Their positions were not hereditary, but their devotion was no less earnest.

The elevator glided to a stop and they quickly removed the crates.

"Here you go." Briggs whispered as he opened the crates and handed each man a molded package of surveillance cameras and two containers one of SpraForm and one of adhesive. Each set off, going to previously agreed upon locations. They first sprayed the foam on the tunnel wall to make a smooth vertical surface and then with a spritz of adhesive attached each camera. The cameras were black, very small and, once in position, were almost impossible to be seen.

"You would really have to be looking for those to find them," commented Williard softly. "They blend right in."

"Yes. Hopefully they will assume they have located all the cameras that were put in here when the mine opened and not be looking for any new ones."

Briggs spoke for all them when he whispered, "It would be nice if we could pick up something before these too are discovered."

Finished, they looked around. There was no sign of their handiwork. In a few spots they could see bits of crystals embedded in the walls. But only in their imaginations could they see the fortune in long gleaming crystals they knew were hidden within those walls waiting to be released from their drab matrix.

Finished with the camera installations they quietly, made a tour of the whole cut, relating each section to the holographic image they had studied.

At the far end of the cut Eindal stood staring at the refuse chute that dropped into the darkness. "The anti-grav units for the refuse," he asked quietly, "are they stored top or bottom when not in use?"

"Top for now," Porter whispered back. "Later, when the lower cuts are opened that may be changed."

"Hmmmm," said Eindal.

"There is heavy security there of course," Porter added, "and heat sensors the full length of the shaft to detect anyone attempting to access it."

Silently, they turned and headed back to the elevator. On the long trip to the surface, each was occupied with thoughts and questions they were not yet ready to express.

Back in the shaft house, they changed back into their business suits, put the coveralls, helmets, glasses and other equipment back into the crates and loaded them into the PersVan.

At the door of the shaft house, they spoke briefly before hurrying to their separate vehicles. Back they went across the dark, wet yard to the gate. Once more, the lights went on, the guard checked them out, and they drove off into the night.

Now they would have to wait and see what the new cameras and the agents Briggs had managed to have assigned to each shift, would come up with. Hopefully, nothing would happen until the Federation ship arrived and set up the surveillance screen they had requested.

- 8 -
Not So Polite Society

The luxurious flyer landed on the brightly lit pad in front of the Carradyne mansion. A remnant of an earlier age of conspicuous ostentation, the building was three stories high with long wings on either side. Lights shone from every window and a steady stream of beautifully dressed people mounted the old fashioned stationary, curved stairway leading to the open entrance.

A brightly uniformed robo-tec assisted Scortzi from the flyer and escorted him to the stairway. Even in that company, heads turned as this tall, handsome, young man strode up the stairs. The pleats of the formal, gold threaded kaiton emphasized his lean hips and long legs. His elaborately embroidered cloak, slung over one broad shoulder, glinted in the light from the tall, ornate light standards that lined the stairway. His long, curly hair was almost as shiny as his kaiton, and on the side of his gold braided headband flashed 5 carats of diamond cornucopia, the insignia of the House of Kalleni. A duplicate pin adorned his blue lapel.

He felt ridiculous. This was the one part of his position that he never enjoyed, never had felt comfortable doing. However, his father had made it clear years before that, like it or not, this dressing to impress, was part of the job. Therefore, he did it as well as he could. Now his smile never wavered as he moved up the stairway through the sibilance of hushed speculation. Arriving at the tall arched doorway, he was announced and ushered forward to meet his host and hostess.

Arnhalt Carradyne, Faraday's President and Chief Executive, met him as he moved into the foyer. Of medium height with pale brown hair and nondescript features his appearance would have been quite unremarkable were it not for the extreme hairstyle and extravagance of his clothing.

He greeted Scortzi effusively. "Master Kalleni, how kind of you to grace our little gathering. I'm so pleased to finally have an opportunity to meet you. May I introduce my dear wife, Sophronia."

Sophronia was a tall, beautiful woman dressed in a simple cream colored gown whose plain style made a perfect background for the long necklace of exquisite Dornatzian beryls and pearls. She was as calm and still as her husband was agitated. She looked at Scortzi and said in a deep, throaty voice, "Welcome to our home, Scortzi Kalleni."

Before Scortzi could respond properly, Arnhalt Carradyne clutched his arm and, propelling him forward, gushed, "I can't tell you how much I'm looking forward to having a chance to get to know you better. We must arrange to talk later. Now, for just a short while, I must play host, but I will rejoin you shortly, in the meantime please enjoy yourself. Your man Manchester is in the gallery, I believe."

He turned to his wife who had been trailing along behind and said, "Sophronia, my dear, you will see that Master Kalleni is well taken care of?" He smiled at them both and turned away to greet new arrivals.

Sophronia Carradyne looked after her husband with a patient smile then turned and offered her hand to Scortzi. "I believe," she said, giving Scortzi a long level look, "that we are to make a grand tour so I can introduce you to a number of distinguished and incredibly boring people.

The last phrase was spoken so quietly that Scortzi at first wasn't sure he had heard her correctly. He didn't have long to consider it as they moved through the crowd with Sophronia making gracious introductions. At the far end of the main salon they went up another beautiful staircase to the long viewing gallery that circled the hall.

Sophronia was an elegant sight as she stopped at the railing and looked out over the crowd of people below. Sensing his eyes on her, she turned, flashed him a bright smile and said, "Well, was that tour grand enough, Master Kalleni? If so, I'll excuse myself and leave you to your own devices. I'm sure you can find female company more to your taste. If not, Alex Manchester is on the far side of this gallery. I must now go and play hostess." Stepping closer, she put her hand on his arm and said softly, "Please, enjoy yourself, if you can, and I will see you again at dinner."

With another radiant smile, she left, sweeping down the stairway and back through the crowd, leaving a bemused Scortzi watching as she threaded her way back to her husband at the main entrance.

An interesting woman, he thought as he moved around the balcony to join Alex Manchester. He and Alex had met earlier at lunch. At first things had been a bit stiff and uncomfortable, however, once they had worked past the intimidating Kalleni name they had found they had many interests in common. Scortzi had been pleased to find that the very proper looking man of medium years had a surprisingly wicked sense of humor. He and Scortzi had taken to each other and would be comfortable working together. With the usual greetings over with, they found an empty corner on the upper gallery. They stood sipping their drinks while looking down at the milling group of fashionably dressed people.

"Alex," Scortzi said quietly, "you must know a lot of people on Soloving, how would you rate this gathering?"

"It's an eclectic group for sure, Scortzi," Alex answered. "There are some of the top government people, some of the leading merchants, not a few famous industrialists and quite a few what I suppose you could call, "Old Bloodlines", all mixed in with some entertainers, some rather famous church representatives and some minor, at the moment out of favor, politicians. I've been trying to figure out what to make of it."

"So it isn't just a meeting of merchants, then," Scortzi remarked, looking around.

"No, not at all. In fact I would say the merchants are in the minority," Alex replied. "Look over there," he whispered sharply. "There's an old spacer. Brillig, I think his name is, Captain Brillig. He was on the original Fischer expedition, must have been 25 or 30 years ago. Made himself an immense fortune, they say."

"Must have done, considering the size of that stone on his headband," Scortzi agreed. "Must be at least 10 carats, wouldn't you say?"

"At least, and if you will glance to your left you can see that his wife has a matching one on her lavaliere," Alex added, nodding discreetly at a lady in a rather exotic copper colored dress.

"Wish Dulsena or my mother were here," Scortzi muttered. "They could tell us to the Toruk how much those two baubles are worth."

"Well, they're too rich for my blood and a lot of other's, too, if I'm reading correctly the looks on the faces of some of those ladies," Alex added.

"Well now," Scortzi said, putting his glass on the tray held by a RoboServ, "let's get out there and mingle a little and see what we can find out, shall we?" They moved downstairs and moved into the crowd. Scortzi strolled over to a small group and in his most engaging manner introduced himself while Alex struck out in the opposite direction. There were a lot of people to talk to and the microphones in their lapel pins picked up everything.

Meanwhile, across the room, a pair of eyes watched Scortzi, measuring, evaluating this handsome young man in his golden kaiton. Was he what he seemed? Could they use him? Another pair of eyes watched the watcher and Scortzi. Suddenly the orchestra played a fanfare, signaling the commencement of supper and the entertainment. Their host and hostess led the way. Alex had just rejoined Scortzi and they started to follow the crowd. They hadn't gone far when a RoboServ approached and requested that Master Kalleni follow him. With a shrug and apology to Alex, Scortzi was led to a place at the head table where his host welcomed him. He found himself seated near Soloving's Cabinet Secretary of Finance, a World Federation Counselor, and a beautiful woman who apparently was an entertainer of some sort. A mixed group for sure.

After the supper and the entertainment, the host and hostess, with a small group of people from the head table, sat at one end of the gallery and watched the flow of people on the dance floor below. The RoboServs kept the drinks coming and Scortzi had to concentrate on the technique that his father had taught him to look like he was drinking when he actually was not. The talk throughout supper had been very general but he wanted to keep a clear head in this group.

The hour grew late and their host and hostess were summoned. As Carradyne rose to leave he spoke to Scortzi. "We really haven't had an opportunity to get to know you," he said. "Would you be able to come to dinner tomorrow so we can have a better chance to get acquainted and just talk trader's talk, which my wife won't let me do at a party." He laughed as he put his arm around his wife.

Scortzi smiled and said, "Thank you, I'd like that. I've spent so little time on Soloving I really need to know more about trade and industry here. Thank you for asking and for having me here tonight."

"Our pleasure, our pleasure, indeed. We look forward to seeing you tomorrow."

With that they moved off. The group broke up and Scortzi overtook Alex who was heading towards the door. Outside, they joined the throng of happy, chattering partygoers descending the old curved steps. "A very pleasant evening," Scortzi said. "Very interesting."

"We won't know just how interesting," Manchester said quietly, "until we can compare notes and…" His voice trailed off but Scortzi understood he was referring to the recordings.

"Yes," responded Scortzi, smiling at Alex, "let's hope they can shed some light on things. Well, at least I managed to get an invitation to return. That's what we really wanted."

* * *

The new day found them, Alex, Lef, Scortzi and Henri Dakkon, the Federation Representative sent by Lisbet Bohrnach, aboard Manchester's personal transport. It was a place beyond the eyes and ears of anyone on Soloving.

The evaluation of the recordings proved to be something of a disappointment to Scortzi and Alex, but Lef and Henri Dakkon were pleased. They seemed to see some patterns in the relationships of some of the partygoers and the very presence of some of the people gave them a place to start their investigation.

"What about Sophronia Carradyne?" Scortzi asked. "Is there anything to indicate she is working with her husband in this?"

"Not so far," said Dakkon. "In fact, it seems that she is quite independent and maintains her own lifestyle separate from that of her husband's. She has her own money and rumor has it that the marriage was not entirely a love match."

"And what is your impression of her, Scortzi?" Lef asked.

"Oh, Scortzi, was quite impressed," Alex put in, smiling.

"Well, Alex, you have to admit she is very interesting," Scortzi said defensively.

"Very," Alex agreed, nodding solemnly.

"And beautiful," Scortzi added. "I wonder if she'll be at the dinner tonight."

"This afternoon," Alex said.

"Yes, I know" Scortzi said. "I'm not used to having dinner so early in the day."

"And, Scortzi," Lef said in his lecturer's voice, "forget about the beautiful Sophronia."

"Beautiful AND interesting," Alex interjected grinning.

"Whatever she is, forget her," Lef said, sternly. "This will be a working dinner, not a time for thinking about beautiful women."

"Lef, Lef, Lef," Scortzi said, copying Lef's tone, "will you never learn? Any time is a time for thinking about beautiful women."

"That's all right, Scortzi," laughed Dakkon. "You think of Sophronia all you want, as long as you get the information we need on her husband."

"Well I'll certainly try, but I don't quite see how. I can't just come out and ask, 'how's the market in black crystals,' now can I?"

"Hardly," Lef said, "but you'll think of something, I'm sure."

"Your confidence is comforting, Lef, but I'm the one who will be going into the enemy camp, so to speak."

"Just remember we'll be listening all the while," said Henri Dakkon.

"If anything happens we can be right there."

"Yes," said Scortzi, as he picked up the miniature transmitter, "what I wonder is, will you be fast enough to help, or just to pick up the pieces."

- 9 -
Dessert to Go

Early afternoon the next day found Scortzi once again mounting the impressive staircase to Arnhalt Carradyne's mansion. His host, who had been visiting with another man, hurried forward across the foyer to welcome him.

The house is even more impressive without the crowds of people, Scortzi thought. Now he could see that the rooms were beautifully proportioned and the furnishings of the very finest quality. Beautiful antique pieces subtly blended with the latest designs, and colors gave the huge rooms a warm lived-in look rather than what could have been, with less skillful decorating, a cold museum atmosphere.

He was introduced to the other five guests who had apparently been waiting for him to arrive before filing into the dining room. This was a sparkling gem of a room with shiny brocade walls and a high mirrored ceiling. The seven of them were seated at a large round table which was laden with exquisitely prepared foods served on antique silver, crystal and porcelain. Scortzi had been told what to expect so was not surprised to find the food was not served in courses, but all at once. With the food in place, the center section of the table then revolved so each guest could serve himself. It was a pleasant informal way and had the additional advantage of not requiring the presence of servers. A definite plus when one needed privacy.

As they settled in place, Scortzi looked at each guest memorizing faces and names. There was Carradyne, of course, not nearly as flamboyantly dressed as the night before, but still wearing a large shoulder brooch, a jeweled belt buckle and numerous rings. His son, Sendel sported even more extravagant jewelery, unlike his son-in-law, Revkin, who was plainly dressed. Scortzi had been surprised to find Captain Brillig, the old spacer that Alex had pointed out, was the fifth guest. The other two men, he was told, were Faraday Division Managers.

Having eaten his fill, Scortzi leaned back in his chair and gazed at the mirrored ceiling, watching the languorous movements of the richly dressed figures sipping their drinks. There were flashes of light as gems caught the flickering lights of the multi-branched glowlight sconces that surrounded the mirrored tableau.

Talk had been very general and it wasn't until the after dinner drinks had been served that Carradyne, in an expansive tone, made a comment that caused Scortzi to come fully alert.

Carradyne's relaxed voice maintained the mood as he commented that, "Of course, it has been hard to be a trader anytime, but now with so many regulations and restrictions it is especially difficult. One has to be constantly ready to take advantage of every opportunity to make a profit. As you, Scortzi, know very well, no?"

Scortzi took a sip of the sweet Drenton wine and matching Carradyne's languorous tones, agreed. "It's always a problem to keep up with the rules and regulations of so many trade worlds and still come out with a satisfactory profit." He paused as if in thought and then, leaning forward, continued in an incredulous tone, "In fact, at times it seems that some government agencies appear to be, well, almost anti-trade. They make things so complicated with all these unnecessary rules and orders."

He leaned back and again gazed at the ceiling watching the reflections waver as heads bobbed in agreement and glasses were lifted again.

"You just begin to think," Scortzi went on, "that maybe you've got all the regulations straight and they get someone new in power who thinks up 105 pages of exceptions and variations." He took a long drink as the heads bobbed vigorously.

"Not like the old days," Scortzi went on, "when trade was determined only by a man's conscience and his willingness to take chances."

"Quite so, quite so," agreed Carradyne, his comment accompanied by a rumble of assent from the others while overhead the ceiling mimed the nods and gestures.

"Conscience, conscience," rumbled Captain Brillig, "That's the key. How can governments dare to dictate to someone's conscience?" he continued indignantly.

"Well," Scortzi added, "each planet has it's own ideas of right and wrong, and that's all right. I just don't like it when those ideas interfere with what I can ship or can't ship and sell or can't sell. That sort of thing is best left up to market demands, to my way of thinking."

"I feel the same way," said Carradyne, "and I think most of the others here agree." A general murmur of assent went around the table. I'm pleased to hear that you agree with us, Scortzi."

"I just wonder," Revkin said leaning forward aggressively, "do you speak only for yourself or for House of Kalleni?"

Scortzi lowered his eyes from the mirrored scene to look across the table into the challenging stare of the man directly opposite him. "Times change," he said slowly in a hard tone of voice. "People and leaders change. Goals may be different. I intend for House of Kalleni to become even greater than it has ever been. If that means bending a few rules here and there, so be it. When it comes to profits, I'm not squeamish."

The two pairs of eyes held, neither giving way until Carradyne's voice intruded saying, "Even if the rules bent are Federation rules?"

Scortzi flicked a smile at Carradyne, leaned back, turned his wine glass slowly in the light and said softly, "The Federation is a long way away."

The words hung in the air as looks were exchanged and Scortzi appeared intrigued with the cut of his wine glass.

Carradyne cleared his throat breaking the silence. "There is a product that has a market waiting for it, but because of it's proscribed status is not filling that demand."

"Wycold Enfolders or Drellix Mind Chips?" laughed Scortzi. "More trouble than they're worth. Any profit margin is too small for the risk of losing license."

"No," said Revkin "Something better, something more profitable than either of those."

At Scortzi's raised eyebrow and skeptical look, he added, "Crystals."

"Crystals!" laughed Scortzi. "Crystals aren't proscribed. We ship them all the time."

"Not blood red crystals," said Revkin softly.

"Oh come on," guffawed Scortzi. "In the first place there aren't any. The curing operations forbid them and besides, there isn't a market for them, anyway. The Black Knights are all dead, just a myth."

"Not so, they can be found," said Carradyne.

"The Fearful Arm of Righteousness has risen all over His universe," rumbled Captain Brillig. "He will no longer be mocked. No longer."

"No longer, no longer," repeated the others.

Scortzi looked incredulous and asked, "You mean to say there is a market for those things? How do you get them from Resdorn?"

"The universe," said Carradyne, mysteriously, "is a wide place and..." He broke off as a large burly man strode in and whispered in his ear. The expression on Carradyne's face turned cold and hard as he turned first towards Scortzi and then the others.

"Antikl tells me that they have picked up a low level transmission coming from this room."

Before the words were well out of his mouth, Scortzi had flung his glass at his host and burst from his seat towards the door. Dodging the guard, his way to the front cut off by Sendel coming around the other side of the table, he raced for the inner hallway and charged up the stairway. Halfway down the upper corridor was another stairway going down, apparently to the service areas, and another up to the next floor. Hesitating only a second he chose the less obvious route and went up the stairs and along yet another corridor. He could hear their voices as they paused, debating as to whether he had gone up or down.

Racing to the window at the end of the corridor he pulled back the draperies only to discover they covered a faux-view, a painting of a window.

The voices were louder now. He turned back to find the door he had seen in passing, praying it would be open. Sliding to a stop, he was just reaching for the opener when the door opened. A hand reached out, grabbed him and pulled him into the room. As the door closed, the girl attached to the hand hissed, “Hurry, help me empty this.”

“This” was a large chest at the foot of her bed. She started hauling out blankets and draperies and throwing them on her bed. They pulled the last ones from the chest just as footsteps pounded down the corridor. Motioning Scortzi into the chest, she closed the lid and piled some of the blankets on top. Ignoring the pounding on the door, she took one of the draperies and rushed over to hold it up to the wall before calling, “Yes?”

The door opened and Sendel rushed in. “Has anybody been in here?” he yelled.

The girl turned, lowered the fabric and looked at him.

“What are you jabbering about?” she said disgustedly. “Why are you charging around yelling at me and making such a commotion?”

“I’m trying to find a man,” he said.

“Brother dear,” Katje said coolly, “I’m 23 years old and I haven’t found one yet.” She turned back, raised the material up to the wall, and, turning it this way and that, said calmly, “Do you like this one or the mauve one better?”

“Awwgh! “Sendel yelled and headed out the door. At the last moment he turned and said, “If you find a man up here call security.”

“Don’t be ridiculous,” she answered, reaching for the mauve fabric. “If I find a man up here I’ll keep him for myself.”

The door slammed with a crash and the footsteps pounded back down the corridor.

She stood in the quiet for a moment before removing the blankets and opening the chest. Stepping back she gave Scortzi an appraising look as he stepped out.

"Well, Master Kalleni," she whispered, "you've gotten yourself into a fix, you have."

Scortzi stood, bowed and whispered, "You have the advantage. You know who I am, but I don't know who you are."

"No, you don't," she agreed. She was a small, slender girl with masses of dark curls framing a beautiful face and flowing down her back. Her eyes were very large and bright blue with dark lashes.

"However," she continued, "who I am is not important right now. We have to decide how to get you out of here before somebody smarter than Sendel starts looking for you. I think the sooner the quicker as my grandmother used to say."

Going to a closet she picked out a cloak and bag, then went back to the chest to gather up the mauve material. Motioning to Scortzi she walked over to a statue sitting on a side table and turned it. A panel in the wall opened and with a jerk of her head she indicated that he was to go on through. Scortzi looked at her for a moment. Finally, having made his decision, he shrugged and stepped into the dark opening. She followed, pausing only long enough to press a button which closed the door.

They were on a very narrow stairway which led upwards at a steep angle. At the top she pushed past him to get to the door. This proved to be such a pleasant experience that for a few seconds Scortzi forgot that his life was in danger.

The girl opened the door and looked about. Motioning Scortzi to stay back, she moved along the wall to another doorway and then walked over to a small flyer. She climbed in and started the motor. A spot light came on and a voice challenged her. She tabbed the communication set and said, "It's me you dolts. Get that light off me! You've ruined my night vision!"

Sendel's voice came over the receiver. "Where are you going?"

"I'm going over to Minette's house, as if it were any of your business. She at least knows mauve from pink, unlike some people we know. Now turn that blasted light off!"

The light was turned off and she quickly manoeuvred the flyer nearer the narrow stair door leaving only a few feet for Scortzi to cover before climbing in on the passenger side. Then, revving the engine, she did such a frog start off the roof that Scortzi was thrown back, scarcely having time to close the door before they were zooming over the rooftops.

Throwing her head back, the girl laughed happily. "Oh, I do love getting the best of Sendel," she chortled.

"Won't you be in trouble when you get back?" Scortzi asked.

"Why should I? I'm just going to Minette's house. We will discuss draperies and things and I will go home. I know nothing."

She sounded so innocent that Scortzi believed she could get away with it. "Who are you anyway?" he asked.

"I'm Katje, Arnhalt Carradyne's daughter."

"You're married to Revkin?" Scortzi asked in a shocked voice.

"Great Narm, no! That's Dorotea. I'm her sister. How could you think I'd marry that self righteous dolt? "

"I don't know anything about him really," said Scortzi.

"There's a lot you don't know, Scortzi Kalleni. For now, though, what I need to know is, can you jump?"

"Jump!" croaked Scortzi, looking out anxiously at the buildings far below him.

Seeing his expression, Katje laughed and said, "Not now. I'll swing over Contemplation Knoll in Placer Park and get as low as I can, then you jump."

She smiled at him and added, "It will be all right. Just bend your knees when you land and roll. You won't get hurt."

"I know how to jump," Scortzi answered in a defensive tone.

"Good," Katje answered. "I don't want you showing up tomorrow with plastene all over both legs."

The ground was coming up fast and Scortzi had one hand on the door handle. Turning he said, "Thanks, Katje. I appreciate the rescue." He pushed the door to one side and dropped. As he bent his legs and rolled, he realized that he had wanted to ask when he could see her again. But, there hadn't been enough time. He sat there on the damp grass in the dark and thought about her, about those long dark lashes and that little dimple that appeared at the corner of her mouth when she smiled.

A spot light flashed as a flyer dropped in low just above him. Lef's voice came out of the darkness behind the light, calling him back to the duties at hand. Somehow, Scortzi thought, as he climbed into the flyer, when this muddle is sorted out, I must see that girl again.

- 10 -
Unthinkable View

Porter hit the floor and was halfway across the room before he really woke up. The alarm ceased its buzzing and flashing as he pressed the panel and said, "Yes! Porter here."

"An alert in K-1." said the voice at the other end.

"I'll be right there," Porter answered.

"Whassa matter?" Remy mumbled.

"Nothing, Dear," Porter said, as he struggled into a coverall. "I just have to go out for a while. You go back to sleep."

The last was unnecessary as Remy had already flopped down and was back to sleep. She'd always been a sound sleeper. Even his scrabbling around to find his other boot didn't rouse her again. Finding his boot he slipped it on and raced for the door, struggling with closing straps as he ran. Out in the corridor he stepped into the lift and just as the doors were closing Williard slid through.

"They did say K-1 didn't they?" Williard asked as he tried to smooth down his ruffled hair.

"Yes. Didn't say what," Porter answered.

The lift opened and they raced past the guard at the door to the flyer waiting for them by the front entrance. Lifting off they headed for Windswept mine where they had installed the cameras.

The flyer was an SC Unit so their approach was silent. They landed near the eastern security building and found Security Chief Briggs and two of his security men in the surveillance room, huddled around the banks of screens. Briggs nodded and pointed to the screens showing the K-1 shaft.

A figure was barely discernable in the dim light. It was leaving the first level and slowly making it's way up the disposal shaft guiding a grav-lift loaded with what looked like a number of crystal bags.

"Can you tell who it is?" Porter asked.

Briggs leaned over and switched on another console to rerun the scenes of the figure as picked up by the cameras when he entered the shaft and then as he headed towards the lateral storage area. On the level he moved very quickly and only as he turned and headed back towards the disposal shaft did a camera catch a glimpse of the face.

"It's sort of blurred," Porter said, "I can't make out the features."

"That's not surprising," said Briggs, "Look at him as the camera catches him at the entrance to the shaft."

"No, that wasn't clear either," Porter said.

"Maybe this will help you to see," Briggs said. "Let me run that series again, this time with a heat spectrometer overlay."

"There's nothing there," hissed Williard.

"That's right," Briggs answered.

"How can that be?" asked Porter. "Even with protective clothing there would be a discernible heat variance."

"What if it's not a man?" asked Briggs.

"Not a man then whaa…Oh No! Not in my mine! No! it can't be! That's sacrilege! Never in a thousand years have robots been allowed in the sacred crystal mines!"

"What's it doing now?" Williard asked. "Is that the inside of the disposal area at the top of the shaft? I can't see clearly."

"Wait! Now he's gone completely! Can't you pick him up again?"

Briggs scanned each console, but nothing could be seen of the blurred figure.

"Anything on the outside cameras?" Porter asked.

"No, we're not picking up anything on any of them."

"Then where is he?" shouted Porter.

"Obviously he is still in the upper disposal area, somewhere," Williard murmured.

"Maybe," said Briggs, "or maybe he has another way out."

Just then one of the other guards said, "There" and pointed to one of the screens viewing the outside perimeter.

"Where is that?" asked Porter.

"On the far side by the canal," said Briggs.

Tabbing his transmitter, he said, "Have you picked him up, boys?"

"Clear as can be, both visual and audio," came the reply.

"Trackers, home in on Unit 4 and proceed with the operation. And be careful, Don't lose him!"

"How did it get from the disposal area to the outside perimeter without our seeing him?" asked Porter.

"It would be my guess that they've cut another shaft over to and then under the canal," Briggs responded.

"Right under our noses," sighed Williard.

"Yes, I'm afraid so," said Briggs. "We had been considering personnel never thinking they would use robots."

"Evil, Evil. Monstrous evil," Porter sputtered. "Well now what do we do?"

"We track it and find out where it goes," said Briggs.

"Have you alerted the rest of the network?" Briggs asked the other security man.

"Yes, Sir, soon as a sighting was made."

"Then all we can do is wait," said Briggs. "Our Units will track him on the ground and the Federation ship, Ristra, will pick him up if he goes off world. We won't lose him."

"I hope you're right, Chief," said Williard. In the meantime, I have a question. How long was the robot on the K-1 level?"

"Not long. Half a twelfth maybe. In and out. That's all," Briggs responded.

"No way it could have cut even one cluster and bagged it let alone several," Porter said.

"Could someone have left clusters cut but still attached?" Williard asked.

"Possible, but just barely. To finish several cuts, bag them and still be out in such a short time…I don't know. It's hard to imagine even a robot doing that," Porter said.

"Yes, and we would have heard more than we did," Briggs said.

"I want to see that film all the way through," Williard said.

"Yes, me too," Porter said, "and I want to see the run for the last shift."

"Security didn't spot anything earlier," Briggs said, "But yes, let's do that. Now? or in the morning?"

"Might as well be now," Porter said. "We won't sleep if we don't."

"Then let's move into my office and let the guards have their station back," Briggs said.

Settled around Briggs' large console they decided to start with the last hour of the shift, running the cameras in sequence. Each camera focussed on a section of the operations, overlapping slightly the range of the camera on either side. Everything seemed normal.

Considering the length of time it took to carefully cut crystals from the surrounding matrix it was not surprising that the figures stayed pretty much in one place, moving aside only for rest breaks. Most small clusters could be removed in a few hours, however, it was not uncommon for workers to take several shifts to remove a large cluster. Most worked alone, however, occasionally, as had happened on this shift, two workers would find they were working opposite ends of the same cluster. In which case they simply worked together on the final cuts.

After the removal the cluster was bagged in the thermal, light-proof bag and placed on a grav float for transfer. In the case of exceptionally large clusters, as many workers as was necessary would leave their positions to assist. The extrication of a particularly large or fine cluster was a cause for elation and the whole crew enjoyed participating. These people were from the elite "crystal families" and took great pride in their work.

"You know," Porter said, keeping his eyes fastened on the monitor, "watching this I can still recall the smell of the freshly cut matrix. There's nothing quite like it."

"Yes," Williard whispered, "but, what I remember is the feel of those damp channels, dark and sort of…I don't know, sort of cozy."

"And the rides up in that slow lift," Porter said. "The feeling of pride I got when I looked at all the full bags."

They looked at each other and both acted sort of embarrassed. It was clear they not only knew these mines, they loved them. As they watched yet another loop of security tape, the fact that they'd earned those memories made them feel confident they could spot anything out of the ordinary.

As the run of the 23rd camera was finishing, Porter said, "Wait! Go back."

Briggs reversed the run and stopped.

"No further, easy, easy, there. Now watch."

"There, see," Porter said. "That man standing by the float with his back to the camera. Hold it there and put 24 on the other screen."

Briggs keyed in 24 and ran it until Porter said, "There. No just a little more, there. See, on the very edge to the left, isn't that the same man with his back to the camera?"

"Yes, seems to be."

"Now watch. Run it slowly, Briggs. He moves more to the right and the worker opposite moves to the left and is hidden behind him. Now he moves back and the other worker is clear again."

"Run this again with the audio," Williard said.

Each worker had a small head set for communication but they were used only rarely and then in hushed tones. The figures moved and this time a whisper could be heard.

"What's going on?"

"Some hold-up at the top of the lift. There, it's down now."

They moved off, guiding the floats towards the lift, leaving the camera focussed on bare walls and floor.

"Nothing," said Williard.

"Maybe, but something feels wrong about it," Porter mused. "Flag it and get the names of those two workers. Now, let's check the rest of the shift." Two hours later they were slumped in their chairs, bleary-eyed, but no wiser.

"Briggs," Williard said, "I've been wondering. Those transmitters you had woven into the new bags, how long will they transmit?"

"The designer said 'several cycles'," Briggs answered. "He wouldn't be any more specific than that."

"Well, that should be adequate," Williard said. "Porter, we might as well get back. There's nothing more for us to do now but wait until we see where that robot leads us."

"Or until he pays us another visit," said Briggs.

"Do you think he will," asked Porter.

"We've been losing crystals at a regular rate. They don't know we are on to them so there's no reason for them not to try again."

"We have to sit here," Porter said bitterly, "and let that abomination come into the mine again?"

"I'm afraid so. We can't let them know we are tracking them. And, even with the best of technology and men, there is always a chance they will give us the slip. We may need for them to try again if we're to make an airtight case against them. Besides, maybe next time we can see where he's getting those clusters."

"Yes," Williard said, as he rose, stretched and walked towards the door, "in the meantime it's "business as usual." That's the plan. Come on Porter. Let's get on back. Security will handle this. It will be morning soon and we still have a mine to run."

"A profaned mine," sighed Porter as he slowly rose and dejectedly walked out to the flyer.

- 11 -
A Little Here a Little There

"You lost it?" Briggs was furious. "How? You were on it all the way from Resdorn! Where did you lose it?"

"We followed him from the lift-off at a small port near Heki on Resdorn," the FIS agent said. "They went straight to Amici InterWorld, where the bag never left the port. It was transferred to a small freighter which had filed for Flornak. Four hours out of Resdorn the signal veered off on a trajectory towards Adele, the smallest moon of Greniff. The ship proceeded on to land at Flornak. Our FIS undercover agents found no trace of the bag or the robot when they checked the freighter on it's arrival."

"Did the freighter carry an explorer flyer?" Briggs asked. "Maybe the robot took off to avoid just such a search."

"That was our first idea, too." the agent said. "However, in checking the original manifest there is no record of any flyer on board. The captain claims he never carries one.

"Since the ship did not stop anywhere," the agent continued, "we considered the possibility that they had liaised with another ship and the robot, with the crystals, made a mid-space transfer. "However the trajectory soon became very unstable and degraded into a free orbit.

"We then thought that perhaps the crystals had been removed from the bag and the bag jettisoned or both the crystals and the bag were jettisoned. Some of our ships have been diverted to the area and are trying to intersect the trajectory, but as you know, it is difficult to locate such a small item and the transmissions seems to be fading. They are still looking, however, and may get lucky."

There was silence with each man pursuing his own thoughts until Briggs said, "You know, they wouldn't rely on some risky retrieval procedure, especially for a number of shipments. That just doesn't make sense. No, they have planned things too carefully to go wonkers with the final step."

"I was thinking the same thing," Briggs said, "That doesn't make any sense."

"What we really need to know," the agent mused, "is where that robot got to. He was observed going on board, but, when our agents checked, the only robot on board was a maintenance model. It wasn't nearly as sophisticated as the one you described as being at the mine. Also, where are the crystals? They didn't find any. No crystals, no bags. Nothing.

"Are you keeping an eye on the Captain of that freighter?" Briggs asked.

"Of course. As a matter of fact we're checking out the whole crew."

"Well," Briggs said, "I guess there's nothing to do but wait until they try again and hope that one of us picks up something."

"Yes. I'm sure sorry things didn't work out better. We'll keep in touch."

* * *

Derek and Dulsena were just coming from a Kal-Van sales meeting when they got the message that a Henri Dakkon and another gentleman were waiting to see them.

Dulsena walked into her office and let out a shout. "Scortzi! How wonderful to see you again."

"Hey! This is quite a surprise!" Derek said as he whacked Scortzi on the back. "To what do we owe this welcome visit?"

Scortzi turned them towards a corner lounge where another man was standing, watching the reunion.

"Derek, I want you to meet Henri Dakkon, an assistant to Lisbet Bohrnach. He's working with FIS on this crystal business. Dulsena, I'm sure you remember Henri from the days of the Rebellion."

They acknowledged the introductions and after everyone was seated and had been served a cold beverage, Dulsena leaned forwards and said, "What has happened that you both are here now?"

"I'm here," Scortzi said laughingly, "because I was a total failure as an undercover agent."

"Not a complete failure," Dakkon objected, "we did get some valuable information and confirmed our suspicions as to some of the people who are involved on Soloving."

"Got it just by the skin of my teeth and only because I was rescued by a beautiful girl who spirited me away up a secret stairway and off in her flier," Scortzi said.

"Ooh, how romantic!" Dulsena said mockingly.

"Yes, it was, actually," Scortzi said.

Dulsena looked at him and from the look he returned she realized the adventure had somehow been important to him.

"Dakkon, here," said Scortzi "is the one who can tell us all about the newest developments."

Dakkon smiled and said, "Well, maybe not all, but there were some things we feel you need to know. Some things that I haven't even told you, Scortzi. First, it seems there has been some trouble at one of the mines on Resdorn. They have found there has been pilferage of crystals and, a few nights ago, the security cameras caught some pictures of crystals being removed from the mine."

"Great Narm, How?" Scortzi blurted. "There's never, ever been anything like that, not that I know of."

"All we know at this time," Dakkon responded, "is that the security chief, a man named Briggs, reported to FIS that a robot had entered the mine and removed some crystals."

"A ROBOT!," Dulsena gasped. "In a crystal mine? Oh Mercy! The crystal families will go wild!"

"Yes. Well, the mine managers and security are trying to keep it quiet until they find out who the accomplices are on the inside. They feel there has to be some inside help because of the time factors. The robot was in the mine for such a short time that it's clear the crystal bundles were all ready for it to collect."

"Did they catch it?" Dulsena asked. "If they picked it up on the security cameras they should have been able to catch it."

"They didn't try. They were trying to follow it. They'd made arrangements with FIS to have a ship ready to follow whoever they had picked up just in case they went off world.

"The crystal bag had been wired with a tracer unit and they were able to follow it aboard a ship but it seems the robot gave them the slip somewhere. The bag probably was ejected and lost in deep space, so that when the ship landed—no robot—no crystals. Everyone on board all very innocent. Couldn't understand why anyone would think they might have such a thing as illicit crystals."

Dakkon's account of the robot's removal of the crystal cluster from the mine and the FIS's unsuccessful attempt to trace him left Dulsena deeply shocked. Having been reared on Resdorn and growing up with all the history and mystique of the crystal mines, she could well appreciate how devastating such a turn of events would be to the crystal families and the more conservative element of the religious community.

Derek's main interest was in how the robot could have slipped through the surveillance net. "Where did the ship land?" he asked.

"Soloving and then Greniff" answered Dakkon, "and that is why I'm here with Scortzi.

"The fact that the ship came to Greniff, with or without the robot, indicates there might be people on Greniff who are involved in the crystal smuggling. They, FIS and Lisbet Bohrnach that is, were wondering if you have had any success as far as getting information from your merchant friends. Have you picked up any hint of anyone trafficking in crystals?"

"Nothing so clear cut," Derek admitted. "We did talk to a number of merchants, however, the only interesting thing we have turned up is the rather sudden success of a trading company run by a man named Jabour Khee. His family for years had a small chain of stores on the

Maatongi Peninsula, dealing mostly in shells and minor artifacts bought by the tourist trade. However, since his father died, and Jabour took over the presidency, the company has grown at an amazing rate. They have opened branches on all four continents and their financial rating is very high. The trade papers are full of Khee's exploits. Of course, we wish a fellow merchant well, but some of us can't see where it's all coming from. Granted his product lines have changed or expanded, But not enough, that we can see, to account for it."

"Interesting," Dakkon said. "Let me see what headquarters can turn up on that. Anything else you can think of?"

"Nothing," answered Derek, "but we were wondering if Chanceller Bohrnach had sent that data we asked for on the Felchor, Flornak, Chaldorn and Soloving circle and the schedule times and shipping weights for Captain Schwecker."

"Yes, here it is." Dakkon responded. "Not much other than the usual."

"Well, we'll take a look at it," Derek said as he took the spool Dakkon handed him. "Is there still that holdover on the run to Felchor?"

"Yes, and we have found he never leaves the port so that may rule out the idea of some extra marital dalliance. The manifests do show a slight increase in cargo weight but not enough to account for the half-day delay."

"Does he supervise all the loading and off loading?" Scortzi asked.

"No, his First Officer handles all of that with the transfer company."

"If he doesn't leave the port, where does he spend this time?" Dulsena asked.

"Roams around the port, has dinner with acquaintances, all seemingly very casual with no pattern," Dakkon answered. "The companions aren't always the same either."

"The new cargo he has added," asked Derek, "what companies is he dealing with?"

"It's all through a cargo packaging firm that deals with hundreds of different shippers."

"I see where you are heading, Derek," Dulsena said, "and I agree that it might be very interesting to find out which companies are involved."

"We can see what we can come up with on that," Dakkon said making himself another note. "Can't promise anything of course. It all depends if we can get someone on the inside or access their records, somehow. Give me a little time on that and I'll get back to you. In the meantime, give us a call if you find anything in your analysis of the shipping data."

"We certainly will," Dulsena said, as she and Derek escorted him to the door.

They watched until he entered the lift, then Dulsena turned to her receptionist and said, "Have Petr handle that meeting this afternoon and anything else that may come up. We don't want to be disturbed unless it's an emergency."

They returned to Scortzi and the next two hours were spent running the spool through their main transputer to see if any patterns showed up. At the end of that time they had only what amounted to a nagging suspicion. They needed the information from Dakkon before they could know if it was really anything of importance.

Two days later they were again huddled over the transputer as they fed in the spool Dakkon had sent over by special messenger.

"Bingo!" shouted Derek. "There it is. Now let's see what he got from the cargo shippers."

"There," Dulsena and Scortzi said, at the same time, as the data flashed on the screen. "We were right. He is in on it."

Dulsena tapped in Dakkon's communication code and few moments later Dakkon appeared on the viewer and they heard, "Dakkon here."

"Dulsena, here. I think we have picked up something. Is this a secure line?"

"No, just a moment." There was a slight change in tone and then Dakkon said, "Go ahead."

"It's the First Officer," Dulsena said. "The shipping manifests are signed by the same man, Rolgar Gritte, on the Flornak to Felchor, Felchor to Dornace, and Dornace to Chaldorn runs, but, on the Soloving to Flornak run there is a Chenyu Pik listed as First Officer. That is true on the last four runs. Doesn't that seem a little odd to you?"

"Yes, it does," Dakkon responded.

"That's not all," Dulsena said. "Two of the companies listed by the cargo shipper are owned by Jabour Khee."

"Ah ha," Dakkon said slowly. "Maybe we do have something."

"I think it would be interesting to find out if First Officer Gritte makes regular trips from Soloving to Flornak." Dulsena said.

"Yes," said Dakkon, "and how Chenyu Pik gets from Flornak to Soloving."

"Yes and I think it would also be really helpful if we had a lot more information about Jabour Khee and his sudden prosperity," Scortzi added.

"We've been working on that," Dakkon said. "We've just placed an agent in Khee's main receiving warehouses. We should be getting a report from him before too long, however, for anything really important we may have to wait until the next time Captain Schwecker makes port."

"There's one other thing," Derek added. "In half a cycle there is the Celebration of Universal Oneness Day. Dulsena and I have made arrangements to attend the ceremonies not only in Rohnseff but in Maashouk, Jontil and Khartouv."

"I'm amazed at such devotion," Dakkon said.

"I'm afraid there's no credit due for that," laughed Derek, "it's just that we thought it might be interesting to see who is conspicuous by their attendance or absence."

"With such crowds, do you think you will be able to tell much?" Dakkon asked.

"Well, granted it is a long shot but we've enlisted others to help and are filming everything to double check later. Who knows we might turn up something of interest."

"I think it's a good idea, however, don't you think it might be a little too obvious?" Dakkon said. "Why don't you pick just one and combine it with something else, perhaps a vacation with your brother, and let us, or your friends, film the others. I'm afraid the other way would put you out in the open on the whole thing."

"Maybe you're right," Derek said, "we hadn't thought of it that way."

"Yes," agreed Dulsena, "why don't we take Maashouk and leave the others to your people."

"Good," Dakkon said, "I'll make arrangements. Just keep in mind that Maashouk is Khee's home area, so take care."

"Don't worry, we will," answered Dulsena. "We have an exceptionally thorough security setup as we are constantly reminded that Nayland Brenev still has people who never give up looking for a chance to get back at our family."

"Well, good. I don't think you can be too careful," Dakkon said. "Get back to me if you pick up on anything new. In the meantime we'll hope for something from the cargo shippers. I'll be back to you."

The line closed and Derek looked at Dulsena and said, "A good thing we mentioned our plans to him. Ours weren't too subtle."

"Subtle!" Scortzi laughed. "You two would have looked very strange indeed racing all over the globe taking pictures like mad. You certainly would have attracted a lot of attention, not to mention putting yourselves in great danger. As you told him, you know very well there are still a lot of fanatics out there who blame you for the Brenev family's downfall. I never have understood your insistence on staying here with these people and their gloomy, oppressive attitudes."

"Scortzi, we've been through that before," Dulsena said. "This was the headquarters for Brenev Industries and we wanted Kal-Van to build on their custom. Besides, I didn't like the idea of running away."

She walked over and slumped onto the lounge. "I've never admitted it before, but I've also kept hoping I could be an influence for change. Show them that a woman could run a business and didn't have to stay secluded at home."

"After so many generations of such teachings," Derek said, as he came over and took her hand, "those attitudes run pretty deep, but I do admire you for trying." He kissed her hand and smiled fondly at her.

Scortzi cleared his throat and said, "Well that's all very noble but I'd rather have you home on Resdorn. You can run Kal-Van from there."

"Well don't fret," Dulsena said, "we won't make our grand peregrination of Greniff. We'll let Dakkon take care of the others while we go to Maashouk. You haven't been there, Scortzi, and we'll have a chance to talk as well as play at being spies. Besides with us and all of Dakkon's people covering each event we will undoubtedly see more. A little here, a little there, as father always says. Maybe it will start to make sense if we can pick up just a few more little pieces."

Later that evening they had one of those little pieces dropped into place by an old friend.

- 12 -
Old Friend's News

The next day Derek and Dulsena were back at the compound preparing for their trip to Maashout. Derek made it a point to tour the grounds each evening and check on the security guards posted around the perimeter of the compound. He had just started back through the orchard heading on the path that lead to the back garden areas. The night was clear with only a small crescent showing of Adele, the first of Greniff's two moons to rise. The air was redolent with the scent of ripening fruit and he took a deep breath and felt quite content. Suddenly he was knocked off his feet from behind. A knee was pressed into the small of his back and his arm was twisted up behind his back. He struggled to free himself, and straining to lift his face from the damp grass, he tried to catch his breath .

"He's gotten careless in his old age, my Derek has," the voice in his ear chortled.

Derek ceased his struggles. The knee was removed and his arm freed. Derek rolled onto his side and looked up into the face of the man squatting beside him. "Gutorm?" he whispered.

Before the other's response was half formed, Derek had doubled up both knees and shot his legs forwards knocking the other man over backwards. Leaping to his feet, Derek stood over the sprawled form. "You scared the hell out of me, you fool."

Gutorm lay where he'd landed and laughed. "Oh I hope I did that at least, my boy," he chortled reaching out to grab Derek's outstretched hand.

"In the old days I wouldn't have been able to get near you. Now look at you." He punched Derek in the middle. "Out of shape you are, boy. Too much high living as Merchant Donovan, I think."

"Hah!" Derek shot back, "So how come an old man like you is out here in the dark playing renegade? I thought you were busy being a trusted elder statesman back on Frayleen, kissing babies and keeping the Storting in line."

"Oh yes, well that does keep me busy," Gutorm answered blandly. "But I do manage to hear of other things from time to time. Keep in touch with old friends." Turning serious of a sudden he said, "It's that I've come to see you about."

"Well, since you made such an effort I guess we have to let you in," Derek said, as he motioned to the man standing off to one side with his weapon pointed at Gutorm.

Taking in this exchange, Gutorm looked back to Derek and said, "Good. But I shouldn't have gotten this far."

"They're the best. Only a few barget hunters slip by from time to time."

Back at the house, the soft blue purple of the summer night softened the high ceiling and far corners of the large room. Lamps with pale peach colored glass shades made soft pools of light over the rich red toned carpet. So formal and cold as a Brenev reception room, the room had, with Dulsena's good taste and eye for color become a warm, comfortable room reflecting the love and good nature of it's occupants.

Gutorm sprawled in a softly cushioned easy chair and watched as Dulsena left the room to check on the children. Now a beautiful, assured young matron, she bore little resemblance to the scared, young girl he'd helped escape from this same compound just ten years before.

At the same time, Derek was watching him. He seems the same old Gutorm, Derek thought. Lean, not a bit of flab on him. The lines in his face are deeper and the blonde hair perhaps a bit thinner. Otherwise he's the same old barget hunter who helped organize the exiles against

Brenev.

Gutorm, sensing Derek's eyes on him, turned to smile at him. "She's still very beautiful."

"Yes, she is," Derek agreed, "and just as brave. It's just that now she's concerned for the children. I'm sure you know why."

"Yes, I do and we need to talk about that. But first, if you would be so kind as to force another glass of that delicious Polcharian wine on me, I'll gather my thoughts and when Dulsena rejoins us I'll explain why this old man has left his devoted constituency to skulk about in your orchard."

A little while later, Dulsena returned followed by Scortzi, who had just flown in from Rohnseff. After the usual small talk, they made themselves comfortable and sat quietly as Gutorm began to talk. He reminded them that the members of BEN, the Brenev Exile Network, having suffered so much at Brenev's hands, had sworn never to give up the search until he was brought to justice.

A few years ago on Frayleen, Gutorm recounted, small groups of fanatics began to be more and more outspoken in their criticism of the established church. Not getting the response they had wanted from the public, they had gone so far as to disrupt meetings, jam religious broadcasts, and harass people going to and from meetings. To the average person, their demands seemed so extreme that most discounted them as crazy fanatics. A few, with more of a sense of history, accused them of being Narmists, defying the law by preaching those out-lawed doctrines of hate and prejudice. The disrupters, of course, denied any such association and declared they were simply trying to call attention to the need for reform.

In the more economically advanced, more conservative areas, these extremists met with little success. In other areas social unrest and less than ideal living conditions provided fertile ground for the germination of the seeds of conflict. It was in these areas that the doctrinal confrontations soon escalated into armed conflicts.

At first, BEN took no interest in these theological quarrels. Then someone reported they thought they had seen Nayland Brenev in the company of one of the leaders of the Narmists/Reformers. There was, unfortunately, only the one sighting and no proof. Nevertheless, based on the reputation of the person who had made the report, two BEN agents joined the dissenters and worked their way into minor leadership positions.

Once inside, it became clear to them that these people were not just a gaggle of wild eyed religious fanatics. They discovered a complete militaristic organization behind the dissenters; well organized, well disciplined, well trained and, most alarming, well armed. They even had camps for training personnel in all phases of a military operation.

Membership had grown as dissatisfied people found within these groups a place to air their grievances and legitimize their complaints. Nor was this growth confined to Frayleen. One agent reported overhearing part of a report in which the names indicated that there were active groups on a number of home worlds.

It was at about this time that the black crystal had been brought to Gutorm and he had taken it to Lisbet Bohrnach on Algoran. No mention was made of Brenev since at that time there was no proof that he was involved.

Meanwhile, the dissenter's conservatively dressed leaders continued to express horror that anyone should consider them Narmists. To the general public, they always presented their arguments for reform in reasoned, tempered phrases. However, this was in sharp contrast to the impassioned harangues delivered at their secret meetings. One recording, smuggled out by a BEN agent, showed one of the leaders shouting, "We want change! We demand change! We will have change! Violence, sabotage and terrorism are simply tools to be used to effect that change!"

"It was at this same meeting," Gutorm went on, "that the BEN agent first heard of 'the mission of the Black Knights'. Since then the phrase has been used frequently amongst the leaders."

"Gutorm, why would a totally amoral man like Nayland Brenev get involved with a group of religious fanatics?" Scortzi asked.

"Manpower," Gutorm answered. "Manpower that he doesn't have to pay for."

"And these Black Knights," Dulsena commented, "they must get something from him in return."

"The crystals," Derek put in.

"Right. But they also get trained fighting men and war materiel. It's a very neat, symbiotic relationship," Gutorm said. "Each gets what he wants."

"But what about afterwards?" Dulsena mused. "Suppose for the moment they're successful, how could they co-exist afterwards?"

"I don't think they expect to. More than likely each one assumes that after the Federation is overthrown, he will be able to do away with the other."

"If they aren't stopped right at the beginning, this could turn into a war of attrition that could go on for years!" Scortzi declared. "No one would be safe!"

"It's more than that, Scortzi." Gutorm said. "Even if they are stopped physically, they will continue." His firm, clear voice left no doubt in their minds that he believed what he said.

"Unless something is done to destroy their belief they won't be stopped by Federation ships or troops."

"How can that be done?" Dulsena said. "Religious fanatics are seldom responsive to logic or reason. Once started they'll be a cancer, growing and undermining the stability of the Federation. What kind of a world will our children have to grow up in?" She looked at Derek, her eyes filling with angry tears.

That terrible question hung there in the silence as each one coped in his or her own way with the fears that it evoked.

- 13 -
Another World

Dulsena took a deep breath reveling in the smell of the ocean and the sound of the sea birds wheeling and calling overhead. She smiled up at Derek who was strolling at her side. This beautiful golden beach of the exclusive resort near Maashouk seemed far away from the angry world they'd been talking about last night. She reached out and took Derek's hand finding comfort in its warmth and strength.

Scortzi had tried to interest them in running, but had given up and was now far ahead of them lost in the crowd of happy sunbathing tourists. Selene and Garrett had been left playing at the water's edge, completely absorbed with building a huge, sand spaceport. Dulcy looked back towards them and could see, Marit, the mother's helper, calming some dispute and keeping things well in hand.

The sun was hot, but the breeze from the ocean and the cool sand underfoot kept them comfortable as they strolled along, veering now and then to pick up a particularly fine shell from the cool wavelets that foamed onto the shore. Stooping to wash the sand from her latest find, Dulsena said, "The information from Gutorm's people about Jabour, do you think it is reliable?"

"Is Gutorm reliable?" Derek responded.

At her shocked look, he said, "If he didn't think there was something to it I don't think he would have made the effort to come here and meet with us last night, do you?"

"You're right, of course," she agreed, pitching the broken shell back into the surf. "It's just so hard to imagine that Nayland Brenev could still have that many followers."

"He pays well, always did," Derek replied. "Besides, he's apparently sold himself as "one of them", someone who has been "persecuted" by the Federation. In their minds he has become this romanticized, idealized hero wronged by the 'big, bad Federation'. I'm sure he and his friends work very hard to promote that idea."

They strolled in silence for a while before Dulsena said, "It's incredible that anyone would believe that about Nayland Brenev. I just keep wanting to believe that people are smarter than that." She sighed and added, "Well, maybe we'll get a better feel of things tomorrow at the Celebration."

She stopped and watched some young people playing a game of kickball, then rejoined Derek, and said, "Being here, watching all this, it's so hard to believe that there really are people planning to overthrow the federation."

"Remember, Dulcy," Derek said, "there are two worlds on this planet; the tourist and commercial, profit oriented businesses, and the orthodox conservative world of the regular residents. They may occupy the same areas, but their worlds are separated, their viewpoints miles apart."

Just then Scortzi reappeared, splashing through the surf. "It's beautiful," he shouted as he neared, "You should have come. The water's perfect."

Dulsena laughed and handed him the towel she had around her shoulders. "Tomorrow," she said. "I've had enough for today. Let's head back to our great sand spaceport. They should have it finished by now. Come on, I'll race you both."

Laughing they ran back, arriving out of breath and just in time to see the others frantically building a seawall to keep the waves from washing away the outer runways. They all joined in, but despite their efforts they finally were forced to stand and watch as the carefully built complex crumbled and washed away. It wasn't until the last launch pad went under and they had begun gathering up towels and bags that

Marit remembered the message she had been given.

"A man came over and gave me this and asked me to be sure you got it, Dulsena."

"What sort of man?" Derek wanted to know.

"Just a man," Marit said, shrugging, "I didn't know him."

Breaking the seal, Dulsena read the hand written message, DO NOT GO TO THE TABERNACLE TOMORROW. GO HOME!

"No salutation, no signature," she said, as she handed the paper to Scortzi. "What did this man look like, Marit?"

"Just a man," answered Marit vaguely, and then, at a look from Derek, thought a bit more and added, "Sort of plump, dark hair, dark eyes, looked rich, wore a lot of jewelry, wasn't dressed for the beach. He gave me the envelope and said to make sure that Dulsena got it. Then he walked away. That's all."

"Probably one of Jabour's men trying to scare us off," Derek said, as he handed the letter back to Dulsena.

"Well he's not going to succeed," Dulsena said. "We're going."

Their attention was caught by a plaintive voice. "Mom, I can't carry all this and Selene won't help."

Dulsena laughed and tucking the note away, said, "Of course Selene will help. We'll all take something. There now, everybody ready? Let's get back. I'm starved!"

"Me, too," Derek said.

"Me, too," Garrett echoed.

"All of you together can't be as starved as I am," Scortzi laughed. They slogged happily up the sandy slope leaving only the crumbling walls of a mighty space station to mark their day's activities.

The, dark haired, dark eyed man behind the sea wall watched until the happy group crossed the terrace and went into one of the suites.

* * *

The next day dawned clear and pleasant adding to the holiday mood of the huge crowds filing into the Najara Tabernacle. Although only one of many tabernacles on the peninsula it was the largest, oldest and most prestigious.

Dulsena, Derek, Scortzi, Marit and the children found their seats in the first row of the balcony. They had chosen those seats so they would be able to get the best pictures of the proceedings. Down below people were milling around while on the podium speakers were taking their seats and technicians made last minute checks.

As the hall filled, Dulsena leaned over and spoke quietly to Derek and Scortzi. "Do you notice anything unusual about this huge crowd?"

"Not really," Derek answered, "it's almost entirely local people, very few tourists. There are some people from Flornak in the next section and a few other off-worlders on the main floor and up in the higher balconies. But I don't see anything unusual about that."

"Yes, but what else?" Dulsena persisted.

Scortzi said, "Mostly males, very few females. But, isn't that typical of Greneff's more conservative populations?"

"Yes," said Dulsena, "but this is extreme in that there are practically no females. Other than the off-worlders, from here I can see only a few in the whole building. That is not usu..."

Just then the chimes rang and the holographic images of the giant crystals slowly appeared overhead ringing the meeting to attention.

The first few speakers were not remarkable but then, each succeeding speaker became more and more vocal in his support of the old ways, mourning the loss of "old fashioned values", the bringing in of foreigners with "wicked" ideas and the resulting laxness in morality that was encouraged by the Federation. They were told that what was needed was the return of "discipline", the demanding of "proper conduct".

Finally, the main speaker was introduced. The crowd went wild. When order was somewhat restored, he began speaking, starting softly and building to a crescendo of repetitive catch-words and propaganda phrases each one forcefully delivered and each one increasing the emotionalism. The people responded by stamping their feet and yelling, until finally the speaker flung his arms high and yelled, "Alvadar!" God shall rule!

The audience came to their feet, arms upraised and their yelling soon evolved into a rhythmic chant that seemed to reverberate through the structure itself. "Alvadar! Alvadar! Alvadar!" and with the last syllable there sounded the great throaty gong of just one crystal - the huge, blood red crystal that had been lowered and now hung in the center of the other pale crystals.

Hurriedly, Derek got the children to their feet and led them toward the exit. Gradun, their security guard, was already forcing his way through the crowd trying to clear a path. Dulsena followed with Scortzi urging them from behind. They pushed through the crush of people who, arms pumping, ignored them. They were too busy screaming their one word cry of unity. Finally reaching the balcony door exit they raced outside and down to the lower parking area where Raynor, having been warned by Gradun, had a flyer waiting. Even back in their rooms at the resort they could still feel the power of that mob and hear that monstrous chime.

Gradun had strongly urged Derek that they should consider leaving Maashout as soon as possible. Now Dulsena said, "Derek I agree with Gradun. We should leave."

"Yes, Please," Selene said in a tearful voice. "I don't like this place anymore."

"I think that goes for all of us, Selene," Derek said as he held her on his lap to comfort her. "We'll leave right away." Kissing Selene on the forehead he set her beside Dulsena and called the resort office, informing them of the change of plans. Marit took the children into their rooms to pack and for the first time Derek and Scortzi were able to surreptitiously assure themselves, that the small cameras hidden in their lapel pins had not been damaged in the crush. Dulsena's slightly larger action-cam hidden in her satchel would have the best record and she had already reassured herself that it was safe. Now, with a glance and a few discreet ocam signals they agreed not to refer to them until they were in a more secure place. Those films showing Jabour Khee and his friends on the stand in the tabernacle would provide the link they needed to connect him with the conspiracy. That and the pictures of that monstrous, blood red crystal. Before the midday chimes rang they were on the shuttle back to Rohnseff.

- 14 -
Mother's Nightmare

Aldrys Schwecker sat on the lounge with her arms wrapped around herself, her hands clutching her thin shoulders, her knees pressed together to stop their shaking. Her head was bowed, her chin against her chest. Her eyes focused on the strip of light that slanted from the open shutter across the shoes of the man seated opposite. Dust motes danced in the light. Every few seconds she glanced up to see that he was still there like some terrible nightmare that wouldn't go away. He was sitting in Arno's rocking chair. Just sitting, rocking, his eyes half closed, his arm lying relaxed across his chest, his fingers only inches from the stun gun in the shoulder holster.

She started shivering again and her tongue searched the corner of her mouth, tasting the blood collected there. Just a short time ago she had come home from shopping and was placing her parcels on the counter in the kitchen. She'd turned to close the door and found the man standing there, right behind her.

"What are you doing in here? Get out!" she'd wanted to shout, but, before the words were out he'd shoved her back against the counter saying, "Don't yell, Aldrys, don't make a sound."

But she had. She'd started to yell and that's when he'd hit her. Hard. With his doubled up fist. She'd been thrown back and sideways and would have fallen if he hadn't grabbed her by the throat, forcing her back against the counter. He'd put his face close to hers and glared.

"Aldrys, I said not to yell. Now do you understand me?"

His hand had moved up her throat grasping her jaw as he repeated the question. "Do you understand me?"

She'd tried to nod but couldn't move.

"Now, we are going to go into the other room and sit down, very quietly. Don't do anything stupid and I won't hurt you again. All right?"

Releasing his hold on her throat, he'd grabbed her shoulder, turning her away from him. His left hand had gripped her upper arm, the fingers digging painfully into the soft flesh while with his right hand he'd shoved her in the small of the back, propelling her towards the lounge in the family room.

Now she sat there, trying to control the panic that welled up inside her. Sat there trying to make some sense of it all.

"We will wait here quietly until the children come home," he'd said. She could hear him over and over in her mind, saying that. Dear God, not the children. What could he want with the children? She felt sick from the terror. The children. If only they would go to a friend's house to study or play. They did that sometimes, calling her for permission after they got there. If they would only do that today maybe somehow she could warn them. Tell them to stay away. Oh, please God, let them do that today. She tried desperately to remember what they had said this morning about their plans for this afternoon. She couldn't remember. She couldn't seem to think. She glanced at this mad man sitting there in Arno's chair. How dare he sit there. How dare he come into her home and threaten her. Rage filled her. Rage at this horrible man. Rage at herself for being so helpless.

She hugged herself even tighter and stared at the shaft of light falling across the man's feet as they arched up and down, up and down as he rocked. Up and down with the dust motes swirling. The only sound in the room was the rustle of her son's little jarbu moving around in the wood shavings of it's cage.

"Dear, God," she thought, "here I am, trapped, just as surely as that jarbu in the cage. And that man is waiting for my children to come home."

The vidphone rang. She leaped up, but, as fast as she was, the man was there ahead of her damping the vid switch, motioning her to answer vocally. A voice responded. Not Joran. Not Sardrys. Just a bored voice babbling something about a delivery being late. Turning it off, she heard her ragged breathing in the silence that lasted only a few moments before being broken by the back door slamming shut.

"Mom, you home?"

- 15 -
Best Laid Plans

Nayland Brenev swept back through the chapel door he had gone out of only minutes before. He raced past the pew, where the messenger had found him, and pushed up the aisle like some obsessed salmon, swimming upstream against the exiting congregants. Before the altar, he lurched to a stop, nose to nose with Marridon and, before his billowing cloak had settled around him, spat out, "What the Bloody Narm are you up to?"

Marridon, still wearing his "Good Pastor Expression" raised his eyebrows and said, "Whatever is the matter Brother Brenev? What is causing you to be so agitated?"

"You know the Narm well what is the matter, or at least you should," Brenev snapped. "I just heard that your people have been demonstrating and causing trouble all over the Federation. Several governors even had to call out the military to get things under control! "Now, we had an agreement. You weren't to do anything until we were ready to act together. I expected you to keep that agreement!"

"Why, I did keep our agreement," Marridon protested. "I had nothing to do with those demonstrations. But, I also can't help it if the feelings of our people run so high that they can no longer contain them. You must realize these good people are full of righteous indignation at the sinful ways that have been allowed to adulterate our worlds for hundreds of years. How can I possibly control such pent-up fervor?"

"I don't know how you can control it," Brenev spat out, "but you bloody well better find a way! I've worked too long and hard for you to mess things up at this late date. You get your people under control and keep them that way, until I tell you otherwise, or they might find their "fervor" gets them more than they bargained for."

With one last glare he pushed past Derrachem, who had witnessed this exchange, and strode furiously down the aisle, shouldering aside the shocked worshipers who had seen this man accost their leader. Totally oblivious to their outrage, Brenev barged out letting the heavy studded door slam shut behind him. In the nearly empty chapel the reverberations echoed and stirred the crystals, still hanging in place, sending shafts of red light bouncing from the stone roof beams to the hard faces of the men gathered around Marridon.

Back in his office Brenev, still too angry to stay still, paced back and forth. Slamming his fist into his thigh with each step he shouted imprecations at Marridon and all his "blockheaded, stupid, undisciplined, muddle-brained fanatics". How could they start something like this, he raged, when he was so close to achieving his goal.

The door opened and Georgg came in holding a wave-jet print-out. "That ain't the half of it, old boy," he said as he handed Nayland the print-out and backed away across the room. Nayland read the jet and went dead still, his face ashen.

"Carradyne, his son Sendel, Captain Brillig and his crew; all the leaders on Soloving in custody on Aldene," he whispered.

He crumpled the print-out into a ball and threw it against the wall. Then, breathing heavily, he stood motionless for a long moment before saying, "They'll talk. Oh, yes, they'll talk. Once they threaten that silly son of Carradyne's with the interrogation booth he'll tell everything he knows." He paused, staring into space.

"So what do we do now?" he said, almost to himself. "We're too short of arms to push the time frame forward. No, no way can we do that. We need those last shipments."

Walking over to his desk he keyed up shipping schedules. "One more cycle! Just one more cycle and we'd have been ready. And that sanctimonious, old fooframi has to go and lose control now! Of all the blasted, Narm be cursed luck!

"We must have those RGD's from Krolinoor to give us the edge over the Federation troops. With just conventional arms we cut our chances in half. It's imperative we have those new fighters and their rolograv depressors. All our tactics are based on using those. We've got to find some way. The Krogtlils insist they can't get them here before Archtith 9. That's almost a full cycle from now."

"That's if they take that back route into the Federation territories."

"Yes, but they insisted on that before they would agree to ship here. They had a big run-in with Federation ships about 20 years ago and were almost wiped out. I don't think there's any way they'd chance another encounter. The head man was very adamant about the need for caution."

"Well, in the meantime, let's get Schwecker over to Dornace.

"What about the daughter? Didn't Varig pick her up, too?"

"No. He just got the two of them. Schwecker has been told what he's expected to do if he wants to see his family again, so I don't expect any more trouble from him."

"Well that puts him in the minority," Nayland grumped. "All right, set up a run to Felchor and get to Jabour Khee about putting on some extra ships and making extra runs. If he gives you any trouble lean on him—hard. Put the word out to each of the Unit Commanders and see if they can scrounge additional arms locally. If we have to make our move early we're going to need any kind of weapon we can lay our hands on."

* * *

Back on Greniff, Jabour Khee decoded the wave-jet print-out and then spent several minutes thinking of all the reasons he couldn't possibly comply. The vid-phone buzzed and when he answered there was no image only a voice asking, "Did you receive a request from our mutual friend?"

Khee started to list all the reasons he'd thought of for non-compliance when the voice interrupted and said, "We don't want excuses, Khee. We want you to arrange matters as requested. You know what we have for sale," the voice added cryptically. "Don't force us to take our item to another market." The phone shut off.

Khee knew the FIS was the other market the voice referred to. Brenev somehow had acquired documented proof of an indiscretion of Khee's from years ago. An indiscretion is how he had always thought of that event, however, he was quite sure FIS would look at things differently. If those documents should fall into their hands it could bring his new empire crumbling to the ground.

"By the Narm," he thought, "with the Holidays coming up every one of the transports is already working overtime. Where am I going to find ships to make extra trips to Dornace and back?" He was finding out it was a dangerous thing to deal with Nayland Brenev. Brenev had made it possible for him to be richer than he'd ever thought possible, but lately he was demanding more and more. This new demand was impossible. Or, if not impossible, would certainly tax his resources to the maximum. However, try as he might he couldn't think of a way to not do it and still survive.

Three nights later two ships bearing the 5 star logo of Khee Mercantile landed at an old, little used port, in a desolate section near Maashout. The cargo hidden in the specially built bulkheads was quickly removed and the ships resumed their regular run into Maashout.

The Federation ship, staying back out of range, had had them under surveillance since their lift-off from Dornace. The Captain now pinpointed the exact location of the delivery and sent the information on to Algoran.

In Maashout, Jabour Khee watched the ships unload and the cargo clear customs. Suddenly he shivered and was swept with a feeling of foreboding.

"An evil spirit just spoke your name" was what his old grandmother used to say when people felt like that. An evil spirit. He wondered if that is what his grandmother would call Nayland Brenev.

- 16 -
Ripples Widening

Back on Aldene, Dulsena and Scortzi followed the line lighted by the guide wand and, as they approached her office, met Lisbet Bohrnach as she was coming out. "Oh, you made it. Good. I have someone I think you will be interested in seeing. Walk on over with me. Oh, but first, give that wand to my receptionist. We don't want security coming down on us."

They started off down the corridor and through a tree filled patio to another reception area. They found that walking with Lisbet was more running than walking. She raced along and, as tiny as she was, slipped through small openings in the crowds of people exiting offices in response to the midday chimes. That left them to make headway as best they could, with many a "pardon me" along the way. They finally came to a stop in a large reception area occupied by only one person, who turned as they entered.

"Katje!" Scortzi said, as he rushed towards her. "Katje. I'm so glad to see you again."

Katje just looked at him and Scortzi's heart fell. All his worst fears about her hating him because of the arrest of her father seemed to be coming true. Then, thank the gods, she smiled.

"So, Master Kalleni, I don't see any plastene," she said looking pointedly at his legs. "I guess you do know how to jump, after all."

"Oh, yes," he laughed. "I made it without any trouble. I made it just fine. You look fine, too," he added.

"You've lost your eyesight since last we met, Scortzi. I look terrible." And, in fact, she did have shadows under her eyes and looked stressed, but certainly not "terrible" as she had said.

"No, no, not terrible at all. Just a little tired maybe," Scortzi said. They stood then, just looking at each other until Lisbet, clearing her throat, suggested that perhaps Katje would like to meet Dulsena. Scortzi laughed and muddled through an introduction before going back to gazing happily at Katje. Seeing that Katje was thoroughly involved in gazing back, Lisbet and Dulsena exchanged glances and moved away leaving them alone.

"I was afraid you wouldn't want to see me again," Scortzi said softly.

"Why would you think that?" she asked.

"Well, it was because of me that the FIS picked up your father."

"Oh, if not you then it would have been someone else. We were expecting it."

"We?"

"My mother and I. We knew he wouldn't get away with it. It was all so crazy."

"Then you and your mother didn't approve of what they were doing?"

"Heavens no! We had argued and fought about it for years. It's a long story but it started when my sister went to visit a friend on Pantro. She met this boy and ended up transferring to a university there.

"He's the one that put all those crazy ideas into her head and after they married he started trying to convince us that what we believed was wrong. Mother and I couldn't see it, however, first father and then Sendel went over to their way of thinking.

"We had been such a happy family, when I was little. But, all the arguing and recriminations destroyed that. It also destroyed my parent's marriage. In order to have some peace at home, Mother finally just withdrew from the battle, refusing to discuss it, and focused her life on her work; you know she is an acknowledged expert on pottery of the Porvasic period. As for me, I finished my classes and started working on my own career as a textile designer. "When they caught you, Mother and I knew it was over. We were prepared to leave. You know it wouldn't have been safe for us there after Father and Sendel were picked up. We'd heard what happened to some other people when the BKs thought they had reported someone. We figured we would be safer here on Aldene."

"Oh, Katje," Scortzi said taking her hand, "I can't tell you how glad I am that you're here and safe and not mad at me. I've thought about you so much and was afraid I would never see you again."

"I wasn't afraid, Scortzi, I knew we would meet again. I was quite prepared to do whatever was necessary to see that we did. Why, don't you remember I told Sendel that if I found a man in my room I'd keep him? Well, you have been warned. I'm really quite shameless when it comes to getting what I want, when it's important."

She looked up at him, with her eyes shining and the little dimple deepening as she smiled at him. Scortzi knew from the feeling deep inside him that she was definitely right. He was hers and she certainly could keep him. In fact, right at the moment, he couldn't think of anything nicer than that she should want to keep him.

Just then Sophronia Carradyne came out of the adjoining room. She spoke with Dulsena and Lisbet then crossed over to Katje. Putting her arms around her daughter she held her close. Sophronia looked red eyed and unhappy but still managed a little smile as she smoothed the curls of hair on Katje's forehead. "It will be all right," she said, and kissed her on the cheek. "They have arranged asylum for us."

With her arm still around Katje's waist, she turned to Scortzi and, holding out her hand, said, "We meet again, Master Kalleni. Although not such a festive occasion as last time."

"No, not festive at all," Scortzi responded after bowing. "I'm sorry things have worked out as they have for you. If there is anything I can do to help, you know I will."

"Very gracious of you. But then I expected nothing less after hearing Katje go on about you," Sophronia responded.

"Mother!" Katje said, blushing.

Lisbet and Dulsena laughed and Lisbet saved her from further teasing by suggesting they catch up on all the new plans over lunch. She led

Dulsena and Sophronia off on another "walk" while Scortzi and Katje lagged along behind, interested only in each other.

Back in the same corridor after lunch, Lisbet was nearly run down by a man rushing from an office. His arms were full of files and record spools and he looked very harassed.

"Goodness, Bentrim, what's the matter? Is there something I can do to help you?" Lisbet asked, reaching out to straighten the jumble of records that seemed in danger of slipping to the floor.

"Help me? Help me? Yes. Can you hide me somewhere?"

"Hide you?" Lisbet laughed. "What are you talking about?"

"Yes, yes, hide me. Not for long, just a day or even a couple of hours. They're driving me crazy!" he moaned.

"Who? Who could have brought one of our most experienced, most efficient Chancellors to such a state," laughed Lisbet, patting his shoulder.

"Priests, that's who!" he cried, bending down and sticking his head forward to look her straight in the eyes. "Big angry priests," he said in a hard, sibilant whisper, biting off each word, "short irritated priests, thin snide priests, fat, little, hectoring priests. All, all of them wanting to know why we haven't done something about these 'Sons of Satan', these 'Messengers of Narm', these rabble rousing, tranquility shattering, ingrates who are flouting the laws and committing sacrilege." And they've sent them all to me. Oh, please, Lisbet," he said pleadingly. "let me hide under your desk for a while. I promise I'll sit there very quietly."

"Poor Bentrim," Lisbet said, trying hard not to laugh. "Can't you hide in your own office?"

"MY office? Great suffering Jambols, no! The protocol people are going crazy in there. These priests are the highest Ecclesiastics on each of their own worlds; important dignitaries that have to be met with all the proper pomp and whoop-de-do associated with their exalted offices. And even if some of them have sent emissaries, instead of coming themselves, these emissaries have to be met with the correct level of deference and ceremonies. And, if they don't come themselves or send their emissaries, they call me on the high priority Fed Net which has its own protocol procedure.

"It has been that way for three days! Three days! I tell you, Ladue has started speaking only Krolach and Sulvar is threatening to quit and move to Polchar and raise bickyloops. I really can't take much more of this." He stood clutching the slipping files and shaking his head.

"Bentrim?" a voice called from inside his office. "Bentrim, are you still here?"

Bentrim gave a strangled cry, clutched his files closer and ran toward the lift. Lisbet and the others watched until he was out of sight.

"Well," Scortzi said, "that gives us an idea of how these demonstrations are affecting the church leaders. Doesn't it?"

- 17 -
Now You See Him…

Back on Resdorn, Rudolf Porter, Bertram Williard and Security Chief Briggs again sat huddled over the green hued screen of the security monitor. Anxiously, they had watched as the intruder retrieved the crystals from the false bottom of the float and loaded them into a bag that had been hidden with them. They had watched as he'd then retreated back along level four and up the shaft leading to the disposal area. When he disappeared from view they knew he had gone into the secret tunnel the rebels had cut leading to the far side of the canal. Scarcely breathing, they waited until a voice said, "We have him."

"Don't lose him. Don't lose him," whispered Porter over and over in the quiet.

"Cold Fire, Cold Fire, this is Blue Parrot." Each of them had started at the sound of the bored sounding voice coming over the loudspeaker.

"We have accomplished this run and are heading on out."

"They've got him!" Briggs said pounding his fist on the table. "They've got a lock on him! They'll stay with him until they land and then pick him up."

"It" not him", Porter grumped. "They'll pick IT up if they don't lose IT somewhere along the way like they did last time," he growled.

It had been a terrible thing for him to sit there and watch that THING, that ROBOT walking around in HIS mine. A thousand years of tradition destroyed.

"Don't worry. They won't lose him," Briggs said. "Not now that they know what to look for."

* * *

Back on Aldene, in an office loaned to them by Lisbet, it was midnight and the bustle and noise of daytime had been replaced by the muted voices of a few night clerks and the soft sounds of the cleaning robots as they readied the offices for another day. Scortzi, Dulsena and the team of FIS economy analysts were tired. From Midday onward they had worked evaluating the multitudinous shipping reports sent in by FIS agents and it seemed they were beginning to see a pattern that might indicate the source and possible distribution of the proscribed crystals. By a process of elimination and a certain amount of guesswork, they had narrowed their search down to the Azeroth system. What was missing was the exact location of the mines and curing facilities. There were two star systems there, one with two small obscure planets and the other with one small planet classified R-2 as not yet sufficiently developed to be ready for admission to the Federation. It was, as usual in such cases, under the supervision of the Federation, which attempted to maintain its restricted status. They were stowing away the last of the files when the VidCom buzzed. Scortzi looked at Dulsena, gave a big sigh and crossed over to answer it. A rather tousled Lisbet looked out at him.

"Just got a call, Scortzi," she said, stifling a yawn. "They've picked up that First Officer you were curious about, Chenyu Pik. Seems they tracked a robot from the mine on Resdorn to a ship which they followed until it landed at Flornak. When they searched, no robot- so the FIS agents picked up the First Officer for questioning, and are detaining the captain and the rest of the crew. The Judicial Clerks will be ready to take testimony in the morning.

"Just thought you might sleep better for knowing that by Midday tomorrow we should have some answers for you."

"Right," Scortzi responded. "That is good news. Thank you for letting us know."

"S'all right," Lisbet said sleepily and the VidCom screen faded.

"Well good!" one of the FIS agents said. "With that, and what we've been able to come up with tonight, we'll soon have what we need to move on these guys."

- 18 -
The Ultimate Slip

“Who is this guy anyway?” the guard asked as he walked along the corridor towards the detention cells.

“Say’s here he’s First Officer on some freighter. Let’s see, hmmm yes, the Ulazza come in from a run to Resdorn” the Deputy answered as he checked his record.

“Must have been up to something pretty bad to have the Judicial Clerks here so fast. They just picked him up late last night.”

“Not our business,” the Deputy said, “You lock’em up, I do the records. Not for us to bother with the whos and whys.”

“Well, Narm! Can’t help but be a little curious, can I?” the guard said defensively. He stopped before a cell and peered in at the figure lying on the narrow cot. He shifted his Nervecept to his left hand and entered the access code. The door slid open. He crossed two steps to the cot and, with his boot, jiggled it vigorously.

“Come on, wake up and face the day.”

There was no response so he repeated the action with more force. “Come on, get a move on. We don’t have all day,” he added as he pulled off the blanket. He took one look, keyed his communicator and hollered, “Get the doc in here, cell 20.”

“Won’t do any good,” he said in an aside to the Deputy, “this guy’s dead.”

"Oh Narm!" the deputy groaned, thinking of the extra records this would require, not to mention the investigation that would follow. "Dumb spacer why'd he have to kick off on my shift."

First Officer Chenyu Pik had indeed "kicked off" or, more precisely, ceased functioning as per orders.

The Head Warder heard the doctor's report and immediately called FIS. They were not pleased, especially when, in response to their query, they were told the Captain of the ship had been released on bond three hours before. By the time they got through to Flornak Control the Captain and his ship were long gone and refusing to respond to FedCom.

"And how the Narm do we explain this," yelled the FIS Regional Supervisor as he slapped the VidCom off. "How do we explain that we tailed a guy all the way from Resdorn just to let him loose from detention! Can anyone explain to me how everything got so bollixed up?" he went on at the top of his voice.

"Well, his attorney was down there last night only a couple of hours after we booked him and since he is a ship's captain with no priors and a good reputation they let him post bond," an agent said ruefully. "How could we know he'd leave?"

This rather plaintive question only made the Supervisor angrier.

"Yes, leave," the supervisor said softly as he glared even more ferociously. "Leave he did. Now can you just tell me how he managed to do that; to "leave" when the ship had been impounded as evidence in this smuggling investigation?

"Great Narm!" he continued at full volume, "didn't anyone try to stop him?"

An agent off to the side hung up a vidphone and said, "I think I can answer that Chief. He had all the proper forms, signed and stamped. The guys on duty at Flornak Control had no idea they were fakes."

"Forged papers! Missing witnesses!" the Supervisor groaned dramatically, "and I've got to explain all this to headquarters!"

- 19 -
Out of the Mouths of Babes

Back on Algoran, Scortzi, Dulsena and Henri Dakkon were explaining to Lisbet what they'd come up with on their analysis when the intercom buzzed.

"Lisbet," the voice of Chanceller Vonct murmured, "I think we have something here that pertains to your investigation. A Captain Arno Schwecker is in my office. He says his wife and son have been kidnapped. His daughter is with him.

"I remembered at the last Council Meeting you mentioned his name in reference to this crystal business you're working on, so I thought I'd better call you. He's told me enough to make me sure it all ties in together. I'm not sure how. Anyway, seems to me that you probably should handle it. I'll have Security escort him and his daughter, ah…Sardrys is her name, to your office. Is that all right with you?"

"Yes," Lisbet answered, "send them over. Kidnapped, you say? Did he say who he thinks did it?"

"Yes, he's made some accusations, but, I think I'd better let him tell you about them. They should be there in about 10 minutes. Let me know what you find out."

The screen went dark. The four of them looked at each other. The captain they suspected of being involved in the smuggling of crystals from Resdorn was there reporting the kidnapping of his wife and son.

What could this all mean?

Fifteen minutes later Captain Schwecker, his daughter, Sardrys, an FIS agent and two Judicial Clerks were escorted into Lisbet's conference room.

Scortzi, Dulsena and Henri had moved to chairs on the left side of the room leaving the antique, high backed chairs in front of the desk for the Captain and his daughter. The Judicial Clerks were seated along the other wall, immediately to the right of the desk, where they could see both the Councilor and the visitors.

At a nod from Lisbet, the first Judicial Clerk rose and from the depths of his grey hood, pronounced this was an official interview, gave his name, the name of the other clerk and the names of those being interviewed. He then named Chanceller Lisbet Bohrnach as presiding officer and added the date, time and names of witnesses.

Judicial Clerks, noted for their amazing memories and astute perceptions, were the heart of the Federation judicial system and testimony given before them was used by Judges to help determine guilt or innocence. Intelligent, impartial, inscrutable and totally incorruptible they insured fair and swift justice for every citizen of the Federation. The incredibly difficult training in mnemonics and psychiatry combined with the stringent lifestyle insured that only the most qualified and dedicated candidates survived to wear the long, hooded, grey cloaks of a Judicial Clerk. Their presence at this hearing increased the tension which had been building.

After the Clerk was seated all eyes shifted to Captain Schwecker. A man of middle years with grey streaked hair, he had the look of a long-time spacer. Lean and fit he probably looked younger than his years ordinarily, but now he looked drawn and haggard like a man who knew he'd bartered away his life's dreams. Lisbet asked him if he understood the importance of the Clerk's presence. He responded that he did. She then repeated the same question to Sardrys who nodded vigorously and said she had learned about them in school.

Lisbet then turned back to Captain Schwecker and asked how he knew his wife and son had been kidnapped. The captain explained that he had come home to find them gone. A few minutes later he'd received a call. He believed it was an off-line call as there was no picture and the voice had the peculiar timbre of an off-line call, which is a radio call rather than a call placed through the regular vidnetwork.

The voice had told him that if he wanted to see his wife and children again he'd better be more cooperative about the revised schedule and not make any trouble. He was told he should remember that he still had a daughter.

At that point Schwecker's daughter, a very self-contained young lady about 13 or 14 years old, leaned forward and took up the narration. She said she had come home to find her father frantic with fear. At first he wouldn't tell her what had happened, however, she had finally convinced him he had to tell her what was wrong.

"I told him I didn't know anything about the Black Knights, or crystals, or any of that stuff, but if we were ever going to get Mom and Joran back home we had to talk to someone who could help us. Everyone knows that kidnappers usually kill the people they kidnap. Don't they?" she asked Lisbet. Sardrys was obviously a strong minded little girl who was trying very hard to be brave. That she wasn't quite succeeding was obvious from the trembling chin she failed to still and the hands that clutched the arms of the chair.

"I'm sorry to say, Sardrys, that you are right," Lisbet answered gently. "However, let's see what we can do to assure that does not happen."

"Captain Schwecker," Lisbet continued, "what is this revised schedule you referred to and who was demanding that you keep it?"

"It's the schedule I've kept for years on my trading route. I go from Greniff to Dornace to Chaldorn to Soloving, then back again. When they, Faraday that is, contacted me about some cargo for them I was real pleased. For a long time I'd been wanting to get in with some of the bigger houses. Well, they had me add Flornak to my run and then, a few months later, Felchor. That made a real long run, but they paid well.

"Everything was fine for awhile." He sighed and moved restlessly in the chair. "Well, then trouble started. They said they wanted me to drop some of my other clients and carry more cargo for them. I told them that I couldn't do that. Why, some of those people had been shipping with me for years. They'd been loyal to me when I was starting out and I wasn't going to dump them now. Well, that's when they told me what I'd been hauling. Crystals. Proscribed crystals," he added as he glanced at the Clerks.

"They told me that I could lose my ticket if the Federation found out about it and if I didn't cooperate they'd make sure they did find out. I'd never done anything like that before. Honest. I just didn't know what to do. So, I just did what they wanted." Again he glanced at the Clerks and then at Lisbet before continuing.

"Finally, not long ago, they called and said I had to shorten the time, you know, spend more time in hyper-drive. I was also told that I would have to make some mid-route transfers somewhere out beyond Frayleen. Well, I told them I didn't want to have anything to do with that. You know, that takes extra equipment for handling and shifting cargo and there are all kinds of problems. As for the hyper-drive business, my crew wouldn't stand for that.

"So, I told them I wouldn't do it anymore and they could do what they wanted. You see, I was gambling that they wouldn't say anything to anybody, because they would be in trouble too. Besides, I didn't like that Black Knight business. I don't want anything to do with that sort of stuff. I never thought they'd," his voice cracked and broke, "I never thought they'd go after my family."

"While I can sympathize with your concern for your family, Captain Schwecker," Lisbet said brusquely, "you showed very poor judgement in not coming to the Federation as soon as you found out what was in those shipments. It should have been obvious that these people are quite prepared to do anything to further their cause. However, you didn't come to us. You went along with them and now your wife and son are paying for your involvement. Frankly, I'm not sure at this moment, how or even if we can do anything."

Captain Schwecker, by now looking quite sick and desperate, said, "But you've got to help them. They'll kill them. I know they will." He thrust his hand through his hair and moaned, "What have I done, what have I done?"

Sardrys, leaped from her chair and, kneeling at his side, put her thin, arms around him and attempted to comfort him. She then looked up to face Lisbet Bohrnach and, in a thin, little voice, pleaded, "Please, Councilor, help us get my mother and Joran back. They didn't do anything wrong."

"We'll try Sardrys," Lisbet responded softly. "Now why don't you wait in the reception room outside while we see what your father can tell us."

Sardrys looked like she wanted to say more, but she rose, patted her father on the shoulder and with dragging steps left the room. The door closed slowly and settled into place with a soft thump. Everyone, but the Captain, had watched her leave. Now, all heads swiveled back to the figure slumped so dejectedly in the ornate chair and to the small, stern faced Lisbet facing him.

"Now Captain," she said sharply, "Perhaps, if you give us every scrap of information you have, we will be able to figure out some way to save your wife and son."

- 20 -
Everyone Has Them

Scortzi walked out of the guest suite at Federation Headquarters and slammed the door, or tried to. The door didn't slam, however, it merely slid into place with a discreet whoosh. He stomped down the corridor, but, the soft carpeting muffled his footsteps. Frustrating! He wanted, no he needed the psychologically satisfying sound of a heavy door slamming into place, the sharp, clear sound of shoe soles beating against a hard surface sending an unmistakable message of irritation and pique.

I FEEL grouchy but I can't BE grouchy, he thought. It was as bad as having his mother there. When he was younger and he'd felt this way she used to say, "Don't be grouchy, Scortzi, deal with the problem." Well, sometimes being grouchy was all you had when the problem refused to be dealt with.

The call from Flornak had triggered this grouchiness. Here he was clear over on Aldene working with the FIS chasing a bunch of religious lunatics, when he should be home taking care of business during one of the most hectic times of the year, and what happens? Somebody goofs up, and they lose two witnesses they'd spent half a cycle trying to catch. Or, to be precise, one witness and a robot; the robot that had been stealing crystals from Windswept Mine. The same robot who, with the aid of a Baluki body skin, had masqueraded as a human named

Chenyu Pik. And, as if that weren't enough, the captain, using forged papers, had taken off and by now was Narm knows where.

What a muddle! The head of Faraday, one of the largest Merchant Houses in the Federation, was under arrest. Katje and her mother were in protective custody; half their family in prison. Aldrys Schwecker and her son had been kidnapped. While all over the Federation, small groups of vociferous people, urged on by a few fanatic priests, were creating disturbances, causing civil unrest far out of proportion to their numbers. And, with the coming of the most Holy Day of the year, when religious fervor was at a peak, things would almost certainly get worse. Why shouldn't he feel grouchy.

Walking towards the chapel garden near Lisbet's reception area he met Dulsena just coming out. Dressed in a pale yellow morning gown, she looked beautiful, but didn't seem her usual sunny self.

"What's up," he asked.

"I just got a call from Derek," she answered, "he said he and the children are all right, but I sense that something's wrong. Nothing specific just more what he didn't say. You know what I mean?"

"Well, Dulcy, remember what it's like at the store this time of the year. He's probably coping with a lot of problems."

"Yes, I know and it doesn't make me feel any better to know I'm here instead of there helping him."

They were silent for a few moments and then Scortzi said, "Dulcy, we're both in a bad mood. They just rang first call for morning chimes. If we hurry we can make it in time. So, will you go with me and walk the path? Then, we'll try again to put all this together?"

At her smile, he put his arms around her and gave her a hug. Then, hand in hand, they hurried to join the people entering the large meditation garden. There they walked the curving path in the proper order around the fountain as the sprays of water rose and fell in cadence with the morning chimes. Step by step Scortzi's irritation fell away until once again he felt he could move in the way of harmony. That was one of the blessings of the chimes. They reminded one of what was really true and the importance of keeping one's life in the way of truth and beauty. How strange that some people should wish to distort that message.

Afterwards, on the way back to the office provided by Lisbet, Scortzi said, "I've been going over the transcript of Captain Schwecker's testimony. One thing he said caught my attention. Right at the beginning when he was telling about the new demands of Faraday's rep, he said they wanted him to make en-route cargo transfers somewhere out beyond Frayleen. Remember?

"If you go out beyond Frayleen you're soon out of Algoran Federation jurisdiction and into Huilla League. Now, in the back of my mind, I seem to remember that when Nayland Brenev was trying to overthrow the Federation, didn't he get weapons from some world out that direction?"

"Yes," Dulsena replied, "you're right. Now what was it?" Her brow puckered as she thought back to that time ten years ago when as a new bride of Loran Brenev she had been caught up in that terrible conspiracy. She seemed to remember that Nayland had not only bought illegal weapons for his troops from that planet but had also hired mercenaries from there.

"Krolden," she said, "Krolidor. Something like that.

"Krolinoor?" Scortzi asked.

"Krolinoor, yes that's it," Dulsena agreed.

"All right, now suppose," Scortzi went on, "that Brenev still has a source there for the weapons he needs. He'd need transport, which brings us back to Captain Schwecker and his ship."

"But," Dulsena put in, "Schwecker's ship is set up with blowers for foam blocks, to transport fragile cargo. That's his specialty, not shipping heavy cargo like arms."

"Yes, but what better way to conceal illegal arms shipments?" Scortzi countered. "Arrange for a minimum cargo of the usual object's d'art and blow your blocks with hollow cores. Rendezvous with the arms shippers, pack the weapons into the hollow cores and blow in some more foam, sealing in a few more fragile items. There you are with your ordinary looking shipment. The same sort of stuff you've been shipping for years. The only difference would be the weight.

No, wait, suppose you don't even seal them right away but wait until the arms are removed in a quick transfer at some out-of-the-way field. You could then blow in the final seal just before landing at your usual port. Who's going to question a slight reduction in weight. Remember, Schwecker's been around for a long time. The customs people are used to him."

"Yes, that's true, but all this is supposition. What if the Huilla League has cleaned up Krolinoor and that source has dried up?"

"That's one thing we need to know, all right. In any case, there has to be a source out there on the fringes of either the Algoran or Huilla jurisdictions where he's getting those arms. Otherwise why the need for Schwecker's being there? We need to talk to Lisbet or Henri and get us some answers."

* * *

Back on Nirubati, Nayland Brenev threw a small Haldornian sculpture against the wall where it shattered and lay in a thousand, glistening shards. Searching for something else to throw he was reaching for a Drellix Mobile when Georgg rushed over and scooped it up.

"Not my Drellix, Nayland. Work off your anger some other way."

Nayland glared and flung himself into a chair muttering something about, "it's a stupid looking thing anyway."

"No it isn't," Georgg rebutted, "you're just mad at everything and everybody."

"Yes," Nayland said in a vicious tone, "especially that fool Schwecker! Why would he be so stupid?"

"Well, that was unexpected," Georgg agreed. "I never thought he would abandon his wife and son."

"Do you really think he's gone to Aldene?" Nayland asked. "What exactly did your informant say?"

"He said that Schwecker was detained on Dornace then left. No one has seen him since. He didn't make his usual run from Dornace to Chaldorn. Never docked, no report of trouble on the flight, no word at all. The cargo he was expected to pick up is still in the warehouse; he didn't notify any of the shippers."

"No distress signals picked up by the patrols?"

"Not that he had heard of."

"You're probably right. He's over at Fed Center singing his little story to anyone who'll listen. So, get hold of Narig Velson and tell him to teach our Captain Schwecker a little lesson.

"In the meantime, get to Khee and make sure he understands about those additional runs."

As Georgg was leaving, the intercom buzzed and the secretary said Captain Swadi was on the vid-phone. Nayland switched lines and Enferdeem Swadi's dark face appeared on the VidCom.

"Aren't you off schedule, Swadi?" Nayland asked.

"Off and not likely to be back on," Swadi replied. "We were picked up. They got the robot."

"They what?" shouted Nayland. "How did that happen? What about the crystals?"

I have them, but they'll be the last. As to what happened. They apparently were on to us at the mine and tracked us from there to Flornak. It was a good thing I had those blank forms you'd given me. I'd never have gotten away otherwise. As it was I just barely got away soon enough to go hyper. What do I do now?"

"Deliver those crystals, get the money and come over here. We have a problem about the weapons shipment. Schwecker's gone to Aldene, or at least we think he has. We've got Khee making some extra runs but he's proving difficult. It might be we'll have to re-think the timing for making our move."

There was a long silence on the line. Nayland watched as Swadi digested this information. "We need those weapons," he finally said. "What about the mercenaries? Can they adjust to a change in the schedule?"

"They're going to have to go along if they want their money."

"Speaking of which," Swadi said, "without additional crystals where are we getting the money to pay for those men?"

"I'll think of something," Nayland replied. "I always do."

Swadi said nothing. Eyes narrowed in skepticism, he remained leaning on one elbow, his finger tapping his upper lip. Silent.

Calculating. "We've come too far on this, Brenev, to have something go wrong now."

"Don't worry, Swadi, you deliver those crystals as usual. You will of course, be sure not to give our good priests any cause for concern about future shipments. Bring the credits to me and, by then, I'll have come up with an alternate solution."

Swadi did not look convinced but he nodded and closed the connection.

As the screen went blank, Nayland's smile of assurance faded and he wished he felt as confident as he sounded. He needed those weapons from Krolinoor and, most of all, he needed those RGD's. If Schwecker was indeed out of it that left Brillig and Swadi for the long runs and Khee for a few short hauls. Not enough. Not enough. He also needed some way to put the pressure on the Krogtlils to deliver those fighters a few days early. Whose markers could he pull to get that done?

- 21 -
Whys and Wherefores

"How much longer are we going to be here, Scortzi?" Lef asked as they walked along the curving hallway. Scortzi stopped and sighed. "I don't know, Lef. Not much longer I hope. In fact, Dulsena and I have talked about it and we'd like to leave before Midday Chimes. So why don't you assume that's what we'll do and have the ship ready to go."

"Good," Lef said, "Kiku and the pilot are getting anxious to get back home. There are all sorts of rumors flying around and they don't like the sound of some of them. They'll be ready whenever you say."

"Fine. We'll meet you at the landing pad out front, in one hour. That will give us time to be at the space port ready to take off just before Midday."

Lef turned back while Scortzi and Dulsena continued on. They'd only gone a short way when they saw Henri Dakkon rushing towards them.

"Interesting development, Scortzi," Henri said as he handed him the latest FIS report. He nodded to Dulsena and, smiling, said, "I think we've had a bit of luck on that Schwecker abduction. Let's find a place to sit down and I'll tell you what we've got."

He guided them into one of the small patio gardens that dotted the building. There they found comfortable seats tucked away under some exotic tree ferns. The air was warm and soft and filled with the scent of flowers. A small waterfall splashed down into a little creek that babbled and gurgled over moss covered rocks.

Such a comfortable, safe place to be discussing such a dreadful crime as kidnapping a woman and her child from their home, Dulsena thought. Her reverie was interrupted by Henri excitedly saying, "A records check of all persons leaving Dornace in the hours following Aldris Schwecker's abduction show that she and her son boarded a flight to Flornak. An attendant remembered that she had appeared ill and the boy frightened. The flight attendant assumed that it was because they hadn't been off-world before, so she tried to put them at ease. She said there was a man on the same flight who appeared to be helping them. She said she didn't know if the man was traveling with them or was just a good Samaritan type. Anyway, she was busy and he seemed willing to help so she'd left them to tend to the other passengers.

"Did the attendant mention seeing anything that would indicate the man was coercing the woman in any way?" Scortzi asked.

"She said not. He just seemed to be assisting them. But of course the guy could have told the Schwecker woman that if she caused him any trouble he would do something to the boy. He might even have told her they had her daughter and if she didn't cooperate she, the daughter, that is, would be hurt, or worse.

"Now, about this man," Henri added. "A routine security check of the persons on that flight flagged a Narig Velson, whose description, by the way, fits the one the attendant gave us. Seems that Velson has, at various times in the past, been brought in for questioning in a number of cases, but has never been charged. Now note this; he had flown into Dornace only the day before. That seems like a long trip for such a short stay.

"There's one other interesting thing the search turned up," Henri said, as he referred to his notes. "Checking Velson's record, they found that he had been on Greniff at the time of the rebellion. In fact, he'd been picked up on suspicion of complicity. However, no charges were filed and he was released. The fact that he was there at that time could be significant and then again maybe not.

"On Flornak, a computer check of Rocallon City services shows that Narig Velson used his card on the public transport from the airport to a stop near his assigned quarters. Certainly to be expected. But," he paused and looked at them, "Aldrys Schwecker and her son used their guest registry identification cards for the same trip."

"Ahhh," Scortzi said.

"Ahhh, indeed. The police also thought that seemed like too much of a coincidence. They're watching Velson's quarters and, maybe, just maybe, we'll get lucky.

"About your idea on the source of the arms," he continued, "Chanceller Bohrnach has filed an official inquiry with the Huilla League. However, as you may know, the Huilla are having problems of their own and aren't terribly interested in minor complaints involving systems on the fringes of their jurisdiction. We received a standard reply of shocked concern at the idea that there might be some illicit manufacture and trading going on, but frankly, I would be very surprised if they are concerned enough to pull any forces away from Fed Center and send them that far from Federation Headquarters and their immediate problems."

"They don't consider manufacturing military weapons and ships as important?" Dulsena asked.

"Not to the Huilla," Henri answered. "There's always been a lot of turmoil there. The concept of a Federation of Worlds is a new one for them. Each world is still very jealous of it's autonomy and finds it difficult to abrogate any power over its affairs to a League. As I understand it, there are even some worlds that are so backward they still have a multiplicity of governing bodies, each working independently. With no strong world government they have problems even finding Council Representatives who are acceptable to all the factions. In many of the regions, disputes frequently get out of hand and end up in open, bloody warfare. So, it's easy to see why the manufacture of war materiel is a thriving business. It's almost certain, that if they found a market over in the Algoran Federation they would have no qualms about passing through a boundary that some Federation has established."

"Without their help in patrolling the boundaries it will be difficult to find out who's involved," Scortzi said. "Schwecker said they wanted him to 'pick up cargo, en route, somewhere out beyond Frayleen'. That's not enough to go on. There's a lot of space out there to get lost in."

"That's true," Henri agreed. "But you yourself pointed out that Brenev had bought arms from Krolinoor for his uprising. The people on that world have always had a reputation for living on the edge of the law. If arms and war ships are being manufactured anywhere you can bet the Krogtlils are in on it somehow. Brenev dealt with them before and it would be logical to assume that he would do so again. We have some agents there, but it's hard to get any information. Those folks don't take kindly to people asking questions about their business. Especially not strangers."

Dulsena spoke up at this moment and said, "This suspicion that the man who abducted Aldrys Schwecker and her son might also be involved with Nayland and the conspiracy is disturbing to me. In his testimony, Schwecker said he carried too many crystals for all of them to have come from Resdorn. He believes that someone has found another source. He says he doesn't know where the source is, but, he was dropping supplies and picking up cargo at Felchor and Port Boragi on Flornak and dropping them at other stops on his usual route. Anyway, when he decides he wants out and tells Carradyne he won't make those runs any more, his wife and son are abducted by a man who may have ties to Nayland Brenev.

"At the same time, someone or some group is pilfering crystals from the Windswept Mine on Resdorn and arranging for them to be picked up by a robot who escapes off world. When the police check the ship at the next stop, the robot escapes detection by wearing a Baluki body skin.

"It would seem that the pilferage at the mine, the marketing of proscribed crystals and the abduction of Aldrys Schwecker are all connected. Then there's this business of smuggling in weapons. I think what we're seeing here are bits and pieces of a very complicated and very expensive plot. Baluki body skins and buying and transporting arms from the Huilla League don't come cheap, you know."

"Well, I don't think there's any doubt who's behind it all," Scortzi said. "It smells of Nayland Brenev; it's the way he thinks."

"I just don't understand it," said Henri. "So he needed a way to make money to buy weapons for some coup he is planning. There are a lot better ways of making fast money than shipping proscribed crystals. Especially when you consider all the curing facilities and whatever that's needed. And then he still has to find a market for them. So why choose crystals?"

"Revenge," Scortzi and Dulsena said, almost in unison. "Nayland Brenev hates me and my family," Dulsena explained. "He blames me for the failure of his plan to overthrow the Federation, for his family being either in prison or re-programmed, and for the Federation giving me Brenev Industries, which is now Kal-Van. He's had 10 years for his hatred to build. I think, when he found out about another mine with inferior, but exploitable, crystals, he immediately saw a way to get his money and his revenge at the same time."

"Yes, that fits," Scortzi said. "With the monopoly on crystals broken the whole economy of Resdorn would be all but destroyed, and the Houses of Kalleni and Kal-Van along with it."

"As for the problems involved with the curing process," Dulsena said thoughtfully, "Maybe he isn't involved with that directly. Think. Who else do we know would benefit from the distribution of these crystals?"

"The Black Knights!" Scortzi and Henri said, in unison."

"Sure, that's why we have black crystals turning up all over," Scortzi said. "It's just as Gutorm surmised. They're in it together."

"Brenev must have taken his idea to the Black Knight and the two are using each other to accomplish their goals," Dulsena added.

"I doubt that Brenev told the BKs about his plan for a new coup," Henri said. "He probably presented it as a straight business proposition on his part. Wanting what he had for sale, they went along."

"A simultaneous uprising of the Black Knights would also be a strong advantage to his scheme," Scortzi said. "It would give him far more manpower than he ever could find on his own. He probably plans that once the Federation is ousted he will move in with his own professional, elite squads to secure his position. He might even think he could then get rid of the Black Knights."

"Ooh, after seeing that crowd at Maashout," Dulsena said, shaking her head, "I wouldn't bet on that. But, who knows what Nayland thinks? In any case he would get the dictatorial powers he has wanted all along and revenge on the Kallenis as well. "I keep remembering that huge crowd at the tabernacle, and those upraised fists, and that chanting. There's an awful lot of power there. It's scary. I'm afraid that putting those two forces together they just might succeed."

"You forget we have one advantage, Dulsena," Henri put in. "We have found out about his plan before he could put it in effect. He rose and, gathering the printouts together, said, "As soon as the President gets this information he's sure to call the council together for an emergency meeting. Would you two please come in as advisors? There are new members on the Council who weren't in office during the uprising. Your knowledge of the crystal culture and your insights on Nayland Brenev may be helpful to them."

Dulsena and Scortzi both shook their heads. At Henri's disappointed look Scortzi added, "All right, Henri, if you feel strongly that it would help, we will," Scortzi said, "but we both really need to get back." And take what precautions we can to protect our families and businesses, he added to himself. He'd seen enough of Nayland Brenev's insane hatred to know that no Kalleni would be safe until he was caught.

"We told Gradun we would be leaving just before Midday," Dulsena said.

"If I get to the President right away," Henri said, "he should be able to convene a quorum by first hour before Chimes. Once in session, it won't take long for me to explain what we've come up with. Then you can answer any questions the delegates might have and leave."

Scortzi looked at Dulsena and asked, "What do you think, Dulcy?"

"All right," Dulsena answered. "We've come too far to stop now. We'll stay long enough to try and answer their questions."

"Good," Henri said. "I'll let you know when we can get everyone together and then send an escort to bring you to the Grand Hall."

He started to leave and then turned back to face them. "I hope you both understand how much we appreciate all you have done. If you hadn't brought this to our attention, I'm afraid we might not have caught it in time. Now, we'll be ready to cope with these maniacs when they do make their move. Thank you."

He made a formal ceremonial bow then turned and hurried off towards the President's office.

"Ready to cope," Dulsena said softly, "I hope so. But, I'm afraid they're underestimating Nayland Brenev."

"Not to mention the Black Knights," Scortzi added. He put his arm around Dulsena and said, "All right, little sister, let's go get packed and I'll tell Lef and Asa we'll be a little later than we planned." I hope we can still make our lift-off time. "Asa usually schedules adequate turnaround time."

- 22 -
Each to His Task

Narig Velson watched the Vid-Com screen fade to black. So, he thought, the Captain had bolted, leaving the little wife behind. Strange, that. Left his son, too. That was a bad thing for him to do. He thought about that and he hated this captain he had never met. His own father had gone off and left him when he was real little. Left him and his mother all alone there on Greniff. In all the years since, he'd never forgiven him. It was wrong for a man to leave his son, especially when someone might hurt him.

Velson was a simple man. Most of the time he did what he was paid to do and never thought of the right or wrong of it. Now he stood there thinking. He had been paid to grab the Schwecker woman and her children. Well he hadn't gotten the daughter, but he did have the woman and her son. He would be paid some more when he was finished with them. He didn't mind too much about the woman, but he was feeling kinda bad about the boy. A son shouldn't have to be hurt just because the father was no good. But, he knew Nayland Brenev. He'd done jobs for him before. Now this Georgg guy said Brenev wanted him to pick them up and maybe kill them if he got the word. He didn't like Georgg. He was always toadying around Brenev. He didn't like Brenev either. He could be really mean and nasty. But, he paid a lot. He stood staring at the dark screen. He chewed on a hangnail and thought about Nayland Brenev and his money and about the boy. Finally, he moved around the room gathering up a few things which he put in a satchel. Then, he let himself out and walked down the dark, dingy hallway. It wasn't right, he thought. It just wasn't right.

* * *

Velson wasn't the only one who didn't like Nayland Brenev and Georgg. After Enferdeem Swadi had counted his money and swept out the door, Marridon, his nose pinched and his mouth turned down, looked at Derrachem and shivered. "That is a hate-filled man," he said with distaste. He hitched his cloak back from his shoulder, shaking the folds free as he did so. It was as if he were trying to rid himself of any residue of Swadi that might still be lingering in the room.

"Nayland Brenev and his co-horts do seem to attract the most unsavory people on any world," Derrachem agreed.

"I don't like having to associate with such rabble," Marridon said, sniffing. "I'll be glad when we can do without them entirely."

"Yes, I agree," Derrachem said. "It's really unfortunate that Swadi had problems getting away from Resdorn. That source is lost now and we could have used some more of the real Resdorn crystals for the tabernacles. So many of the Felchor crystals are such poor quality."

"Well, if all goes well we soon will have control of the mines and curing facilities on Resdorn and we'll have all we need," Marridon said, seating himself at his desk.

"I wonder," Derrachem said pensively, "if our people in the mines were able to get away."

"I hope so," Marridon said. "However, if they were not that fortunate, they have their instructions. They have sworn they are prepared to accept martyrdom before allowing themselves to be taken into the interrogation booth."

Marridon activated his screen and called up a file. "Now let's get on with this. We have more to worry about than just crystals. The time has arrived. The battle cry will soon go forth.

"The report from Fa'lel on Greniff?"

Derrachem checked his records and said, "82 Divisions, 790 Units reported ready."

"Soloving?"

"Sixty Divisions, 570 Units reported ready, but need additional communicators to coordinate with Brenev's troops."

"Pass that back to Brenev. Chaldorn?"

On down the list they worked numbering the faithful, the followers of the Black Knight ready to march against the foe in this holy war.

* * *

Back on peaceful Aldene, Scortzi stood in front of the Algoran Council Administration Building and watched as the terrace floor opened up and their flyer rose from the depths of the underground hanger below. Dulsena arrived just then and said, "Scortzi, guess who I found calling for a flight back to the space port; Katje and her mother. I hope you don't mind, I offered them a ride in your ship."

Scortzi swung around and saw Katje and Sophronia standing back a few paces. He smiled and said, "I'd be delighted to have the company of two beautiful ladies even for such a short trip."

Seeing Katje glance over his shoulder he turned red faced and stammered, "Three, three beautiful ladies. Excuse me, Dulsena."

The three 'beautiful ladies' laughed at his discomfiture and Dulsena, moving forward, smiled and patted his arm. "That's all right, Scortzi, I realize I'm just a little sister. Come Sophronia, Katje, we'd better get in. Lef's anxious to leave."

Once aboard, Derek and Asa stretched out and went to sleep. Gradun and Lef were up front with the pilots. The rest were in comfortable lounge seats.

The flight back to Belnoir seemed too short for Scortzi and Katje who sat, heads together, looking out at the beautiful countryside. Katje turned her head slightly and laughingly made some comment to Scortzi. Watching from a seat behind them, Dulsena caught her breath. How like Mother she looked just then, she thought. Funny, I hadn't noticed that before.

Sophronia, watching the three of them, wondered how serious this infatuation of Katje's would prove to be. The young Kalleni certainly seemed smitten and the check she'd had made on his background indicated he was a person of integrity from a good, well respected family. Bright and personable, obviously. But, was he also strong and patient enough to cope with Katje. Then again, his sister, like Katje, seemed to have a mind of her own and it was easy to see she and Scortzi got along well.

Her thoughts were interrupted by Dulsena asking, "You surely aren't planning to go back to Soloving are you, Sophronia?"

"Oh no," Sophronia responded, "that would be very unwise. My brother is a professor at a small university and he explained my situation to the head of his department. They were kind enough to offer me a position as guest lecturer."

"They were thrilled with the idea of having you," Katje put in, looking back over her shoulder. "And they should be. She's THE expert on Solvangian pottery from the Porvassic Period. A little University like Saronia is…"

"Saronia? at Cuomari on Resdorn?" Scortzi asked excitedly.

"Yes," Sophronia said, "I was just telling Dul…"

"Saronia!" Scortzi interrupted, "Why that's wonderful. That's not far from Weneche. Why didn't you tell me, Katje?"

Sophronia just shook her head and smiled at his enthusiasm.

"Not far at all," Dulsena put in dryly. "What's four or five thousand kilometers?"

"Right," Scortzi agreed, smiling at Katje. "I could visit you at Cuomari or you could come to Weneche. Everyone comes to Weneche. You could meet my mother and father."

He was still beaming happily at Belnoir Spaceport, as they picked up Asa and headed for the ship, "Bright Star." The Merchant Kalleni thought everything was working out just fine.

Dulsena laughed and then asked Sophronia, "what time is your flight?"

Sophronia shook her head and said, "what flight? We had to stay longer than we planned on Aldene, and lost our reservations, so we will have to find another."

"Oh", said Scortzi, "I'm sure Asa can work out something."

The Kalleni name opened a lot of doors and options. Sophronia and Katje would continue on with Scortzi and Asa. Four more days of Katje's company suited Scortzi just fine.

After brief goodbyes, Dulsena and Derek were anxious to get home to the children, and hurried after Gradun to their flyer. Kol-Van, with all its holiday problems was waiting

- 23 -
Bright Star Home

Bright Star made a smooth lift off and soon the webs were released and the window covers raised. Scortzi left Sophronia and Katje enjoying the starry view from the first level lounge and made his way towards his suite of rooms. Most of the loose ends of this trip had been, or shortly would be, tied up.

Rolf Blenton had, courtesy of Lisbet Bohrnach, made a swift and secret return to Resdorn from Aldene and Lef, despite his objections, had been sent back with him. Blenton had then made a deliberately obvious return trip to Soloving. He was back at work apparently with no one the wiser as to his real reason for going to Resdorn.

Back on Resdorn, according to mine security agent Briggs, they had identified the people on each shift who were responsible for the pilferage. They were ready to move, in concert with the FIS, as soon as they received word from Lisbet. More than likely, that would happen before he arrived at Weneche. As for finding the source of the inferior crystals, that was a job for FIS. Scortzi felt he had done what he could. He needed to get back to work. With what Captains Brillig and Schwecker could tell them, they would soon be able to take care of Nayland Brenev and whoever else was involved in this uprising.

Captain Schwecker especially should be pleased to cooperate. Agents on Flornak had picked up a man who had quite readily told them where the Schwecker boy and his mother were hidden. He had also told them a long involved, completely implausible tale about how it was he who had rescued them from Nayland Brenev and now needed protection from him.

Now, as Scortzi approached his suite, all the activities of the last few days seemed to recede and once again his thoughts were centered on the reports Asa would have waiting for him. People soon would be celebrating the holidays, but he and the rest of the staff of House of Kalleni were already working on previews and sales campaigns for eight cycles from now. No more time spent on secret intrigues, he told himself. It was back to being Merchant Kalleni doing all the endless things one dealt with in a large, multi-world business.

Back in his suite, he and Asa weren't even through the first spool when the ship gave a great shudder and alarm klaxons wailed. Window covers slid into place and a voice kept warning them to take their seats and fasten all webbing. Scortzi's first impulse was to go back to the lounge where he'd left Katje, but just then another great shudder passed through the ship.

Never in all the trips Scortzi had taken off world had he ever been on a ship where there had been an emergency. There had been incidents years ago, but nowadays the technology was so advanced that people had become complacent about traveling over great distances. The only thing he could imagine was that they had been hit by a meteorite or some such thing.

The deafening klaxon ceased suddenly and the silence was broken by a voice identifying itself as the captain. The ship had experienced some mechanical difficulties," the Captain said, "however there was no danger. Everyone please keep calm and stay in their seats until repairs could be affected." He went on to assure them they would be kept informed.

"Well," Asa said in the sudden quiet, "mechanical difficulties, indeed."

"Yes," Scortzi said in a skeptical voice. "Well I guess we might as well go ahead and work."

"Yes," Asa said, releasing his webbing and rising, "I have those figures on the weaver's estimates over here somewh…" the ship gave another lurch, flinging him violently against the bulkhead. Scortzi, still seated though not webbed in, rode his chair to a jarring stop against the same bulkhead, getting a fierce whap on the back of his head in the process. Dazed, he turned his head and saw Asa lying off to his left, apparently unconscious from his fall.

Scortzi struggled to get up, but the deck now slanted upwards at about a 45 degree angle and his chair was lying halfway on its back. Finally, by rolling over onto his hands and knees, he managed to get to his feet. His head was still swimming and before he could regain his balance a fourth, even more powerful explosion, flung him backwards into, and half over, the table, which had been securely bolted to the deck. That table was now the only stationary object in a room full of flying papers, record spools and various objet d'art. Yet another lurch sent Scortzi sliding back off the table and down to a sitting position.

The loud klaxon, which had resumed its whooping after the third explosion, ceased. In the semi-silence that followed, Scortzi could hear nothing but the ringing in his own head.

Sitting legs astraddle on the sloping deck, he watched dazedly as a record spool vibrated from its temporary landing place and rolled down to rest near Roger's head. Oh God! Asa! He scrambled on his hands and knees towards Asa, who lay there so quietly, with his head at an awkward angle

"Asa," he whispered. "Oh, Asa." Desperately he tried to find a pulse. He couldn't seem to find it. He tried to straighten the body, wildly thinking if he could only get him straight he would be able to breath better and be all right. Panting with the exertion, trying to keep his balance on the tilting deck, he pulled Roger's body around. Again he searched for a pulse. In the neck. In the wrist. There was none. Kneeling at Roger's side, he finally realized he wouldn't find one.

As the sounds of his own ragged breathing calmed, he become more aware of noises in the corridor. Katje! He'd left her and her mother in the lounge after the takeoff. He had to get to her. Just then the klaxon sounded again and the ship, giving another lurch, slowly righted itself.

Getting to his feet he staggered to the door and palmed the opener.

Nothing. He hit it again, harder. The door creaked and slid open a few centimeters and then stopped. He grasped the edge with both hands and pulled with all his might but it only grated open a few more centimeters. He heard someone running down the corridor and yelled for help. Part of a face appeared in the open crack and then another pair of hands grasped the edge.

"On three, pull," a voice said. "One, two, three!" Nothing.

"Again," Scortzi yelled.

This time the door slid the rest of the way.

"Thanks," he told his rescuer.

"Sure," the man, who wore a uniform and flight engineer insignia said hurriedly. "Anyone else in there?"

"My secretary. He's dead."

"Sorry," the man said as he started jogging off down the corridor.

"Hey! Hold up, what's happened," Scortzi yelled, racing after him. "Did we get hit by a meteor or something?"

"We've been told not to say anything. The captain will be making an announcement soon."

"Well you must have some ideas about it," Scortzi persisted.

"I have an IDEA we have some serious damage. I KNOW we have some people who have been injured. Know anything about emergency medical aid?"

"I've had some training."

"Well then, if you want to help, see what you can do for those who are injured. This is a liner, Narm-be-burned, not a Fed warship. We only carry fifteen Robo MedTecs and one supervising Physician. Now we've got dead and injured all over the ship, and they'll need all the help they can get."

They'd reached the door to the lounge and the Engineer stopped suddenly, put his arm in front of Scortzi to stop him, and said, "People are scared. Do what you can to keep them calm. We have enough problems without having people panicking. Tell them we're in no immediate danger and that the Captain will make an announcement as soon as he can."

Scortzi nodded and they walked into what only an hour before had been a beautiful observation lounge. Now it was a shambles: tables and chairs overturned, art objects and glassware flung about. People with various injuries were being assisted by others who, although still on their feet, seemed dazed and disoriented.

A woman clutching a bloody cloth rushed towards the Engineer. "Where are the Med-Tecs," she cried. There are people injured here. We need some help!"

"We'll get help up here as soon as we can," the Engineer assured her. In the meantime Master uhm…"

"Kalleni," Scortzi said.

"Yes, Master Kalleni here will help you."

"Are you a doctor?" she demanded of Scortzi.

"No, I'm not, but let's see what we can do to make these people a little more comfortable, shall we Madame…?."

"Keruth, Elmay Keruth. I was on my way to see my daughter and her family on Resdorn," she added distractedly.

"Well, Madame Keruth," said the Engineer, "I'll leave you and Master Kalleni to do what you can here." He raised his voice to get everyone's attention and said, "We want all of you to stay here in the lounge until…"

"Sir, my wife," interrupted an older man with a large bump on his head, "my wife is in our cabin I've got to find out if she's all right."

"I'll get someone to check all level one cabins immediately, Sir. Don't worry. We will check all the cabins and get back to you. It may take a little time, so please be patient and stay here in the lounge. We'll do the best we can."

"We want to know what's going on!" another man yelled.

"I'm sure the Captain will be making an announcement very soon."

As the Engineer headed out of the lounge, Elmay Keruth shouted after him, "Announcements are fine, but we need some MedTecs."

"Well, let's see what we can do here," Scortzi said. In a loud voice he said, "Is there a Physician here?" No response.

"Anyone with emergency aid training?"

A few hands showed and two people moved forward. To Elmay he said, "Show us the ones you think are the most seriously injured. We'll start there."

"There are two ladies over here," she said over her shoulder as she headed over to one side, "who were helping a man who looked real bad. The lady who was next to me has a cut on her head and was bleeding badly. That's where all this came from," she said waving the bloody cloth. She was heading for a small group gathered around someone lying on the deck.

Scortzi had been looking for Katje and was relieved now to see she and her mother were the ones who were helping the injured man.

"No MedTecs, but that officer said this man could help," Elmay Keruth said to them as they came up. The only one who looked like they believed this was Katje.

"Well," Scortzi said after checking the injured man, "This man obviously needs more expert medical attention than we can give him. You two do what you can. I'll go and try to find a MedTec."

"And get some Robos in here to clean up this mess," someone else said.

"Yes, where are all the Robos? This is disgraceful!" another one shouted.

"Don't worry about clean up," Elmay said softly to Scortzi, "get a physician. This man won't make it if he doesn't get help fast. As for the others, we'll do what we can until the MedTecs get here."

As Scortzi hurried out a voice came over the loudspeaker asking everyone to pay attention as the Captain would now make an announcement.

Everyone listened intently as a deep, resonant voice said, "This is Captain Shonjik. As you all know we have experienced some problems. There has been a series of explosions and the ship has sustained some damage…"

"Do tell," Elmay said in a scornful stage whisper.

The Captain continued, "…but we expect to facilitate repairs and be able to land safely. If everyone will stay calm we will have you back at Rohnseff Spaceport as soon as possible. I will keep you informed of our progress. In the meantime, please be patient and assist the crew as much as you can. Thank you."

This brief announcement, meant to be reassuring, didn't answer any questions and left the passengers irritated and frightened. When, a few minutes later, a grim looking Scortzi returned with only one Robo and one MedTec, their anger was directed at him. "Is this all the help you could find?" someone snapped.

"Hold it," Scortzi yelled, "I was lucky to get this one so let him get to work and then I'll explain."

Elmay took the Tec in charge and led him over to where Sophronia was tending the injured man, while Scortzi faced the angry group that crowded around him.

"The crew has been instructed not to talk, but from the bits and pieces of information I could gather it would seem that the first explosion was in or near the engine room. The others were in the Crew and Tecs quarters and near where the robos were housed. A number of off-duty crewmen were killed or injured and a good many of the MedTecs and Robos destroyed or damaged. The infirmary was also badly damaged and the supervising physician and his staff seriously injured. The few MedTecs that are left are trying to cope with all the severely injured down on Level Three. Problem is, with the Infirmary damaged, supplies and equipment are limited so they're working from Emergency Kits. The few Robos that are left are helping make structural repairs so we can get back to Greniff. From the looks of the rest of the ship, we're lucky to be here. This lounge is one of the least damaged areas. It looks like we're just going to have to take care of ourselves for awhile."

Into the shocked silence following this announcement, the voice of Madame Keruth rose loud and clear. "All right, if that's the way it is let's get moving. All who have injuries come over here where the MedTec can see you. The rest of you help get this place in order."

Looking at the Robo, she said, "You get hot soup and drinks for the wounded and after that find something to eat and drink for everyone else.

It was soon obvious that Elmay Keruth and Sophronia Carradyne were efficient organizers who didn't need Master Kalleni to tell them how to get things done.

The MedTec and Elmay were helping the more seriously injured, trying to stabilize them for transport to a temporary infirmary on level three. Those with minor injuries were tended to by Sophronia, Katje and others and made as comfortable as possible. By the time the Captain made his second announcement, confirming most of what Scortzi had said, those who were able had managed to straighten up the lounge and were helping the Robo serve what would have to pass for luncheon.

Meanwhile, Scortzi, in response to the pleas of the man who was worried about his wife, went back into the corridor near his suite. He tagged a Steward and talked him into checking the man's cabin. There they found her, a little lady with bright blue eyes sitting very straight in her chair, webbed in and clutching her satchel in her lap.

They walked in and the first words she said were, "Why are you boys out walking around? The Captain said to stay in your seats."

It took a while to convince her it was all right to release her webbing and come with them. Finally, indignantly shaking off their attempts to assist her, she got up and, clutching her satchel in front of her, marched out of the cabin and down the corridor towards the lounge. The two "boys" laughed and the Steward whispered, "I learned a long time ago that when it comes to little old grandmas it's just easier to let them have their way."

He gave Scortzi a brief salute and went off to check the rest of the cabins while Scortzi hurried to follow the lady making her way back to the lounge. He thought it was more than likely Sophronia and Elmay would now have help in running things.

- 24 -
At Any Cost

Many hours later, in the pale light of the waning moons, the Bright Star once again slid into dock at Rohnseff Spaceport on Greniff, this time at a servicing area, away from the regular terminal. Captain Rhys Xholan, Spaceport Officer, supervised the docking personally. Anxious friends and family members, faces gaunt with worry, waited silently behind temporary barricades for the injured to be grav-lifted to the lines of medical personnel waiting to one side. Port personnel escorted weary passengers, past the Medvans, through throngs of media people, to the flyers that were to take them to temporary lodging until new bookings could be arranged.

Scortzi had watched until all the injured were removed before accompanying Asa's body to one of the transports which would take it, with all other victims, to a temporary morgue that had been set up in one of the large service areas.

His mind felt dull and heavy. Asa Rogers was dead. Impossible. He kept going over and over those last moments. If Asa hadn't loosened his webbing. If he'd been here...If he'd done that...But he hadn't and now Asa was dead. He couldn't imagine working without Asa. For years he'd always been right there, anticipating what he needed, taking care of all the details.

When he had gone to his cabin to pack up his things before landing, he'd been struck anew at how much Asa had done for him. How much he had counted on his being there. In with Asa's personal effects there had been a picture of his father. "Oh Lord," he had whispered, "how can I tell him of his only son's death."

Now, standing by Captain Xholan's private flyer, watching the sad exodus from the Bright Star, he had an eerie feeling between his shoulder blades. The sort of feeling you get when you know you're being watched. He glanced around, but couldn't see anything; the lights flooding the area made dark caves of the surrounding hangers.

Unseen by Scortzi, a man in a worker's jumper, watched from well back in one of these "caves". He saw Scortzi. Saw the tall, handsome man with his pleated kaiton and shiny little cornucopia pin. "You lead a charmed life, Master Kalleni, you do indeed," he said softly to himself as he drifted back into the black shadows.

Rhys Xholan was an old friend of Rimini Kalleni's and had been a great help to them when Dulsena made her escape from her husband Loran Brenev and his brother, Nayland, during the uprising. Since then, Scortzi had made it a point to visit him whenever he was on Greniff. Now, as the captain made his way towards him, Scortzi could see how drawn and haggard he looked. He was obviously deeply troubled. The handshake confirmed it; "danger" the ocam signs said into Scortzi's palm. "Danger" said the fingers on his back as Xholan outwardly greeted him as an old comrade. "Wait" said the fingers on his knee as the flyer took them to the administration building. Not until they were in Xholan's private office, safely in the confi-unit, could the danger be given a name.

"Nayland Brenev," Scortzi said, "I'm not surprised."

"Nor I," Rhys Xholan responded,"but, I must admit, I had hoped that we'd heard the last of him." He loosened his uniform vest, gave a great sigh and then continued. "When one of Gutorm's men, a man named Kretz, came to me last week to warn me about Brenev, all the memories of that terrible time came flooding back. Narm! It's a bloody shame we didn't catch that devil along with the rest of his family," he said heatedly. "The man is a cancer in the body of society. He spreads corruption and dissension wherever he goes."

"Isn't that the truth," Scortzi agreed, "it would have saved all of us a lot of trouble if we could have sent him off to be re-programmed."

"Hunh!" Rhys blurted out, "Probably would have burned out the circuits trying to reprogram that bit of garbage!"

Scortzi laughed and said, "You're probably right. Kind of nice to imagine it though, isn't it? Little sparks coming off his hair, toes curling up, guys in white coats saying, 'more power, more power'."

They both laughed at that thought then Scortzi said, "Well maybe someday. Now, how about this man of Gutorm's, what did he have to say?"

"Said he'd been assigned to infiltrate Brenev's cell here. Seems that the "local boy" still has a lot of people who sympathize with him and his family. By the way, after I'd talked to this man I immediately talked to the Governor. He told me he'd just received a message from Fed Com about the B.K.'s working in league with Brenev. It all confirmed what Kretz had said. Seems things are coming right down to the wire and they expect trouble over the Holiday."

"It's outrageous that they would disturb the most holy days of the year," Scortzi said, indignantly.

"Well, that was one of the things Kretz was most adamant about. It would start over the holidays. Exactly when he couldn't say. Only the leaders know that. He just knew that the men had been put on alert and told to be ready for a call."

"Why did he come to you?" Scortzi asked.

"Gutorm. He'd told him to come to me if there was a threat to Dulsena. Seems Gutorm anticipated that Brenev would come after her and he knew I was her friend and possibly in a position to help her.

Rhys's voice changed and he became very serious. "It's not just Dulsena he's threatened, Scortzi. Kretz said all your family has been targeted. Viewed with that in mind, doesn't it seem a bit coincidental that the first liner accident in years was on your flight to Resdorn. Strange that it was serious enough so you had to come back here to Greniff?"

"Oh Rhys, that seems a bit paranoid. There were hundreds of passengers on that ship."

"They weren't interested in the rest of them. Just you."

Scortzi sat back in his chair and, meeting the steady gaze of his friend, said, "Rhys, are you saying you seriously think that Brenev arranged that accident just to get back at me?"

"I'm saying I think it's something to bc considered."

There was silence following this until Scortzi said quietly, "There were two others on that liner who may have been targets, too."

"Oh? Who?" Rhys asked.

"Sophronia Carradyne and her daughter Katje."

Scortzi told Rhys about their fleeing from Soloving to Aldene and how their testimony helped implicate Arnhalt Carradyne and his friends in the conspiracy between the B.K.s and Brenev.

"If the B.K.s knew they were on board that ship it's reasonable to suppose they would try to get to them, too. Other people who turned informants were condemned as heretics or traitors and were killed.

"Rhys," he added "Katje is...Katje is very important to me."

Rhys sensing Scortzi's distress, reached for the VidCom but it buzzed before he could reach it. At his response, a guard reported that the Merchants Kalleni and Donovan wished to see him.

"Dulcy and Derek here!" Scortzi blurted out. "What are they doing here?"

Captain Xholan told the guard to direct them to his office and then transfer his call to the security chief. The chief appeared on screen and Rhys arranged for protection for Sophronia and Katje. This done he rose to welcome Dulsena and Derek before turning to Scortzi and saying, "To answer your question, Dulsena and Derek probably are here because the media has been flooded with news about the Bright Star ever since it happened. Undoubtedly, they were concerned about you."

"Of course we were worried about you, you dolt!" Dulsena confirmed as she walked in the door. We've been glued to the News Vu Screen for hours. When we heard you had landed back here we got right in the flyer and came to take you back to the compound. At least now you can spend the holidays with us," she finished brightly.

"Yes, Dulcy, that's one good thing," Scortzi said. Then turning serious, he added, "Dulcy, Derek, Rhys thinks that maybe the accident on the liner was a plot to get to me. I suggested that it might have been directed at Sophronia and Katje, too. He...But wait," he stopped himself, "wait, there's something wrong with that idea, Rhys. They would know we would be on First Level and yet that was the least damaged area. The explosions were all near the engine room and on Third Level."

You're right, Scortzi," Rhys said, "that doesn't make sense."

"Unless," Scortzi said slowly, "unless that 'accident' didn't happen when it was supposed to."

At their surprised looks he asked, "Do you remember what happened just before we were to take off?"

"There was a delay," Dulsena answered slowly.

"Exactly," Scortzi agreed.

"That woman from Polchar who insisted that her pet, whatever it was, travel with her," Dulsena added.

"Yes, we were about 7 minutes late taking off because of that," Scortzi said. "If we had been on schedule the explosions would have occurred just as we were going hyper. If that had happened it wouldn't have mattered which level we were on, there wouldn't have been any survivors."

They stared at him, the shock clear on their faces.

"Wait a minute," Derek said, "Dulcy, didn't you say that Sophronia and Katje changed their plans at the last minute so they could travel with you and Scortzi?"

"Yes, that's right! They couldn't have known that they were going to be with you."

"They changed their plans?" Rhys asked sharply.

"Yes," Dulsena answered, "Scortzi suggested they travel with us and, of course, Katje agreed that was a great idea. Why, Rhys? What are you thinking?"

"The Al-Luz," Rhys said cryptically, looking at Dulsena and Derek.

"What are you talking about?" Scortzi asked sharply. "What about the Al-Luz?"

"That was the liner Sophronia and Katje were originally booked on," Dulsena answered. "It's lost. Its last communication was just before it was to go hyper and it hasn't been heard from since."

They sat in shocked silence as the implication of this train of thought sunk in; Bright Star and Al-Luz. Then Scortzi shouted, "Those Krolargitz!" He leapt from his chair and strode to the window. Looking blindly out he pounded his fist against the wall beating out each word. "Those filthy Krolargitz! Asa, all those other innocent people killed because Nayland Brenev wants someone out of the way! Because Nayland Brenev orders it!"

Scortzi couldn't seem to get enough air. Each great ragged breath grated in the silence. With effort he finally calmed himself and then turning to face them, said, "Dulcy, Derek, there's something else that has happened and I think you should hear what Rhys has to say."

Rhys told them about Kretz and what he'd said about the Kallenis being targets. Dulsena was horrified.

"All the Kallenis?" she whispered. Mother, Father and the children. Oh Blessed Lord, NO!" She jumped to her feet, "Derek the children! We left them at the compound, with Marit!" She looked frantically at Scortzi and Rhys.

"I don't think they will have done anything just yet, Dulsena," Rhys said. "I don't believe they will make a move against your home or family until they are ready to implement their plans elsewhere. However, I do think it would be a good idea to have extra security people on duty."

"They already tried to kill Scortzi!" Dulsena shouted. "Why not me, too? Or the children? Nayland Brenev has a lot more against me than against Scortzi."

"An attack on a liner could be made to look like an accident," Scortzi said, "A deliberate attack against private property and individuals right here on Greniff couldn't be so easily explained. No, I agree with Rhys. He'll wait until they are ready to move elsewhere."

Dulsena, very agitated, pushed herself up from her chair and walked over to join Scortzi at the window. She stared out at the spaceport below. "Would it help for us to take the children and go to Resdorn?" she asked.

"I don't know, Dulcy, maybe, but..., I don't know. He has agents everywhere," Scortzi answered.

Derek got up and, moving to Dulsena's side, put his arms around her. "Gradun is with them and we will put on extra security people, like Rhys suggested. It will be ok. Remember, we have the advantage of knowing ahead of time so we won't be caught by surprise. It'll be all right."

Dulsena, stiff and unresponsive, closed her eyes as if in pain, thinking of the last time the compound had been under siege and the bloodshed that had followed. "I don't want them at the compound," she said firmly.

"Then we'll find some place you think is safer," Derek said. "There must be some place."

The flight back to the compound was short but to Dulsena it seemed to take ages. She watched as the countryside below took shape in the pale dawn and thought of another flight over this route. A flight that had ended in the deaths of two men and a mad scramble through the forest to save her own life. Derek squeezed her hand as if he too were remembering those days.

She smiled at him and said, "Do you remember that creekbed and the sneltzen trees?"

"I'll never forget," he answered. "Even with mud all over your face, you were the prettiest thing I'd ever seen. Certainly the feistiest."

"And you just about killed me off running me all over the countryside in those horrible, wet shoes," she laughed.

"Well, if you had just once admitted you needed to rest, I would have stopped."

"Not me! Unh huh. I wasn't about to let you think I couldn't keep up." She turned and looked out the window again. "We were so young," she whispered. "Now here we are, we've built good lives and are so happy and Nayland Brenev comes back from the past to make us miserable again. Oh, I'd so hoped he was dead! How can one person contain so much evil?"

Derek put his arm around her shoulders and felt the stiffness, the tautness. "This time we'll stop him, Dulsena! I promise you, this time we'll stop him."

- 25 -
Just a Hunch

"Ah yes!" Lisbet said as she scanned the report that Henri Dakkon had just handed her. Jabour Khee. Do we have anything else on him?"

"Not much, I'm afraid," Henri said. "The only thing that may be pertinent is what Merchants Kalleni and Donovan pointed out and that is that Khee Mercantile has enjoyed a sudden, unexplained, economic success over the last five years. Other than some inquiries about his tax records several years ago his file is quite unremarkable."

"There isn't any doubt about who received the goods at Maashout?" Lisbet asked.

"No. They had the ship and landing field under surveillance the whole time."

"Interesting," Lisbet murmured. "What do you plan to do about Khee?"

"Nothing right now. We will, of course, keep him under surveillance, and we can pick him up for questioning at any time. We would just like to see who else or what else comes to him."

"All right. I'll trust your judgement on that for now. So what about the Schwecker business? Anything new on that?"

"Not really. Nareg Velson is sticking to his story about rescuing them, but Aldrys Schwecker's version of what happened is totally different. It's almost sure he is working for Brenev. They just haven't made the connection. He should start talking soon.

"Good," Lisbet responded, "I'm glad that little girl will get her mother back unharmed. Now what have you heard from the Huilla, anything?"

"No, and I don't really expect to. They've got their hands full with problems in toward Huilla League center, and they aren't about to fret about a few illicit arms shipments.

"Actually, considering the time constraints, we, the task force members that is, have focused our attention on Trilbus for three reasons. One: Brenev has dealt with them before, two, they have a reputation for dealing with whoever has the money and the third reason is something we hit on in staff meeting. An intelligence note sent in from Trilbus has it that there are rumors flying about of a "new" weapon that will be a big money maker. The informant couldn't get any more specific but seems people expect Polcharsh, one of the oldest armament dealers on that world, to profit greatly from some newly developed technology that 'will revolutionize the industry' for them."

"Hmmm. If there is something like that around Brenev would want it. It would help to make up for the difference in manpower. Anything else?" She leaned back in her chair and watched her assistant, feeling he had left something unsaid.

Dakkon had been put in charge of an emergency task force trying to integrate all the intelligence reports they were receiving; trying to see a pattern, anything that would help the Federation stop this uprising before it got started. Now Dakkon rubbed the back of his head, frowned and then slowly answered, "Not really."

"Not really?" Lisbet said. "What is this 'not really'? Is there something or not?"

"Well," Henri said hesitantly, "in one of our discussions, it was pointed out that someone else was 'out beyond Frayleen'. They were talking about the Krogtlils on Poldar."

"Oh yes, I remember them," Lisbet said. "I was stationed on Pantro when they tried their little trading venture on Arno. Are they still crossing Federation lines?"

"Well you know the Krogtlils. They're pretty aggressive when it comes to their technology. They're always developing something new and if there's a market they aren't too particular about where it is as long as they get paid well."

"Is there anything to link them with Brenev?"

"No, or rather not much. Dulsena thinks that Nayland had some dealings with the Krogtlils during the Rebellion but she isn't sure and we haven't been able to confirm that there has been any contact recently. And we don't have anything else. It's just that...I don't know...it's just too convenient to ignore. It fits." He shook his head and added, "it isn't much to go on, but the group bounced the idea around and the more we talked the more it seemed like something to consider."

"I sense that you seem to be leaning more towards the Krogtlils than the group on Trilbus," Lisbet said.

"No, not really," Dakkon responded slowly, "It's just a feeling. No way to explain it, really."

"I've learned to trust your hunches, Henri. It might be wise to check it out more fully as well as following up on Trilbus.

"Yes," answered Dakkon, "I think that would be a good idea. One thing's for sure, Brenev will have contacted one or the other and maybe both. In any case, I'll let you know what turns up."

Henri had just reached the door when Lisbet asked, "Henri, how long has it been since we lost a major liner?"

His hand poised above the opener, Henri stopped, frozen. Turning slowly, he met Lisbet's level gaze. "A very long time."

The question and answer hung there in the silence.

"One of YOUR hunches?" he asked Lisbet quietly.

Lisbet gave a little shrug and said, "Like you said, it's too...well, too much of a coincidence."

Before midday chimes had rung, a call from Rhys Xholan changed a nebulous hunch into a grim fact.

- 26 -
Fleets Out

On board AFS Dauntless, ComTec 1st Class Colbar raced towards his post in Com Central and almost ran into his buddy, Shoilon, who was heading the other way. "Watch out for Morgyn," Shoilon whispered, "he's really bucking for Firsts on this operation."

Colbar's eyebrows went up while he mouthed a silent, "Oh?" Shoilon simply rolled his eyes and jerked his chin up in a gesture that clearly said, "You know Morgyn".

The subject of this exchange was Lt. Lim Morgyn, the Communications Officer. Now, hands clasped behind his back, head down and forward, he stopped pacing back and forth long enough to peer accusingly at Colbar as he slid into his station and logged in. Colbar, trying to look cool and in control, inwardly breathed a sigh of relief that for once he had logged in early. Not by much but not late either. Thank the gods!

The other Tec was conscious of this exchange even though his eyes were focused on his screen and his ears filled with the sounds transmitted by the computers.

The computers received the data sent by the ship's aerials, the sonobuoys and the MAEs (magnetic anomaly monitors) orbiting the Federation borders between ships to monitor any vessels entering their space. They could determine the type of vessel, range, speed and course.

They were also programmed to compare a ship's location with shipping schedules and flight plans and to report any ship found where it wasn't scheduled to be. All this information was simultaneously transferred to the ComTecs for evaluation and recorded for future reference.

The ComTecs were human filters trained to catch any anomalies, that might slip past the literal, facts only, monitoring of the computers. They brought a human dimension to the evaluations. On a large operation such as this, stress could build rapidly so the ComTecs only worked two hours at a time.

All the additional gold braid aboard ship, not to mention the huge number of ships involved, had made it clear that this exercise was of major importance. This knowledge kept the Tecs alert on two levels; fine tuning their surveillance screens, while at the same time trying to catch any hint that might be wafting about as to what this whole to-do was all about. The officers were being very close-mouthed and by-the-book. So far, all any of the Tecs had learned was that a whole net of Federation ships, traveling at top speed, had been assembled and slipped into position to patrol the outermost edges of the Algoran Federation border with the Huilla League. It was an incredibly long distance to cover and even with the orbiting probes they'd positioned between ships their surveillance equipment was stretched to the limit. Still, "they WOULD", they had been told by the fierce, beetle-browed Lt. Morgyn, "repeat WOULD find ANYONE entering Algoran territory". Speculation as to why this was so important ran the gamut from a massive invasion by the Huilla to some ship full of survivors with a deadly, contagious disease. Colbar had speculated with the rest of them, but didn't really believe any of the talk.

Actually, from the spread of the ships, it seemed to him that they were focusing on Trilbus and Krolinoor. He even thought he had a pretty good idea why. His dad had been stationed for a while on Pantro, near the Federation border, and had told him about the problems the Fed ships had with the weapons dealers from those two, and about the Krogtlils coming in as far as Arno. That had been twenty years ago, but his dad had always said, "We haven't heard the last of them."

Added to what his dad had said was what he'd learned on his own about the Krogtlils: You never could know what they'd do. They could have decided to go halfway around the territory before attempting an entry or they could have invented something which would prevent detection all together. All these ships could be cruising up and down out here for nothing. Well that wasn't his problem. His problem was to stay clear of Bucking-for-Firsts Morgyn.

* * *

I saw them, Enferdeem, I saw them with my own two eyes." Entok, an old friend of Enferdeem Swadi's, clutched his drink with both hands and leaned across the dirty, drink spattered table towards Swadi. "I've never seen so many Fed ships! Never! Cruisers, battleships, littler ships, I don't know what they were, but off they went, one after another."

He looked furtively around the little bar before continuing. "My sister's son, Safet, you remember Safet? Yah, sure ya do. You met him at the wedding. Little guy, thin, lots of hair." He took another long drink and wiped his mouth with a sleeve that had obviously been put to that use before.

"Well anyway, you know he works at the base in Pantro. That big new Fed Fleet Base." Entok took another swallow, looked around again, and then leaning even further across the table, slowly, in a hoarse whisper said, "Well, Safet told me they've been workin' 'round the clock, loadin' ships with supplies like they do for extended patrols. 'Round the clock, he said, 'Round the clock'."

He sat back in his chair and nodded sagely. Then leaning forward again added, "People don't like that, you know, what with the holidays comin' up and all. Don't like it at all."

He put his head down even further and looked up at Swadi with narrowed, knowing eyes. "Anyway, the place is packed. Military, high up military, comin' in from all over. You can bet somethin' very big is goin' on, somethin' very, very big," He looked at Swadi and nodded, his head bobbing up and down over the drink clutched with both hands.

Enferdeem Swadi watched this man savor being the bearer of what he considered important news. However, not for one moment, did he give any indication that this bit of information was of any interest to him personally. Expressing only mild curiosity at the strange actions of Fed Fleet, he led the conversation on to other things. Shortly afterward, he laid some money on the table and excused himself to "take care of some business".

Out in the harsh sunlight of Arno, he hopped onto the beltway and as quickly as possible moved towards the fastest lane. Old Entok's news had disturbed him far more than he'd let on. Even if, allowing for the drinks, there were only half as many ships as he'd said, it could make things very difficult indeed. With such tight surveillance it would be almost impossible to rendezvous with the Krogtlils as planned. Worse than that, if the Krogtlils picked up on that many Fed ships they might just turn around and scuttle for home. That could be devastating to their plans. They had to have those Krogtlil fliers to disable Fleet Headquarters and the other major bases. Normally, most of the Fed ships would be back in their home ports for the holidays. The whole idea of striking on the holidays had been based on that. It had seemed like a good plan.

Now, if what Entok said was true, instead of being in dock, hundreds of ships were out on some exercise. So, their plan to disable the fleet by hitting all the ports at the same time wouldn't work.

Patting his pocket to make sure his code transposer was there, he worked his way to the edge of the beltway, jumped off and headed for a bank of vidphones. Brenev wouldn't like this news at all. Swadi doubted that the arrogant twit even had a backup plan. He remembered his supercilious voice saying, "I'll come up with something. I always do." Swadi's lips curled in a sneer. "We'll just see what you come up with. In the meantime I'm not waiting for you 'to come up with something'. I'm putting the Paladin Sequillat on alert. It just might be that we'll be calling more of the shots instead of the great know-it-all Brenev."

- 27 -
Uneasy the Heads

The crystal goblet flew through the air, spraying a plume of green liquid, before crashing against the white wall and falling in a glittering fan to the floor. Nayland Brenev stood, his chest heaving. Narrow eyed he watched as a few crystal splinters, caught in the viscous liquid, slid slowly downward leaving long, green stains; stood motionless, until the last tiny shard had dropped onto the white napped carpet below.

"Idiots!" he said softly. Then louder and louder and louder until he was shrieking, "Idiots!, idiots!, idiots! I'm surrounded by idiots!" Hands clutching his head he reeled around the room.

The door opened slowly and Georgg peered in before entering. "Does that include everyone?" he asked calmly, closing the door behind him. He got a vicious snarl in answer. With abrupt, jerky movements, Nayland slowly lowered his arms and adjusted the fringe of his short, elaborately embroidered tunic.

"Tell me Georgg," he said biting off each word. "Our advisor, this Fed Fleet Narmed be damned great expert who was supposed to know so much about Fleet procedures, didn't he say the Fleet ALWAYS tries to have most of its ships berthed for the one big holiday of the year?"

"I believe that's what he said," Georgg answered, "but he also said that was true if all was quiet in the territory."

"He also said," Nayland went on in a steely voice, "that with the

Huilla busy with their own problems, and the new treaties with the Beloitz, that he saw no reason why that wouldn't be the case this year. Right? Right!" He pivoted suddenly and glared at Georgg.

At Georgg's puzzled nod he continued, "So, can you tell me why Captain Enferdeem Swadi should call just now and tell me that hundreds, not a few, please note, but hundreds of Fleet ships have been sent scurrying out on some fantastically huge exercise or manoeuvre or whatever the Narm they call it!

"Noooo," he said, shaking his head, "instead of heading home to the wife and kiddies for the holidays they're out there, Narm knows where, playing soldier! Right where the Krogtlils were to meet Enferdeem!"

"Unh ho," Georgg breathed, and slumped into the nearest chair. "I can see why you're upset."

"Upset!" Nayland said sarcastically, "You can see that I'm 'Upset'. That's brilliant of you Georgg. Just brilliant! Nine years of planning. Nine years of dealing with crazy fanatics. Nine years of scrabbling around for money, for weapons, for troops and materiel. And for what? To have those stupid, idiotic fanatics of that crazy old coot, Marridon destroy it all by jumping the gun and rioting in the streets. If it hadn't been for them the Feds wouldn't have been put on alert!"

He threw himself into his chair and chewed on his knuckle. "And that stupid Carradyne! Letting himself be duped by that Kalleni whelp! How could they have been taken in by that fop?" he shouted.

He leaped from his chair and stormed around the room, raving, "It was a bad day for the Brenevs when they got mixed up with that family! If it weren't for that worthless tart of Loran's and her family, my people would still be in their rightful home on Greniff. I'll never rest until they're all dead, dead, dead!"

Nayland, it would seem, had conveniently forgotten that he was the one who had insisted Loran marry Dulsena Kalleni in an attempt to get her family's support, or at least their money, for his rebellion. Considering the moment, Georgg thought it prudent not to mention this fact.

A commotion in the outer room brought Georgg to his feet. He reached the door just as it was thrust open and a wrathful Marridon, black, hooded cloak swirling about him, strode in. He raised his arm, his finger pointed straight and steady at Nayland. "Because of you," he thundered, "the Paladin Sequillat have been called to arms!"

- 28 -
Serenity/Insanity

The call to evening chimes finished as Brothers Eindal and Harrik walked towards the path leading to the fountain. It had been a sunny, clear day and as the light dimmed and the bell flowers began to close the evening breezes stirred the yellow leafed Volnar trees. Brother Eindal took a deep breath. The air was redolent with the scent of sweet linnaeus blossoms. As he stepped onto the beautiful mosaic walkway and the first chime rang, his attention was diverted from his devotions by the sound of Brother Latkoe calling his name. Heaving a great sigh he stepped from the pathway and held his hand up in a rather imperious gesture. This halted both Brother Latkoe's forward rush and his quavering tenor pipings at the same time.

"Couldn't it wait, Brother?" rumbled Eindal quietly, with ill concealed irritation. Immobilized before the still upheld hand, Brother Latkoe blinked nervously and shook his head. "Fed...," he squeaked. He stopped, gulped and, lowering his voice several tones, said, "Admiral Toomey's aide wants to talk to you." Not until the hand was lowered completely did he turn to scuttle quickly back towards the door to the chapel.

Brother Eindal looked back towards Brother Harrik walking serenely along the path. Planning to catch his attention he started to wave and then thought better of it. "Let him be, let him be," he muttered to himself.

With longing he looked at the Brethren lost in meditation on the serene pathway. If this is the call we've been waiting for, he thought, there won't be many more quiet moments to enjoy for a while. He tucked his arms into his sleeves, gave a great sigh and trundled after Brother Latkoe.

Not long after, he once again stood at the side of the fountain. The last chimes had rung and the worshipers had left. He stood alone in the dusk, hands clasped in front, his head bowed. The news he had received weighed heavy on his heart. They had been successful. The surveillance had paid off. They'd found those who had forsworn their heritage. As hard as it was to believe, all were members of old crystal families, lured away from the path of Harmony. Sad day for them. Sad day for their families. As of now only security and a few of the brethren knew of the pilferage problems and no one would be taken into custody until word was received from the Federation. Fortunately, only Windswept was involved and a "problem" in one of the curing facilities had "required that it be shut down for a short time". This had been a decision made to prevent any more crystals being taken before the mine could be rededicated.

There would be much grief and soul searching among the mine folk when the news was released. Even more troubling was the terrible fear that there was a great deal more pain and suffering yet to be born than just grief at pilferage. Dark, evil forces were at work spreading grief and pain far beyond Windswept Mine, beyond their little world. He knew they were there. He felt them deep in his bones, in his heart.

- 29 -
A Different View

Marridon stood looking outward from the great arched portico of the tabernacle at Maashout. The flight from Nirubati had been uneventful and he was happy to be out of that world's everlasting rain. He'd almost forgotten what it was like to see a clear sky. Now, the bright colors of the surrounding gardens seemed startling in their brilliance. He had been told that they'd had a rain shower the day before, but today was clear and beautiful. He chose to regard this as a good omen portending a clear success in their endeavors.

He and Derrachem had chosen this place as a base from which to direct the call to Apocalypse. Greniff, unlike some of the other home worlds had been swift to embrace the truth and, being Brenev's home planet their military support was the strongest here, too. This would, they felt confident, ensure a swift victory. At evening chimes, in just a few days, he would issue the call. Oh glorious, long awaited day!

He knew Brenev was worried about the delay in getting the aircraft from the Krogtlils. However, he, Marridon was not worried. He would rely on the strength of Right and, of course, the fervor of the Black Knights. Deliberately turning away from the colorful view, he strode through the great doors into the cool darkness of the tabernacle. The great red crystals would soon ring out in victory.

* * *

Enferdeem Swadi handed over the final payment to the Krogtlil, M'glenkenduk, as agreed. In its place he was handed what looked like an antique brass cylinder covered with writing. This, he was assured, was a proper receipt. Strange that a people who survived by selling the very latest in technology should use such an antiquated method for confirming a deal.

The fighters had already been loaded and now he and the strange little arms dealer stood and watched as the pilots, who had been trained by the Krogtlils, boarded the carrier. What they were watching was being repeated on four other large Krogtlil carriers. One thousand fighters with their pilots and their support units to be flown out to their assigned rendezvous points. These fighter ships had been armed with the very latest attack weapons that the Krogtlils claimed were far more powerful than any found in the Fed Fleet arsenal. Swadi hoped they proved the claims. Their whole attack strategy depended on these aircraft, and their pilots, performing as described.

"You're sure your idea of crossing the frontier will work," Swadi asked M'glenkenduk again. "There are a lot of Fed ships patrolling the border."

M'glenkenduk shrugged and continued to watch as the last of the pilots disappeared into the ship. "Who can ever say they know anything for sure? All I can say is that it has worked before. With any luck it will work again."

"Luck!" snorted Swadi. "I don't want luck! I prefer to deal with matters in such a way that I don't have to depend on luck."

"Well," the placid Krogtlil responded, "Luck was kind to you this time. You heard of the Fed maneuvers and got word to us in time so we could change our meeting place. Perhaps, luck is a better friend than you think." His thin lips twitched in a brief smile. He would have smiled more if it weren't for the so serious man standing at his side. Tiresome, he thought. So tiresome to deal with people like this man.

Always so serious, so humorless. Seemed like customers for these products were that way. Not so with Krogtlils; they enjoyed life. They enjoyed developing and manufacturing new machines and products. There was a lot of satisfaction in figuring out how to do something better than anyone else. But the people who bought these machines of war didn't seem to enjoy anything at all. They were like this dour faced man, so dissatisfied with everything. Sad. It was as he had often said to his friends, maybe they needed to learn how to make things.

M'glenkenduk was an old man. He had been selling his company's products for many years, but, still he had his own home workshop where he spent many long and happy hours. In all his years of selling he never had learned to understand people who spent good money to buy weapons. The Krogtlils made them because strange people, like this man, wanted to buy and were willing to pay enormous amounts for them. However, most Krogtlils considered it bizarre behavior. "Where could there be joy in destroying something," they asked each other. "Everyone knows that joy comes in building something, figuring out how to make something new or better."

"No explaining it," he muttered to himself.

"Pardon?" Swadi asked leaning forward.

"Oh, nothing, nothing," the old man smiled again. "You have your receipt, right?" At Swadi's nod, he continued, "Then I say fare thee well and, even if you're not seeking it, May you have Luck." As he sauntered from the flight deck into the quiet of the observation deck, he smiled again. "Not to want Luck. What a sad man. Could one such as that ever really have good fortune? He thought not. Never to create, only destroy. Surely such a life did not bring good luck.

"At least he took the 'receipt'," he muttered to himself, smiling again. The efficient little timing device hidden inside the pretty cylinder would cause it to self destruct once he made the hyper jump. Mustn't leave anything to connect Swadi and his ships to the Krogtlils, just in case the sad Captain's luck wasn't good. Not that M'glenkenduk would wish such a thing, but even Krogtlils didn't leave everything to Luck.

* * *

Nayland Brenev watched as Nirubati receded to a dot of light. He was webbed in already for the jump into hyper space. Now that the final countdown had started he found he was anxious to get on with it. He and Georgg had all the records and soon he would be directing affairs from his own home base. It would be good to be back on Greniff. Good to destroy those usurpers who had taken over his home. His heart pounded and his head ached to think of that woman living in his house, running his company. He forced his clenched hands to relax. "Calm. I must stay calm," he muttered. "My revenge will come."

* * *

"Are you sure you saw something or were you just imagining it?" The sarcasm in Lt. Morgyn's voice sawed at Colbar's nerves.

"I dunno Sir, I sure thought I saw something."

"You thought you saw something," Morgyn said softly. "You woke me up, got me out of a nice warm bunk and up here because you THOUGHT you saw something?" Morgyn's sarcasm was now tinged with disgust. "Would you then be so kind as to tell me again what it was you THOUGHT you saw?"

"Yes, Sir. Well, I couldn't sleep so I got up and keyed in on this reserve board. I was just noodling around and then I thought I saw something way over, on beyond where the last of the monitors was dropped. I cross checked with the computer and it had logged it as a meteor shower. But, somehow it just didn't look right for that. It wasn't much, just a glimpse, but it caught my eye. See, here it is on the run-back."

They both watched intently as Colbar ordered the segment rerun and then rerun yet again.

"You're right, it isn't much," Morgyn said. "Let me see it again."

For the fourth time they studied the little flashes that appeared and then just as suddenly disappeared. Morgyn straightened up and then rocking back and forth, pursed his lips and whistled a few notes softly. "Well, lucky for you there does seem to be something there. Let's see if there's anyone else on patrol near there who might have seen something."

"How did you know about it?" Lt. Severe of the F.S. Intrepid asked. "We just picked up on it ourselves."

"Oh you know us, Leo," Morgyn responded blandly, "always alert, always on top of things."

Colbar leaned back in his chair, crossed his arms and grinned smugly at Morgyn. You owe me one, he thought to himself, and that never hurts.

- 30 -
The Evil Some Men Do

"Well, maybe we were given the wrong information," Henri Dakkon remarked to Lisbet Bornach. They were reclining on slightly slanted couches in Henri's private reception area. The lights were low so they could take full advantage of the view of the stars twinkling in the clear, cold night. Separated from this chill vista by a glass wall, the room itself felt warm and cozy.

Because of the emergency, all members of the Choiterem as well as the Federation Council had stayed on Aldene rather than going home for the holidays. There hadn't been much of a holiday mood what with reviewing the reports coming in and one meeting after another.

Henri glanced at Lisbet. There were dark smudges under her eyes and she looked wan and tired. He remembered catching a glimpse of himself in the mirror a little earlier, and knew he didn't look any better. Having gone into the holidays with a terrible sense of foreboding they had spent the entire five days expecting the worst. All the data sent in by the FIS field agents had seemed to support the depositions and the rumors that the Black Knights would make their move on the holidays. Now, as the last hours crept by, it began to look like there had been a change in plans. The resulting let-down seemed to bring out the bone deep weariness each felt.

"All the information, all the data collected indicated an attack coinciding with the holidays," Lisbet said softly. "I don't know..." Her voice trailed off as if she couldn't let herself believe they had been so misled.

Henri got up and walked over to an exquisitely carved refreshment cabinet. Picking up a small carafe he walked back to refill Lisbet's glass. "I must order some more of this excellent wine. I found it at a charming little winery on Polchar last year and perhaps I can get some more of the same vintage altho..."

The glass wall shattered thrusting a thousand star-lit shards of glass throughout the cozy room. The cold night crept into the room as Lisbet and Henri each realized they would never again taste the warm summer wine of Polchar.

All over Aldene the beautiful, earth embracing, garden filled, buildings of the Algoran Federation collapsed into nothingness. Out beyond, on a dozen planets, all over the Federation, government facilities and spaceports shared this intrusion of death. The Krogtlils had earned their money.

- 31 -
Ungodly Barbarism

Rhys Xholan, Scortzi and Governor Koihn, accompanied by the Governor's guards, were relaxed and enjoying the ride from Krie Auditorium back to the Governor's Palace. The concert had been excellent and afterwards, at a late supper, they had lingered talking with the performers. Down below, the lights of Rohnseff shown brightly as the last of the holiday revelers filled the streets. The pilot made the last turn heading for Government Square and suddenly Rhys shouted, "What the Narm!"

The lighted towers of the old section of the Government House had risen slowly into the air and then fallen back downward. The sound of a powerful explosion reached them and the shock waves rocked the small flyer. Immediately, further to the south, there was a series of explosions and flames and smoke roared up from the direction of Rohnseff Spaceport.

All around them flyers, especially those that had been nearer Government House, were struggling to stay in the air and at their assigned level. A few didn't make it and were crashing into the levels below. Rhys' pilot switched on the lights that identified their craft as a government vehicle and began to demonstrate why he had been chosen for his position. Moving from level to level, seeming to anticipate openings before they were there, he slipped into and out of the wobbling mass of fliers and headed downward to skim the topmost level leading to Government Square.

"Can you see the Governor's Palace?" Rhys yelled. "Has it been hit?"

"Can't tell from here," the pilot answered.

"Get us there," Governor Koihn snapped. "If it looks all right drop me off. I know you need to get to the port, Rhys. Scortzi, do you want to come with me or go with Rhys?"

"I'd better go with Rhys, but I'll be in touch in case there's anything you want me to do."

The pilot came in fast and Koihn and his guards jumped out. Before Scortzi had the door completely shut, the flyer was up and racing for the port.

"Before you land," Rhys said, "fly over and let's see just what we've got here." Coming in from the north, it seemed that the local and domestic flight areas weren't too badly damaged. It was when they reached the inter-world facilities that the destruction became evident. Flying through the smoke and flames they suddenly were over a clear area where nothing was burning: there was nothing left to burn.

"Gone!" Rhys' voice was harsh from the shock. "There's nothing there!"

"It's as if all those buildings, all those launch areas never existed!" Scortzi said softly. "What could have done something like that? I've never heard of anything that could do that! What's happened?" He looked at Rhys with a horrified expression.

"I don't know. I don't know," Rhys answered, staring at the void. All the major docking areas for inter-world shipping were gone, completely gone. There was only a large, steep sided hole where they had been. All around this well defined void, everything was burning out of control.

"Great Narm!" the pilot whispered. "The people that must'a been there. They'd never had a chance! Not a bloody chance! What the Narm could have done something like that?"

Rhys simply shook his head. The pilot swung the flyer into a sharp turn and flew back over the void again then through the smoke of the burning rim. Beyond the fires, the passenger terminals and services areas, although obviously badly damaged, were still standing.

"Put us down at the terminal nearest my office," Rhys told the pilot and at the same time reached for his radio. That small action seemed to free-up his numbed brain. "Got to get help," he said to Scortzi. "Port Service can't handle this."

A few minutes later they landed just beyond the park leading towards A-B terminal building and raced into a nightmare. The dead and dying were lying where they had been flung by the force of the blast: men, women, children crying and pleading for someone to help them. Only a few were being assisted, sometimes by people who seemed almost as badly injured as they were. Others, far too many others, were obviously beyond anyone's help. People were wandering around, seemingly too dazed to understand what had happened. There were moans and cries from the wreckage and one man screaming, "Reena, Reena," was frantically pulling at the remnants of a wall that had collapsed, apparently with his Reena underneath. One woman had opened her large suitcase and was methodically refolding and replacing all the clothes.

The thin wail of sirens caught their attention. A few and then a stream of emergency flyers began arriving. MedTecs, loaded with supplies, quickly set up a triage station while their supervisors organized the rescue operations. Soon, everyone who was able was scrabbling through the wreckage trying to extricate those trapped beneath while the Tecs attended to the wounded and prepared them for transport.

Fire fighting equipment, their warbling calls adding to the cacophony, raced towards the fires on the perimeter of the void.

"I hope there are enough of them," Rhys said, "if those fires spread out of control, the whole port'll go. Let's get back to my office and see if we can get some order out of this chaos."

A thousand thoughts tumbled through their heads as they raced outside along the arcade leading from the terminal towards the park and Rhys' office. They stopped suddenly as several large military transports with the Grenechan double crescent moon insignia, flew in and landed immediately to their left. The doors opened and Militia

Men with rescue equipment poured out and headed for the wreckage.

"Thank God General Althain kept his men on alert throughout the holidays," Rhys said. "Now, according to plan, the troops will spread out to secure the ground areas while the Grenechan Air Patrol will protect the flight routes in and out." Although neither said it, cach wondered how or even why any large craft would choose to land in the midst of this chaos.

"Captain Xholan!"

"Captain Xholan!" Rhys realized he was being hailed by two people running towards him from different directions; one was Colonel Jehanin of the Militia and the other was a woman he recognized as a reporter for G.N.N., Grenechan News Network. They both were converging on him when they all were blinded by an intensely bright flash overhead. One of the transports had exploded. Men were dropping, screaming into the inferno below. They'd never even had a chance to use their grav-lifts.

"Someone's firing on those troop carriers!" Colonel Jehanin reversed and ran back towards the transport bellowing, "Lieutenant, Get some men and find out where that's coming from! Sergeant get these civilians under cover!"

Abruptly, air pallets were reversed and the injured who had already been loaded onto ambulance flyers were off loaded and all were hurriedly guided back into one of the underground parking areas.

Rhys dodged the reporter who had been talking steadily into her transmitter and ran towards the flyer that his pilot was manoeuvering under cover. Scortzi anticipating his move had beat him there and now handed him a grav-lift from the storage rack in the cabin and buckled one on himself.

"Stay close, Stovern," Rhys shouted, "I may need you in a hurry." Slipping quickly into their harnesses they kicked off and headed for the Administration building at full power.

With Rhys leading the way, they headed towards the balcony just outside Rhys' office. As they were slipping out of their grav-lifts they were again accosted by the reporter and her cameraman who had followed them.

"We need a statement, Captain Zholan," the G.N.N. reporter demanded as she balanced on the balcony rail.

Rhys glared and tried to wave them off, but it was obvious they couldn't be gotten rid of that easily.

"Come on, Captain, the public has a right to know what has happened. If we get it from you we at least will know it's correct."

"All right, all right," he growled. "Right now all I know is that there's been some sort of attack. We don't know the extent of the damage or any other details, yet. As soon as we know something we'll let you know."

"Can you tell us how many deaths or injuries there have been?" she insisted, thrusting the microphone in his face.

Rhys grasped her by the shoulders and propelled her around to face to carnage. "Look at that. Just look at it. How could I possibly know the answer to such a question?" he shouted back at her. He strode into his office and tried to slide the door closed behind him. He pushed, but the frame was tilted and the cracked glass panels stuck partway. He turned and glared at the reporter and her cameraman as if to say that door or no door his office was closed to them.

His assistant, Li and one of his clerks, was already there clearing away debris and broken glass. The office while damaged was usable. "Do we have communications?", Rhys asked.

"All domestic lines have reported in but none from off-world," Fielding responded. "Norbert, from Emergency Services has called in a couple of times on a field unit. He's working with fire-control and said he'd call back as soon he could figure out what was going on."

"Good, good," Rhys said, while with a sweep of his arm he cleared part of the ceiling from off his desk. "What about Egys-EX and Maas-EX?" These were the other large ports on Greniff. Each of the three large continents on Greniff had a major spaceport: Grenek with Rohnseff Spaceport, Gohmeron with Egyerius Spaceport and Kandrabad where Maashout Spaceport was located. There was also a small island confederation politically affiliated with Egyerius. "We got a very garbled transmission from Egys-Ex," Fielding answered. "Maas-Ex came in very clear, but the radioman said there was something strange about it. The form wasn't correct and neither were the I.D.s. He says it was as if someone not familiar with the protocol were sending."

Scortzi and Rhys looked at each other, each thinking of the last time Scortzi had been in Maashout.

"Well," Scortzi said, "If someone unfamiliar with the protocol is transmitting messages from Maashout, it doesn't take much guessing to figure out who's behind it".

The whine of flyers overhead had become so loud that these last words were shouted. There was another great flash of light. They rushed to the broken-out window to see that the sky was filled with flyers. Bright flashes of light, showed Grenechan ships locked in combat with flyers bearing a strange, never-before-seen insignia, double crescent moons intersected by a large blood-red crystal.

* * *

By midday, Rhys and Colonel Jehanin had set up a joint command center. The air battle was, at least for the moment, over and the invading flyers had been driven off. Now the injured were being reloaded onto the few remaining emergency vehicles in working condition and, hopefully, would make it to the hospital without being attacked again.

The firemen, who had worked on despite the battle overhead, had made some headway in checking the advance of the fire, but it was far from being under control.

Now Scortzi, Rhys, his Port Security People, the Governor's Assistant and his staff, and Colonel Jehanin and his aides were in Rhys' conference room for a joint briefing.

"They've hit Government House, fortunately most of the delegates were home for the holiday, and as you know, they've wiped out the off-world spaceport and the port telecommunications center," Colonel Jehanin said, biting off each word. "In Rohnseff, a few of the transport lines were sabotaged including the major arteries into the western edge, levels 9 through 22. Maintenance estimates they will have them running again in about two days. Assuming of course they are not attacked again. They're now working under heavy guard.

"There were numerous attempts to take control of the power system, and although a few power plants were damaged or destroyed, the rest of the system has taken up the slack.

"Simultaneous attacks were made on the main Municipal computers, but, fortunately, the troops stationed there held out and were able to protect them. The subsidiary/back-up computer systems also were well enough protected so that most were undamaged in spite of sabotage attempts. We're fortunate in that, due to prior warnings from Intel-Service, precautions were taken and the attempts to sabotage the power and computer systems failed."

Everyone knew that "fortunate" was a weak word for that statement. In a city of 22 million built on 25 levels, a power outage was a catastrophe. Literally, whoever controlled the Municipal Computers ruled the city: the power distribution center, the public transport, the clearing of identification cards for food, goods and services. All these and much more were controlled by the computers. They kept the city running. Without them - no air, no water, no lights (and in the lower levels of the city they depended totally on artificial light), no food distribution, no nothing. With the computers the city lived and they had a chance to fight back. Without them there would be chaos.

"We've implemented the emergency plans developed after the Brenev Rebellion," Johanin continued.

"Did any of those plans consider such extensive loss of government facilities?" Rhys asked.

"Some were 'worst case scenarios', but the first strike damage has been, in many cases, greater than we had expected," Johanin admitted reluctantly. "So, we're just going to have to salvage what we can and come up with alternate procedures for the rest."

After two hours, each one had been briefed on areas of responsibility and had left. Rhys, Li and Scortzi, having been up for over 30 hours, were exhausted. Now, at the insistence of Rhys's staff, they were going to try and catch some sleep. On their way out an assistant stopped Rhys and said, "Excuse me, sir, that last group of aircraft that came over, who were these guys anyway? Nobody I've talked to has ever seen that insignia. They aren't Huilla. So who are they?"

This question was being repeated over and over millions of times on all three continents of Greniff, as well as on all the continents of every planet in the Algoran Federation, with one notable exception, Nirubati. They hadn't asked who was involved, but had sent a long, rambling announcement explaining their support for the "forces of righteousness". It would seem that they had either declared spiritual allegiance to the Black Knights, or been bought by Nayland Brenev. Not necessarily with hard cash. After all, the promise of booty and adventure had been buying men's loyalty for countless millennia. There were always those for whom causes or a man's grievances, noble or ignoble, were simply opportunities for plunder and pillage. For them, The Black Knights cause, together with Nayland Brenev's money, would do until something, or someone, else came along.

- 32 -
Apocalypse Now

On board the FS Alliance, an aide came in with a printout for Commodore Alzendro Pilchard. He read it and in sonorous tones announced, "The insignia we've all been wondering about—I have just been told it belongs to the Paladin Sequillat." Some in the group recognized the name—others did not. It was a name from the long ago, dark and bloody past of the Federation, which had come back like an unwelcome specter to give new shape to their nightmares.

The buz of speculation continued until Commodore Pilchard's aide stood and called for attention. The grim faced group of military leaders settled into their seats as the Commodore stepped forward to the head of the table. Alzendro Pilchard was a tall man with a long, thin face and the pale non-descript hair of a blond turning grey. He was not a favorite of those officers who liked their commanders to be sociable and charming. He was, nevertheless, admired by everyone for having reached his position on merit and hard work. Now he stood, erect and silent, waiting until he had everyone's attention. Finally he spoke.

"Ten years ago a mad man named Nayland Brenev attempted to overthrow the Federation. He did not succeed. His family was captured and either re-programmed or banished to the prison planet Perdita. His fellow conspirators were either killed or reprogrammed. Brenev himself was never caught and apparently, is now making a second attempt to gain dominion.

This time he has more help than just his mercenaries. He has been joined in this insurrection by the outlawed organization calling themselves The Black Knights. There have also been a few reports, so far unsubstantiated, that Narmists and the Paladin Sequillat are involved. I can see from your expressions that you realize how this escalates matters.

"What we have here is an explosive combination of unlimited greed and ruthlessness allied with religious fanaticism. We've just experienced what these people are willing to do to achieve their goals." He motioned to Major Collins, his aide, who stepped forward and said, "On the screen before you is a brief list of the extent of damage from their coordinated sneak attacks. You will find the same list on your individual monitors. There is additional, more detailed information, on the destruction throughout the Federation, or at least as much as we've been able to collect to this time, in Appended Data 3, and on Greniff's damage reports on Appended Data 4, which can be called up to clarify any answers. Data Sheets 1 through 4 give background information on Nayland Brenev, The Black Knights, the Narmists and the Paladin Sequillat.

"I'm sure the first question you want answered is what type of weapon was used to cause such massive damage in an incredibly confined area." Heads nodded and a few rumbles of agreement were heard.

"The answer is, so would we." He paused for effect then added. "We believe it is a new bit of technology from, who else?, the Krogtlils." This announcement brought forth a new burst of rumbles and some more heads nodding. Obviously many had come to the same conclusion.

"At the moment we have no proof for this, however, several events have led us to believe this is so."

He went on to say that earlier there had been intelligence reports describing 'a super weapon or weapons from out beyond Frayleen'.

"This may be the weapon responsible for the extensive damage experienced so far. A short time later, from data picked up and analyzed by our ship the Intrepid, Fed Forces were able to intercept a group of transports believed to be carrying fliers and personnel. We cannot prove it, but the evidence seems to indicate that these transports also came from the Huilla League Territory. The transports were very large, capable of carrying several hundred fliers with attendant support personnel. The ships refused to respond to queries for identification and warning shots were fired. No communications forthcoming, the Federation ships opened fire. Two of the transports were destroyed and a third was severely damaged. It attempted to go hyper and apparently destructed as a result. We do not at this time have reports as to how many transports escaped, nor do we know if there had been prior shipments. A complaint has been filed with Huilla League.

"At the moment, we have three objectives: one, stopping Brenev and his group from getting any more of these weapons, two, protecting ourselves from a repetition of these attacks, and three, assessing the extent of the damage already incurred.

An angry voice from the back spoke up. "It looks to me, from this list, that all the major spaceports and government complexes in the whole Federation have been wiped out."

"They've all sustained serious damage," Collins responded, "but in most cases can be made marginally operable and.."

"Do we have contact with Algoran yet?" a voice shouted. "We've been trying to get through and can't! What's the situation there?"

"Yes, what is being done?"

"And what are we supposed to do in the meantime? Are we just going to sit here and wait for them to attack again?"

Major Collins looked towards Commodore Pilchard, who nodded and stepped forward. "No we aren't going to sit around and wait. You know better than that, Heldik. What we have done is call up all the reserves, although, and I feel we must be candid about this, not all the reserves have responded. However, those who have reported are working under the supervision..."

"Wait just a minute" Heldik Holken interrupted, "do you believe the reserves have gone over to Brenev?"

"At this time we do not know why there has not been full response. We hope it is because of the damage to communications, but..."

"But you can't say for sure?"

"No, we can't say for sure."

At this there were more rumbles and head shakings as Pilchard resumed his comments. "As I was saying those who have reported are working under the supervision of the port technical personnel, to convert the minimally damaged domestic flight areas to accommodate interplanetary service. Both surface and air fleets are concentrating their forces on protecting not only the ports, but the various municipal complexes controlling the life support and transportation systems. Admirals Ashouk of Memphis and Uhati of Gohmeron will explain the defenses for each of their areas. For the most part they have instituted those actions called for under the Memphis Tri-Lateral Agreement with which you are all familiar. As for Algoran. We are in touch through Fleet transmissions. They are receiving messages from Algoran and are prepared to refer them on to the appropriate units."

"Messages from whom?" a voice asked. "We've heard that every major Federation facility on Aldene was wiped out!"

"Well like most rumors that is an exaggeration. There is no doubt about it, the damage to Algoran facilities was extensive. We aren't trying to whitewash that. However, we believe a few groups have re-formed and are trying to pull together some sort of interim government."

"What about the President? His cabinet?"

"What about Jorgenson, the Chancellor of Defense?"

The gabble continued until the Commodore held up his hand and said, "Please, let me finish and then I'll try to answer individual questions. Something is interfering with transmissions from Aldene. Periodically we can get through, but it's all very garbled. We're working through a relay set up with a patrol ship, but, so far, we have not been able to make contact with the President or Vice-President. A very brief message did seem to indicate that all of the Chancellors, including, I'm sorry to say, Lisbet Bohrnach are dead." There was a sharp intake of breath from someone in the room. Lisbet, a citizen of Resdorn, had been well liked and trusted. If she and all the Choitarem were dead, the Federation was leaderless.

"If we can't reach the President or Vice-President, should we assume they too are dead?" someone asked.

"What about the Council Delegates?" someone else shouted.

The Commodore held up his hands and shouted, "Please, quiet please. Be patient and I'll give you all the information we have. He cleared his throat and went on. "From what we understand the Secretary for Education and Cultural Recognition is presently acting as President."

The room again exploded into a torrent of comments. One loud voice was heard over all the others, "ECR is a low level cabinet position! Is there no one else left?"

"We haven't enough information to confirm or deny that," the Commodore responded. "All we know is the few transmissions we are receiving are from ECR Chancellor Benneton."

Vice Commodore DeVrys, a white haired contemporary of Commodore Pilchard rose and gave Pilchard a piercing look. "Commodore, are you telling us that for all intents and purposes, Algoran is gone?"

"I'm not saying that at all, Froeken, I'm saying that for now we are receiving transmissions from Aldene through the Fleet Communications network and have instituted defense procedures as outlined in the Memphis Tri-Lateral Agreement."

"What do we tell the people?" another voice asked, "An announcement will have to be made. The media people are going crazy out there with wild speculations!"

"If you will call up Appended Data 6 you will see a copy of a suggested press release."

"Not enough! You have to hold a media conference, explain what we know and ask for the people's support."

"Yes, the people have a right to know and then they'll rally 'round."

"Will they?" Vice-Commodore Devrys' dry voice overrode the others. "I think we have overestimated our support on Greniff and furthermore this fact sheet you handed us bears that out. Where's the damage report on Maas-X? What was destroyed on Kandrabad? I'll answer that for you. From the data given here Maas-X wasn't damaged and the only installations destroyed were the Administrative Headquarters on various Federation bases."

At the looks of incredulity, he added. "Go ahead, check me out. Think! Greniff is Nayland Brenev's home planet. Intelligence has been telling us that Maashout, and Kandrabad in general, are a hotbed of Black Knight support. I don't think the Federation is going to get any help from Kandrabad, Memphis Tri-Lateral Agreement or not!

The words hung in the air. All heads turned towards Flight Admiral Ashouk, Secretary of Defense for Kandrabad. The expression on his face as he stared at his clenched hands was confirmation of Devrys' opinion. So there it was, Algoran Federation leadership was apparently gone and now, it would seem, Greniff was a world at war with itself.

Before they could cope with that thought an aide came in with the message that they were receiving another message from Chanceller Benneton.

"Put it on the viewer," Pilchard snapped.

A man's face appeared on the screen. The picture quality was very poor and the voice faded in and out. The audio picked up in mid-sentence,"…never heard any more after that. They say it's gone; all gone. We know there was an incredibly bright light that lit up the night sky for hundreds of klics and then all the communications networks went out.

"Chanceller Benneton," Pilchard said slowly and distinctly, trying to be understood over the static, "has there been an attempt to re-establish some sort of government headquarters. Where are the President and the rest of the cabinet?"

Benneton's image wavered and they scarcely heard his response. "I don't know where any of them are. No one answers our calls. We're just here alone. We're Education and Cultural Recognition, you know. No one ever tells us anything important. We're supposed to promote cultural things like drama and art and music. Yes, music. Music is very important, you know. Yes, music is what we do. Music like…" He hummed a few words and then rose to walk around the room directing an invisible orchestra.

"Benneton!" Pilchard yelled, "What are you doing? What are you going to do about re-establishing the government? Is there anyone else there I can talk to?"

"Anyone else? Oh no, there are only a few of us and we're all alone here. No one answers our calls." He put his hands on his hips, leaned forward and glared, "They just will not answer our calls. Well, if that's the way they're going to be we'll just go on with our work. That's all we can do." With a showy pirouette, he began tripping around the room singing. "All we can do tra la, tra la, all we can do tra la la la la." Benneton then struck an heroic pose and began to sing loudly. As the transmission broke up and the screen filled with snow, the song was replaced with static.

* * *

The flyers swooped low over the compound below. Nayland Brenev, his body tense, his face pressed against the window searched for remembered landmarks at his old home. Black thoughts and old hatreds tumbled over and over in his mind. He recounted them, fed them, built up his fury.

"My home, my compound where my family and I were so happy until Loran brought that viper of a woman into our midst. It was she, she who caused the destruction of my home, my family, my life."

The veins throbbed in his forehead and he was shaking so hard he had to brace his arms on the window frame to steady his night scope. He forced himself to be calm, to think, to compare what he saw with his memories. They'd changed things, he thought. Well those changes, along with all other traces of their occupancy, could be erased. He rubbed his eyes and again strained to see.

There were only a few lights on and everything seemed peaceful. The flyers made a tight banking turn and came over again, fingers poised over triggers ready to return any fire from below. Nothing. Nayland Brenev moved the scope back and forth, checking the house, the storage sheds, the gardens and orchard. He was completely puzzled by this lack of response. He knew that the sophisticated surveillance system KalVan had installed had undoubtedly picked them up long before this, so what kind of game were they playing?

"Fire, fire! Do something!" he hissed. He wanted them to fight. He wanted an excuse to bring their home down around them, to make them see it and watch them suffer.

There was no response to their demands for surrender. No movement at all. Impatiently he motioned the pilot to land. The other transports followed. Soon dozens of men broke down the entrances and poured into the compound. They raced from room to room weapons at the ready. They found no one.

Nayland stood in the center of the largest reception room, fists clenched and his face scarlet with rage. "Noooooooo!" his long drawnout cry of fury echoed in the empty room. "They have to be here so I can kill them myself. See her as she dies!"

But they weren't there. Dulsena, Derek and all the other KalVan executives had, at Gutorm's insistence, taken their families and scattered to places of asylum far from Nayland's mad hatred and violence.

- 33 -
Old Hurts, New Betrayals

It was evening at Maashout. Marridon was walking in the gardens that overlooked the tabernacle site. It was a pleasant clear night. Both moons had risen and it was one of those few cycles of the year when both were in first phase at the same time. Now they hung there in the purple blue sky, two slender crescents, while in the tabernacle the great red crystals hung ready to chime. The inspiration for the Paladin Sequillat logo was more obvious than Marridon cared to think about. Hopefully no one else would think to mention it. There had been far too much dissension about them being involved in what was to have been a Black Knight holy war. Too much dissension altogether. His face was forlorn as he remembered the great argument he had had with Derrachem.

"Derrachem, Derrachem, old dear friend. Why can't you understand? We did what we had to do. What else would you have had us do with Aldene? We couldn't let the Federation government continue. Did you really think we could stop them and not kill them. Were you really that naive?

"Monstrous you call it. How could you say that to me? That would make me a monster. No, I cannot believe you think I am a monster! My people don't think I am. I have been aware that your faith has shifted and wavered over the last few years, but I never thought it had gotten to the point where you would doubt my divine calling to lead." Derrachem had just looked at him with a forlorn expression and quietly asked, "Oh, Marridon, have you never doubted? Have you ever, even once, questioned who you are and what you are doing?"

He had been so shocked he hadn't even answered. Derrachem had simply turned on his heel and left. After all their years together, all their dreams, he had just left him standing there. Now, as he stared at the two silver moons shining over the tabernacle, he thought of the people who were thronging into that great edifice. My people, he thought. My people. "Oh, Derrachem," he moaned, "you should have remembered that I am the Black Knight." I lead my people on the path to repentance, he thought. How could you not want to be here by my side? All these years and now, when we are so very close to achieving our goal you fail me. Oh, Derrachem.

He sighed and then, straightening his shoulders and with his head up, he walked down the path towards the back entrance to the tabernacle. Whatever his personal disappointments and betrayals, he must be strong, his work must go on.

It felt strange to have someone else help him with his robes of office. For so many years only Derrachem had done that for him. For just a moment he again felt grief, but an instant later it was replaced with a wave of anger that shook him from his very depths. How dare Derrachem pass judgement on him, The Black Knight. Such wickedness! Such yes, yes that was the word Derrachem had used. Such monstrous wickedness to turn against him like that.

He vented his indignation by giving his cloak a final shake and then, with the first tones of the chimes, strode onto the podium. It was only as he stood, arms upraised in a gesture of blessing, that he realized something was very wrong. Other than the chimes there was hardly a sound and only a few shouts of praise. Most of the people in the huge building stood and were strangely quiet.

His first words rang out loudly in the silence. He meant to give them encouragement by recounting the progress made against the Federation. He listed the territories taken and the major battles won. There was a little response led by his most ardent admirers, however, nothing as it should have been. Uneasily he continued. He summed up his recital and concluded by shouting the battle cry of the Black Knights Alvadar Anzegh, crying out for them to join in the battle. But, instead of a great response, a great affirmation, voices rang out shouting, "Forward but not with the Narmists!" Others picked up the chant, "Not with the Narmists! Not with the Narmists!"

Marridon finally got them to quiet down but before he could say anything a man with an amplifier shouted, "You deceived us and now we are in an unholy alliance with those Narmists who call themselves the Paladin Sequillat. You betrayed our trust!"

The crowd yelled and shouted in agreement. A few others dissented but they were shouted down.

"We are not in league with them," Marridon shouted back. They have just joined us for this battle against the Federation."

"Semantics," the man shouted back, "Their forces and their aircraft, bought incidentally from the godless Krogtlils," he shouted to the crowd, "are fighting alongside our warriors. That makes us in league with them and I for one am not going to fight side by side with those godless apostates!"

The crowd went wild. Those who agreed with the speaker shouted and thrust their arms upward repeatedly to emphasize their shouts. Those who still backed Marridon shouted just as stridently back at them. Others who had just learned of the Krogtlil's involvement, now joined in at full voice.

The worship service had turned into a mad melee. Marridon knew he could not get it back under control alone. He signaled for the great chimes to be lowered even further and the volume increased. Now the blood red lights flashed over the faces of the still shouting people, flashed over the upraised arms and weaving bodies as some resorted to fisticuffs to make their arguments. The huge chimes ringing out at full volume adding to the cacophony.

Suddenly, horror of horrors, the largest of the chimes shattered. Then others. People screamed in fright and pain as slivers of crystal flew everywhere. Now the red lights flashed on the red of blood stained faces and bodies. Marridon, who had rushed forward to the edge of the podium, fell with a prolonged wail into a crumpled heap. His hands moved convulsively, futilely trying to remove the long shard of crystal that protruded from his chest.

Gradually the throng quieted to sobs and tears, as more and more people saw what had happened to their leader.

"A sign," the man with the amplifier suddenly shouted. "A sign! A sign!" the others picked up the chant.

The people rushed for the exits, helping the wounded as they went. Out they raced. Out of the great tabernacle, leaving Marridon lying there with the blood red lights flashing over the hall, flashing across his body, and glinting off the long shard of crystal that still protruded from his chest. The hall became very quiet. The hands, still clutching the red shard, were now quiet, too. The Black Knight was dead.

From his place at the far side of the podium, Brenev had stood transfixed by what he had seen; the shattering of the crystals, the pleas of Marridon cut short by the spraying crystal shards. His body guards had forcibly pulled him away. Expertly they rushed him and Georgg out the back entrance of the building, out towards their flyer. A few of the raging mob caught sight of them and raced to intercept them, calling to others even as they ran. Wild eyed, blood streaming from numerous cuts and slashes, they vented their fury. The hubbub of noise drowned out the words, but there was no mistaking their intent as they closed the gap.

The flyer barely made it off the ground. With only seconds to spare, they slipped from the grasping hands of the maddened pursuers. The pilot climbed quickly and shot into overdrive leaving Nayland Brenev with one last view of the tabernacle surrounded by a sea of upturned, angry faces shouting at him, people waving their fists at him.

Stunned, Nayland drew in great, gasping breaths. He was so furious he could scarcely breathe. That idiot! That crazy old man had ruined everything for him! He should never have turned the volume up on those crystals. How could he have been so stupid? He knew they weren't as strong as the real Resdorn crystals. Now, because of his bungling, he'd lost the support of those religious fanatics. Even before they were well started he had messed things up so the Paladin Sequillat had gotten involved as well. Now here he was, left to pick up the pieces. He would be hard put to keep things going with just the mercenaries. Things were already going badly since the information he'd paid so dearly for, had turned out to be all wrong. The fleet had not dispersed to their various ports for the holidays, but had been very much in evidence all around the perimeter of the Federation. Only Aldene had been neutralized. The terrible damage that was supposed to have been done to these "easy targets", had instead been minimal. As a result strong Fed Forces were now counter-attacking everywhere. Even on Greniff, which should have been the easiest victory of them all, they found themselves fighting hard for every objective. It was almost as if the people had changed somehow. Surely not that many had been affected by the heretical ideas of KalVan. Impossible!

Georgg watched Nayland and started to say something then stopped. He knew there was no way to talk to him when he was like this. He just hoped there would be better news when they got back to headquarters.

As it turned out there was good news, but not news about battles fought and planets won. This was a turn of events so unexpected that no one could have anticipated it.

- 34 -
Added Leverage

Upon returning, Brenev had immediately called for an update on his troop's progress. He was not pleased with what he heard. In almost every area the Federation forces were routing the combined Brenev/BK fighters. With a swipe he cleared the viewing screen. With another abrupt movement he ordered a call to all his commanders. They had to know what had happened. They had to be prepared, for undoubtedly things would get even worse when the BK troops heard what had happened at Maashout.

As he waited for word that the gathering was complete, he read a transmission from Enferdeem Swadi demanding that Paladin Sequillat Commanders be given equal ranking and authority with his officers. The sound of his response echoed through the hallways reaching even the small, guarded room at the end of the building.

In that small room Marit raised her head and listened to the muffled shouts. She was sitting on a small lounge with her arm around Garrett who had fallen asleep with his head in her lap. She had been trying to avoid Selene's angry, accusing eyes. How could she explain her reasons for doing what she had done, she wondered. Selene was a child. She couldn't understand about a vow of revenge she had made to the memory of her sister. The child couldn't understand the hurt she had felt at seeing her sister slowly die of grief when her betrothed was taken off to Perdita. How could Selene know of the part her mother had had in bringing such grief.

She couldn't help it. She glanced again at Selene and encountered the same hard, unforgiving look. She wished she could explain how hard this was for her. In the many cycles she had cared for them she had learned to love them and now she couldn't help it if she had to do something that was going to hurt them. Worst of all she really liked Dulsena and Derek. She tried to push that thought out of her mind. She would carry through with her plans. She had sworn to do this and she had gone too far to back out now. She knew the children were the only way to get Dulsena and Derek to surrender to Brenev. Afterwards she was sure she could talk Nayland Brenev into letting her take Selene and Garrett some place where they would be safe.

She looked at Selene sitting so straight with her arms crossed over her chest, still staring at her.

"It will be all right, Selene," she said, placatingly.

"No it won't. Not unless you take us to our mother and father as you were supposed to do," Selene answered in a small hard voice.

"Why did you kill the pilot? He was just doing what he was supposed to do. You are the one who is bad. You've brought us here instead of to the port so we could go to Resdorn to be with our grandparents. I thought you were our friend but you aren't! You are mean and I hate you!"

"Oh, Selene, you don't understand," Marit cried, "I had to do it."

"No you didn't!" Selene shouted. "You're a liar and I don't believe anything you say!"

Garrett stirred at the angry shouting and sat up. "Come over here, Garrett. Stay away from her," Selene said.

Garrett moved over to sit by Selene and she put her arm around his shoulders. "Marit isn't our friend anymore, Garrett. Don't talk to her. Stay with me."

Garrett stared at Marit with a hurt expression and Marit burst into tears.

"She's crying," Garrett said softly, looking up at Selene.

"She ought to," Selene said bitterly, "she's a big liar."

Just then the door opened and a man motioned to Marit and said to bring the children and come with him.

Selene sat still and held Garrett down when he started to get up. "Stay where you are, Garrett. We won't do what they want."

The guard walked over, roughly grabbed Selene by the arm and pulled her to the door.

"Selene!" screamed Garrett and rushed after her, clutching her around the waist.

"Selene, please do what they ask," pleaded Marit. I don't want them to hurt you."

"A lot you care, you liar!" Selene said as she was hustled down the long corridors. When she lagged, the guard pushed her between the shoulder blades sending her lurching forward. Garrett, tears streaming down his face, struggled to keep up with them.

Finally they stopped before a door and the guard knocked. The door slid open. A tall man with dark hair and a mean look was seated behind a desk. Slowly he stood and, with his hands on his desk, leaned forward as if to see them better. Then he smiled, but it was a smile that made Selene shudder and for the first time she felt really, really frightened.

- 35 -
Returns of Vengeance

Rohnseff Spaceport was a shambles. Construction crews were working around the clock in an effort to convert the domestic flight areas to an inter-world facility, however work was hampered by the periodic air attacks. What was accomplished was makeshift. Fierce battles had been fought all around the planet. The Federation troops had been forced back towards Rohnseff City and were now fighting to defend the municipal support systems from the very strong combined Brenev/BK forces. So far they were holding their own. The port facility proper was flooded with thousands of refugees who had fled there seeking a way to leave Greniff. It was their last hope as Brenev had control of most of the airfields outside of Rohnseff.

Scortzi and Derek had been frantically pressing KalVan and Kalleni freighters into service to transport their personnel back to Resdorn. Siburi had refused to leave until she had collected all the important records from the store as well as all the jewels and other easily transportable valuables. She had firmly pointed out that they would need whatever they could salvage to start over again somewhere else. After she had personally supervised the loading of these items into a small freighter, she and her secretary had joined the long line of passengers waiting to board the remaining operational ships.

Now, Scortzi and Derek had their hands full working with KalVan security to hold spaces for those who would be arriving from the KalVan summer compound where they had fled after Gutorm's warning. Derek held his position amidst the bustle at the boarding ramp of the last KalVan freighter anxiously awaiting Dulsena and the others to appear so they too could be off. He was worried. He knew that back at the compound all the transportation left to them had been three small fliers. Into these they would have had to load themselves and the few remaining personal items they could manage, fly to Rohnseff, over territory held by the rebels, and then jockey for space to land along with all the other flyers converging there. Hopefully all this would be done without encountering hostile attack.

Katje and Sophronia were the first to appear at the ramp.

"Where are the others?" Derek asked.

"They should be along any time now," Sophronia answered. "They were right behind us. We were first in because Katje was piloting and she doesn't let much of anyone get ahead of her, no matter what." Katje just gave Derek a look, shook her head and prodded Sophronia on up the ramp.

They had just boarded when Dulsena's pilot appeared, loaded down with bags and parcels, followed by Dulsena who shouted, "Where are Marit and the children, Derek? We lost sight of them when we were coming in. Have they already boarded?"

"Haven't seen them yet," he replied, helping her with the bags she was carrying, "but, they should be here any moment."

"Derek, I'm worried about them. I didn't see them land," Dulsena insisted. "You can't imagine what it's like out there. It's wild."

"Kanute is with them. He'll take care of them," Derek said. He didn't want to admit that he was worried too. They should have stayed together!

As Dulsena went aboard Derek turned to her pilot and said, "When did you see them last?"

"It was just as we started down into an approach pattern. She was right. It's a real mess out there. I had my hands full getting down and wasn't paying any attention to where they were. Kanute is a good pilot though and I can't imagine he wouldn't get them here safely."

"Yes, I know he is but I still don't like it. Well, you go ahead and stow all this stuff and then get on board. Your family's waiting for you. I'll wait here until they come."

Derek didn't just wait. He called all the landing areas trying to find out if someone had seen them land. Nothing. Scortzi, when he was told of the problem, pulled some men from the loading crews. They searched all around, but no one could remember seeing that flyer land, nor had they seen Kanute and the children. But, as all were quick to point out, who could find anyone in that crowd?

By the time Scortzi got back to the freighter Derek, and Dulsena who had refused to stay on board, were frantic. They had already begun to suspect something terrible had happened when they got a call saying they were to go to Rhys Xholan's office immediately.

At the temporary office building they were ushered into a conference room and met there by a grim faced Rhys Xholan. "Please sit down all of you," Rhys said. "You're not going to like what I have to say any more than I like saying it.

"Derek, Dulsena, I have had a message from Nayland Brenev. He has your children."

"What!" shouted Dulsena. "How, how could he have them? They were right behind me when we came in to land?"

"It seems that Marit took them to him."

"Marit took the children to Brenev? But why? Why would she do that?" Dulsena cried, unable to comprehend what she was hearing.

"He says that Marit's sister was betrothed to Nayland Brenev's cousin and he was one of those sent to Perdita. Marit's sister, according to Marit, died of a broken heart and she blames you."

"She blames me? All this time!" Dulsena wailed. "All the time she has been with us she has been planning to do something like this? I can't believe it! We really liked Marit. We trusted her. She seemed to genuinely love the children. How could she do something like this? Oh Derek, what are we going to do?"

"More to the point," Scortzi interjected, "is what does Nayland Brenev want you to do. He didn't send that message just to gloat. He wants something. What is it?"

“You’re right,” Rhys said, “He wants Dulsena herself to ‘come and get them’. He says that is the only way.”

“You mean trade them for Dulcy,” Derek said.

“Derek,” Rhys said reluctantly, “I don’t want to say it but yes, perhaps that is what he means.”

“He wouldn’t let them go no matter what,” Scortzi said flatly.

“No I don’t think he would either,” Rhys agreed, “however, there may be a way.”

“How, what way? What can we do?” Dulcy asked desperately.

“I apprised Commodore Jehanin of this situation,” Rhys answered. “He is of the opinion that we may be able to turn this to our advantage. If Brenev is so anxious to have his revenge on you, Dulsena, that he is willing to divulge his location we may, with the Commodore’s help, give him something else to think about. The general thinks that a lot of fighting spirit will be lost if Brenev is removed. After all, the support he has is mostly loyalty to him personally and from the mercenaries he pays. If the Federation could capture him they believe that support would collapse.”

“Well let’s try!” Dulsena cried. “We have to try!”

- 36 -
The Dragon's Lair

Dulsena stood in the clearing on the hilltop and tried to get her bearings. It was dark and very quiet. The usual night sounds had not resumed after her flight in. A sudden POP! sent her nerves jangling. It was only a piece of metal on the flyer contracting in the cool night air. She felt very alone.

The instructions received at Rhys's office had been explicit; she was to follow them exactly or the children would be killed immediately. A wave of panic washed over her. No, she thought, I can't think of such a thing. I must take it one step at a time and count on Derek and Commodore Jehanin. Derek. Leaving him had been so hard. Hard for them both. Neither would admit that they didn't have a lot of confidence in the plans they'd made. They just knew they had to do everything they could to get Selene and Garrett away from Nayland Brenev.

With new resolve, she took the small communicator from her pocket and turned it on. It had been set at the frequency the instructions had directed.

"I'm here. What now?"

"Look to the south," a voice replied. "Do you see the beacon on the hill?"

"Yes, I see it. It's not very bright," she replied.

"Bright enough," came the reply. "You brought the grav lift as directed?"

"Yes."

"Good. Put it on and head for the beacon. When you get there you will receive further instructions."

"Why don't we quit all this skulking around and you just tell me where I can find my children?" Dulsena said sharply.

"Patience, patience. All in good time. Now get started."

Dulsena slipped into the grav unit harness and, lifting up and over the trees, headed for the pale light on the hill. She landed without incident and again keyed in the communicator.

"I'm at the beacon. Now what?"

"Take off the grav unit and leave it there. Did you bring the light as we said?"

"Yes, I have the light."

"Turn it on low and shine it forward at knee height."

Dulsena turned the light on high and then immediately onto low at the same time the voice said, "ON LOW!"

"Sorry," Dulsena said, "I'm not familiar with this light."

Well that proved one thing, she thought to herself. They could see her even if she couldn't see them.

"Shine the light in an arc until you see an opening in the cliff wall."

She did as she was directed and said, "I see it. It's very small."

"It's big enough. Granted you will have to crawl in for a short way, but then you'll be able to stand."

Dulsena stared at the small opening. This was bad, she thought. Jehanin's cruiser would not be able to monitor her if she were underground. Well, she had no choice.

She started for the tunnel when the voice said, "Turn the communicator off, Dulsena and put it on the ground by the opening. She did as she was instructed. Now she really was alone.

* * *

Aboard the cruiser, the Tec adjusted his scanner and then said, "We've lost her."

"Keep trying," Major Aylesbury encouraged him.

Derek looked stricken. Where could she be? Think, he said to himself. Think. She was in the mountains south of Maashout. Rugged terrain. Wooded. Who lived there? A few scattered hunters, some woodcutters, a few miners…A few miners? he repeated to himself. "Miners," he said out loud. "There are mines in those hills. She has probably been led into some mine shaft."

"Get the mass spec on to that hill," the major said to a Tec, "and find out if there are some shafts or cuts in that area."

Soon a pattern of lines appeared on the screen.

"Oh Narm!" the major said, "it looks like a maze of tunnels going in all directions. She could be in any one of them."

* * *

Dulsena crawled along the rough tunnel until it opened into what appeared to be a large cavern. Inside, the main walkway was clearly marked. It led her across to where it entered another tunnel. She could at least stand up in this one and she moved along as quickly as she could. Several times she came to "Y's" and there were markers indicating which way she should go. A short distance further on, the tunnel narrowed to a rough ledge cut along one wall. Cut from some shalelike rock it was composed of flat, sharp layers that were slick from the water that was trickling down the wall. Anxious to be out of there, she was hurrying when her foot slid out from under her. She caught at the wall to regain her balance while at the same time, with a rattle, a section of the path dislodged from underfoot and slid off the ledge. A moment later there was a splash. Dulsena, her heart pounding, balanced carefully and leaned over to shine her light downward. There was an abrupt drop off and only darkness. Over the sound of her pounding heart she could hear the rushing of water down below.

Straightening carefully, she caught her breath and decided that it might be prudent to go more slowly.

Sweeping the area forward with the light, she saw that the small rivulets had now become almost a solid sheet of water cascading down the walls and across the walkway. She crept along the ledge with one hand on the wet wall and the other holding the small light. Even going slowly she still slipped several times. It seemed ages before the ledge sloped down and widened out into another smaller cavern. At least here the floor was sandy and relatively dry. Another set of markers pointed the way she was to follow.

As she followed this new tunnel she thought of how gleeful Nayland would have been if she had fallen off that ledge into the black, racing waters below; how satisfied he would be to have her lost forever in that dark, unmarked grave.

"Too bad, Nayland, I made it," she shouted out loudly. It,It It It, her voice echoed eerily through the caverns. In a whisper she added, "So far".

She went on for quite a ways and then suddenly the light changed and she found herself once again out under open sky. Ahead a dim light flickered on and then moved back and forth. A voice said, "Follow me."

A dark figure led the way downhill along a crooked path. Twice they were stopped and challenged by guards who appeared out of the darkness. They were allowed to continue on after an exchange of passwords. At last they came to a group of buildings and she was led into a small room. There she was forced to strip and submit to a detailed examination before being left alone to dress and wait.

Fortunately they had allowed her to keep her own clothes. The Commodore had expected the communicator would be confiscated and the homing device found. The idea had been that, hopefully, this would divert their attention so they would not look further and find that the fabric of her jumpsuit was inter-woven with communication fibers. And, even if they took her clothes, there was still another back-up in the small device that had been implanted just above her hairline.

After a long wait, two guards came and got her. She was marched down a long corridor and shoved into a small room. The door slid closed with a dull thud behind her. In the total silence, she looked around her at the bare, white room. There was a small cot with a thin cover folded at the end, a chair and a shallow annex with an ancient

PCU. No ornamentation anywhere. Nothing. She assumed she was under surveillance, but couldn't see the viewers. Well, no matter, she thought, it probably won't be long before they take me to Nayland. She fervently prayed that then she would be allowed to see the children and that they could see her. How frightened they must be, she thought.

She paced anxiously, three paces over, three paces back. Four paces up, four paces back. No sound penetrated the cold white walls. Time went by. She couldn't know how much time exactly as they had taken her chronos. But nothing happened. Nothing. She called, but no one answered. She pounded on the door. No one answered. She was entirely alone in this featureless, windowless cell, cut off from everybody.

* * *

Back on board the Dauntless, the general had insisted that Derek try to get some rest. Exhausted and sick with worry he had finally agreed after extracting the promise that they would waken him if anything happened. Now he dozed fitfully, terrible images running through his dreams."

Earlier he had watched as they monitored the communicator on an erratic journey across the mountains. Its signal had been clear. It was also clear that Dulsena was no where near it as it was the only signal. There was no trace of the other two. The waiting had become almost unbearable when they had suddenly picked her up again. Apparently she was back on the surface. They tracked her down to a valley and then on up the other side. There the movements became short with times of inactivity in between. They could only conclude she had been confined somewhere. Later, as the night wore on, Derek and the Tecs at their monitors had watched as the object of their surveillance moved back and forth, back and forth, before finally settling into one spot and staying there.

Commodore Jehanin, had moved silently up behind Derek, put his hand on his shoulder and together they had watched this cessation of movement.

"Sleep, Dulsena," Jehanin had whispered gently. "Sleep. We don't know what problems and challenges tomorrow may bring."

"As for you, Derek," Jehanin had continued brusquely, "You must try to rest. You'll need to be alert tomorrow for your family's sake."

Derek, exhausted and sick from worry, had given in and gone to his quarters, flopped on the hard bunk and stared at the ceiling. Jehanin's words echoed over and over through his mind. "We don't know what problems and challenges tomorrow may bring." Problems, problems, problems. The words pounded through his nightmares.

- 37 -
Revenge Is Mine

"What do you mean they've left," Nayland yelled. "Get through to Bilchard or Bilchow or whatever his name is and tell him to move his troops in and cover for those blasted BK quitters. We'll have to get reinforcements to Polchar, too. And what about this crazy communique from Pantro? It doesn't make any sense!" He continued striding around the room shuffling readouts, flipping through telespools pulling up charts on the enormous viewscreen that covered one end of the room. "Where are the reports from Dornace?" he yelled, "They're overdue. Isn't anyone around here capable of doing anything besides me?" He swirled around and glared at Georgg. "Well? Well? Can't you say something?"

"I have, but you don't listen," Georgg said in a sad, tired voice.

"So, tell me again," Nayland said in a mockingly patient tone. "See, I am listening. I am sitting down here and I am listening. So tell me something worth listening to."

"Bilchord doesn't have any troops to move in. They have all left," Georgg said very distinctly. "All the Black Knight's forces have disbanded. When they quit, the troops you had hired pulled their wages and left, too. Forces led by your old nemesis, Gutorm Anfinrud have routed your troops on Frayleen and Polchar. Resdorn, as you well know, was Fed aligned from the start."

He paused as Nayland made a face and gave a dismissing wave, then he proceeded. In the Muonior System, Pantro and Arno have decided they are more interested in trade protected by the Federation than in rebellion. Only on Soloving are there still a few scattered cells resisting. Flornak, Dornace and Chaldorn have also decided that the Federation provides more of an incentive for trade and besides the destruction of Aldene caused a surprisingly strong groundswell of disaffection. Those three, along with Resdorn and Algoran were the first to form the Federation and they have old alliances. As for Nirubati, there are still a few holdouts who are fighting, but the Feds are bound to overpower them before long. Oh yes there's Felchor. Well, the Feds aren't even bothering with Felchor. Other than those mines with the poor crystals, it's a worthless place and they can afford to wait until it is more convenient to go in there and wipe up. So, other than your old family supporters here on Greniff, there just aren't any troops to speak of anymore—anywhere.

Your great rebellion is finished, Nayland. You might as well face up to it."

"It can't be finished! It can't be!" Nayland shouted as he jumped up and strode around the room. "There has to be something more we can do. Something we haven't thought of. You're always such a pessimist, Georgg. Now think, think. We still have weapons and flyers," he said, trying to sound optimistic.

"Not enough to do any good," Georgg responded.

"Well there must be enough to do some damage somewhere. If nothing else we will use them as a diversion to draw their attention away from here until we can leave."

"Leave and go where and do what?" Georgg asked, biting off each word.

"Don't worry about that, don't you worry. You know I always have a plan. Just help me figure out what we can do with those weapons."

"Nayland, get out while you can!" Georgg shouted.

"No, no, no." Nayland shouted back. "Besides, there's one bit of unfinished business."

"What is more important than us getting away to Huilla while we still can?" Georgg asked impatiently.

"We still have visitors here, Georgg. You don't expect me to leave before I have entertained them properly, do you?"

"Visitors? Oh, that again. Let it go, Nayland. Let's just leave."

"Oh no, if everything else is gone, as you seem to think it is, I can still get that much out of all this. I really can't put it off any longer."

- 38 -
The Eye of the Serpent

Dulsena opened her eyes; the lights coming on had awakened her. The food service door slid open and she hurried to her feet. She had learned that the food had to be removed quickly or the door closed and nothing more would be offered until the next mealtime. She removed the small tray, set it on the table and then made her way to the PCU. This was the tenth morning she had been through this routine. When she had been brought to this old country home she had assumed she would be taken right in to see Nayland Brenev. However, that hadn't been the case. Instead she had sat day after day without a word from anyone on the outside. She had tried to get someone to tell her what was going on; she had yelled and pounded on the door, but, all her efforts to get someone to come or talk to her had been in vain. Finally, she had to accept the fact that she was trapped and no one was going to talk to her until they were ready to.

It was so frustrating especially when her mind was in a constant turmoil worrying about the children, imagining what Nayland might do to them. She had no better idea now than when she came as to where they were or if they were all right. It made her sick to think that they were at the mercy of such a man. She knew very well what he was and what he was capable of doing, even to innocent children. As for herself, well, she was sure Nayland would think up something particularly unpleasant for her. For a few hours on the first day she had been afraid they had shut her in this cell and then everyone had left. It was only on the second day, with the arrival of the food trays, that she was reassured that there was still someone out there. Other than those few seconds a day there was no contact with the outside world. Alone, in this stark, white cell, she had seen no one and heard nothing.

The food they shoved through the door twice a day was rough fare and barely palatable. Nevertheless, she forced herself to eat it. She was determined to be in as good condition as she could be for whatever was to come. That was her only defense, to be as strong and alert as possible and if that meant eating pitan and that disgusting mixture, of whatever it was, that is what she would do. Defiantly she finished up the last morsel and put the tray in the disposal unit.

Then, stripping off her clothes down to her undergarment, she stood in the center of the tiny room and began the latz warm-up exercises and the self defense routines that Cogn Toc and Lef had drilled her and Scortzi on for so many years. She had started doing them several times a day aware that she had been lax about them during the last few years. It seemed there was always so much to do; work at the store, trying to keep up with the children and her responsibilities running the compound. It was clear that her decision was the right one as she had found herself short of breath and stiff after the first few workouts. Now, after ten days, or what she thought was ten days, she felt herself getting back into the rhythm, making the transitions more smoothly. She went through the routines and her thoughts kept pace. There were no women's sports on Greniff, no games or tournaments. That was one of the things she missed about Resdorn. She and Derek had organized games with Garrett and Selene and the children of the executives who lived in the compound. That had been fun, but not like organized events. There were a lot of things she missed about Resdorn and, as they had packed for their flight away from Greniff, she had found herself remembering things and places she wanted the children to see and people she wanted them to meet back home.

Thinking of the children, she stretched a little further than was comfortable, kicked more vigorously. She wished she were bigger, stronger, more capable and yes, less afraid. She was so desperately afraid of Nayland. Not for what he might do to her but afraid for the children and how he might harm the rest of her family. Visions of Maashout Tabernacle came to mind. There had been such immense, raw power there. Perhaps the force she had felt, the energy that had reverberated through that huge hall, had been enough to completely rout the Federation forces. Perhaps by now the whole of Greniff was controlled by Brenev. Perhaps even the Fed ship and those tracking her had been forced to retreat. Did she still have backup or not? Those questions and doubts had haunted her as, hour after hour, she had stared at the four walls of this cell. Maybe she had simply walked into this trap for nothing. She would be powerless to help her children, if indeed they were still alive. What if…Maybe…If only…"Stop it!" she shouted. "Thinking like that won't help and will drive me crazy."

She repeated the exercise routine, stretching further, lunging harder. By the time she finished the workout she was soaked and panting. Like an automaton she went through the cool down exercise, then took a deep breath and headed for the PCU. Faith. She would keep her faith and try to be prepared for whatever happened. However, in the warmth of the PCU, the tears came. "OH, Selene, Garrett" she cried, "I'm trying, I'm trying. I pray for strength and help. We need it so much."

When, many long, white hours later someone finally did come, she was taken unawares; lying on the cot she had dozed off. The door opening awakened her and a hard-faced guard ordered her to follow him. She was led through long, mostly featureless corridors until at last they went through a high doorway into another, much older, more ornate part of the structure. There thick rugs covering the stone floors and heavy, colorful fabrics covered the old fashioned furniture. Sunlight streamed through tall deep-set windows and flashed off the antique metal armaments that hung on every wall. High up on the walls just under the groined ceiling, brass tipped spears jutted outwards. Each was hung with a patterned, triangular banner with a long point. Most of the banners were faded attesting to their great age. Beneath them, hung long rope talagents of colored, multi-stranded rope. The only other place Dulsena had ever seen anything like them was in a museum she had gone to with Loran. She had learned that each talagent represented the combined lineages of one of the old royal houses. This must be one of those old houses. At intervals on each talagent, silver or gold emblems were fastened denoting an honor bestowed. Interspersed with these were small ribbons and lengths of fringe. Each ribbon knot and fringe retold, if one were knowledgeable and could read them, the stories of fateful alliances and momentous battles. Some she passed were very old and faded while others appeared to have been added later. All of these items were relics from the devastating wars before the Federation came to power. Certainly, whoever owned this property had family that had been here for many, many years.

The guard stomped on ahead and Dulsena followed. The talagents glittered and swayed slightly as they passed. So many warriors had gone off to battle well armed and backed with the latest machines of war, she thought. Now here she was, about to battle for her life and the lives of her children, without a weapon of any kind except her wits.

They reached the end of the hall and stopped before some very tall, carved wooden doors. The guard knocked loudly four times. Nothing. He knocked again, muttering under his breath. Just as he was raising his fist to knock again, the door started to open. A young boy was struggling to pull it open.

"Where's your father?" the guard growled, "and why isn't he here to open the door?"

"He's off some'ere. Old Brenev sent him off to do somethin'," the boy whined.

The guard pushed the door open and waited for Dulsena to come through. They were now in a stark white corridor and the calm of the ancient hall they had just left was replaced with a dreadful din. People, most of whom were in uniforms she didn't recognize, scurried here and there shouting orders and questions. A hover cart shot around the corner barely missing the guard who barked something unintelligible at the frazzled looking man in a rumpled uniform who was guiding it. He responded with something equally vulgar sounding, without ever looking up from the stack of record boxes he was trying to keep from sliding off the top. He careened off down the corridor imperiling everyone along the way.

The guard's muttering grew louder and even fiercer as he stomped along forcing his way through the crowd. At last he stopped before a door, knocked, then waited and knocked again.

The door swung open and there, across the room, was that familiar dark countenance, Nayland Brenev. Dulsena had thought she was ready for this moment, but she was shocked at the force of the feelings that rushed through her at the sight of this man. He looked up and she felt her fists clench as he smiled at her. SMILED at her!

"Where are my children?" she said fiercely.

"Oh, still the same Dulsena, so impatient, so demanding," Nayland said smoothly. "The years have not taught you how to get along with people."

"I get along fine with people of conscience. It's vicious, blood thirsty savages like you I have a hard time being civil to. Again, where are my children?"

"Oh you do have hard words for your old brother," he said smiling, but his eyes were hard.

Steady, Dulsena told herself, You have no weapons but your wits. Keep them together. Observe.

"Nayland, let's stop this fencing. Where are my children and what do we have to do to get out of here?"

"Do, Dulsena? Why nothing at all. You can see your children any time you want. I'm feeling magnanimous right now. After all, everything has gone my way. The Federation has been routed and my troops are in control. I am back on my own dear Greniff, which I have missed so terribly during all the long years of my banishment due to your meddling. But no," he said waving his hand gracefully, "that is all behind us now. We must look only to the future. You will be with your children and I shall rule from our old home here on Greniff. Of course, it is too bad that none of the rest of my family can be here since they have all been reprogrammed or sent to Perdita by your precious Federation. No we wil…"

His voice droned on but Dulsena was watching him carefully. He was lying! Not for one minute did she believe what he was saying about his forces winning. The body language was all wrong, the inflections, the eye movements. All wrong. Everything he was saying was a lie, or almost everything. She focused on his eyes. They were unnaturally bright, wild looking. His movements were jerky in spite of an obvious effort at self control. The words rushed out alternating more and more grandiose claims of victory with more accusations and claims of insults and persecutions by the Federation. He had risen from his place behind the large desk and, as he talked, he paced quickly back and forth and became more and more agitated.

Dulsena watched spellbound. The blood pounded in her ears as all the signals hammered home the thought—this man is not rational. In fact it was becoming very obvious he was quite mad! Now she was really worried. One can sometimes predict what a sane person will or will not do, but, there was no way to know what a mad man would do. She was going to have to be very, very cautious.

- 39 -
Chimes of Darkness

"Come, Dulsena, we must not keep you waiting longer. You want to see your children, don't you?"

The tirade, monologue, whatever you wanted to call it had stopped. Now Nayland Brenev, his eyes glittering, nodded to the guard to open the door and, with an elaborate, courtly gesture, waved Dulsena through. A small group of guards was waiting. They formed a line on either side of her and began to follow after Nayland.

The crowd in the corridor had thinned out considerably and the few people that were left stopped and silently saluted as Nayland passed by. Mostly Greneche, thought Dulsena. Some looked terribly sad and something else, what was it? Wistful. Yes that was it. Wistful. Others appeared angry, frustrated. She wondered if this did not confirm her assessment that far from having the wonderful victory that he had claimed to have, that perhaps quite the opposite was true. All the activity she had seen earlier suggested a retreat, not victorious confidence. She was right. She knew she was right. But wouldn't this make Nayland even more dangerous? He had nothing left to lose.

They exited the building and emerged onto a large paved area, a terrace that had been built on a large promontory that jutted out from the mountainside. The air smelled strange. She couldn't identify what it was, but, as they got closer to the furthest point of the promontory, she could look back up the gorge and see lava belching forth from the truncated top of a volcano and flowing down the sides. Even as she watched, a new explosion of flame and sparks burst hundreds of feet into the air. More steaming, scarlet lava bubbled and roiled down the sides. Even from a distance the heat was incredible and the stench was nauseating. Horrified, she stopped, repulsed by the sight. Nayland turned and saw she had stopped. Imperiously, he motioned her forward and one of the soldiers shoved her ahead. As she approached the wall at the edge she could see that the whole area below was filled with a glowing, red, molten river.

Her heart was racing and she could hardly breathe. She was terrified!

"Why are we here?" she shouted at Nayland. "You said you were taking me to see my children."

"Oh I am, I am. Why, there they are now. Right on schedule." He laughed and pointed.

She leaned over the stone wall and saw, coming from the castle-side of the gorge, a small open cage-like basket moving slowly outward from below where they stood. It hung from cables strung across the gorge and inside were two small figures, clinging tightly to the bars of the cage. She could hear the terrified wails of Selene and Garrett. "Mama!, Mama!" The cries burned through her and Dulsena thought her heart would stop.

"NO!, NO! Oh God! NO!" she shouted as she beat her hands against the stones. She whirled and swung at Nayland, but, the soldiers blocked her way.

"Even you couldn't be this monstrous!" she shouted. "You can't do this! They're just children. They haven't done you any harm. Take your hate out on me. I'm the one you blame. Leave them alone. Please! I beg of you. I beg of you."

"She begs!" Nayland laughed. "Do you see that? The great Dulsena is begging me." he laughed even louder and the soldiers joined in.

"Let them go, Nayland."

The soft voice from off to the side, took Nayland by surprise and he turned in amazement.

"Georgg?" he said quizzically. "Now, Georgg, you know I can't do that."

"Yes you can, Nayo. You don't need them. Let them go."

"We've been through this before, Georgg," Nayland said sharply. "Don't try to change my mind again. They die and she will watch them."

He turned back to Dulsena, "You can see can't you, Dulsena, that this is how it must be? You can see I won't let even my greatest friend change my mind so you know nothing you can say will make me change it. Ah, but wait, there is one way left, isn't there. Oh Yes. You can pray. You were always so good at that. Pious little Dulsena listening for your crystals and praying, praying. Well you will hear the crystals ring again today and you will pray. Oh yes I'm sure you will pray very hard." He laughed again.

Then suddenly, grasping her by the left shoulder, he propelled her around ending with his arm tight across her body under her chin. At the same time he twisted his right hand in her hair and forced her head sharply around so she was looking directly at the basket swaying over the gorge.

Speaking softly in her ear, he said, "You see how the basket is hanging there, swinging above that great molten river? Well the catch holding that pretty, little basket is controlled by one of your precious crystals. Yes, it is. And, like all good Resdorn crystals, there is a microchip at the top. Now when I send the signal the catch will open and the basket will drop. And you, dear Dulsena, will watch it drop, down, down and you will remember the suffering you have caused me. Now isn't that appropriate, Dulsena? Appropriate that I should use one of your own Resdorn crystals. Such a nice touch don't you think?"

He gave her head a fierce shake, abruptly released her and pushed her away from him. Laughing, he reached inside his tunic for the control unit. Just then a small figure rushed past Georgg and a great laser blast caught Nayland in the chest throwing him against the low wall. The momentum flung him out and over. Everything seemed to go into slow motion. Dulsena gasped and watched as the dark body, spread eagled, was silhouetted against the roiling, scarlet lava. Down, down it floated into the smoke, down towards that hellish nightmare scarlet river.

"Nayooo" Georgg rushed forward and his long anguished scream was cut short as he was caught in the laser fire directed towards the small figure who had killed Nayland Brenev.

Dulsena spun about and stared at the battered figure crumpled on the stones. "Marit?"

"She didn't know," came the whisper. Georgg attempted to rise, but fell back from the pain. "She didn't know," he whispered. "She thought he was going to let her take the children away afterwards. She didn't know."

A flier shrieking across, barely above her head, brought Dulsena to her senses. Other fliers were coming in from all directions. The guards began running towards the castle firing ineffectively as they ran. Dulsena pivoted around and searched desperately for a glimpse of the basket. Through the melee she saw a larger Fed unit sweep in, enclose the basket in a retrieval net and sweep away with the precious cargo. Turning she saw the whole promontory was now full of men, with more pouring out of every exit. Federation uniforms. Fed troops! There were others too, who were not in uniform, who fighting through the melee, were heading straight towards her. It was easy to recognize the two men leading them—Scortzi and Gutorm.

"Dulcy, are you all right?" Scortzi shouted through the tumult.

"Yes but Derek, where's Derek," Dulsena asked as she pulled away from the shelter of Scortzi's arms.

"He's fine," both Scortzi and Gutorm said at the same time. "He's on the ship that just netted Selene and Garrett," Gutorm added.

"We thought the children would need him to be there," Scortzi explained.

"Nayland's dead," Dulsena shouted. "Marit shot him. He went over the edge into the gorge. Marit's dead too and so is Nayland's friend Georgg. It looked to me like his troops were all leaving. Is it over? Did the Federation stop them?"

"Yes, except for cleaning up of various pockets like this one." They looked around the promontory and could see that the Federation forces had finished rounding up the remaining rebels and were putting them in restraints for transport. Gutorm's communicator buzzed and as he keyed it a voice could be heard saying, "Report, please."

"Dulsena is safe and in good shape," Gutorm reported into his communicator. "Brenev is dead as are Marit and Georgg Nulek. The situation here is under control and we should be at the rendezvous point within an hour."

"Understood. Commodore Jehanin requests you check in with him as soon as possible. There are some people here who are anxious to see Dulsena."

"Yes, Sir. We will do that."

He keyed off and said, "You heard the man. Let's go."

They started across the terrace towards the door when Dulsena said, "Wait", and hurried back to the wall and looked over the edge.

The cable was still there, dangling over the smoky, red hell beneath. Another explosion and a bright red spray shot out of the mouth of the volcano and drifted down to settle on the roiling turmoil below.

"I wanted to make sure," Dulsena said to Scortzi as he moved up beside her. "I wanted to make sure he's really gone."

They stared down at the hellish river beneath them, then in a whisper Dulsena said, "Marit did it, you know. She shot him. Poor Marit. She did us such great harm and then died trying to set things right." She looked down again at that roiling red abyss. There was no trace of Nayland Brenev. He had suffered the horrible fate he had planned for her innocent children. "Yes," she sighed, "I do believe it now is over."

She swung around and said, "Let's get out of here. I want to see my children. Oh wait," she stopped with a puzzled expression. "You said that you thought Derek should be there when they got the children. How did you know what was going to happen?"

"Commodore Pilchard got a message from a man telling him what Nayland was planning to do and when."

"A man? Who? Georgg? He tried to talk Nayland out of it," Dulsena asked.

"No, we don't think it was Georgg. When they asked him for his name he refused to give it and said just to say you were the daughter he never had."

"Daughter he ne…Luis. Luis Roncallo," Dulsena whispered.

"Yes, I think so. You know he never was caught after the rebellion.

Apparently he was still working for Brenev, but drew the line at killing your children."

"But, Scortzi, that was so long ago. How can you be sure?"

"Remember Marit giving us the description of the man that gave her the note that day on the beach; plump, dark hair, dark eyes, looked rich, wore lots of jewelry? What better description could you have of Luis Roncallo?"

"You're right," Dulsena said with wonder. "Well thank the Lord he still felt that way. Without his info..." Her voice cracked with emotion. "Without his information the children would have gone down into that." She waved her arm weakly at the gorge. We couldn't have stopped it could we?"

"I don't know, Dulcy," Scortzi as he put his arm around her shoulders. "I do know it made it a lot easier for us to save them."

"Well, whatever Luis Roncallo has done I will always be grateful to him for that," Dulsena said. She gave a big sigh and said, "All right, come on let's go see those precious children."

As the three of them hurried towards the doorway, she added, "Say, where were you guys, anyway? You did cut it a bit close! If you'd only..."

Scortzi and Gutorm looked at each other and shook their heads. "You see Gutorm," Scortzi said, "I told you she would be fine."

- 40 -
Harmony Restored

Dulsena awoke. She was back in her old room on Resdorn. She and Derek and the children were staying, much to the delight of Rimini and Palomith, in the family home until they could arrange for their new house. Once again, as she had countless times in the past, she watched the sheer, yellow terrace draperies blowing in the soft morning breeze. The sunlight streamed through the bright golden Volnar trees and flashed and glittered across the white and gold floor tiles.

The little sparkles of light reminded her of Siburi. What a woman. What a good friend. After the attack on the Rohnseff Spaceport, she had helped get most of the KalVan executive staff and their families onto various freighters and flown to safety on Resdorn. She and her Secretary had insisted in staying on Greniff long enough to clean out the vaults of all the jewels and more valuable art objects before making a heart-stopping escape in an old, long since retired freighter with a balky hyper drive. They had landed in Resdorn just yesterday. Thanks to her there would still be a KalVan.

So many friends, she thought. Rhys, who had done all he could for this troublesome daughter of his old friend; Gutorm, who always seemed to be rescuing her; Lisbet Bohrnach and Henri Dakkon who would always be in their memories. And, most of all, there was Scortzi, dearest big brother, dearest friend who would go anywhere if she needed him.

There's evil everywhere, she thought, but always, always there's more good than evil and the good will overcome if people of faith just keep trying.

She rolled over and watched Derek sleeping so quietly. She reached out and gently touched the dark hair curling moistly over his forehead. How sweet to be lying here next to him in this beautiful, peaceful home with her children safely asleep in the adjoining rooms. But, soon she must waken them so they would be ready for morning chimes.

She rolled back, sighed and stretched. Today would be the first of many busy days. In fact, for the next three days all of Resdorn would be celebrating. All normal activities had been set aside. Instead there would be parties, parades, concerts and every sort of entertainment imaginable. This grand celebration was not only for the suppression of the Brenev Rebellion, but was a great outpouring of Thanksgiving that Resdorn, for the most part, had been spared the terrible destruction that some of the other worlds had experienced. Of course, as Brother Eindal and Rudolf Porter were quick to remind any who cared to listen, the mines had been compromised, but, the few people who had collaborated with the BKs had been removed, their names stricken from the rolls of the crystal families and, after the ceremonies today, Windswept Mine would reopen.

Since Dulsena, Derek, Scortzi and their group had been so closely involved, working as they had with the Federation in bringing down the insurrection, they found themselves very much THE CELEBRITIES. They had been praised, toasted, interviewed, featured, written about, speculated about, and pursued constantly since their return to Resdorn. MMB had even wanted to interview the children on one of their newscasts, Resdorn Today. She and Derek had managed to forestall that. They were trying to limit the children's appearances to happy affairs more suitable to their age. Unfortunately, it was impossible to shield them entirely from incidents that reminded them of their ordeal in captivity and the scarring trauma of hanging over that molten rive.

However, by concentrating on the "exciting" recovery by their father in the "for real Fed ship", to use Garrett's words, and the reunion with their mother and Uncle Scortzi, the children had seemed to recover quickly.

For the adults involved the scars would always be there. The loss of good friends like Lisbet Bornach, Henri Dakkon and most of the Algoran Federation leaders, was sorely felt. There was also great anger at the wanton destruction of the beautiful Algoran facilities on Aldene. It would be years before they could be rebuilt and functioning as before. But, as Rhys Xholan had reminded them, it could have been worse. What if that young tec on the Intrepid had not spied those transports coming in from Krolinoor? Not having those additional aircraft and weapons had tipped the scales against Brenev. They'd also been lucky in spotting those fake crystals and in picking up on so many little pieces of the plot. All those little pieces fitting together had kept them from being completely caught off guard.

There were celebrations here on Resdorn. However, there was mourning and hardship in many places. No one would be celebrating on Greniff where the destruction had been extensive and the population hard hit. That was true of some other worlds, too.

So many innocent people dead and so many who were not innocent; Nayland Brenev and Georgg, Derrachem and Marridon. All dead. Their search for glory and power had brought such pain. And then there were those who'd fought for greed. Brenev's mercenaries had taken heavy losses. The rest, the ones who had gotten away would, so she had been told, be philosophical and simply look elsewhere for smaller wars of greed and revenge. Always the thought that the next one would pay off.

The war was over but there was no peace. The Black Knights, leaderless and disillusioned, railed against the Paladin Sequillat, who in return stoked their smoldering anger and blamed Brenev, the Black Knights, and the Narmists for failure of their holy war. The Narmists, meanwhile, blamed everyone including God for everything.

She shook her head at the folly of it all. Then she smiled to herself as she thought of last night. She and Derek had been on the terrace enjoying the peaceful summer night. They had just come from a festive family gathering where Rimini had proudly announced that the Chimes of Bonding would be rung for Scortzi and Katje before the next holidays. Derek had moved up behind her and, wrapping his arms around her, held her tight. With her head laid back against his chest together they had looked out at the star-filled night.

"Somewhere," she had whispered, "among those sparkling lights are Greniff and Aldene and Soloving. That other bright dot over there might be Jorbar with its planet Frayleen. Gutorm is back there with his family just as we are now here, safe on Resdorn." She smiled at the thought.

True, the Federation had been torn apart and many worlds had suffered terrible destruction. But, eventually there would be steps toward reestablishing relationships. And, as usual, the merchants had been the first to call for re-opening the trade alliances. As had been the case since the beginning of time, the possibility of mutual profit opened many borders, even when ideologies found little common ground for discussion.

There was still much to be done, but for now, this moment, she was content. She would take comfort in the progress of each new day and in the thought that always there would be the crystals. Comfort in knowing that always there were thoughtful people happy to come and walk together on the path of harmony in response to the call of the Chimes of Resdorn.

The End

Preview

The Chimes of Resdorn

Book Three

Kalleni Beyond

Prologue

The collision claxon sounded, rending the air with its ear splitting demands to be heard. Captain Alior slammed down his cup, splattering an arc of brown liquid over info spools and desk. He rushed from his small cabin to the bridge, almost colliding with Ralan, his First Officer, who reached the door at the same time. Standing behind Rol Denghi, who was manning the navigation board, they peered at the image on the screen.

"What is it? Where did it come from?" Ralan asked sharply.

"Beats me. It must have been in hyper. It just suddenly appeared," Denghi answered. "Its course is very erratic."

"Yeah, it's veering all over the place," Ralan muttered.

"Hail them. Let's see what's going on," Alior ordered.

The hail went out. There was no answer.

"Repeat it," Alior snapped.

Finally a voice could be heard, however, the transmission was poor and kept breaking up.

"Let me try another frequency," Selvo, Alior's Crew Chief, said. Like each crew member on board he had several jobs and doubled as Communications Officer, although he wasn't licensed: He simply knew a little more about it than anyone else on board. Freighters, even large ones such as this one, ran on the rule minimum crew - maximum payload.

"Let's try it this way," he muttered, tweaking and adjusting the slides. This time the transmission was a little clearer. "We're the...out of...nau. There was an explosion in the...charge and we've sus...ned numerous injuries. Are you in a position...sist us?"

"This is Captain Singh Alior of the freighter Shanka out of Atore. How may we assist you?" Captain Alior asked.

"Believe we are...ger...breaking up. Can...transport to your ship? We've had losses, but believe we'...jured and ten...ostly all right. We need help...injured...perately."

"We have no doctor on board," Alior responded, "and our medical facilities are meagre."

"Ship is losing...integrity. Seems...not...ny choice."

"How many are in your crew?" Alior asked, as he exchanged looks with Ralan. Both were aware the crew's quarters and basic supplies were very limited. Loaded to maximum as they were, it would be hard to find space for any additional people let alone accomodate those who were injured.

"I don't like this," Selvo blurted out. "Not with all the rumors we've heard about pirates preying on ships along the border."

"They're probably just that, Selvo, rumors," Alior said. "We haven't heard anything definite. Anyway, can't see pirates operating out of a small, banged up freighter. Still..."

"It wasn't always damaged," Selvo said, frowning at the image on the screen. The captain grunted, acknowledging the comment. He ran his hand over the bristly dark, grey curls then stroked the long white sideburns as he weighed what little information he had. Selvo was right - there had been rumors. On the other hand neither the Merchants Network nor the Alliance had issued an actual warning, so how much weight did a lot of bar talk carry? Ralan's voice broke into his thoughts,"Can we turn down a request for assistance if they really are in trouble?" The question hung there.

Captain Alior shifted his stance then stood, arms crossed, watching as the freighter yawed then slowly leveled off. "You checked all the weapons yesterday, didn't you, Ralan?"

"Yes, Sir. They're all loaded and ready."

"Then issue them. Make sure everyone is armed and have a party waiting near LD 4. We'll bring them in there."

"Selvo, tell them they can begin transporting their wounded in ten minutes. We'll open cargo bay 4. In the meantime, apprise the crew of what is going on."

Ralan rushed off and Selvo transmitted the message to the stricken ship. Alior walked to the captain's seat, reached underneath and pulled out his own weapon. He'd carried it when he was a young ensign serving in the Federation-Huilla wars and it had been on every ship he'd served on since then. He'd checked it once in a while and had actually worn it a few times when they'd gone into some rough ports. However, the last time had been years ago and now he found he had to loosen the belt a couple of notches before it fit around him. He thumbed the check switch and the charge showed full.

"Narm, I never thought I'd have to wear this again," he muttered, angrily. "What are things coming to when we have to be armed aboard our own freighters?" There was no answer, nor had he expected one. They waited, watching the stricken ship drift to and fro.

The crackle of another broken transmission broke the silence. "We're ready to transpor…tain, the wounded will…first."

"Is the crew in place at LD 4?" Alior asked Selvo who was double-checking the weapon Ralan had handed him. Selvo nodded. His brow was furrowed and his jaw set. It was obvious he didn't like what was happening. Rol Denghi set his laser close to hand and then reached down and drew out the long, thin blade fitted into his boot sheath. This was a new one. His old one had broken in a bar fight in Kefau and he'd replaced it before he left port. He now placed it on the other side of the console. Cutting his eyes sideways, he saw Selvo watching him. They exchanged wry looks and Selvo rubbed his nose, an old private signal of theirs when something didn't smell right.

"LD ready, Captain. The shuttle doors are opening," the voice came over the intercom. The bridge crew watched as a vessel detached from the listing freighter and headed their way.

"Pretty good size for a freighter shuttle," Selvo muttered.

They watched it as it jockeyed for position then nosed in. There was a slight shudder as it docked. The captain counted slowly to ten, thumbed the intercom and asked, "What condition are these men in? Do they look in bad shape?"

"Bandages look bloody. Some are being carried," was the response. We're sending them on. "Still coming. Still coming. Twenty one, twenty two. That seems to be it."

"Twenty two? Twenty two?" the captain repeated as he turned towards Selvo. "Where the Narm are we…" Suddenly, the door to the bridge slid open and three men rushed in. They might have looked bloody and bandaged, but they moved fast. The captain was cut down by a full laser blast even as he reached for his weapon. Selvo tried repeatedly to fire, but his weapon seemed to be empty. He was cut down as he looked with bewilderment at the bright weapon-ready light on the worthless laser.

Rol Denghi stared at the stranger standing there grinning, mocking him as he pressed the trigger again and again with no result. He threw the useless weapon at the man's head at the same time lunging forward with his blade in the other hand. The stranger fired. The blast slammed Rol back against the console. He learned of death slowly as he slid down, his hand convulsively gripping the handle of the still unblooded blade.

Drulek, Captain of the "damaged" ship, strode in and looked around with satisfaction. Ralan followed him in.

"Your disarming of the weapons was a great help, Ralan. Very quick and efficient."

"Just make sure my payment is as quick and efficient," Ralan said, grimacing at the sight of his dead shipmates. "I'll check on the others in the cargo area," he added as he headed out.

He had not quite reached the door when the laser blast caught him full in the back sending him sprawling onto the passageway.

"Quick and efficient," Drulek laughed.

"He did help us," Drulek's second said.

"Yes, he did, but you remember our orders: No witnesses."

- 1 -

Derek finished the punch line of his story and waited for a reaction from Scortzi. Nothing. Scortzi sat, chair tipped back against the wall, leg swinging, eyes focused on something across the square. His empty glass hung from his fingertips.

So, after I turned purple," Derek went on, "what was left to do? I simply boltraxed right through the cadoc." He chuckled and took a drink.

The leg stopped swinging, the chair slowly lowered and Scortzi swiveled to look at Derek. "You did what through the what?" he asked. "What the Narm are you talking about? What does that have to do with selling rojette to Arnheim?"

"Oh, I finished telling about Arnheim a long time ago. You've been off, thinking about something else. I wanted to see if I could get your attention."

"Hunhh!" There was a long pause. "Boltraxed through the cadoc, did you. Well, if you ever figure out how to do it let me know." He grinned at Derek and said, "Well, I guess you're right. I was letting my mind wander. Just thinking about us and Felchor and some of the things that happened way back then. You ever think of those times?"

Derek shook his head and said, "Not any more. Try not to."

"Felchor. I never thought I'd ever see it," Scortzi went on. "Just a name from the rebellion days, all tied in with Nayland Brenev and the Black Knights."

"Well, it's easy to see how they could hide out here during those years," Derek said, disgustedly. "Backward place, miserable climate and apparently it's even worse in other places."

"That's hard to believe," Scortzi said, as he pushed away a lizard that was trying to climb up the leg of the small table that held their drinks. "And yet that man at the repair service was telling how it's thriving now, doing better than it has in years. Wonder why. Seems kind of odd."

Printed in the United States
71492LV00004B/73

9 781424 130894